IRONCLAD DEVOTION

A MYTHOS LEGACY NOVEL

Also By Jami Gold

Unintended Guardian (A Mythos Legacy Short Story)
Treasured Claim (A Mythos Legacy Novel, Book One)
Pure Sacrifice (A Mythos Legacy Novel, Book Two)
Stone-Cold Heart (A Mythos Legacy Novel, Book Four)

IRONCLAD DEVOTION

A MYTHOS LEGACY NOVEL

JAMI GOLD

BLUE
PHOENIX
PRESS
PHOENIX, ARIZONA

Cover Design by Melinda VanLone of Book Cover Corner
Content Editing by Jessa Slade and Marcy Kennedy
Line Editing by Erynn Newman of A Little Red
Copy Editing by Julie Glover
Cultural Advising by V.S. Nelson
Author Photo by Mark Oxley/Studio 16

Blue Phoenix Press
18337 E San Tan Boulevard, #9435
Queen Creek, Arizona 85142
Visit our website at bluephoenixpress.com

This is a work of fiction. Names, characters, places, and incidents are a product of the author's imagination or are used fictitiously. Any resemblance to actual events, locales, or persons, living or dead, is coincidental.

The author acknowledges the trademark status and trademark owners of various products or copyright material mentioned throughout this work of fiction, including the following: Bikers Against Child Abuse, Harley-Davidson, Crayola, Tinker Bell, ZZ Top, Duck Dynasty, The X Files, Candy Land, and Iron Man. The publication and use of these trademarks is not authorized, associated with, or sponsored by the trademark owners.

Ordering Information:
Quantity sales. Special discounts are available on quantity purchases by corporations, associations, and others. For details, contact the Publisher at the address or website above.

Ironclad Devotion / Jami Gold. -- 1st ed.

Publisher's Cataloging-in-Publication Data
provided by Five Rainbows Services

Gold, Jami.
   Ironclad devotion : a mythos legacy novel / Jami Gold.
      pages cm. – (Mythos legacy, bk. 3)
   ISBN: 978-1-942928-06-5 (pbk.)
   ISBN: 978-1-942928-05-8 (e-book)
   1. Fairies—Fiction. 2. Navajo Indians—Fiction. 3. Magic—Fiction. 4. Love stories. 5. Paranormal romance stories.   I. Title.
PS3607.O436 I76 2015
813`.6—dc23

                                                2015916516

To join the author's mailing list and take advantage of
pre-order-only sale prices for new releases, visit
jamigold.com/mail

For members of B.A.C.A. and other protectors of the innocent —
You are real-world superheroes...

Chapter One

HEAT IGNITED UNDER KIRA'S SKIN, SINGEING A PATH TOWARD her wrists. She shoved the pain into a back corner of her mind and resisted pulling back her long sleeves or gloves to check the damage. The answer was always the same.

The dark tattoo-like streaks weaving across her body were spreading. *Effing A.* Soon, the tribal marks growing like vines would reach their destination, and then she'd be out of time.

Despite the burning stings, no twitches of agony broke through her controlled expression, the better to avoid questions. Kira instead focused on Emily beside her, the little girl's fear detectable even in the dim light inside the local biker haven, Moose's Bar and Grill.

Ideas for how to reassure the child piled high in Kira's mind and then stalled. How had she ever thought she could manage this? Her history gave her insights into how best to help the girl, but mothering instincts fell far outside her capabilities.

Kids were the purest source on Earth of joy, happiness, and all those other feel-good emotions, so her bond with Emily had been a guilt-free conduit to the energy she needed to survive. But now she was failing them both, and the negative surge of Emily's worry cut deep. Fatally deep.

She stroked one of the girl's dark-haired pigtails and gave Renee Cushman a warning glare across the table. "What do you mean, the adoption process is on hold?"

Emily's case manager pursed her lips. "Maybe we should speak privately."

The girl's determination to plead her case flared across their connection, and Kira nestled Emily under her arm. "I promised I wouldn't do anything behind her back." The child had been lied to enough already.

Renee tilted her head, unable to disagree. "The Phoenix police have been going through everything from the crime scene, looking for evidence to link Tito to the..." Her gaze darted to Emily and back. "Murder."

"*Evidence?* How much more do they need? An arrest record two miles long for drugs, domestic violence, and child abuse isn't enough?"

Oh yeah, the girl's dearly-departed mom sure had known how to pick 'em. The one good thing she'd ever done was involve the leather-clad, intimidating members of Bikers Against Child Abuse to help Emily. Crissy Braxton might still be alive if she hadn't gone back to her abuser and kicked Kira and the rest of B.A.C.A. out of the picture. She might still be alive if she hadn't done a lot of things.

Renee opened a file folder. "Tito has the arrest record, but the previous charges against him haven't stuck, so the police are being extra thorough this time." She shuffled pages on the table. "Anyway, they found a note recanting the information Crissy reported on Emily's birth certificate."

Kira's heart sunk so low it fought for space with her stomach. "A note."

"Crissy gave a name. A man's name. Claimed he's Emily's father."

Emily trembled against Kira's side, and pain flared along Kira's forearms again. Damn it.

A beefy palm slapped the bar behind her. "You have *got* to be shi—"

"Moose," Kira snapped a warning, recognizing the protective— and profane—tirade building in her former foster father's mood. She couldn't have him jeopardizing her adoption chances even more.

"—kidding me. She can't be punted off to someone she's never met."

Moose was the only man Emily *didn't* fear, and that was only because he'd been her primary B.A.C.A. contact along with Kira. The rest of the men in B.A.C.A. were tolerated—but never trusted. Trust was in short supply after Emily had spent her six brief years in the company of Crissy's boyfriends, who could all compete for *Worst Male Specimen of the Year.*

"Of course we wouldn't just hand her over. We'll first verify the claim and see if this guy even wants to be involved. But if he does..." Renee sighed. "If he does, then he'd have supervised visitation rights while we complete the background checks and home study certifications. Assuming all that goes well, the judge would award custody."

Kira latched onto each *if.* Maybe he wasn't really the father. Maybe he wouldn't want to be a single dad. Maybe he wouldn't pass the background checks. This guy was probably just like all of Crissy's other boyfriends, right?

No need to change her plans for how to survive. And more importantly, no need for Emily to worry about something that wasn't going to happen. Kira wouldn't *let* it happen.

"So this is just a delay, not a rejection."

"Prin..." Renee, using the only name humans knew for Kira, gave her a patient look. "We always knew this adoption would be a long shot. *I* know about all the great work you've done with kids through B.A.C.A., but any judge would look at you..." She paused meaningfully and waved, indicating the tattoo-like markings visible on Kira's exposed skin at her neck and temples, the ever-present leather gloves and biker attire, and the wild colors of Kira's hair, currently hot pink with orange tips. "And worry about your parenting skills."

Moose's heavy boots thumped from behind the bar. "That's discrimination, pure and simple. We're all licensed for the foster care system, so the state thinks we're good enough for *that.* Besides, Prin is a better person than ninety-nine percent of the people out there. She'd give her right arm for this kid."

"*I* know that, but the court could find an excuse if they wanted to. Concern for Emily living in a trailer behind a bar—a *motorcycle* bar. Something."

"Don't give me that crap." Moose crossed his arms. "There's no state law against kids being *in* a bar, much less living near one."

Renee's shoulders lifted in a shrug. "Regardless, if all the other conditions are met, short of Emily's court-appointed guardian convincing a judge that this guy shouldn't get her because of issues discovered during the investigation, a biological parent has priority."

They'd escaped Tito's obscene request for custody unscathed because of the abuse charges, and given Crissy's taste in men, this was sure to be the same. No problem. "And I'm her court-appointed guardian, right?"

"Yes, we established emergency guardianship for you when we first started the adoption process." Renee clicked the end of her pen several times. "But so help me, Prin, if I think you're not acting in Emily's best interest, I'll go to the judge myself and have it revoked."

"Of course." No matter how much Kira wanted to keep Emily close for survival reasons, she wouldn't ignore what was best for the girl.

She looked down, meeting her foster daughter's dark eyes. With Emily's faith in her renewed, the drain on her energy ceased. Too bad the growth of her magical power lines couldn't be reversed.

If only that problem didn't matter. If only she could find a way to stay here for Emily's sake, even after the magical circuitry tying Kira to her faerie homeland completed its connections—and yanked her back. If only Lirdeag wasn't there, waiting to capture her.

She squeezed the girl and forced a smile. "Emily's happiness is the most important thing."

And there was no way Emily would ever be happy with a strange man.

THE RED GLOWING METAL CURVED IN A PERFECT SPIRAL UNDER ZAC'S precise strikes. Well, *almost* perfect. The scroll leaned a bit to one side, but with a couple of hammer blows against the anvil, he forced the work piece into a flat plane. Satisfied, he cut the swirl off the iron rod in preparation for the next step. If only life in general could match the plans in his head so easily.

A bright light flashed above him, signaling an incoming call on his business line. He glanced at his work piece lying on the dirt floor of his shop. The next step could wait.

He stripped off his gloves, plucked out his earplugs, and wiped his face with the closest towel. Nothing like working around a nearly two-thousand-degree fire in the Arizona desert. And the temps would rise another twenty degrees by next month as the full heat of summer cranked up the outdoor blast furnace. Pity the poor air conditioner.

Cool air met him in the doorway of his front office, and he picked up the phone. "Thanks for calling Chased by Fire. This is Zac."

"Zachary Chase?"

"Yes, ma'am. How can I help you?" He stubbed his boot against the door to the shop, closing it and keeping the heat of the forge away from the blessed air-conditioning. The air register blew directly on him, and it still wasn't enough.

"My name is Renee Cushman, and I'm with the Arizona DCS. Do you have a minute?"

DCS? Curiosity and his desk chair beckoned. Artistic blacksmithing wasn't a sitting-down kind of job, and kicking up his boots for a minute sounded good.

"Sure." He removed the protective leather apron shielding his clothes from burns and unbuttoned his shirt, letting the A/C reach his chest.

"Did you know a Crissy Braxton?"

"Crissy?" He sat down hard in the chair, his muscles tight under his skin. "Yeah, why?" Then the verb tense the woman had used filtered into his thoughts. "Wait, *did*? Is she..." He winced. Maybe he'd heard wrong and was jumping to conclusions, but he wanted to know for long-overdue closure's sake. "Is she dead?"

"Yes, I'm sorry to be the one to tell you. She was murdered a couple of months ago."

"Murdered?" Bloody hell. What could have led to *that*?

"Don't worry, you're not a suspect or anything, but may I ask you to be more specific about your relationship with Crissy?"

This call was making less and less sense. "Uh, I haven't seen or talked to Crissy in years, but we lived together for a while." He did the math in his head. It had been right before he'd left on his six-month trip to England for his journeyman training. "About six and a half years ago."

"Is it possible she was pregnant when your relationship ended?"

Chills rippled across his skin. The implications of the woman's question stampeded around his gut. A million thoughts followed, tangling between his heart and his brain. His mouth broke free of the impasse, words bursting out without stopping at his brain filter for approval.

"First of all, the relationship didn't end with the usual breakup. She left me when I was out of the country on a work trip. I came home, and she was just gone. No note. No forwarding address. No answer on her cell. Gone. Secondly..." He took a deep breath, gained control over his mouth, and prepared for the news. "I used protection every time, but yes, ma'am, there's always a chance."

"In their investigations into the murder, the police found a note written by Crissy. She names you as Emily Braxton's father."

Emily. A daughter. His pulse pounded in his ears, and every-thing else slipped away.

The universe seemed to tilt, as though shifting its rotation. Dizzy, he clenched the arm of his chair, but nothing could bring the spinning to a halt.

The woman's voice cut through the haze.

"What?" His question came out as a croak, his throat dry and constricted.

"I said, if Crissy's note is accurate, I need to know if you'd like to be involved in Emily's life."

"Of course I would." Despite his lack of parental role models, he'd figure out fatherhood. Somehow.

The woman's sigh carried over the telephone speaker. "Due to Crissy's death, we can't complete the usual affidavits and forms, so we can't legally establish paternity until a DNA test confirms the relationship."

"What's the quickest way to get that done?" After everything that had happened with his own mother, he couldn't let this girl think she was alone.

Five minutes later, Ms. Cushman had set up an appointment for him at a paternity testing office down in Phoenix. In forty-eight hours, the courts would have their answer, and then he'd be able to see his daughter.

He hung up the phone and drummed his fingers on the desk. It would be a long forty-eight hours.

Instead of giving in to the fervor pulsing through his body, urging him to do something about the situation—this very minute—he sat in his office long after the call had ended. His life had completely turned upside-down, and yet he wasn't freaking out. Maybe the opportunity to avoid his parents' mistakes was giving him access to a secret source of calm.

Rather than feeling panic, regret ate away at his lungs, stealing his ability to breathe without guilt. He'd already missed out on six years with his daughter. All because Crissy had ditched him.

He'd thought her betrayal of leaving him was bad. And hell, it *had* been bad. He hadn't been that blindsided since the cops tackled him in front of his old office and slapped him in handcuffs for his father's business fraud.

But this betrayal hurt on a whole different level. She'd left him—while *pregnant*—and then shut him out of his daughter's life. Why the hell had Crissy done that?

Whatever the reason, he *would* be there for his daughter now.

Chapter Two

KIRA SLAMMED THE CELL PHONE ONTO THE BAR AND PICKED UP a nearby beer bottle. Moose grabbed the bottle's neck before she could smash it against the phone's touchscreen.

His eyebrow waggled. "Mind if I return this beer to the nice man who ordered it?"

She released her grip on the glass and let him set the bottle in front of a tourist. Judging by the guy's wide grin, he'd gotten exactly the kind of show he'd hoped to have for his visit to a biker bar.

Pansy ass.

A tug on her jeans brought her back to the trouble at hand. Emily looked up at her, the worry in her expression already sending tingles of heat to Kira's wrists. "Was that Miss Renee? What did she say?"

Kira tilted her head back and muttered under her breath, "Oh *fuck* me."

She was *so* dead. For a moment, the temptation to lie sat on her tongue. But the truth would be evident soon enough, and risking Emily's trust wasn't worth one night of peace.

"Remember that test I told you about when we went down to Phoenix?"

"When they put that stick in my mouth?"

"That's the one. That man Miss Renee mentioned last time took the test too. She just got the results back." She crouched down and met Emily's eyes. "He *is* your father."

"I don't want to go with him!"

Fire blazed along the lines under Kira's skin, matching the vehemence of Emily's negative emotions. Kira sagged against the back wall, unable to hide the effect of the energy drain. How could she recover? If this kept up, the Mythos plane might suck her back any second for a forced recharge.

"I know, Fairy." She purposely used Emily's road name, the one given to her when she became a member of the B.A.C.A. family. The one they used when they promised to keep her safe from her abuser. "But tomorrow..."

She glanced up at Moose, who was hovering close, and gave him a *pay attention* look. Then she returned her gaze to Emily.

"Tomorrow, he wants to meet you. Just *meet* you. You'll still be coming home with me. Moose is going to call the family tonight, and we're all going to the meeting with you. This guy's going to know right from the start that we're your family, and that if he messes with you, he's messing with all of us."

"Like an initiation?" Emily's six-year-old tongue struggled with the big word.

Kira managed a smile. "Well, he won't get the cool vest or bandanna. But yes, we'll show him what he has to deal with if he wants to know you."

"Will Rocky be there? And Bear? And Tiny? And Tin Man?" Emily's list of all the biggest and most intimidating men of the B.A.C.A. chapter made her priorities clear.

Moose bent over, letting his "wild man" beard tickle Emily's face. "I'll call every family member, Fairy. You won't be alone."

"You'll *never* be alone." Kira forced herself away from the wall and leaned forward on one knee, getting closer to the source of her energy drain. "This doesn't change the fact that we're family."

Emily planted her hands on her hips. "My mom made promises too. But she kept using, and she let him hurt me again. She lied."

Each observation was an accusation stabbing Kira with Emily's distrust. And with each one, the tattoo-like marks under her skin slithered, burning, closer to the power nexus on her palms.

Even if she found a way to avoid returning to her homeland for the necessary energy charge when the circuit completed, the maturation of her magical connections would allow Lirdeag to track her energy—and her. She'd gone into hiding for a reason. She could empathize with Emily's situation far more than the little girl could guess.

"I know. I'm sorry your mom couldn't keep her promises. But have *I* ever broken a promise to you?"

Emily sighed dramatically. "No. 'Cept the time my mom made you break it."

Sometimes, her attitude was more like a teenager than a six year old. Just more evidence of how much she'd already survived in her young life.

"Exactly my point." Kira opened her arms and hoped the worst was over. "Now come on."

Emily let Kira drag her into a hug. They collapsed into a huddle on the floor. Emily giggled at the near-tackle. At least Kira could protect her ward from *something*—awareness of her complete exhaustion if nothing else.

"Okay, tomorrow's going to be a big day. Why don't you let Moose tuck you into bed, and I'll be there in a few minutes." When she could stand again.

After they left for her trailer out back, Kira sensed someone watching her. The tourist was leaning over the bar, looking down at her. His amused arrogance gave her the strength to stand.

"Got a problem, asshole?"

Face-to-face with her now, his smile dimmed for a second, but then he recovered, and a smirk curved his lips. Typical.

The bar was close enough to Phoenix to attract the college boys looking for a thrill of imaginary danger. Like Moose would ever allow bar fights. On the other hand, brawls in the parking lot? That was a completely different matter. All the local bikers had learned to steer clear of her.

Tourists lacked that clue. She half-suspected some of the fraternities gave their pledges an assignment to come here as part of a hazing ritual. Their horny presence had come in handy before as an energy pick-me-up, but she'd given that up to focus on Emily and the girl's healthier source of energy.

Not that her plan was working so well.

The college-boy tourist leaned closer. "Well, I *did* hear you ask someone to fuck you, and I was wondering if I was supposed to join you on the floor."

She opened her mouth to tell him that he'd have a better chance with the exhaust pipe on her Harley. Before she got the words out, a wave of power from his horniness slammed into her.

Shit. She was desperate for energy, especially in preparation for whatever tomorrow would bring. And sexual passion—the other main source of pure connection to life's spirit—was the irresistible junk food equivalent of what she needed to build up her strength.

Her expression fell into a mask she'd perfected over the years. Enough come-hither sexuality, vulnerable innocence, and tattooed-biker-chick danger to amp up his anticipation.

"When Moose gets back, meet me by the tree behind the building."

She walked away before the guy could reply. Half the time, the tourists would chicken out and never show.

The last couple of years of frantic experimenting to figure out her limitations and abilities had taught her a few tricks. The odds were slightly better—and their energy higher—if she dropped the invitation into their lap and left them to build up their courage alone.

Fifteen minutes later, she crowded the college boy against the tree trunk, hidden from any random eyes by the deep twilight. Not that they would seem out of the ordinary, being fully clothed and only standing near each other and all, but she didn't need anyone paying attention to her magic in the next step.

Her script—phone-sex-worthy dirty-talk designed to get them ready to blow their load before they even touched her—worked perfectly once more. At the height of his anticipation, she removed her glove and touched her bare fingertips to his temple. His eyes turned glassy and unseeing, and energy surged into her. Hell yeah, this was what she needed.

Her aura blazed with his feel-good emotions. And she'd made him feel *really* good.

Who needed actual sex? She'd tried the bump-and-grind a few times, but it didn't do anything for her. The energy released during the mental simulation she used was more important. Holding off the growth of her magical circuitry so she could remain on Earth was top priority.

A minute later, she set his temple free and replaced her glove. The trance's influence would last for another couple of minutes. Enough time to get him back into the bar so his surroundings would match the last memory her magic let him keep.

Sabotaging people's memories always made her skin crawl, but she couldn't let them remember her magic either. Desperate times and all that.

Thank goodness her relationship with Emily was close enough that she didn't need to use this brute force approach to feel energized by emotions. She couldn't stomach *taking* anything from the girl who had already lost so much.

The guy followed her lead, lurching zombie-like beside her. Inside the bar, she shoved him onto his stool and slid an ice water into his grasp. Her magic didn't physically harm anyone, but a drink of water would clear his mind of the remnants of the trance. If tradition held, Moose would be kicking him out soon, and he needed to be safe to drive.

She joined Moose at the other end of the bar and set up glasses for him to pour the next order. He eyed the tourist's glazed expression. Luckily for the sake of her secret, Moose always assumed the occasional dazed customer was simply stunned, figuring she'd given them a sharp enough earful to make their brain bleed.

"That guy bothering you, Prin?"

"I can handle myself." Even though she'd aged out of the foster system several years ago, Moose still treated her like his daughter. Sweet, in a sometimes-annoying way.

The tourist chose that moment to sip from the water. When they fully exited the trance, their first words were always unpredictable, dependent on where their memory left off. This one leaned over the bar, as though still looking for her on the ground so he could offer to fuck her there.

Oh *lovely*. Moose would kill him.

She stood in front of him and beat him to the conversation. "You need to leave and not come back."

One time was all she allowed herself with any guy—and never with anyone she knew. She didn't need anyone poking around her abilities, seeing too much or uncovering the truth.

"You sure?" He jiggled his brows and stretched out his arm, as though to grab her. "I could make it worth your while."

She gave him a glare harsh enough to peel paint off a gas tank. "Don't touch me, and don't make me hurt you. Ask yourself why the three-hundred-pounders in the bar leave me alone, and then go home."

He let his arm drop, and as she knew would happen, his male ego took over so he wouldn't feel rejected. "Your loss, bitch."

Beside her, Moose laughed at the guy's retreating back. "You know, Prin, I almost feel sorry for some of the guys you turn down."

"Not that one, I hope." His smirk had been the unattractive kind of arrogant.

"No, not that one. But one of these days you'll have to let a guy get close to you."

She stepped back and scrutinized him. "You been hitting the bottle when I'm not looking?"

"Princess." His use of her full human-known name spiked her pulse. Whatever he was about to say, she didn't want to hear it. He settled his large palms on her shoulders, preventing her escape, and looked her in the eye. "No matter what happens with Emily's adoption, this experience has brought out your mothering instincts."

Her? Mothering instincts? Moose must have hit *several* bottles.

Her expression—incredulous, no doubt—didn't dissuade him from pushing the issue. "I'm serious. Don't sell yourself short. Maybe you should think about getting out of here and finding a husband."

She scoffed and tugged out of his grasp. "I don't need a man around to have a kid."

Marriage meant bad news. She'd been evading Lirdeag, her fae intended, since her desperate escape at the age of five, so why would she volunteer for an Earth-bound version of the deal?

She avoided Moose's gaze by wiping down the bar and then tossed the towel into the bin. "Speaking of kids, I'm turning in for the night. I told Emily I'd be there soon, and I don't want to break any promises."

"All right, I won't keep you. Besides, we'll be meeting up with the others early."

The reminder of the next day's schedule pressed on her chest, and her breath caught. The energy infusion had erased her worry about winking out of her existence here, but the other worries about Emily remained.

She needed to be ready for anything tomorrow.

Chapter Three

THE BAR'S PARKING LOT SET THE STAGE FOR THE MEETING between her, Emily, Moose, and nearly twenty other B.A.C.A. members the next morning. Emily basked in the center of the gathering and shyly thanked each one for coming. Even the men. Maybe now—when she knew these "big brothers" had her back for meeting a stranger—she might start to let herself trust them.

For her part, Kira dressed in her full leathers—no jeans for her today—to be as intimidating as possible. She'd also made her changeling hair take on a vivid, not-found-outside-of-a-Crayola-pack red shade. The color complemented the flames of the custom paint job on her Harley. *Angry* biker chick fit her mood for the day.

Everyone wore their B.A.C.A. vests—Emily's in denim and the rest in black leather. Patches covered their vests, some displaying the B.A.C.A. logo of a tattooed fist surrounded by the words "Bikers Against Child Abuse" and others stating their motto of "No child deserves to live in fear."

Moose touched the motto patch on Emily's vest. "You're not scared now, are you, Fairy?"

"Not right now." She gave him a weak smile. "I'm in the family."

Kira hugged her close. "All your big brothers and big sisters will stay with us as long as you want. And Moose and I will stay with you the whole time. You'll never be alone."

Renee Cushman arrived and took in the crowd from inside the car, her eyes widening. A *whirr* signaled the opening of her side window. "I take it this means you're ready to go."

Kira nodded toward the road. "Where are we headed?"

"Just a few miles away. His address is out with those horse properties that back up to Cave Creek Regional Park."

"Dirt roads." Kira eyed the group. They'd be thrilled. Not.

She returned her attention to Renee and jerked her chin. "Take it slow through those sections. Street bikes are allergic to flung dirt and rocks messing up their chrome."

Renee shook her head and caught Emily's eye. "Sure you don't want to ride with me, sweetie? I've got air conditioning and no dirt."

Emily answered by stepping back and slipping her small hand into Kira's.

Kira tied the B.A.C.A. bandanna do-rag style onto Emily and helped her into her helmet. In addition to the lack of restrictions on passenger age, Arizona didn't require motorcyclists to wear helmets, but B.A.C.A. always made the kids wear them. Once Emily was securely behind her on the seat, Kira slid on her sunglasses to complete her "look."

Almost like a precision team, the others followed suit and started up their bikes. The rumble burst across the pavement, and the pedestrians touring the art galleries down the road jerked to a stop. Yep, they were intimidating, and that was the whole point. The B.A.C.A. kids had encountered some scary people, but their family watching over them was scarier.

Her lungs expanded, taking in a deep breath. She was damn proud to be part of this group.

Luckily, the pavement held all the way to the turn-off for the driveway. Fancy-ass homes stood watch in the neighborhood. Big horse spreads with bigger houses.

What was an ex-boyfriend of Crissy's doing here? This area was nothing like the inner city hellholes Crissy had lived in the whole time Kira had known her. Not that it mattered. Money didn't buy a guarantee of living abuse-free.

The bikes crept up the winding dirt driveway. A couple of horses behind a fence reared as they passed. She'd calm them in a minute, but for now, it was more important to make an impression.

Ironclad Devotion

Renee stopped her car at a courtyard entrance. Swirling wrought iron filled the archway to the courtyard and lined the top of the adobe wall surrounding the residential section of the property. The metal's signature properties vibrated Kira's aura as soon as she pulled in front of the gate.

You've got to be kidding me. Iron? An iron fucking gate. And more iron surrounding the place like a damned anti-fae fortress.

Did the guy have a fear of faeries? If not, she was about to give him one.

She could handle the cast iron parts of her bike's engine in close proximity because—despite the word *iron* in the name—cast iron wasn't pure at all. Steel was a little trickier, a little purer. She could tolerate it touching her bare skin for short periods, and it wouldn't seriously hurt her as long as it didn't pierce her skin. But wrought iron—or the "mild steel" they often used for the decorative stuff—was dangerous. The purest iron in common use.

At the very least, any touch to her bare skin would cause instant energy-drain. At worst, it might kill her.

The leather gloves and full-length clothes she wore even in the heat of summer protected her from accidental contact, but purposely touching the near-pure iron might burn her even through the gloves. And *this* was where Emily's father lived?

She gunned her motor extra loud in protest, and the others followed her example. A man burst from the front door. "What the hell is going on? Are you *trying* to terrify the horses?"

At the reminder of the animals, Kira cut her engine and helped Emily down from the bike. While she unfastened Emily's helmet, Kira snuck a peek at the guy.

Her heart sank. Even though his striking face and muscled body looked nothing like Crissy's usual gangbanger or junkie type, he shared Emily's dark hair and eyes. The Native American influence over his genes was stronger, with broad, high cheekbones and deeper coloring that reminded her of the wind clan faeries, but there was no mistaking it. This cowboy-hat-and-boots-wearing man was Emily's father.

A cowboy with an unhealthy addiction to iron. Lovely. Just lovely.

Chapter Four

ACA WHOLE OUTLAW MOTORCYCLE GANG BLOCKED THE FRONT gate, and Zac skidded to a stop halfway down the steps in his front courtyard. What the hell?

The invasion force finally shut off their engines and gathered in the middle of his driveway, shades on, arms crossed. Red hair caught his attention in the center of the gate. The curvy, leather-clad woman picked up something behind her and walked away, following the gravel back toward the road.

Well, this was *his* house, damn it, and he wouldn't let *anyone* just waltz in here. Skull-and-crossbones tattoos or no.

An older woman with short gray-streaked hair emerged from the lone car in the driveway and met him right as he yanked open the gate. She read from a pile of paperwork. "Zachary Chase?"

"Yeah, who the hell are you?"

"Renee Cushman. We spoke on the phone."

Crap. Yelling and swearing probably wasn't the best impression to give Emily's case manager. "Of course. Sorry, ma'am."

"No, it's quite all right. Sorry for the..." She looked over the motley crew behind her, as though debating the right word. "Welcoming committee. I didn't know we were going to have an escort, or I'd have warned you." She fanned herself with the file folder in her hand. "After we get into the air conditioning, I'll explain their connection to Emily."

He scanned the crowd of burly guys—and several burly women. "Emily's here? Where?"

Ms. Cushman spun around, searching, and pointed down the driveway. "There, Prin has her."

The red-haired, leather-clad woman he'd first noticed was standing at the horse fencing, a child on her hip. *Emily.* The woman reached over the rail toward his aggressive stallion, and the smile on Zac's face broke into open-mouthed horror.

"No! Don't, ma'am! Bullet's been known to bite."

The redhead didn't acknowledge his warning, and he ran toward them, fearing he'd be too late, especially after how worked up the horse had gotten with the motorcycle noise. But instead of charging the fence—Bullet's usual way of expressing dominance to those he didn't respect—the stallion approached the woman meekly, his head and tail lowered.

Impossible.

Zac's steps slowed in the middle of the driveway, still twenty feet away, giving him time to try to make sense of the scene. The redhead stroked Bullet without a care in the world for his teeth. Those teeth that had just recently stopped trying to bite *him.* The stallion nickered at her touch.

The woman's murmurs carried over the dirt drive. "I'm very happy to meet you too. May I introduce my friend? This is Fairy. She'd like to pet you if that's all right."

Bullet thrust his head forward, within range of Emily's reach, as though the stallion could suddenly understand English. Emily giggled and rubbed his face.

After his daughter had her fill, the woman spoke again. "Thank you. I would greatly appreciate it if you and the others could help me keep Fairy safe. She's very important to me."

Zac started forward, ready to introduce himself, when his stallion shocked him once more. The animal lowered his front half, like a circus-trained horse's approximation of a bow.

How did Bullet even know how to *do* that trick? That position—one foreleg forward, one foreleg back, head curved down—wasn't normal horse behavior by a long shot.

His daughter asked the question that sat on the tip of his tongue as well. "What's he doing?"

"He's showing that animals and faeries are friends, and your name is Fairy, right?" The woman returned a bow, graceful despite Emily on her hip. "Thank you. I am honored to have your assistance."

Hearing her two sentences back-to-back—one directed toward Emily, the other directed toward Bullet—added to his confusion. Her attitude when speaking to Emily was casual, matching her motorcycle-riding, leather-clad appearance. In contrast, her words to Bullet were formal, almost musical, and a complete clash with her persona.

Which was the real her? And more importantly, what the hell had she done to his damn horse?

Zac took another step toward them, and Bullet instantly stood upright and tossed his head, back to his normal self. The woman angled her face toward Zac, her expression changing from smiling to stone-faced in a second.

Violet eyes seized his attention and didn't let go. He wanted to get his first real glimpse of his daughter, but the girl hid, tucked against the woman's far hip, so he had no choice but to give in to the redhead's gaze.

Colored contacts? Had to be. Eyes couldn't naturally be that color. These weren't just *sort of* violet. They were as violet as could be. Yet the color shimmered in rainbow speckles below the surface of where a colored contact would sit, proving his theory wrong.

His hands clenched and then released. That wasn't natural. For that matter, the rest of her face wasn't natural either.

Even though the color already made her eyes stand out, thin tattoos also outlined them, like in the ads for permanent eyeliner. But unlike the pictures in those ads, her tattoos extended onto her temples with swirls and curving lines. The artist in him couldn't help memorizing the design for future ironwork projects.

Only those dramatic eyes and her dark lips colored her milky-white skin, like a goth and a biker chick rolled into one. And somehow, her look came together with a regal beauty.

A frown formed on her face, and she jammed her sunglasses over those mesmerizing eyes. The spell broken, he could finally tear his gaze away and seek out Emily, peering around the woman's shoulder. She clung to the redhead, her expression round and fearful.

A broad grin stretched his mouth. There was no doubt this beautiful girl was his daughter. He recognized himself in everything from the curve of her wide-set eyes to her thick, dark hair, unconstrained by the bandanna falling off her head.

"Hi, Emily." He tipped his hat to the woman. "Howdy, ma'am."

Emily buried her face in the redhead's hair. He hadn't been expecting this little girl to welcome him—a stranger—with open arms. Not really. She'd just survived her mother's murder after all. But his heart still felt like it shrank in his chest.

This wasn't yet another betrayal to add to his collection though. He needed to remember that.

Behind him, Ms. Cushman's voice carried down the driveway. "Can we *please* go inside? I'm dying here."

He smiled at Emily and the redhead and extended his arm back toward the house. "This way, ma'am."

He'd be polite and welcoming to this group Emily obviously trusted if it killed him. And it might.

Now that he wasn't running to warn the woman about his horse, he had no choice but to notice the gang almost blocking his way to the front gate. Sleeveless T-shirts and vests showed off their tattooed biceps, and as if that wasn't intimidating enough to walk past, several carried sidearms. And here he was with all his weapons locked safely away like a normal person.

At the top section of the patio, he checked behind him. Only Ms. Cushman and an older bearded man, who looked like he could be a missing member of ZZ Top or *Duck Dynasty*, had joined the redhead and Emily inside the courtyard. The others remained standing guard in the driveway. Maybe that was a good sign.

"If the rest aren't joining us, could one of you close the gate? Otherwise the javelinas will get into the courtyard and eat all the plants."

As ZZ Top yanked the gate shut, Zac's gaze was once again drawn toward the redhead. Everything about her struck him as not natural. Not just her looks, but the way she effortlessly held Emily on her hip despite her short stature, the way light seemed to bend around her, adding a rainbow brightness to the area. Hell, the way his garden's flowers were more noticeable after she walked past.

This redhead didn't follow the laws of nature. She couldn't be categorized. And that nagged at him like a piece of metal that wouldn't bend the way he wanted.

He let the group into his house, holding open the iron-accented wooden door. "Come on in."

The redhead might have sworn under her breath as she entered.

"This is beautiful, Mr. Chase." Ms. Cushman looked up, taking in the two-story entrance and upstairs loft. "I don't get a chance to see many homes with this level of craftsmanship. Was this all part of the house when you bought it?"

"Thank you, ma'am. And please, call me Zac. My father is Mr. Chase."

Ms. Cushman laughed and examined one of his sconces on a stone pillar. "Fair enough. Feel free to call me Renee."

He made a mental note to try to remember that, but he tended to fall back on his *ma'ams* and *sirs* in uncomfortable situations, just like how upsetting situations sometimes brought out the British slang he'd picked up during his journeyman training.

"The woodwork and stonework was mostly in place. I made all the ironwork, like that sconce light, myself." At her widened eyes, he explained, "I'm an artistic blacksmith. Light fixtures, stair rails, gates, furniture accents, and other artwork. If you've seen that open-scroll cowboy boot in Old Town Scottsdale, you've seen my work."

"Oh yes! Every time I take snowbird visitors to Old Town, they want pictures with the giant boot." She gave him a genuine smile. "Very impressive."

He removed his cowboy hat, now that they were indoors, and used that excuse to hide his face for a second. Should he cringe at Renee's praise—or at the redhead's scowl? Any minute, World War III might break out in his foyer.

Chapter Five

ZAC HUSTLED THE GROUP DOWN THE HALL TOWARD THE DINING room. At least there, a table would stand between them all.

Renee reached toward the iron and colored glass chandelier over the tabletop. "Gorgeous. I think I should start saving my money for a present to myself."

Once they were all seated, Renee indicated the bearded man. "This is Jack Forester, but he usually goes by his road name of Moose. You might have heard of him from Moose's Bar and Grill in downtown Cave Creek."

Zac nodded. He'd passed the biker hangout many times to deliver pieces to the art galleries the next block over.

Renee swung her arm toward the redhead, now with Emily on her lap, at the end of the table. "This is Princess. And this, of course, is Emily Braxton."

His daughter emerged from her cower long enough to exclaim one word. "Fairy."

"Oh yes." Renee grinned. "Her road name is Fairy."

He didn't want to think about how or why his daughter had a *road* name, but he tried to express interest. "Fairy, huh?" He gave Emily what he imagined a fatherly smile would look like. "You like Tinker Bell?"

The redhead snorted, twisting the you-don't-have-a-clue-what-you're-doing dagger in his chest.

Emily rolled her eyes. "Tinker Bell isn't a *real* faery. Prin says *real* faeries are strong warriors, and that's what I am. Strong."

The redhead squeezed her tight. "Yes, you are, Fairy."

Zac buried his wince. "Of that, I have no doubt."

Without meeting her eyes, he looked at the woman holding Emily. She'd taken her sunglasses off, and he didn't want to get distracted again. "I'm sorry, ma'am. I didn't catch your name."

"Princess."

"No, I mean your real name."

The redhead nailed him with her gaze. Even with the muted illumination of the room, sparkles continued to light up her eyes. "For as long as I've been on Earth, Princess has been my only name. No last name. No middle name. Just Princess. My friends call me Prin for short. *You* can call me Princess."

Yowch. Maybe he could categorize her after all.

Both Renee and Moose called out a chastising "Prin." But she ignored them, keeping her eyes on him. Challenging. Daring him to piss her off.

Well, for as long as *he'd* been on Earth, he'd tried not to be stupid. "Princess it is then."

Just as he was about to put her firmly into the *bitch* category, she broke off their eye contact and smiled in the direction of the hallway. Her end of the table brightened. A trick of the sun?

A second later, Honey, his half-deaf yellow Labrador, padded into the room. He stood to put her into one of the back rooms before she could freak out about all the strangers in the house.

Honey passed by him in favor of going straight to Princess and Emily. Of course she did.

Princess shifted Emily on her lap and bent down to the dog. The tabletop blocked his view, and he leaned over to see what the woman was doing this time. She was whispering in Honey's bad ear, and the dog's tail was wagging so hard her back end swung side to side.

He was tired of things that didn't make sense. "She's deaf in that ear."

Princess sat up and raised her brow. "Your point?"

The woman caught Emily's gaze. "See? They're all going to watch over you. Are you ready to tell the rest of the family they can leave now? They're probably getting hot out in the sun."

Emily nodded, and the two left the room, heading toward the front door. A moment later, Honey followed them, without so much as a glance in his direction.

He took a step, about to chase after them, but instead pivoted back to Renee and Moose. "What's her deal? And why haven't I even been able to approach my own child yet?"

The two looked to each other, and Renee opened her hand. "I'll share Emily's story and leave Prin's to you."

Moose sat back from the table, rolling a gold coin around his knuckles, and let Renee take the lead.

"Zac, there's a reason I wanted to explain the situation in person. That same reason is why I said on the phone that I didn't think it would be a good idea to set up a meeting right away. And that reason is related to why the others are all here. But you insisted, so here we are."

He shifted his jaw, chiding himself, and returned to his chair. "I'm listening."

"A couple of years ago, your daughter entered the Child Protective Services system because Crissy's boyfriend—in addition to abusing Crissy—was sexually molesting Emily."

Zac's mouth went as dry as the desert outside even as nausea rolled through his stomach. How could someone *do* that? To a *child*? An even tinier child than he saw here today.

He wanted to deny it was possible. Something that bad *couldn't* have happened to *his* daughter. But he hadn't been there, had he?

His gut spasmed like he'd been sliced open, and acid seared up his throat. He hadn't been there to protect his daughter from the worst kind of crime imaginable. His limbs trembled, and he clenched the arms of his chair. He'd failed her already.

Heat rose in his chest all over again at how much Crissy had screwed him—and Emily—by cutting him off from her.

Renee's continuing explanation dragged Zac back from his roiling emotions. "Moose and Princess—and all those bikers outside—"

At the same time as her reminder of the invaders at the gate, motorcycle engines started up and drove off.

"—are members of B.A.C.A., Bikers Against Child Abuse, a volunteer organization dedicated to making kids feel safe again.

Members are trained by mental health professionals on how to help the kids, and they have to go through the same background checks as police officers. They stand watch outside the kids' homes, they escort them to and from school, and they sit with them in court as they face their abusers. In short, they're the good guys, dedicated like you wouldn't believe, and what they do *works.*"

The welcome bit of positive information distracted Zac from the tightness in his ribcage, and he peered at Moose with fresh eyes. The patches for the organization covered his leather vest, and now the show of force and weaponry made sense.

Renee waved toward Moose. "Emily's first CPS case manager put Crissy in touch with B.A.C.A., and they made Emily a member of their biker family, so she'd know someone always had her back. Moose and Princess were her 'primaries,' the members on call for her twenty-four-seven. Unfortunately, unknown to CPS, Crissy got back together with her abuser, and he convinced her to cut Emily off from her B.A.C.A. family."

Wait a minute... "How could CPS *not* know Crissy had returned to her abuser? Wasn't anyone paying attention?"

"Honestly? No."

His body tensed so hard his chair jumped, scraping the wood floor.

Renee dropped her gaze before Zac's glare set her on fire. "I don't know if you remember reading about CPS's problems last year, before the reorganization into DCS, the Department of Child Safety, but Emily's case was ignored. The reports from Prin and Moose were never investigated until the governor's task force reprioritized case assignments."

At least the woman was honest. He ground his teeth and willed his muscles to relax. No killing the messenger.

Renee fluttered her arms, as though trying to shove away the past. "Anyway, we learned of the boyfriend—and the continuing abuse—just a few months ago, and we'd started proceedings to re-move Emily from the home when Crissy was murdered."

Damn, that was one ugly-ass picture. And not a lick of it made sense.

"I don't understand why Crissy would put up with that. The

Crissy I knew wouldn't have stood for someone abusing her, much less a child. *Her* child."

"Her boyfriend was also her drug dealer, so he had a lot of power over her."

"Crissy was doing *drugs*?" What the hell had happened to her while he was in England?

"I take it she wasn't on drugs to the best of your knowledge when you were together?"

"*No.*" He shook his head, adding to his emphatic answer. "I wouldn't have been with her if she was."

She'd known enough about his history with his mother to know that was a deal-breaker. Crissy had sworn her teenage experimentation was long in the past, a foolish mistake never to be repeated. If he hadn't already witnessed Emily's resemblance to him, he might have asked if Renee was sure they were speaking of the same Crissy Braxton.

"Well, I'm sorry to say that she struggled with drug addiction for years. And she had a history of allowing guys like that into her life. Almost every man Emily's known has hurt her in some way."

Zac leaned back in his chair and stared at the ceiling. Bile threatened to bubble up his throat, and he couldn't swallow away the nauseated sensation. His arms shook with the effort to *not* destroy something. To *not* rampage like a madman. To *not* lose his ever-loving mind over thoughts of what she'd witnessed, what she'd lived through.

How was he supposed to just *accept* this? And if he was struggling this much, what had it done to Emily?

No wonder the poor girl was terrified. She had no reason to trust him—and every reason *not* to.

Chapter Six

THE ACHE IN ZAC'S CHEST FROM CRISSY'S BETRAYAL TURNED hot. He would sell his soul for the chance to prevent Emily's torture. But that chance didn't exist.

All because of Crissy.

He stood and paced from one end of the room to the other, his feet unable to stay put. "I don't understand any of this."

He rubbed the back of his neck, as though *this* pain could ever go away.

"Hell, I never even understood why she left me." His arms swung out, indicating the house. "I mean, I wasn't living in this place yet, but we weren't desperate for money. Yeah, I was going to be gone for six months, finishing the last of my blacksmith training, but we'd talked about getting married after I came back. Why would she leave—when *pregnant*—if that's all she had waiting for her?"

Renee flipped open her file folder. "You're a member of the Navajo tribe, correct?"

He stopped pacing. "Technically, yes. I'm one-half Navajo. My mother did all the paperwork when I was a child." What the hell did that have to do with anything?

"Have you ever heard of the ICWA, Indian Child Welfare Act?"

The phrase rang a bell, but he couldn't place it. "Not really, no."

"The ICWA states that when a child qualifies as a member of a

Native American tribe, the tribe can transfer jurisdiction for custody cases to tribal court. I suspect Crissy feared losing custody of
Emily. Even if you'd terminated your parental rights, the tribe
could still gain jurisdiction. Under their jurisdiction, priority is
given to placing the child within the tribe. Even placement with
strangers in the tribe is considered preferable to placement with
non-Native Americans."

"Why would she worry about losing custody?"

But even as the words fell from his tongue, he suspected the
truth.

Renee met his gaze. "Emily was born with drugs in her system."

Zac dropped into the nearest chair and propped his hands on
top of his head, breathing deep. *Of course.*

Sometime while he'd been in England, too busy to maintain
regular contact, she'd started using again. And because she *did*
know that drug use was a deal-breaker for him, she'd left. Then
she'd discovered her pregnancy, learned that she'd have close to
no rights in a custody case if the tribe gained jurisdiction, and
decided to keep Emily's entire existence a secret from him to
prevent the tribe from ever knowing about her.

He wanted to rage at the insanity. He'd never lived on the
reservation. Hell, he could count on one hand the number of times
he'd even visited the Navajo Nation in his whole life.

His Native American heritage from his mother's side was simply a fact of genetics, not anything he practiced. Especially not that
spiritual mumbo-jumbo she'd talked about. His mother had given
up the right to influence his life when she'd left him and his father
decades ago.

But because of those damn *genetics*, he'd lost his daughter for
six years. Then Crissy had let others harm his daughter to the
point that—even beyond the grave—she was *still* keeping him from
Emily.

Emotionally and mentally, the girl might never be able to trust
him. And without trust, how could he ever reach past that pain to
help her?

He dropped his fists onto the tabletop with a bang. Life was just
one big damn betrayal after another.

"I'm sorry, Zac. I truly am." Renee closed her file folder. "If you'd like to step away, I'd understand. Due to Emily's involvement with our department, complications I didn't even go into with Crissy's murderer trying to force Emily to testify in a separate case, and the issues she has with strangers, I think the State of Arizona could make a good case to retain jurisdiction."

Moose had remained quiet during Renee's story, his haunted gaze a reflection of how Zac felt. Now the big man tapped his gold coin on the table.

Renee nodded and cleared her throat. "If you abandon your attempt to gain custody and we can keep her in our courts, she'll be in good hands. Prin's fostering her now and had already started the adoption process before we learned of your existence and Emily's tribal qualification. Emily wouldn't be a victim of the system if we could help it."

"Prin?" Zac waved toward the doorway. "You mean Princess was trying to adopt her before Crissy's note threw everything for a loop?"

No wonder the woman hated his guts.

"That's about the sum of it, yes."

Emily's life could be worse than growing up in a good-guy motorcycle gang. Hell, her life *had* been worse. But he refused to be like his mother. He couldn't abandon his child. He'd hate himself if he didn't even try. Not every child got to have a father, but he was here and wanted to help.

"On the other hand," Renee echoed Zac's thoughts, "I'd be remiss if I didn't point out that studies show that girls with involved fathers are less likely to have issues with drinking, drugs, and teenage pregnancy."

He couldn't argue with that. Crissy had grown up without a father, and look how *she'd* turned out. He wouldn't risk Emily doing the same if he could help it.

Whether Emily knew it or not, she needed him. And he would be there for her.

He lifted his chin and pressed his shoulders back. "I need to be part of Emily's life. What's the next step?"

"I hope you understand why we won't turn a child in the system over to a non-custodial, biological-only parent right away. Especially to a male parent in a case like Emily's." Renee clasped her hands together. "We first have to do a thorough investigation, similar to how we'd evaluate and certify a potential foster home or adoptive family. That means background check, home study to certify a safe environment, references, and so on."

"Understood. How long are we talking about?"

"The whole process takes about ninety days. In the meantime, you'll have supervised visitation rights. You'll arrange for those with Emily's court-appointed guardian." Renee gave a half-hearted shrug. "That's Prin if you hadn't guessed. She'll be the one supervising all visitation and retaining custody until the process is complete."

His jaw slackened, and his confidence level dropped with it. Princess held the reins on his relationship with Emily. That should prove...

Irritating.

No. He swallowed and gathered his focus. He'd find a way to make this work. For Emily's sake.

Negotiating with Prin for visitations wouldn't be irritating. It would be *interesting*.

His flowing emotions must have been playing out on his face because Renee exchanged a knowing look with Moose. She gave Zac a grim smile.

"I don't think I need to tell you that it would be in Emily's best interest to find a way to work *with* Prin, not against her. I know it might feel like you two are in competition here, but I also know Prin will do what's best for Emily. And Emily trusts Prin, more than she trusts anyone else. Becoming Prin's enemy won't help you build a relationship with your daughter."

"To win the trust of my daughter, I have to win the trust of Prin." A sarcastic chuckle burst from him. "I mean, *Princess*."

"Exactly."

"Thanks for the tip." He turned to Moose. "Now, what can you tell me about Princess that will help me deal with her?"

The man guffawed and pocketed the coin he'd been playing with. "You have no idea what you're asking."

"Then help me understand."

"First of all, I won't betray Prin. More—"

"I wouldn't ask you to." Honor and loyalty were in too short supply in the world already.

"Good. Because more than just the biker code, she's the closest thing I have to a daughter. My late wife and I would have adopted her twenty years ago if the system had let us."

"The system didn't let you?"

"She showed up—out of nowhere—in front of my bar one night." Moose shifted his gaze, triggering Zac's honed-by-necessity radar for potential lies. "I think she was running from something, but I don't know what."

Moose returned his attention to Zac. "She said her parents had been murdered but refused to give their names. For all anyone knows, she didn't *know* their names since she was so young. The cops never found a record of a murdered couple that matched, there was no missing persons report, and no one could get a real name out of her, so the state never cleared her for adoption. They thought they were punishing her by keeping her in foster care limbo until she revealed her name, but I think she got exactly what she wanted. She usually does."

Conniving or an innocent child? "How old was she?"

"About five. She's been with me as my foster daughter ever since. I'm not sure how much—if anything—she remembers from before then."

Had her parents really been murdered? Or had something else traumatized her into silence?

A five year old running away from who knows what. Although, if Moose's "tell" was to be believed, he knew more than he was saying about what she was running from. Maybe it was so bad that he hoped *she* didn't remember, and he pretended cluelessness so he couldn't answer her questions about it.

"Anyway..." The man crossed his arms. "The second reason I can't give you any tips is because in many ways, she's a mystery to me. If my Roxi were still alive, she might be able to give you some female insight. But as it is, I see her chew up strangers—men—and spit them out on a regular basis. So all I can do is wish you luck."

Foster mom and child, both having issues with men. Yeah, *interesting* might not be the right word for the situation.

Chapter Seven

HIRLING EMOTIONS CLOUDED ZAC'S THOUGHTS, AND HE dropped his gaze to the dining room table. Now what?

"Christ." Moose slipped a cigarette pack from a pocket. "After being reminded of all that shit again, I need a smoke. Mind if I head outside?"

"Want some shade?" Zac stood from his chair, eager for the interruption. "I can show you to the covered patio out back."

"Yeah, thanks, man." Moose followed him to the hallway.

Renee called from the table. "I'll work on the forms for you to get this process started."

"Thank you. I'll be back in a minute." Zac dropped Moose off at the back door and then concentrated on the sounds from the rest of the house.

Assuming Princess hadn't ditched them all and taken Emily away with the rest of the bikers, they had to have disappeared around here somewhere. Voices carried from the family room down the hall.

He stopped at the doorway and eavesdropped. Anything he could learn about their relationship might help him make this work. He peeked around the corner. Princess and Emily were sitting in the middle of the floor, and Honey was snapping at something in the air.

"Almost done, Fairy. Your eyes still closed?"

Emily was facing the entrance, and her eyes were indeed closed. "Yep."

"Remember, you'll only be able to see my surprise if you believe in magic."

Princess sat with her back to him, but she extended her hand in front of her, beyond where her shoulder blocked his view. She'd removed one of her gloves, and swirls of colored light gathered on her palm. A moment later, the light fluttered away like a butterfly. Honey chased the apparition, drawing Zac's attention to the fact that dozens of the colorful *things* floated around the room.

"I believe." Emily's voice was giddy, anticipation bubbling out of her.

Princess lowered her hand and replaced her glove. "Okay, you can open your eyes now."

Emily's eyes popped open, and she squealed at a pitch that nearly left him deaf. "I see them. I see them."

"Yes, and only very special people can see them." Princess held out a finger, and one of them landed on her for a second before taking off again. "If you believe that the world is bigger than all this crap you're having to deal with, you can see magic. Crap is just crap. Don't let it get you down. Remember that magic is real."

Not the most kid-appropriate language, but the message of not letting stuff get you down was a good one. Then again, the language could have been worse coming from a biker chick, and given Emily's history, she probably *had* heard worse.

His daughter barely blinked at the sight around her. "Can I touch them?"

"You might be able to get one to land on you. Hold your finger out like I did."

Emily did as directed. While his daughter was distracted, he slipped into the room and settled on a chair in the corner to get a closer look at Princess's "magic." Like Emily, he held out his hand.

"Stay very still." Princess helped Emily keep her arm stable. "You don't want to scare them off."

"What are they?"

"I call them faerie flies."

"Like butterflies for faeries?"

"Yep. Do you like them?"

He'd been so busy watching Princess and Emily that he'd stopped keeping an eye on his own hand. Warmth brought his focus back to his finger. One of the "faerie flies" had landed on him.

His breath caught, and he kept it that way for fear of making the thing disappear. More colorful than a real butterfly, this one glowed, translucent, in every bright shade imaginable. He could see through it to the potted plant next to him, yet he could sense *something* on him. As though a special prism directed the heat and white light of the sun to split into a clump of rainbow colors and gather at a certain spot.

He hadn't been to many magic shows, but he'd never even *heard* of a trick like this one. Princess could play Vegas with this kind of talent. It was extraordinary.

He slowly brought his hand closer. Tiny sparks shot off from its form, dual-winged like a butterfly, opening and closing. The points of light bursting around the wings reminded him of an Independence Day sparkler or a too-hot iron rod just pulled from the forge.

"I *did* it." Emily's joyous cry drew his attention to where one of the apparitions had landed on her finger as well.

"Yes, you did." Princess helped Emily bring her arm gently down to where she could get a better look. "Remember this moment, and always believe that there's more to life than you think, so never give up."

Emily noticed him in the corner. "Does *he* believe?"

She'd attempted to whisper, but like kids seemed to do, she'd misjudged her volume.

Princess twisted toward him, scoffed, and then faced Emily again. "He thinks we're playing an imagination game because he can't see them."

"Funny." Sarcasm rolled off his tongue. He didn't need this woman treating him like an *other* in front of Emily. Or in his own home for that matter.

"Our game amuses you?" Princess didn't bother to face him.

"No, but your story about how I can't see your faerie flies does."

She spun around, her brows pinched together.

He nodded toward his finger, where one of the apparitions still rested. "What part of *that* am I not supposed to be able to see in this game of yours?"

Her gaze took in the thing on his hand, and then she scrambled to her feet. The fluttering glow on his finger winked out of existence.

She rushed toward him, and he stood to meet her. Letting her have the position of power in their body-language showdown would be a bad idea.

She looked him up and down, as if searching for an answer to a question he didn't even know. Finally, she asked him outright, "What *are* you?"

"I'm not the bad guy you think I am, ma'am. As Emily's father, I want a chance to show her that not all men are horrible." He twisted her speech to Emily around on her. "Don't you want her to grow up believing there's more to men than just that? So fear doesn't hold her down?"

He hadn't intended on confronting the woman right away, but he couldn't let her undermine him in front of Emily. Either Princess would prove herself able to put Emily's needs first—or he'd just made a bigger enemy.

Her mouth opened and closed several times with her obvious internal debate. The movement drew his gaze to her full, lush lips. He forced his attention away before his thoughts could follow, but his gaze landed next on her entrancing violet eyes. The speckles shimmering in her eyes intensified, her cheeks flushed, and he'd swear her hair became brighter red.

He braced himself to be slapped. Or worse.

Chapter Eight

K IRA COULDN'T PUT A FINGER ON IT, BUT SOMETHING ABOUT
this man's energy was different. *Something* made him
unlike anyone she'd ever met.

His eyes bore into hers, dark, unreadable. And yet, so like
Emily's.

Black hair fell down his forehead past his eyebrows and over
the tops of his ears. The long strands touched his collar, curling
slightly at the contact. Sparse stubble grew only where a mustache
and goatee would be, giving evidence of his Native American
genes. Less body hair—just like faeries. A dent in one cheek hinted
at a dimple.

She tore her gaze away. The dimple mocked her, knowing she
wanted to see it in full bloom.

Her focus instead landed on the T-shirt that nearly strangled
his biceps. Who needed biceps that size? Just because he spent day
after day hammering metal into shape didn't mean he had to be
so...

Full of raw, tempting power.

Damn it. She wasn't sizing him up for a potential energy boost,
so what the hell was she *doing*?

His *looks* had absolutely nothing to do with how he'd seen her
magic. How he'd done the impossible.

Hell, she hadn't even been sure *Emily* would be able to see her faerie flies, but she'd needed to *try*—to do something—despite the risk of removing her glove. Anything to keep the girl from freaking out even more.

The moments after the rest of the family had ridden off had cornered Kira into dealing with a chaotic shift from Emily's peaceful acceptance to a full-on panic attack in the middle of the driveway. Even the dog's presence hadn't calmed her crying and flailing.

Desperation had driven Kira to break her own rules about hiding her magic, and she'd called on her clan's ability to control fire and light in a last-ditch attempt to distract the girl before she lost all of yesterday's emergency energy surge. She'd been damn lucky her plan to allay Emily's fears had worked at all.

So how had *he* seen them? Until the marks under her skin completed the power circuit on her body, her magic wasn't powerful enough for anything more than minor tricks of light.

Humans simply didn't retain enough of their connection to the purity of life and wonder to see her low-level magic. Even most children nowadays were infected by the mundane, their ability to experience true awe tarnished by video games, mindless school lessons, or horrors at home. And *no* adults escaped the inevitable slide into banality.

His ability came from something else. Something she'd never seen.

She didn't like mysteries. *She* was supposed to be the mystery, not anyone else.

Impulsively, she ripped off her glove again and grabbed him by the wrist. His emotions flowed into her through the connection. One way or another, she'd get her answers.

"Who are you?" Step one: Identify the enemy.

A simple touch of her bare skin didn't put the person into a trance, but the physical contact sharpened her natural ability to read others' feelings. The truth couldn't hide from her.

"Zachary Chase, ma'am." His emotions were as calm as his voice. Her grasp on his arm hadn't fazed him at all. In fact, he seemed to like it. "I go by Zac. And I'll even let *you* call me Zac too."

He cracked a smile at his joke. His eyes crinkled, and his dimple burst into existence. She gasped. Holy hell, did she love her a good dimple. And this one—beside his bright smile that stood out against his rich skin color—was deadly.

She needed to get him to stop smiling. Now.

"Why do you want Emily?"

"Like I told you, ma'am, I think I can help her, and she deserves that chance. Don't you think it would be in her best interest to *not* fear every man she comes across? Think about her at school—or at work when she's older. Besides, children shouldn't live in fear, right? Isn't that the motto of your group?"

Nothing but sincerity flowed from him.

She checked over her shoulder. Honey and the faerie flies were still distracting Emily across the room. Kira turned back to him. "Have you ever abused anyone?"

"No, ma'am." Hot anger flared in their connection, and instinct nearly drove her to jump back from the heat. "And I'd like to kill every one of those sons of—" He cut himself off, and self-chastisement smoothed his emotions again. "—jerks who hurt her."

"Do you do drugs?" The last thing Emily needed was more addicts in her life.

"Never." Something flickered at the edge of his thoughts.

He wasn't lying—not by a long shot—but strong emotions lay behind his reason for avoiding drugs, and he kept them bound and gagged in a corner of his mind where he wouldn't have to think about them.

His dimple peeked out again. "I don't smoke and rarely drink, if those are your next questions."

"I grew up in a biker bar. Smoking and drinking aren't on my judgment list." Her choice to do neither was strictly personal and no one else's business.

"Is that why you came here? To judge me?"

She tilted her head, struggling to read the layered emotions of his question. On the surface, he wanted to appear indignant. But underneath, beyond where she could usually detect, he welcomed her judgment. He wanted her approval and was confident he'd get it if she gave him a chance.

"Yes. I'm judging whether you're as much in Emily's best interest as you think you are." Before he could feel satisfied at her answer, she listened for Honey's yips, assuring her that Emily wasn't eavesdropping, and changed the subject. "Do you love your daughter?"

The jerk of his head made reading his emotions unnecessary. He had no plans to ever love anyone.

In other words, he was no better than she was when it came to parenting instincts. If he wasn't going to love Emily, why would it be so much better for her to end up with him?

By the time he answered, his thoughts had put up a front. "I haven't even gotten a chance to know her yet, so it's a bit early for love. But yes, I care about what happens to her."

"Why'd it take you six years to care?"

The strongest emotions she'd felt from him yet burst across their connection. "I'd have cared about her before she was even born if I'd known she existed. *I* would never abandon a child."

"You broke up with Crissy before knowing she was pregnant?"

"No, ma'am. She broke up with me. When she disappeared."

While she'd asked the last couple of questions about Emily, acute pain had grown in her chest. Yet a moment of self-diagnosis revealed that she was okay—*he* was the source. She was feeling his emotions just as strongly as her own. Her heart wasn't aching, but his was. Piercingly.

He'd lost his daughter through no fault of his own, and now he feared he'd lost her forever.

The strength of his emotions—and her ability to read them so deeply despite just meeting him—meant ignoring his desire to help Emily wasn't an option.

"Okay." She bit her lip, wishing she could take back the word.

But her strong connection to his feelings—far beyond the levels she normally perceived, even with physical contact—meant the consequences of his extreme negative emotions would be dangerous. Besides, she wouldn't turn the girl into a pawn between them.

His body stiffened, making him tower over her even more. From his wrist, hope trickled. "Okay, what?"

"Okay, I won't get in the way of you trying to help Emily." The dimple bloomed again, and she glanced away and released his arm. "Fair warning—she doesn't even trust the other family members. And I won't *force* her to give you a chance."

"Understood."

She lined up her fingers to put on her glove. He grasped her bare hand, and her gaze shot back to his.

No one *ever* dared touch her without permission, much less touch her exposed skin. Not if they were smart.

This man proved just how *not smart* he was by rubbing his work-roughened thumb over her bare knuckles. "Thank you. I'm grateful Emily's had someone like you in her life."

That damned dimple made another appearance, and all her retorts died in her throat. His genuine sentiment and charm were dangerous to her tough-girl image. She was liable to let him get away with something ridiculous—like touching her.

His eyes twinkled. "Does this mean I get to call you by your name?"

She gave him a glare, but her heart wasn't in it. His negative emotions must have drained her too much to make the effort.

He angled his head, and despite the seeming impossibility, his dimple deepened in his cheek. "Please?"

Between his boyish grin and the dimple that could melt hearts, abnormal giddiness bubbled in her chest. Her resistance crumpled.

"Fine." She rolled her eyes, and a hint of a smile curved her lips. "You can call me Kira."

His eyes widened—and her brain clicked into gear. *No...*

She froze from the inside out, even as her blood heated up with her pounding heartbeat. Why the hell had she said that? She finally had the presence of mind to draw back from him, but the damage couldn't be undone.

No faerie ever revealed any part of their true name. That was *How to Be a Faerie 101*, drilled into her since birth. Anyone with her full true name would have complete power over her, and someone with even just a part of her name could affect her free will.

Hell, the whole reason she had to stay away from the Mythos plane was because Lirdeag, the traitorous faerie who'd proclaimed himself her fiancé, had tortured her parents to discover her first name, Kiratania.

And now this man—this iron-strengthened *enemy*—had the first part of her true name. Thank goodness there were nine more parts to her name, but still...

He looked almost as shocked as she felt. He barely breathed. "Your name—your real name—is Kira."

"Forget I said that." Her voice rasped in her throat, and her limbs shook with the effort to *not* move closer to him at the sound of her name on his tongue. Without another choice, she touched her fingers to his temple to wipe out his memories. "Forget my name. Call me Prin."

"Prin." Emily's call grabbed her attention, and Kira spun around, her legs still shaking so hard they barely held her up. The girl's face lit up with a hundred smiles. "Look."

Honey had herded the remaining faerie flies around Emily, and a dozen rested on top of her arms and head. One even sat at the end of her nose.

"That's wonderful, Fairy." Her words came out between hyper-ventilating breaths.

Thank goodness Emily hadn't been listening to their conversation. She'd hate to mess with the girl's memories too.

Behind her, Zac's deep voice rumbled with concern. "Are you okay?"

Shit. She didn't know how much she'd erased his memories. How confused was he?

Without waiting for her answer, he cupped her elbow and guided her to the leather chair in the corner. She was too grateful for the support to snap at him for touching her. Again.

Before anything else could go wrong, she put on her glove. Stupid. She *really* should have known better than to expose her skin and magic. Her internal rules existed for a reason.

Only after she was safely protected once more did she look up to gauge his memory loss. "I'm fine now, thanks. It's been an in-tense day. How are you holding up?"

His face scrunched up, as though he was debating his answer. No way was she going to remove her glove again to see where his confusion lay.

"Parts of today—learning about everything she's been through"—he glanced at Emily—"have been horrible." He returned his gaze to Kira. "But parts of it have been amazing. I got to see your magic trick—that I have no idea how you pulled off. I got your approval for my attempt to build a relationship with my daughter, and I greatly appreciate that."

His teasing grin brought out his dimple. "And you gave me permission to call you Prin, so all in all, I'd call this a good day."

Her lips couldn't help matching the curve of his. Even beyond his charm, his words proved the memory manipulation had done what she needed it to do. Thank goodness for that.

If the fae had a god of *Undoing the Stupidest Thing You've Ever Done*, she'd have needed to pay tribute. Big time.

Chapter Nine

ZAC LEANED AGAINST THE CHAIR AND KEPT HALF AN EYE ON Emily and her joy with the magic trick. The other half of his attention stayed firmly on the redhead sagging into the leather cushions beside him.

Kira.

He couldn't believe she'd told him her real name, and judging by her reaction, neither could she. She'd shaken like a newborn colt and had seemed only a third as stable. Thank God she hadn't passed out on him. If Emily had seen that happen, he'd have probably gotten the blame.

Kira.

Had she really never told anyone that name before? If so, why had she told him?

Regardless, he had a job to do, and that was more important than whatever her reasoning might be. The first step in gaining Emily's trust was gaining Kira's trust. That meant he had to respect her wishes, show her that he could be trusted with this secret. She'd agreed he could call her Prin, and since that's all he'd been asking, he was happy to oblige.

Back when Renee had said Kira would do what was best for Emily, he'd had his doubts. But now he knew what worked with her—sincerity. Heck, if anything, her interrogation had proved just how much she cared about his daughter.

Renee stepped through the doorway. "Ah, here you all are."

Moose followed Emily's case manager into the room, and his eyebrow lifted as soon as he spotted them in the corner. Maybe he'd expected Kira to have ripped his head off by now.

Zac stood up from where he'd been half-sitting on the arm of the chair. "Sorry for disappearing on you, but Emily and I were marveling over Prin's magic trick. She's amazing, you know."

Both Renee and Moose looked confused, their foreheads drawing tight.

Renee's lips twisted, the corners tugging into a smile. "No, I didn't know." She lifted her file folder. "Anyway, I have those forms ready for you to sign so we can get the process started."

"Great." He turned back to Kira. "Are you okay, or do you still need a hand?"

She swallowed, her throat bobbing as she looked up at him. "I'm fine."

Emily came closer to them—voluntarily getting within ten feet of him. She'd dropped her arms and left the apparitions behind. Her gaze shyly touched on him before landing on Kira. "We really *are* special. They can't see them, can they?"

His focus jumped to Moose and Renee, who hadn't given a second glance to the glows flying around the room. Had they seen the trick before?

Kira stood and gave Emily a wink. "Of course not. There's nothing to see."

He scanned the room. It was true. The apparitions had vanished without a trace.

He just barely managed to stifle rolling his eyes. Maybe she'd hoped he'd make a fool of himself. "I think you like messing with people."

She laughed, a genuine burst of musical delight. "A girl has to entertain herself somehow."

A moment later, they'd all gathered back in the dining room, and Zac spread out the forms for starting the custody proceedings. As far as he was concerned, there wasn't a question of whether or not he should sign them. He would have taken responsibility for his daughter six years ago if given the choice, so he'd make the same decision now.

The only question was how to approach the issue with Emily. He caught her gaze across the table, where she once again sat on Kira's lap. "Do you know what these papers are for?"

She glanced up at Kira, who nodded encouragement to his daughter despite her back being as stiff as one of the iron rods in his workshop. "It's okay to talk to him, Fairy. You know I'll never let anything happen to you."

Emily ducked her head and whispered, "They're for letting you take me away."

Her response made it clear what she was most concerned about, and that made his job easier. "You're only half right, Fairy."

She looked up at his use of her road name. He'd purposely used it to emphasize his next point.

"Yes, these papers are for letting me be your dad, but I'm not trying to take you away from anyone. Prin and Moose want to keep you safe, and I want to do the same. I think we'll be able to do a better job of taking care of you if we're all working together. So Prin and I are going to be spending a lot of time together with you for the next few months. This is about us being together, not anyone being taken away. Do you understand that?"

Emily tightened her hold of Kira. "Does that mean Prin still gets to be my new mom?"

Uh... His eyes sought Kira's, but she was no help. She straightened her shirtsleeve, completely ignoring him. Her message was clear: *You walked into that one, so don't look at me to help you.*

"Well." He swallowed. "These papers are just the beginning of the process, not the end. The important thing for you to understand right now is that Prin *will* be in your life. We have months to figure out *how* that will work."

"I won't do anything unless I can keep Prin."

Custody judgments didn't take what kids wanted into account until they were older, but pointing out that fact would be like detonating a nuclear bomb. Destructive with nothing to show for it.

Without another choice, he offered, "I promise to try to keep Prin in your life."

Emily crossed her arms and narrowed her eyes. "Prin doesn't break her promises, so you better not break yours. If you do, you're no better than my *mommy*."

The adults around the table froze, unprepared for the level of anger she'd directed at her mother. He doubted any of them blamed her, but he wasn't sure it was healthy for her to have that much negativity built up inside. On the other hand, if someone should point out Crissy's good aspects to balance out Emily's perception, he was the wrong person for that job.

"I agree. Your mom made a lot of mistakes. While no one's perfect, and I'm sure I'll make some mistakes, I hope to God I can do a better job than her." If he couldn't top *that* low bar, he didn't deserve to have Emily.

She gave him a glare dark enough to suggest she'd picked up the technique from Kira. "We'll see."

It wasn't a ringing endorsement, but that slight willingness to give him a chance to prove himself was probably the best he was going to get.

"Yes, we will." With that, he signed the papers to start the custody process.

Either he'd prove himself a capable father, or he'd fail to do better than a lying drug addict who'd sat by while her child was molested. He should have felt confident. Instead, he felt utterly lacking in the skills needed to deal with Emily's emotional issues.

God help him, but he might need to keep Kira around for his own sake.

Chapter Ten

K IRA'S STOMACH CLENCHED HARDER AT EACH FORM STACKED into the signed-and-done pile. Zac had talked a good game, claiming he wasn't trying to take Emily away from her, but the girl hadn't given him a choice about agreeing to include Kira in her future. His words meant nothing.

In reality, he was signing Kira's death warrant. She didn't want to lose Emily for either of their sakes, but if he was as good as he thought he was, the girl would survive. Kira, on the other hand...

How was she supposed to gain energy if he interrupted her connection to Emily?

Yet shutting down *his* relationship with Emily would treat the girl as a pawn. Not to mention that Kira would then face his negative emotions *and* Renee could then justify taking the girl away anyway. Bastard.

She was stuck. Effing A.

Back when she was a child, she'd created her own energy. That nice little convenience had disappeared along with her childhood. Now the banality of the Earthen plane slowly ate away at her essence, making her more vulnerable.

The positive emotions she absorbed from others had become less effective at delaying her inevitable maturation, and negative emotions were now more destructive, forcing the tattoo-like lines to develop faster, coming closer to completing the circuit that would allow her to tap into the energy of the Mythos plane.

Other faeries would be eager to reach that step, embracing it in their teen years, but the magical strength she'd gain wasn't worth the danger. Not when her freedom—and that of her people—was on the line.

Her thoughts circled around her limited options, imitating the swirls of Zac's pen. She could go back to her previous method of collecting energy from the bar's tourists. Of course, with summer season upon them, those college visitors would be few and far between. Besides, like junk food, that energy felt good while it lasted, but it never lasted long enough now that she was getting older.

Should she foster and adopt another child? Or volunteer at a children's hospital? She shifted in her chair, unable to find a comfortable position with the threat of burning through yesterday's remaining energy reserves itching under her skin.

Emily was a special case. Kira knew her issues, knew how to gain her trust, knew how to help her. A random child at a hospital or foster agency wouldn't have that connection to Kira, so she wouldn't gain any positive energy right away. She had enough trouble balancing the positive and negative energy while dealing with Emily. Working with another child might mean she'd receive all of the negative and none of the positive, like her connection to Zac. And without positive energy on a regular basis, every little setback condemned her more.

Zac signed the final form with a triumphant flourish. "Ta-da."

"Wonderful." Renee—the traitor—gathered the pages into her folder. "I'll get this into the system right away."

"To celebrate, let's raid my refrigerator and grab lunch."

Zac's charm worked on Renee as well, and the woman laughed. Oh, ha ha, so funny.

Not.

Kira picked at a cluster of grapes while he regaled the group with promises to cook for them later. Even Emily seemed interested in trying his Navajo fry bread tacos, a recipe from his maternal grandmother. Traitors all.

After lunch, he insisted on showing off his house. From the gourmet kitchen to the pool patio, not a single room or outdoor area was safe from his iron obsession. Door handles, bed frames, patio furniture, blah, blah, blah. Each one pressed against her awareness with a threatening vibration that increased her irritation.

Renee gushed over his work so much Kira suspected the woman was trying to get a free piece out of him. Either that, or the fifty-something woman wasn't beneath flirting with a man close to half her age. Ugh. Just because he was as gorgeous as all get out didn't excuse behavior like that.

Worse, the last part of the tour took them to his workshop next door. And she couldn't beg off because Moose had left to get the bar ready for the evening crowd. Renee would question her ability to be Emily's guardian if she bailed on the *supervised* part of a supervised visitation, so she had to enter the heart of the iron beast.

He was oh-so-proud of his business, pointing out the separate drive for his Chased by Fire workshop. In the front room, a desk and computer sat on one side for his office, and a couch and chairs filled the other, the coffee table between them covered with port-folios of his work, which Renee promptly flipped though with more compliments.

Then the moment Kira had been dreading came to pass. He opened the door to the back room, and she had no choice but to carry Emily into the dangerous space. Her chest was so tight her lungs barely took in any air. She stood in the center of the most open area and prayed he wouldn't come near to show off any of those medieval-looking tools arranged beside an anvil.

Emily had demanded to be carried for the entire tour, her discomfort with the proceedings clear, so at least she wasn't pressuring Kira for a closer look.

Renee scanned the dirt beneath their feet and the windows along one wall. "A dirt floor? And I was expecting this room to be dark. Is that one of those inaccuracies of movies?"

"Dirt is more comfortable for standing on all day, and more importantly, can't catch on fire." He hitched his thumb toward the windows framing a view of the open desert. "And many blacksmiths *do* like dim workshops. We can't work in direct light because we judge the temperatures we need by the color the metal glows, but this indirect light from the north side isn't a problem for me."

He motioned Kira and Emily closer. "Come test how heavy this hammer is."

From Kira's hip, Emily kicked her legs, as though that would steer her ride closer to the show. "*Prin.*"

Under her breath, she grumbled. "I'm not moving, Fairy. If you want to get closer, you'll have to get down and walk over there yourself."

Before she knew what was happening, Emily slid from her grasp and took a few hesitant steps toward Zac. Of all the times for the girl to get an attack of bravery.

Kira wrapped her arms around her chest, making herself as small as possible. Without Emily in her arms, she felt more exposed to the threat of death around her.

Emily stopped about four feet from him and glanced back, probably checking to make sure Kira was still there to protect her. *Yeah, yeah, just don't get yourself in trouble and make me go over there, kid.*

Zac gave her a grateful look, as if she was encouraging Emily to approach him. Not even close, He-Man.

He crouched down and held out a hammer at arm's length. "Try this one."

Emily snatched the hammer, poised to step back from him, but the weight threw her off-balance, and she staggered until getting her other hand around the handle. "Wow."

"Pretty heavy, huh?" He grinned. "Now imagine swinging that hundreds of times a day against metal that's so hot you can bend it, and you'll understand my job."

"Cool."

Renee shook her head. "I didn't know people still did this for a living. How do you even get started in something like this?"

"Actually I wasn't much older than Emily when I started hanging around the farrier at my dad's ranch. The guy who shoes the horses," he added before anyone could ask. Because everyone had been waiting on pins and needles for *that* explanation. "Anyway, I loved the idea of bending the unbendable to my will."

"And you started with him when you were old enough?"

He stood and brushed his palms on his jeans. "I apprenticed as a teenager, but my dad didn't let me pursue it. He insisted I go to college. It was only after my job with him fell through that I took it up full time."

A flicker of something, some emotion he wanted to hide, rippled across the space between them. Kira almost missed the subtle clue amid the distraction of all the iron threatening to kill her, but his emotions were strong enough for her to feel from this far away.

Interesting. Maybe that was the opening she needed.

Yes... If he was hiding something big, he might not be eligible for custody. And if she faked being his friend, she could get close enough to learn all his secrets. Especially if she risked more time out of her gloves.

She smiled, and her new bestest buddy caught her grin and returned it. Bingo.

Chapter Eleven

AT KIRA'S SMILE, ZAC'S GUT FLIPPED OVER IN HIS CHEST. GOD, she really *was* stunning.

The dark contrast of her all-black leather clothes and eye tattoos accentuated her porcelain-fine skin. And he never would have thought he'd say it, but her ink was damn beautiful. Sweeping curves and lines that he could only hope to make half as graceful in his work.

"Here, Mister." Emily's voice dragged his gaze away from Kira.

She struggled to lift the hammer. He grabbed the handle, his fingers brushing Emily's around the wood. She squeaked and ran across his workshop to Kira, who scooped her up.

"It's okay, Fairy. I'm not going anywhere." She graced him with another smile. "Mr. Zac doesn't know that you and I don't like being touched without permission, but now he knows. Isn't that right, Mr. Zac?"

Kira had an aversion to being touched? Could have fooled him, considering that she'd touched him first. Apparently, *that* was okay since she could give herself permission.

"Yes, now I know." He went along with her lead and met both of their eyes in turn. "I'm sorry."

Kira nodded, not a trace of annoyance in her expression. Did she really have an aversion, or did she fake it for common ground with Emily? For the sake of gaining her trust, he should probably err on the side of caution.

In contrast, Emily buried her face in Kira's hair again at his apology. Wonderful.

"Emily?" he tried. She didn't look up. "Fairy?" One eye peeked out from between Kira's red locks. He wanted to move closer to emphasize his words, but he had a feeling that would make things worse. "How about I show you how sorry I am? Maybe make you a little figurine as a gift. Anything you want. How does that sound?"

Kira shook her head. "That's not necessary."

Renee clapped. "Oh, that sounds fabulous. I'm so jealous. What do you think, Emily?"

A muffled "maybe" was her only reply. He'd take it.

"Can I talk any of you into staying for dinner? We have enough time that we could make those Navajo fry bread tacos. I'm pretty sure I have all the ingredients."

"I would *love* to. Really." Renee hugged her folder to her chest. "But I need to get back to the office and enter these into the system."

He glanced at Kira, fully expecting her to turn him down. She squeezed Emily against her. "I think I know someone who wanted to try that recipe. Am I right?"

Emily searched Kira's face, her brows close. "Moose isn't here."

Kira pressed her lips together, looking for all the world like she was trying not to laugh. "Well, there's going to be a lot of time these next few months where it's just you, me, and Mr. Zac. And you *know* I can handle him. Remember last week when I had to kick out those five Vegas bikers?"

Emily's eyes brightened. "Oh yeah, they walked funny after you were done with them."

Renee's brows popped high, and Kira pursed her lips even tighter. He wasn't sure whether they were telling the truth or pulling his leg in a prearranged tall tale. And Kira's expression didn't help, as she looked like she was trying to reassure Renee and Emily with opposite stories at the same time.

He broke the standoff by holding up his hands. "I'm not stupid. I promise to behave."

After Renee said her goodbyes and let him know she'd be in touch, he brought Kira and Emily into the kitchen, where he gathered the mixer, deep fryer, and ingredients for the meal. Kira set Emily at the table at the far end of the long room and put her to work tearing up lettuce while she joined him at the counter. Silence filled the void of Renee's chattiness, but it wasn't an awkward kind of silence.

Every time he reached for the next ingredient or utensil, Kira was at his side with the proper item. Like a doctor and nurse team who had worked together for years, she anticipated his needs practically before he realized them himself.

Thanks to her efficiency, he'd mixed and rolled the fry bread dough and chopped the vegetables in record time, and he couldn't hold back his amazement. "How do you do that?"

"Do what?" She didn't look up from preparing the ground lamb for the next step, no trace of teasing in her voice.

"Knowing what I'm going to need before I do."

"Oh... That." A moment passed. Finally she offered, "I've worked behind the bar with Moose for as long as I can remember." She chuckled. "*Long* before I was legally allowed back there. I'm just used to the job, I guess."

Her explanation made sense, but he couldn't help thinking there was more to it than that. One more thing that made her seem unnatural. Add it to the list.

He glanced back at Emily, who was having a bit too much fun with her assignment. They'd have lettuce confetti by the time she was done.

"How has she been adjusting? I mean, not just to Crissy's death, but to the changes of her school and everything."

"She hasn't been in school yet."

"But she's six." He started the meat, and Kira was ready with the cheese and grater, like his own personal mind-reading assistant. "Wasn't she supposed to be in kindergarten this year?"

Kira scoffed. "Tell that to Crissy."

Her gaze shot to Emily, but the girl showed no sign of eavesdropping. Although the kitchen was open, the breakfast table was far enough away as to be in a different room.

She resumed in a whisper. "You'd hardly recognize Emily from when I first took her in. I don't know how often they even had food in the house. Crissy's neglect was complete. No food, clothes, or medical care. Enrolling her in school never happened. She was so far behind it's been easier for me to homeschool her these last couple of months." Her voice sharpened, as though expecting him to argue with her decision. "Her emotions are strong and unpredictable—she's both too mature and too immature for her age—but she's not stupid. She'll be caught up and ready for first grade in August."

Wow. Just when he thought he knew how awful Crissy had been—and more importantly for his ongoing sanity, how dedicated Kira was—the truth surprised him yet again.

He set down the cheese block and grater and gave her his full attention. "Thank you. I mean that."

His hand empty, he longed to embrace her with his gratefulness. He'd promised himself to err on the side of caution though, in case she really did have an aversion to being touched. The struggle to resist reaching out to her warmed his face, and his skin itched like an ill-fitting shirt.

"I can't thank you enough for everything you've done for her." Was that overkill? "I mean, I know you did it for her and not for me, but I still appreciate it."

Her lips curved. "Yeah, I did it for her. But appreciation is always nice."

Was this the same woman Moose had warned him about? The one who spit out men daily? Hard to believe, as this woman was downright friendly. And sweet. And caring.

And looking at him questioningly.

Crap, he'd been staring at her. He returned his attention to the ground lamb browning in the skillet.

She was just so damn fascinating to watch. He'd never been this close to anyone like her before. Not just the motorcycle chick aspect or the tattoos, but her whole package. The competing personas and unexpected behaviors that screamed *unnatural*, and yet she somehow made them seem normal. At least for her.

Her hair had fallen behind her shoulders when she'd checked on Emily. Tattoos emerged from the hairline at her neck and curled forward to under her ears. Those marks followed the same graceful curving pattern, like a tendril of a vine unfurling.

His thoughts skipped down the path of wondering how far her tattoos extended under her clothes. Was she ashamed of them?

Was that why she wore long sleeves and gloves?

He broached the subject as a test. "I like your tattoos."

"Hmm? Oh thanks." Her voice was flat, perfunctory.

"Who came up with the designs?"

She twisted away, glancing at Emily. Definitely not a comfortable subject for her. She avoided his gaze for another moment, her lips tight. He continued watching her, patient enough to wait for a response.

"They're all mine. Custom." The words were clipped and sharp.

Not the answer he was expecting. She'd designed custom artwork, went under the needle for who-knew-how-long, and then acted like she was ashamed of them. That made no sense.

When the oil in the fryer was ready, Kira once again read his mind and called to Emily. "Fairy, you want to watch Mr. Zac make the fry bread?"

She was scary-good at that. Maybe he should be worried about her knowing too much about his thoughts.

After Emily was firmly on her hip, Kira saw his expression. "What? Did I guess wrong?"

"Nope." He winked at Emily. "I can guarantee you'll be safe around me. Your foster-mom knows my thoughts better than I do."

Kira blushed, the color obvious on her bone-white cheeks, and ducked her head.

Emily gave him a shy smile. "Yeah, she does that to me too."

"Hmm, we might have to gang up on her." He exaggerated his sneaky expression to ensure Emily knew he was joking. "What do you think would happen if you thought *go left* really hard, and I thought *go right* just as hard?"

Emily's smile burst into a full-on grin—the first he'd seen from her. "Her head might *explode*."

"You think?" He shook his head in mock disgust. "We'd better not do it then. That'd be awfully messy."

A giggle escaped from his daughter, and his chest expanded at the sound. Blood pounded through his body at double-speed, and he pressed his fist onto the counter.

It was a damned miracle. He could do this. He really could.

Kira looked up and caught his eye, her brow cocked.

He uncovered the bowl of fry bread dough, and under his

breath, he asked her, "How am I doing?"

She stepped closer, presumably to give Emily on her far hip a better view. Her proximity gave him a whiff of her scent. Similar to the rest of her, the aroma was natural and yet not. Sweet scents from nature, like bay leaves and cloves with a hint of ginger, didn't smell like normal perfume, but the fragrance was enticing all the same.

Her shuffling noises as she moved masked her answer. "Better than I expected."

Maybe that was the real problem she had with people. Too many had disappointed her, not living up to her expectations. He could definitely relate to that.

And maybe that meant he knew better than most how to relate to her and gain her trust. Thoughts like that could almost make a man giddy.

He dropped a flattened circle of dough into the sizzling oil. "My grandmother—my *shima sani*, if I'm remembering the Navajo word correctly—taught me this recipe when I was about your age, Emily. I'm sure she taught me others too, but this is the only one I remember." He tapped the disc to keep it below the surface. "It's one of my favorite meals, so I hope you'll like it too."

Kira leaned forward so Emily could see into the fryer, where the dough was bubbling up. Her long sleeve rubbed his arm, and she didn't seem to react negatively to the contact. "Is your grand-mother still alive?"

He didn't move back from the casual touch. "I don't know. After my mom left us, we stopped visiting my grandparents on the reservation. My father never got along with them, and my mother's abandonment didn't help with that."

A tight ball landed in his stomach, nearly stealing his appetite. Revealing that much about his history hadn't been on his list of things to do today—hell, he'd rarely revealed that much to anyone—but maybe the gory details would make him easier to relate to. Especially if Kira had truly lost her parents when she was young.

"Sorry about all that." Her lips formed a wry grimace. "We make quite the messed-up threesome here, don't we?"

"That we do." He flipped the fry bread and chuckled at Kira's anticipation of his need for a stack of paper towel sheets.

"Although we seem to work well together."

A healthy amount of pink tinged her cheeks again. He bit his tongue and refrained from commenting on it. He almost wanted to make causing that color his new goal.

Several minutes later, a fresh stack of fry bread and all the fixings stood ready, and he showed them how to assemble their Navajo tacos. Satisfied *mmms* echoed from around the table, where Emily had chosen to sit in her own chair rather than on Kira's lap. Every bit of progress gave him hope.

Of course, with dinner drawing the day to a close, he now had to come up with a plan to see them again—like a child visitation version of planning a second date. They both seemed to like animals, so maybe something along those lines would work.

"What would you say to going to the zoo in the morning, before it gets too hot?"

Kira focused on Emily. "What do you think, Fairy? We haven't been to the zoo yet."

"Do they have lions?"

"Yep." He winked at Kira. "And tigers and bears too."

At Emily's smile, Kira returned her attention to him. "I have her in several counseling and play therapy sessions during the week. But this weekend should work for us."

In other words, not tomorrow. He bit back his disappointment at not seeing his daughter every day, but considering their "supervised visitation" arrangement, giving up all that time to babysit his visits would be a lot to ask of anyone.

Besides, it wasn't like Kira didn't have a healthy, for-Emily's-own-good reason for the delay. The time apart would let him catch up on work too. Especially a special project he owed a certain someone.

"Sounds like a plan." He finished the last bite of taco. "Emily, have you given any more thought to what you'd like me to make for you?"

"You really could make me *anything*? Even though it's metal?"

"Sure can."

Emily stilled, her expression serious. "Prin, should I ask for a fairy? Or something else, like a dragon?"

Kira's face tightened. "I don't know that you should ask for anything. It's really not necessary."

"It's not a big deal." He stood and stacked the dishes for clearing the table. "I *want* to make her something."

"Well..." Kira wiped her mouth with a napkin. "You're Fairy, so maybe a fairy would make the most sense."

"But I like dragons too."

"Hmm, that could be tricky. Dragons and faeries are enemies."

"They are?" Emily's eyes rounded, and she scooted closer.

"Yes, faerie magic is one of the few things that can hurt dragons, and dragons have power over metal, and some metal can hurt faeries. I heard the faeries had to kick them out of their world, the fighting was so bad."

Emily's shoulders drooped. "Oh."

He fought a grin. Who'd have thought Kira would be such an imaginative storyteller?

Emily sat up and met his gaze. "I'd like a dragon, please. Maybe if I'm nice to it, faeries and dragons can learn to be friends."

Kira covered her mouth, her eyes scrunching, like she was holding in her reaction. He could relate, not knowing whether he should laugh or cry at his daughter's sweet conclusion.

He managed to give Emily a serious nod. "A dragon it is then. And if anyone could teach them to be friends, I think it would be you."

She beamed at his praise, and he left the table with an armload of dishes before he could ruin the moment by swinging her into a hug. Would wonders never cease? He *was* doing this. He was winning both Kira *and* Emily over.

After learning about Emily's history, he'd worried that he'd *never* be able to have moments like this with his daughter. And here he'd accomplished more than he'd thought he'd ever be able to do—in one day. Who knew he was a miracle worker?

No, that wasn't quite it. He glanced back at Kira and Emily at the table.

Who knew that they'd all work miracles together?

Chapter Twelve

KIRA PACED BY THE LARGE FRONT WINDOWS OF MOOSE'S BAR
and Grill, watching between the hanging neon beer signs
for Zac's arrival. In contrast, Emily sat at the empty bar
and entertained herself by drawing. How had Kira become the one
more anxious about the situation?

She puffed out a breath, attempting to eject the stress inside her
ribcage. Should she be upset that Emily was slipping away from
her? Or grateful that Zac's gentle handling had resulted in Emily
no longer draining Kira's energy with panic attacks? The line
between good news and bad news eluded her.

Worse, so far, her plan to uncover his dark secrets hadn't elicited anything except a sense of closeness—maybe even friendship—
with him. And *that* definitely wasn't in the plan.

Tires crunched on gravel outside, pulling her from her
thoughts. A red Ford pickup truck with a huge engine compart-
ment and dual rear wheels drove into the bar's parking lot.

Oh, *hell* no. How was *that* thing better than her and Emily
riding to the zoo on her Harley?

His truck was clean and new-ish, not in bad shape or anything,
but it didn't have an extended cab for a back seat. How were all
three of them supposed to fit in the front? She'd never make Emily
sit next to Zac, and that left her to take that oh-so-comfortable
middle position. If that beast was a stick shift, she was going to

impale him on it.

"He's here, Fairy." She grabbed the pack with their water bottles, a necessity in the desert, no matter the temperature.

Emily stuffed her drawing materials into her mini-backpack and scampered over. "Can I bring these with me?"

"Yes, as long as I don't have to remind you again about your hat."

Emily giggled and ran back for her floppy wide-brimmed hat. "I'll remember."

"Uh-huh."

They headed toward the door just as Zac entered. He did a double take at her tiger-shaded, orange-ish and black striped hair and then tapped the front of his cowboy hat. "Howdy, ma'am, Emily. You all ready for a fun day?"

"Yeah, change of plans though." She edged past him out the door. "Emily and I will take my bike there."

He chased after her and Emily around the building's corner. "That's not a good idea."

"Why not?" She stopped, one foot ready to bolt toward her bike in the back lot. "How is it better for all of us to squish into your truck?"

"I'd rather not have to witness all the cars trying to kill you and Emily."

She stepped closer to him and then thought better of it. "I have *never* been in an accident."

Zac closed the gap she'd left between them. "Maybe that means you're due."

"Are you accusing me of being willing to risk Emily's life?"

Humans couldn't compete with her reflexes. She could get her, Emily, and her bike out of danger before other drivers could get near them.

"No, ma'am. It's the rest of them I don't trust." He locked onto her gaze and held his palms up, sincerity oozing from the gesture. "Please. There's so much I never had the opportunity to protect her from. Don't take this away from me too."

His request was from one person who cared about Emily to another, and the earnestness behind his words couldn't be ignored. He'd be overprotective now, simply because he finally could.

Overprotectiveness in the long term wasn't healthy for most people, but in the short term, feeling cared for was just what the girl needed.

She glanced at Emily, who'd shut down, her emotions emitting nothing. *Note to self, no arguing in front of her.*

"Okay." She let Zac lead them back to the truck, where he held open the passenger door.

Ten feet from the truck, Emily halted, her stiff posture reflecting that she'd figured out the seating situation.

Kira leaned down and whispered, "I'll sit in the middle. It's okay."

"But—"

"I can handle him, remember?"

Emily nodded, a mixture of bravery and gratitude now flavoring the emotions floating to Kira's side. Zac caught her gaze, understanding the gist of their quiet debate.

"My promise to behave is still in effect."

Like he *could* do anything to her. She climbed into the truck and gave him a grin. "Too bad. I was looking forward to giving someone a good fist to the face."

His eyes widened, and then a laugh burst from him. "I'll see if I can find someone for you."

"Good plan."

She offered a hand for Emily to climb inside. The truck's large tires made the first step a mountain to the girl. Technically, Emily shouldn't be in the front seat at all *and* in a booster seat in the non-existent back, but what choice did they have? Besides, the girl's normal transportation was a motorcycle, so Kira wasn't one to talk.

After Zac closed their door, Kira set their packs on the floor and helped Emily with her seatbelt. A glance at the truck's controls confirmed it was an automatic transmission.

Bummer. No face punches, no impaling—how was she supposed to entertain herself?

As Zac settled behind the wheel, his broad shoulders and powerful biceps brushed her sleeve. Following her rules around him wasn't getting any easier.

His scent, a raw mixture of smoke-hardened strength and

animalistic power, filled the enclosed cab. If he were a stranger walking into Moose's place, she'd have sniffed closer, intrigued— and then escaped the other way. Guys like him were too unpredictable compared to the college guys who all seemed to follow the same script.

The brute-force mental connection she used on tourists required her to stay distant and unaffected, and maintaining that dispassionate attitude wouldn't be possible with him. His primal appeal was too distracting.

So were the thoughts skipping through her head right now.

Damn it. It would be a long day.

Chapter Thirteen

N OT SOON ENOUGH FOR KIRA TO AVOID DANGEROUS THOUGHTS, they arrived at a still-mostly-empty parking lot for the zoo. "Are you sure they're open?"

"Members get early entry. I bought a membership online the other day so we'd have more time before it got too hot."

Huh. His foresight was impressive.

He opened his door and grabbed a bag from the back. She waited for Emily to jump down and then joined them on the asphalt. Heat already wafted up from the pavement. Good thing temperatures didn't bother her, especially with her need to wear long, protective clothing to prevent direct contact with ferrous metal objects.

He pulled sunscreen from his bag. "Did you spray yourselves already?"

Damn. Again with the foresight. Way to make a girl feel inadequate for not thinking of that. As a fire clan faerie, her skin wouldn't burn, but Emily's would.

She held her hand out for the can. "Fairy needs to be sprayed."

He hesitated, a flicker of annoyance that she was taking over flashing through his emotions. Just as quickly, he passed her the spray.

Good boy. He was catching on. The necessity of spreading her arms and legs for the sunscreen could be triggering for Emily, especially if a man was looming over her.

After she finished, she plopped the girl's floppy hat onto her head with a don't-lose-this look. Before she could return the can, Zac took off his cowboy hat.

"While you have that, could you get the back of my neck? When I do it myself, most of it ends up in my hair."

Even though the sunscreen was the spray type, and not lotion to be rubbed in, the act still felt too intimate. Too much like the kind of thing she'd do for a friend—if she had any friends. But given his unruly hair, he was probably telling the truth.

She lifted the curling ends of his locks off his neck. What would the strands feel like without her gloves? Would the skin of his neck feel soft, or would it be hard like its chiseled shape?

She shoved the random thoughts away. Not going to fall for that again.

He fanned his hat along his neck after she finished and then tipped the brim onto his head. "Thanks. How about you? Need it for your face?" He glanced at the cargo box in the back of his truck. "Or I might have a spare hat for you."

Her with a cowboy hat? She almost snorted at the idea. "I don't burn."

His brow cocked. "No offense, ma'am, but your skin is as white as they come. You're a burn waiting to happen."

"Nope. I'm this color because I don't tan either."

He took the can from her and mumbled something under his breath about how he'd believe it when he saw it.

Once through the entrance with their bags and water bottles, Emily studied the map. "Should we go in a big circle?"

Zac shook his head. "It'll get too hot for us to see everything. We can come back as many times as you want though, so let's start with the lions if those are your favorites."

He moved to take the map from Emily, but Kira held out her arm and blocked him. "Lead the way, Fairy."

While Emily started toward the Africa Trail ahead, he looked at Kira's forearm across his chest. "You know, for someone who doesn't like being touched, you sure seem to touch others a lot."

"Or maybe you enjoy putting me into situations where I have to touch you." She dropped her arm and followed Emily.

He matched her pace, his eyes twinkling. "Would I do that?"

She ignored his teasing. Mostly because he'd been right the first time.

Of all the people she shouldn't touch, Iron Man topped the list. Yet somehow she kept letting herself come into contact with him.

She changed the subject. "I understand you wanting to be protective of her. But you have to let her find her confidence too."

Emily consulted the map again and made a left turn. With her wide-brimmed hat, she looked like a mini-explorer embarking on a safari.

Zac shifted his bag on his shoulder. "You're telling me that even though I just found her, I have to let her be independent."

"A bit, yes." The advice could just as easily apply to her own desires to keep Emily close.

He sighed. "Fatherhood isn't for the weak."

Out of the corner of her eye, she noticed the giraffes in the grassy field beside them ambling closer to the fence. Damn it. She spent so little time around nature that she'd forgotten about that complication.

Showing appreciation for their respect was the least she could do for these confined animals. She needed a way to honor them without calling attention to their behavior. The day would certainly be interesting. Emily would love seeing the animals up close, but who knew what Zac would make of it.

"Fairy, look. While we're here, let's stop and see the giraffes." She crossed her palms over her chest and bowed to the animals. "I'm pleased to meet you all."

Like most animals, their voices rang out in her mind as impressions, not clear enough to be understood as words. The overriding thought was that they wanted to know how they could be lucky enough to meet a princess of the legendary fae during their lifetime. A member of the royal family probably hadn't walked the Earthen plane in several centuries, and yet their spirits still recognized each other as friends and allies.

She acted like she was directing her words to Emily, bending down to the girl's height, but answered their question. "Fairy, aren't these lovely creatures? We're blessed to see them during our visit today."

The giraffes bobbed their heads, tickled by her words.

Emily imitated Kira's bow, her arms crossed and palms placed below her collarbone. "Thank you for coming to see us."

The giraffes ducked their heads again, not able to understand Emily's words, but honored by her attempt all the same.

"Great job, Fairy. You'll be like a real faerie in no time." She sensed Zac's gaze on her and hustled them away. "On to the lions."

A few minutes later, Emily had successfully led them to the lions' enclosure. She peered around the yard. "Can you see them?"

Zac pointed to a dark area. "There. Along the back wall. They're resting in the shade."

Kira held out her arms, and Emily allowed her to pick her up. The girl leaned, searching for the best view.

"I can see an ear and half a head." Emily's disappointment was evident even without the use of Kira's abilities. "Can you make them come closer?"

Zac's gaze jumped to Kira, but she ignored his reaction to deal with Emily's question. "I can't do that."

"Oh." Emily hid against Kira's shoulder, but not before a tinge of blush colored the girl's cheeks. From her buried position, she mumbled, "I thought maybe you could do magic with animals."

Damn it. So much for not calling attention to the animals' behavior today. She could either disappoint Emily or make the animals' reactions obvious to Zac. Lovely.

Maybe she could get the lions' attention without blatantly using her ability. She raised her volume so her voice carried over the enclosure. "Even if I could, it would be rude to interrupt their nap. We faeries should have more respect for animals than that."

As she hoped, one of the lionesses opened her eyes.

"Look, Fairy, they're waking up. Let's give them a minute."

The lioness saw her and grunted to the others. Soon, all the lions gathered at the edge of the ravine between their yard and the fence.

Emily's eyes widened, and she spoke in an awed whisper, "You did it." She slipped down from Kira's hip. "They're beautiful."

"Yes, they *are* beautiful." Kira bowed to them in thanks. "We're sorry for disrupting your nap, but we're so grateful to see you."

The male shook out his mane and lifted his chin. A roar exploded from him, the bellow rolling over and through them, echoing off the enclosure's back walls and the mountains beyond the zoo's borders. Her ribcage vibrated in resonance, and she felt the noise deep in her soul.

The sound was one of dominance—and of welcome. On behalf of all the animals, he thanked her for her visit and chided her for even thinking of not announcing her presence and allowing him this honor.

She bowed again, warmth flooding her cheeks. She hadn't been welcomed like that since... Ever.

"Wow." Zac tapped on his cell phone, which he'd apparently used to video record the exchange. "I don't think I've ever heard a full-strength lion roar like that. Makes me glad for the fence."

Emily tugged at her jeans. "What did he say?"

Kira didn't look at Zac to catch his reaction to the question. "What makes you think he said anything other than *rowr*?"

"You're all pink."

Kira touched her face. "Am I?"

Zac leaned forward, checking out Emily's claim, and grinned. "Either you're blushing, or you're already getting that sunburn you claimed you wouldn't."

She replied loudly enough for the lions to hear. "I'm just so pleased we were able to witness that greeting from these majestic animals. It made me feel very special, and I'm thankful." When Zac gave her an odd look, she changed the subject. "Although, maybe you're right, and the heat is getting to me. Fairy, I'll wait in the shade until you're ready to move on."

She bowed once more to the lions and retreated to the shady bench across the walkway. Without thought, her hands covered her face, as though she could bury her head in the sand like the ostriches that were probably somewhere around here too.

Blushing? She'd left the Mythos plane so long ago, and when she was so young, that she sometimes forgot *who* she really was. A faerie, sure. A princess, yeah, whatever.

But leave it to these animals to remind her that the truth was even more extreme than they knew, unaware of faerie politics as they were. She was the last remaining member of the royal family. Her freedom here on the Earthen plane was all that kept Lirdeag from claiming the throne and gaining full control over the fae.

"Hey." Zac's deep voice disrupted her thoughts. "You okay?"

She sat up and gave him a blank look. "Why wouldn't I be?"

He took his hat off and ran his fingers through his hair. Then he sighed and sat beside her. "I'll be honest. I never know what's normal or not around you." He replaced his hat. "Like, I can't even tell if things are as off-kilter as I think they are, or if I'm just imagining everything."

He gazed at Emily, who'd dragged out her drawing supplies and was sketching the lions. His hand waved toward the enclosure.

"I mean, either the heat *is* getting to you and I should be doing something to help. Or..." He grimaced. "Or a lion made you blush."

"You don't need to do anything to help me. I'm fine."

"Can you drink some water? Just in case."

She took a swig from her water bottle. "There. Happy now?"

"Yes. That's better than thinking I had to go in there and beat up a lion to defend your honor or something."

At the mental image, she laughed, a belly-deep sound she couldn't hold back. "Now who's delusional and needs to drink some water before the hallucinations get worse?"

He took a drink from a bottle and winked. "There. Happy now?"

"No." She shook her head in exaggerated disappointment. "Maybe I *wanted* you delusional."

A gut-busting laugh burst from him. "Oh, I bet you do. You want me so mixed up I don't know up from down. All the better to entertain yourself."

"Oh, come now." She gave him an innocent look. "You make it sound like I'm a horrible person."

"No. You're the best person I know." His earnest tone surprised her—and him too. He stood and backed up several steps. "I'm going to check on Emily."

The distance didn't affect her ability to share his powerful emotions though. Inside, he crushed his thoughts so hard she almost winced in sympathy. Something about his past made him reluctant—no, more than reluctant—made him *incapable* of seeing people as *good*. Adults especially.

And then there was her.

Chapter Fourteen

CROSS THE ZOO WALKWAY FROM KIRA'S BENCH, ZAC LEANED against the fence and pointed out something about the lions to Emily. The girl scribbled several more lines on her page, and then glanced back at Kira.

She ambled over. "Is that the I'm-ready-to-go-now look?"

"I think so. Did you want to see my drawing?"

"Of course I do." She stood to one side so Zac could see as well, without him having to get too close.

Emily held out her notebook. Considering that Kira was capable of stick figures, Emily's drawing could have qualified as professional quality in comparison.

"Wonderful, Fairy. Well done."

Zac echoed her praise. "Wow. That really *is* good." He crouched beside Emily. "If I said that I think you inherited my artistic talent, would you take that as the compliment I mean it to be?"

A shy smile curved her lips. "You really think so?"

"Yes, Fairy." His voice contained only sincerity. "I really do."

Kira indicated the lions, who still hung out by the ravine's edge. "We should thank the lions for being such good subjects too."

Emily put her drawing materials away and then faced the lions. "Thank you for your help."

The male huffed, like a sighing grunt. Kira was about to walk away when a sense of concern washed over her from the enclosure. She covered her question to the lions with a glance at Emily.

"Any problems or is everything good now?"

She barely registered Emily's thanks for the help, her concentration instead on the thoughts of the lions. The male bellowed a low grunting roar, asking if she was safe. And then he added something about a "seer."

A *seer*? She didn't know what that would refer to, much less why she wouldn't be safe. And between the animal's limited communication ability and her need to *not* raise Zac's suspicions any more, seeking clarification from the lion wasn't possible. Instead, she gave the male another bow, promising to be careful.

While they'd stopped at the lions, the zoo had started filling up with other visitors. Most adults took one look at her and gave their group a wide berth. Whether or not Zac ever experienced discrimination for his Native American genes, her appearance was more intimidating.

At Zac's suggestion, they next aimed toward Monkey Village, a walk-through exhibit with tiny squirrel monkeys. Their trek was one detour after another, as she stopped to acknowledge the rhinos and cheetahs and otters and every other animal along the path who wanted her attention.

At the jungle-style enclosure for Monkey Village, no mesh or glass separated the sidewalk from the trees arching overhead, and only the exhibit's rules kept visitors from reaching out to touch the Chihuahua-sized animals.

"They're so cute!" Emily clasped her hands, probably to keep herself from cuddling one of them like a stuffed animal.

The monkeys' high-pitched, almost bird-like chirps crescendoed as they entered. Just as quickly, the monkeys ran into their building at the edge of the enclosure.

"Wow." Zac eyed Kira. "Animals that don't love you? How'd that happen?"

The truth pressed her lips into a thin line. The monkeys' intentions would cause trouble soon enough, and she needed to head them off.

No brilliant ideas came to mind. No too-idiotic-to-ever-work ideas came to mind either.

Before she could come up with anything, the animals scampered out again and circled around their group on the nearby tree branches. They held out offerings of fruit wedges—and worms and grasshoppers—in their little hands.

Zac's disbelieving gaze burned hot on her cheeks. She bowed to the monkeys. "Thank you. We're honored, but we can't accept your gifts. This opportunity to visit with you is quite enough."

A zoo staff member came over, checking to make sure they weren't breaking any of the exhibit rules no doubt.

"No feeding the—" She saw the variety of foods in the monkey's hands. "What's going on?"

Kira played dumb. "What do you mean?"

The employee frowned at them. "Keep your arms down," she ordered, even though none of them had made a move.

The woman unclipped her radio, as though about to call security. Kira and Zac made quite the pair—a tattooed motorcycle chick and a wholesome-as-apple-pie cowboy hanging out together might even be a sign of the apocalypse—and now, between the two of them, her appearance worked against her.

To her surprise, Zac spoke up. "Maybe the monkeys are having a food party before it gets too hot."

The staff member gave him a look as blank as her tone. "A food party."

"Yeah, like a potluck. Is one of them pregnant?"

A chuckle escaped Kira, and it took all her concentration not to lose it completely.

"Don't worry, we're leaving." She bowed to the animals. "Enjoy your celebration. We wish you well."

Kira led their group toward the exit. The monkeys followed, leaping from branch to branch and balancing on the railings beside them.

Emily squealed. "They're so cute. I wish I could hug them."

"That would definitely break the exhibit rules." Kira understood the desire though.

The zoo staffer stood by the exit, ensuring they made it out without any hitchhikers.

At the door, Emily waved to the animals. "Enjoy your bugs and worms and things."

"Yes." Zac grinned. "It looks like they brought a good variety for their potluck. Good for them."

Kira gave them a final bow and ducked out the door behind Emily and Zac. By the time they made it to the walkway outside, she couldn't hold back her laughter.

Zac shook his head, and his dimple deepened. "Hanging around with you is definitely entertaining."

She gave him a wink. "You're welcome."

He might not know what to make of everything, but he was handling the oddities well enough to step to her defense. And *that* was more unexpected than anything to do with the animals.

Zac herded them to the shade and called for another water break. All the detours they'd taken along the path to Monkey Village had eaten up most of the morning. But Emily was thoroughly enjoying herself, and that's what mattered.

Children's giggles and splashing sounds caught their attention across the walkway. They weaved through a collection of umbrella-shaded benches and came to the edge of a rock face, where a waterfall crashed onto a splash pad. A dozen or so kids shrieked around the shooting jets of water. Some played in swimsuits, obviously regular zoo visitors who knew to prepare. Others let their clothes get sopping wet. At least the joke about Arizona being a "dry heat" was true. The sun and low humidity would dry out those clothes in no time.

Emily looked up at Kira, a plea in her eyes. "Can I play?"

"I don't have a problem with it." She took Emily's hat and backpack. "But we're guests of Mr. Zac, so he gets a say too."

Emily turned her puppy-dog eyes on Zac. "Can I play?" She fanned herself. "I'm really hot."

"Sure." Zac waved toward the play space. "We're here to do anything you want."

Emily took off so fast she probably didn't hear the end of his sentence.

He chuckled. "She's really something."

"Oh, she's something all right." Kira claimed an empty spot on the benches with a good view of the splash pad. "If this keeps up, she'll know how to manipulate you five different ways by dinnertime."

Zac took the seat next to her. "You say that like it's a bad thing. After everything she's been through, she could use a bit of spoiling."

Kira couldn't argue with that.

She opened her wallet. "By the way, you're trying to spoil *her*—not me. How much do I owe you for the entrance fee?"

"Nothing." After she narrowed her eyes, he shrugged. "I'm serious. The membership included a guest. That's you today."

"Thank you."

On the splash pad, Emily ducked under the waterfall and into the cavern. Out of sight.

Kira set her backpack and pile of Emily's things at Zac's feet. "I'm going to check the inside. Make sure she's okay."

She dodged the jets of water on the splash pad—leather didn't appreciate getting wet—and edged around the waterfall. A dim hallway, lit by colored bulbs and sculpted to look like the stalactites and stalagmites of a cavern, stretched to another exit on the right. Several drenched kids ran in the opposite direction, leaving happy squeals in their wake. Halfway along the walk, stairs led up to a slide, both looking like they'd been carved from rock. Emily's giggles led Kira to the mist-filled exit at the other end of the path.

She stepped onto the rope bridge outside, and Emily spun back toward her. "Isn't that cool, Prin?"

"It is. You be careful though, okay? We can't see you when you're in there, so no getting injured."

"I will be."

Kira settled beside Zac and pointed out the exits and water slide. "Seems okay. Probably the biggest danger is being run over by other kids."

"At least most of them are pretty little and can't do much damage."

"Uh-huh. We'll see how you handle it the first time you see Emily bleeding."

His horrified look gave her exactly the reaction she was hoping for. Predictability could be fun.

"Man." He shook his head. "That was just mean. Maybe I shouldn't have fought off the hordes who tried to steal your seat while you were in there."

"Sorry." Her twitching lips probably gave away that she wasn't sorry in the slightest. Since when was banter as much fun as biting someone's head off? "Thank you for fending off the invaders."

"Oh, it was awful." His brows pulled down in mock distress. "They threatened to steamroll my dead body with their strollers if I didn't give in to their demands."

"Is that all?" She *tsked.* "You're lucky. They could have set their toddlers to chewing off your feet so you couldn't even get away."

"I think you came back just in time."

"I *am* pretty scary looking."

His gaze swept over her like a caress from her thighs to her neck. Her skin heated more under his regard than it had all morning from the sun. After a leisurely visual tour of her body, his sparkling eyes met hers.

"Positively frightful." He winked, making it obvious he thought nothing of the sort.

On the splash pad, Emily made her twentieth trip into the cavern. Seconds later, she reappeared at the bottom of the water slide only to run in again.

At least *someone* was cool. Maybe Kira could dunk her face in the waterfall. She needed a distraction—for both of them.

"I must be losing my touch. I don't think you're intimidated by me at all."

A genuine smile brought his dimple into sight. Along with it, sheepish embarrassment tickled her senses from his emotions.

Good. A part of him was still intimidated by her. She couldn't let this fake-or-maybe-not-fake friendship ruin *all* her fun.

"Well." He cleared his throat. "I wouldn't go *that—*"

A massive energy drain in her limbs stole Kira's attention. "Emily!"

She stood and searched the splash pad for any sight of the girl.

Zac rose to his feet beside her. "What?"

"Something's wrong." She ran for the cavern entrance and yelled over her shoulder. "Watch for her at the exits."

The energy drain continued, burning along her skin. But Emily wasn't inside the play structure. She wasn't anywhere.

Chapter Fifteen

"**E**MILY!**"** KIRA SPRINTED BACK TO ZAC, LEAPING OVER toddlers playing in the puddles. "See her?"

"No." He scanned the area, his attention latching onto an employee. "I'll—"

Kira felt it then—a tug through the connection she'd established to Emily over the past couple of months. She couldn't explain it to Zac, so she just took off running down the walkway leading back to the zoo entrance. *I'm coming, Emily.*

Damn it, she'd taken her eyes off the splash pad to joke around with Zac. How could she have been so stupid?

She shouldn't have neglected her duty for even a second. Much less to—she needed to be honest and call it what it was—*flirt* with the last man on Earth she should get close to. Damn it, damn it, damn it.

No animal enclosures lined this part of the path, and only a few young families strolled along the pavement. Where was Emily? She staggered, another wave of Emily's panic and fear taking what little strength she had. *No!*

Movement around a bend caught her eye, and she pushed herself. She *had* to find the will—the strength—to save Emily. She had to.

Her feet steadied under her enough to stumble around the path's curve. Two men, their backs to her, strode down the walkway. Little legs flashed between theirs.

Emily. Being marched in front of thugs who looked just as out of place at the zoo as she did.

"Hey!"

The shorter man spun toward her. "Take the girl. I'll handle this."

Emily thrashed past the legs. "Pri—"

The taller man covered Emily's mouth, picked her up, and ran. Kira somehow found another gear and gave chase. The shorter thug stepped in front of her.

She shoved him aside with enough force to throw him to the ground, focused only on the taller man with Emily. Almost. His saggy jeans were within her reach.

She lunged forward and caught his waistband. A yank tugged him backward, and he fell on his ass, his pants now down by his knees. Emily landed in a tangle on top of him.

Before he could make a move, Kira leaned over him and punched him in the face. The impact crunched his cheekbones. Solid. Satisfying.

No one messed with her Emily.

Worry about the girl's drenched clothes ruining her leather didn't cross her mind. She picked up Emily, stomping on the guy's nuts while she was at it, and hugged her close.

"It's okay. I've got you. I've got you. No one can hurt you."

Emily's arms waved beside Kira's shoulder. "Prin. Look out!"

Kira whirled, ready to fight one-handed if need be. The shorter guy rushed toward them.

Another figure sprinted from beyond the path's curve. Zac.

He leaped at the man, and his flying tackle took them both down in a knot of limbs. More footsteps pounded on the pavement nearby, but Kira cared only about any danger to Emily. She needed to be ready for whatever would come next—and prayed she'd have the energy to deal with it.

The short guy and Zac rolled to the edge of the walkway, Zac coming out on top. Security officers screeched to a stop around them. Zac landed several punches before security hauled him off the thug.

The security officers twisted Zac's arms behind his back, assuming him the bad guy.

"My daughter." He panted. "They tried to kidnap my daughter."

Kira stepped forward with Emily. "It's true." She indicated the two downed thugs. "We chased them here from the splash pad."

Emily spoke up. "They said they had a gun."

The officers released Zac, and he stumbled toward Kira and Emily, his wild thoughts crashing into her. Before she knew what he was doing, he wrapped them both in a hug.

"Thank God you're okay." He squeezed them against his body, his animalistic scent overwhelming her. "Thank God you're okay."

The power of his relief swept through her like a giddy tide—washing away the tension in her muscles at the forced contact. Instead, his touch felt...

Good.

His emotion filled her chest, expanding it with warmth. Her heart sped up, beating stronger, beating with more determination, beating in time with his.

Energy flowed through her blood. The drain caused by Emily's fear reversed. The marks under her skin had no doubt slithered closer to their destination, but she—her strength—was whole once more.

Whether he'd admit to loving his daughter or not, Zac's feelings for Emily were pure and sincere enough to provide Kira with energy. His positive emotions invaded her essence just as easily as his negative ones. This changed everything.

She had a new power source. But only if she encouraged Zac's relationship with Emily.

Effing A.

Giving in to the inevitable, she loosened her stiff spine and protective hold on Emily. The more she relaxed into his embrace, the more freely energy traversed the connection. Finally, she melted against his chest and soaked up every ounce of positive emotion.

If this was the way things had to go, she'd make sure she wrung everything out of the arrangement she could. Make the risk of losing Emily to him as worth it as possible.

Even if she had to get closer to him than she'd ever planned.

Chapter Sixteen

ZAC SLOWLY LET HIS DEATH-GRIP ON KIRA AND EMILY LOOSEN. They were safe. Everyone was safe.

The craziness that had filled his head, playing every worst possible outcome, gradually quieted to a dull, throbbing headache. His delay of a few seconds to yell for security had carried Kira out of sight, and he'd beaten himself up over that decision with each stride that hadn't caught up to them. Even now, with both of them safe in his arms, his stomach still twisted into knots so tight they might be there permanently.

Safe in his arms... Bloody hell, he'd engulfed them without thought of their phobias—or whatever that aversion to touching was.

He pulled his arms away. "Sorry."

Pressure at his side disappeared, Kira releasing him as well.

Wait, she'd hugged him back?

"It's okay." Kira gave him a smile with no trace of complaint. "We understand, don't we, Fairy? We're all very happy to be safe and together."

Emily burst into loud sobbing. Kira looked at him in alarm and then sat on the nearest bench. She rocked Emily on her lap. "Shh, shh. It's okay. It's okay."

Damn it. His hug had been the last straw for her.

Emily tried to say something, but sobs reduced her to burbled, unintelligible syllables. Kira stroked her still-damp hair. "Shh. Wait until you get your breath. I'm not going anywhere."

He picked up his hat from where it had landed on the edge of the path and stood there, unable to do or say anything to help. His hands clenched, and his knuckles burned at the stretch, reminding him that he'd pummeled the asshole. He'd have kept at it too, if the guards hadn't dragged him off.

That at least was something he'd been able to do to help. Now, all he could do was just stand there like an idiot and hope for another opportunity to apologize.

"Excuse me, sir?" One of the security officers approached. The others held the two abductors, their wrists now zip-tied behind them. "The police are on their way, and I need to ask you to stay here until they arrive."

"I need to go back and get our backpacks and water bottles." He indicated Emily. "She's going to need a drink once she recovers."

The officer extended her arm for Zac to lead. "I'll go with you."

Back at the splash pad, he slung the three packs over his shoulder and claimed Emily's nearby hat. During the return to Kira and Emily, the security officer at his side shook her head. "I'm so sorry. We've never had an abduction attempt here."

That was likely true, so why Emily? Why after everything she'd already been through would this happen too? Unless the incidents were related...

Could someone be trying to prevent Emily from speaking up about what she knew? The more he thought about it, the more that was the only answer that made sense.

By the time he and the security officer made it back to the bend in the path, the Phoenix police had arrived and were taking statements from the gathered zoo employees. Emily's sobs had quieted, and he dug out her water bottle from the packs.

He sat beside Kira, but not so close—he hoped—as to set Emily off again. He held out her bottle. "Here. You should drink after all that."

Emily didn't recoil from his hand. She seized the bottle and gulped, proving how much the crying fit had taken out of her. Zac gave Kira her bottle, earning her thanks as well.

A cop ambled over. "Y'all ready to answer a few questions?"

"Yes." Kira answered for all of them. "As long as you promise to copy the detective investigating Crissy Braxton's murder on all reports, and make sure he's present for their interrogations." She indicated the two assholes, now being passed over to the police.

Interesting. She'd reached the same conclusion he had. Either they were both imagining things, or there was a fair bet they were right.

"I agree. This wasn't random." On a hunch, he leaned toward Emily. "Do either of those men look familiar?"

Emily twisted in Kira's lap. The cheekbone of the one Kira had taken down was a misshapen black and blue blob. The one he'd punched had blood drying on his chin. They both winced in doubled-over pain. Neither of them looked quite the same as they had before.

Emily whispered in Kira's ear. Once the other officers led the men out of earshot, she conveyed Emily's message. "The tall one is known as Boner, and the shorter one is Loco."

The next forty-five minutes passed in a barrage of questions about the incident itself, with the zoo employee who'd heard Zac's yell back at the splash pad corroborating their story. The fact the cop seemed least inclined to believe was how Kira had downed one of the men by herself.

She gave him an innocent smile. "I'd be happy to demonstrate how I did it if you don't mind a couple of broken bones."

The cop laughed and looked at Emily. "I'd say you're in good hands with these two looking out for you. Just to follow protocol though, I should warn y'all that it's safer to call the police than to take matters into your own hands."

Right. Emily would have been long gone if he and Kira had followed that plan.

After the police finished with them, Zac faced Emily. "I'm sorry for overwhelming you with my hug. I was just so happy you were safe that I forgot not to touch you. I didn't mean to upset you."

"That's not why..." Emily swallowed hard, the tears right at the surface once more.

Kira stroked Emily's hair back from where it had plastered to her face. "Take your time, Fairy. We're ready to listen whenever you're ready to talk."

Emily took a determined breath and spoke slowly, each word a struggle. "Them grabbing me was like the badness all over again." She curled into a ball on Kira's lap. "But you told me to believe in magic."

Kira kissed Emily's forehead. "That's right. I did."

"So I wished someone would save me." She looked at Kira. "And it worked. First you saved me. And then..." She gave him a shy smile. "My daddy saved us both."

His throat thickened like he'd been riding on the trail all day, and his eyes moistened to the point of stinging. He blinked as fast as his heart beat against his chest to clear his eyes, but his lungs took up the burning pain. Probably because he'd stopped breathing.

Emily had called him *daddy*. Today was magic indeed.

After a minute, his throat loosened enough to speak. "That's a daddy's job, Fairy. Every little girl should have someone who would do anything to keep her safe."

That was the truth in his case at least. He'd do anything for this little girl. Anything.

He reached toward her but didn't touch her. "For too long, you didn't have that someone, but now you do."

Emily hooked her fingertip around his. It wasn't much, but it was enough. "Thank you."

"Thank your foster mom too. She knew before I did that something was wrong."

Mother's intuition? Or something else?

For once, he didn't care. The important thing was that she'd known quickly enough to save Emily. The woman was—quite frankly—amazing.

"She always knows." Emily laid her head on Kira's shoulder. "I'm glad."

"Me too, Fairy." He held Kira's gaze long enough for a blush to heat his face. "Me too."

Kira squeezed Emily against her. "So when you started crying, was that just happiness and relief? Or was it about something else we should know?"

A tear rolled down Emily's cheek and into the corner of her smile. "Happiness."

The weight on his heart evaporated at the news. He *hadn't* upset her with his hug, and he *hadn't* betrayed her trust. Overwhelmed, he rested his hands on the bench for balance. His arms ached with the need for another group hug, but he didn't want to push his luck.

"And hey." He almost said Kira's name but caught himself in time. Instead he grinned, breaking the serious mood before tears rolled down his cheeks too. "Prin got to punch someone in the face after all. So all in all, this was a good day."

"Yes, I did." Kira positively beamed. "And it was *excellent*."

He chuckled. "Remind me never to piss you off."

"Nuh-uh. If someone's dumb enough not to figure out on their own that I'm not to be messed with, why would I help them?"

His laughter shook his whole body. "What am I going to do with you two?"

Before he could stop it, his mind provided completely inappropriate images of what he could do with Kira. Emergency distraction needed.

He snapped his fingers. "I know. Let's get ice cream."

"Ice cream? We haven't had lunch yet."

"So?" He slung all their bags over his shoulder again. "If any day calls for eating dessert instead of lunch, it's today."

Kira *tsked* and stood, still with Emily on her hip. "There's so much spoilage around here I'm surprised it doesn't stink."

He sniffed and led them toward the exit. "Mmm, smells like ice cream to me. What do you think, Fairy? Feel like some ice cream?"

Emily gave him a big grin. "I vote with Daddy."

Kira opened her mouth, faking a shocked face. "I see how it is. Well, I refuse to be the bad guy here. So I say we go for ice cream"—she leaned close, like she was about to whisper something scandalous—"*and* hot fudge."

His cheeks ached from smiling so hard, and his chest warmed at their banter. He pumped his arms more vigorously than needed for his walk down the pavement. Anything to burn off the urge to hug them both again.

Today had brought both the lowest lows and the highest highs. And as weird as it would sound to anyone else, he'd rank this as one of the best days of his life.

Chapter Seventeen

K IRA CRADLED EMILY'S HEAD IN HER LAP. AFTER A LONG DAY, the poor kid had conked out in Zac's truck during the drive home. She didn't even stir when the tires crunched over the gravel in Moose's parking lot.

Kira pointed Zac to the side drive leading to the rear lot. "Can you pull back there? That'll give me a shorter walk for carrying her to bed."

The singlewide trailer Moose had given her came into view.

"This is yours?" Zac drove around, stopping when the passenger door faced the front steps.

"Yep. Home sweet home."

It didn't look like much to him, she was sure. The outside aluminum was dingy, an un-trendy bluish-green color lined the top and bottom, and just a battered wood picnic table decorated the front. The only part of the place younger than thirty years old was the A/C unit on the side.

But it was where she'd grown up after escaping to the Earthen plane, so it was home. And until last week, she'd thought Emily would grow up here too.

Zac held out his hand. "Give me your keys. I'll get the door for you and then come back for your bags."

By the time she'd balanced Emily against her shoulder and slid out of the truck, he'd unlocked the door and was holding it open for her to carry her load of dead-weight inside. The kid didn't wake for the walk to her bedroom or the de-shoeing process on her bed. She was out for the night.

Kira slid the bedroom curtains closed. Thanks to Arizona's non-use of Daylight Saving Time, light started creeping into windows between four-thirty and five o'clock this time of year. That was one wakeup call she didn't need.

Every extra hour Emily stayed down in the morning meant more sleep for Kira. Faeries liked their lazy, lay-around time, and that had been in dreadfully short supply since Emily had moved in.

Out in the main room, Zac walked in with their backpacks and Emily's hat.

"Thanks." She took their stuff from him and set the pile on the kitchen counter.

He didn't appear to be in a rush to leave. Instead of heading toward the door, he hooked his thumbs in his jeans' belt loops and scanned the room. The inside of the trailer wasn't much to look at either, with its worn carpeting and linoleum, faded floral wall-paper, and one-step-above-a-trashy-garage-sale furniture.

He took off his cowboy hat and laid it beside the backpacks. "This doesn't look like your style. Too much beige."

"It's not." She leaned a hip against the counter. "Moose gave it to me after Roxi died. Too many memories for him, I think. I grew up in the bedroom Emily has now. If this could be called a style at all, I'd say it was an Early 80s Roxi Special."

"That explains it." He rocked from heel to toes.

Was he waiting for something? This situation was weird enough, and the awkward factor was climbing quickly.

Yeah, she needed to let him close enough to Emily to create those good emotions, and yeah, she had to get close enough to him to be able to share them. But that didn't cover hanging out together when Emily wasn't even around. That would seriously be what was known as a *bad idea*.

Finally, he waved toward the table and chairs in the kitchen. "I don't mean to impose, ma'am, but if you don't have other plans, I'd like to stay—"

What? Her heart beat double time for a second until his next words registered.

"—and talk about what happened to Emily today."

"Oh. Right." Her heart dropped into a funk. Stupid, irrational thoughts. When he started heading toward the table, she redirected him. "Sound carries down the hall from there. We can use the couch."

He eyed the lone sofa in the living room area doubtfully. "All right."

"There's no roaches in it. I promise. I keep a clean house."

"Sorry, I wasn't implying..." His apology faded with his inability to think of a good way to express whatever *was* causing the discomfort she sensed from him. He picked up his hat, as though changing his mind about staying, and fiddled with the brim.

She selected two cups from the cupboard. "Want something to drink? I think I drank two gallons today, but I still feel dehydrated."

"Sure. Water is fine."

She filled their glasses, carried them to the couch, and pointedly sat at one end. Still with his hat in his hand, he stood in front of the couch at the other end, looking for all the world like the last thing he wanted to do was sit next to her. What, his truck bench was acceptable for such close quarters and her couch wasn't?

Well, la-di-da. Her place wasn't big enough to fit a couch *and* a chair.

"Obviously, I don't do a lot of entertaining."

"I'm sorry. I'm making you uncomfortable. I assure you, ma'am, that was not my intention. It's just..." He blushed deeply, the color reaching his hairline. "This is the first time we've been alone— without Emily, I mean."

She stifled a nervous laugh and tried to dial down the urge to tease, flirt, whatever. Those irrational impulses would be the death of her.

But it was hard. So hard. Flirting had always been a means to an end and not just for the fun of it, so now she couldn't help the desire to play.

"So I *do* intimidate you. Good to know." She set her water down on the end table, spun sideways on the couch, and patted the cushion in invitation. "Guess it's my turn to promise I'll behave. For now."

That wasn't *too* bad. Right? He and his dimple and his positive emotions for Emily made it *way* too easy to be overly friendly with him.

His tension broke into a chuckle, and he sat beside her. He took the offered water and set his hat on his knee. "Thanks."

He circled the glass on his thigh, leaving a condensation ring on his jeans. Not that she was noticing his thighs. Or how well-developed they were. Or how snug his jeans looked over those thighs.

He interrupted her too-obsessed-for-her-own-good thoughts. "I didn't want to frighten her by talking about the incident at the zoo earlier, but I think we have a serious problem."

"Yeah, you'll notice I went along with your 'ice cream for lunch' distraction."

There was no question Tito's thugs had targeted Emily. That was no random encounter.

"Okay, let's be logical about this." She took a sip from her glass and forced the day's circumstances to make sense. "Let's ask ourselves why this happened today. Why not weeks ago?"

"I'll bite." He finally settled into the cushion, facing her, and drank his water. "Why?"

"I think Tito's afraid to come near here." She returned her cup to the table and gave him a wry smile. "I don't know if you're aware, but bikers have a reputation, and this place is infested with them. Even the kitchen and wait staff are bikers."

"So you think she's safe here. Even though he knows where she is. And you want me to risk my daughter's safety on that assumption?"

"Okay. Let's hear your theory."

"That's the thing." He rested his arm on the back of the couch and propped up his head. "Unless it was coincidence because he just found out where she was, I don't have a better answer. But I think the bigger question is *why* do they want her? Do they think she witnessed the murder?"

"No." The idea punched her in the stomach. For Emily's sake, she didn't want to believe that. "She told the police she didn't. She told *me* she didn't. Besides, if Tito and his gang really thought she was a threat, they'd probably try to kill her. Not kidnap her."

He recoiled and tucked his arm against his ribcage. "Kill her?"

"Well, that would be more straightforward than—"

"No, you're right." His hand clenched. "Damn. So why would they kidnap her?"

A jolt stiffened her muscles as something the police had mentioned months ago came back to her. "Tito has a history of escaping criminal charges. He's up for something big involving the Feds, and he's been trying to make a case for compelling Emily to testify to prove his innocence."

"Kids aren't reliable witnesses. Any lawyer would tell him not to bother."

"I think he's desperate. He even tried telling the cops he was her stepfather to gain custody and everything. I think since he was able to manipulate Crissy, he figured he'd be able to manipulate Emily, if only he could get his hands on her. Maybe now that you're in the picture, he's decided to get more aggressive."

"And he thought we'd be okay with him *stealing* custody?"

"Don't ask me to explain stupid. Besides, for all we know, he just missed having someone around to abuse and torture."

Unable to help it, she glanced toward the hall leading to Emily's bedroom. Her memories flashed back to the torture Lirdeag had inflicted on her parents. He'd forced her to watch, hoping her pleading would break them faster. All because they knew some-thing he wanted to control—her name, and by extension, her.

Shudders rippled through her limbs, the horrors of her child-hood experiences breaking through her carefully erected mental wall. She'd survived by never thinking about her parents. Never thinking about her royal heritage. And never thinking about the homeland she'd had to abandon to keep her people safe. Today had brought those thoughts to the surface, and vulnerability lurked inside her fragile shell.

If Moose hadn't been in the right place at the right time all those years ago, Lirdeag would have captured her and enslaved her people. She needed to be there for Emily the same way. Yet infalli-bility wasn't possible.

She was just one person. A faerie-person, to be sure. But that didn't make her infallible.

She pressed a trembling fist to her stomach, worry gathering like an iron ball eating away in her gut. She'd messed up plenty of times. This time, if she messed up, Emily would suffer.

"Hey." Zac reached toward her. "Don't you freak out on me now. You've kept it together all day far better than I have. Remember, it all worked out okay today."

Scenarios for all the ways she could fail to protect Emily played in her mind, and she shook her head so hard a strand of her hair stuck to her lips. "I can't be the reason someone gets hurt again."

"You're not doing this alone." He slid his finger along the strand, carefully not touching her face, and pulled the hair out of the way. "I'll be there to help every step of the way."

She met his gaze. Did he know how perfect that statement was? How much that was exactly what she needed to hear?

Did she dare trust him?

For all her talk about Emily not trusting others, she was just as bad. She trusted Moose. Not only because he'd taken her in and asked no questions about the events he'd witnessed the night she showed up out of nowhere, but also because the years since then had proved him honorable. Her attitude toward everyone else? Not so much with the trusting thing.

But she might *have* to trust that Zac would have her back for this. He cared about Emily, no question. Was that enough for her to trust him? At least on this issue?

For Emily's sake, she didn't have a choice.

Chapter Eighteen

K IRA SLID OUT HER CELL PHONE FOR THE WE'RE-HEADING-OVER call Mr. Overprotective insisted she make before they left. The better to freak out on an appropriate schedule apparently. Which, given how late they were running for this outing, might not have been the worst idea.

She zipped up the backpack of supplies and called down the hall. "Come on, Fairy. We were supposed to be there half an hour ago. You ready?"

Emily entered the kitchen, a mopey frown on her face. "Do we *have* to go?"

"What are you talking about?" Kira dropped everything onto the counter. "When Mr. Zac mentioned this horseback ride last week at the zoo, you were a ball of excitement. What happened?"

The girl looked down and shuffled her feet. Kira slid into a kitchen chair and motioned for Emily to take another. "It's okay. Let's talk about this."

Their outing could wait. No matter how much she might want to hustle them out the door, her duty to Emily was more important.

Emily needed to believe that she—and her feelings—had worth, and that meant listening and taking her concerns seriously. Her worries shouldn't be dismissed simply because she was "a kid" or "making things inconvenient."

Kira prepared her patience for getting to the bottom of the issue. "Is this about Mr. Zac, the horseback ride, or something else?"

Silence filled the room. Kira reached out with her abilities and played Twenty Questions to dig deeper.

After several minutes, Emily slid down in her chair. "Horses are big."

Kira inhaled, comprehension seeping into her thoughts. Being unable to protect herself from bigger, intimidating beings was something the girl already had too much firsthand knowledge of in her six years.

"Yes, they *are* big." Kira tightened one of Emily's pigtails. "But they'll be very gentle with you. I'll make them promise. And if, after you meet them, you don't want to ride, we don't have to do that part. Okay?"

Emily considered the deal for a minute. "You promise it will be okay?"

Her tone made it clear that this was one of those promises Kira dare not break. On the scale of promises, this was an easy one. Zac's horses were probably well behaved in any case, much less with her request upping the stakes.

"I promise."

Emily nodded and picked up her hat without being asked. Kira left a voicemail for Zac and then grabbed their bag. Compared to all that drama, the trip to Zac's was a breeze—and free of any stalkers sent by Tito.

Along Zac's driveway, a waving cowboy hat caught her attention, flagging them onto a side drive leading toward the barn. He did a double take at her hair. Again.

Today she'd opted to change her locks to a bright blue with yellow at the tips, two colors horses saw easily. Considering that faeries of her clan could make their changeling hair take on any imaginable hue instantly, limiting herself to a single change each morning for the sake of human understanding was already a huge sacrifice. She refused to give it up altogether. After a second, he accepted her new look with a raised brow and approached her bike.

She killed her motor and helped Emily down. "Sorry we're late. Not sure if you got my message."

"No problem." He wiped his forehead and replaced his hat. "I just finished saddling the horses for a training stroll around the corral before we hit the trail."

Air whistled through her teeth with her grimace. "Yeah, about that. The reason we're so late is that we had a *concern* delaying us this morning." With her emphasis, her gaze cut sideways to Emily, still cowering beside her bike.

To his credit, he caught on to the issue right away, his expression serious. "Does this concern mean we shouldn't go riding at all?"

"Unknown. I figured we'd play it by ear, but suffice it to say that we won't be doing even the training ride right away."

He sighed and nudged his hat backward. "I'll unsaddle them."

Kira and Emily stood to the side while Zac went to work. By the time he exited the barn from putting away the tack, all the horses understood the reason behind the saddle shuffle. As expected, they all promised to take good care of Emily. But she'd remained apart from Kira during the debriefings, showing no interest in meeting the horses.

Zac ensured the horses had fresh water and then set his hat aside. The sun was already beating down, and he was probably miserable from all the physical exertion. Kira took a step toward him, but before she could say a word, he dumped a full bucket of water over his head.

The deluge soaked his hair and most of his shirt. Rivulets streamed down his face from his long locks, and he bent over and shook out his head, leaving his hair a charming mess. His now see-though shirt clung to his chest and showed off every muscle.

Kira tore her gaze away. Holy hell. That wasn't a visual she needed. His sculpted chest was *not* something she should be aware of, much less be thinking about. And that please-run-your-fingers-through-me hair? Not a temptation she needed either.

She pivoted toward him only when his boots crunched closer. His hat was back in place, but that was the only dry thing above his belt. Not that she was looking below his belt.

He waved toward the house. "All right, let's get into the air conditioning and figure out the schedule for the day."

Through the back door, he snagged a towel and wiped down his head. If anything, the result increased the lure of his hair. Especially now that he left his hat off and the locks stuck out in every direction, begging for her attention.

She clenched her hands behind Emily, who rode Kira's hip. What the hell was wrong with her? The guys at the bar never had this effect on her. In fact, no part of sex or even the *idea* of sex ever had this effect on her. Why was she suddenly acting like a hormonal human teenager?

She was supposed to feed off feelings like this in others, not rev them up in herself. Maybe *she* needed a cold bucket of water poured over her. Too bad cold water was non-existent from the taps during the Arizona summer.

They settled around the table, where Emily demanded to sit in Kira's lap. Between that and wanting to be carried, the girl was obviously struggling today.

Zac's frustration crept across the table toward Kira. Damn it. He was back to sharing his *negative* emotions with her.

How the connection had gotten so strong between them already, she didn't have a clue. Twenty years of growing up with Moose hadn't resulted in anything this close. As helpful as her connection to Zac had been at the zoo last week, it was damned inconvenient now.

Before his emotions worsened, Kira shared Emily's concerns, pausing occasionally to confirm she'd gotten the details right.

Not for the first time since they'd sat at the table, Zac swept his fingers through his hair. "So that's why we couldn't start right away."

His tone held too sharp of an edge, and Kira gave him a warning look. "Her worries aren't something to be ignored."

"I know, I know." He sighed. "I just don't know where we go from here. How do we fix it?"

"We ask *her*. She has to be in control of her life as much as possible."

Wasn't that what anyone wanted?

Chapter Nineteen

O VER THE NEXT COUPLE OF HOURS, KIRA MANAGED TO DRAW Emily from her shell, agree to meet the horses—and even step into the corral with them. On a hunch, she had Zac grab a horse brush and tie up the horse he thought Emily should ride.

She called Emily over to the gentle older mare, named Candy. "Do you want to try brushing her? She'd like it. If you're friends with her, she'll make sure to take extra good care of you."

Zac demonstrated how to use the soft brush and then held it out for Emily to try.

The girl cocked her head. "She likes getting brushed?"

The last bit of frustration Kira felt from Zac dissolved into his chuckle. "She'd let you do it all day if you wanted. Especially with this brush. This one's her favorite."

Emily took the brush and gave Candy one stroke, and then another and another. With each one, Kira retreated toward the edge of the corral. Soon the girl was happy on her own and cooing to the animal like a dear friend.

Zac joined Kira by the fence. "How did you know brushing would help?"

It'd be fun to pretend she was an expert at this stuff, but making Zac feel bad wouldn't help whatever was going on with their connection. Besides, his dimple hadn't shown all morning.

Logically, encouraging his attractiveness would be bad for her resistance. Logic. Right. Call her a sucker for improving his mood.

"I didn't." She gave him a sly smile and then looked away.

Playing with fire—at least fire she couldn't control—was *so* not smart. She focused on the facts instead.

"Emily's seemed, for lack of a better word, *fragile* all day. With everything that's happened to her lately, it's not surprising. Ever since I took her in, I've tried to give her as much control as possible because she lived without any for so long. She has too much experience with having things *done* to her—as a victim. And no offense, but you coming into her life is yet another event that's beyond her control."

She checked his expression. He didn't seem upset by the observation.

It *was* the truth.

"Anyway, she needs to feel empowered, not only about her own life, but in general. Caring for an animal can be very empowering, not to mention establishes a bond."

"Thank you. I'd have stood around with a deer-in-the-headlights look all day if it weren't for you."

His genuine smile, complete with his dimple making its first appearance of the day, tickled the hair at the back of her neck. She swallowed the moisture pooling in her mouth. What a scrumptious man.

And totally off the menu.

As she glanced away, he cleared his throat. "Now what? We're almost to the hottest part of the day."

"We could either wait for another day, or..." She eyed Emily's quick smile at Candy's side. "We could try again this evening."

He looked toward the large hills behind his property. "If she's okay after a few circles of the corral, we could do a short loop through the park as a sunset ride."

"That might work."

Emily readily agreed to the new plan but pouted when Zac turned Candy loose to seek shade. Kira tried not to think about how they'd fill the hours until it was time to go. The reality was even worse than she imagined, as Zac led them to his workshop.

He directed them to the couch in his front office and

disappeared into the back room. Not having to face the iron-hell room was good. Then he brought out a wrought iron dragon shape, about two feet across from wing-tip to wing-tip.

Kira sucked in a breath and swore quieter than a whisper. "Oh *fuck* me."

Zac glanced her way but didn't seem to have understood her muttered words. Thank goodness. She needed to stop that swearing habit, especially around guys. She should have learned her lesson after that college jerk had misinterpreted her grumble the other week.

"What do you think, Fairy?" He held it out to her.

Beside Kira on the couch, Emily took the death metal. "Wow, that's cool."

Kira scooted away as far as she could without attracting attention. Swirls of iron extended in every direction, from its wings, its tail, and the fire shape protruding from its mouth. Emily flipped the abomination this way and that, checking it from every angle. Kira slipped to the side and stood from the sofa before one of its limbs touched her.

Zac gave her a questioning look.

She attempted a smile. "That's really something."

"Thanks. I think that's the most artistic piece I've ever made. I've just felt—I don't know—free and open to ideas lately." He gave a self-conscious shrug. "I know you can't take it home on your bike, but I could bring it by later."

Her muscles tensed so hard she recoiled. "Oh no. That can't come into my house."

He rubbed his chin, his expression even more confused.

"I mean, it doesn't belong there." She waved, her hand fluttering randomly. "That's between you and Emily."

His head tilted. "You think it should go into the room she's going to have here? Something to start making it feel like her room?"

"Yes." She latched onto his misunderstanding, even though she didn't want to think about the day Emily would no longer be with her. "Exactly."

His eyes widened. "Okay then." He turned to Emily. "Do you want to pick out the room you're going to have in a couple of months?"

Her brows tight, Emily looked to Kira for confirmation. Everything she wanted to say, every promise to never let her go, every rage about the unfairness of the situation, all dropped into an abyss below her heart. Life sucked right about now.

She couldn't allow the iron into her home without risking death, yet she couldn't explain why. Her only choice was to allow this betrayal to Emily's trust. She stuffed her frustration into the same void she used to hide the pain when her marks burned new skin.

Her voice plummeted into the emptiness as well, flat and dejected. "It's okay, Fairy. It won't happen for a while yet, but you're allowed to start making some of this place yours."

Emily's gaze dropped down to the iron dragon, conflict playing out on her face. Damn it. How had it happened again? Once more, Kira was stuck debating the benefits and risks of Emily allowing the next level of closeness with Zac versus feeling betrayed by Kira's pressure. Both options spelled her death.

And with that damned deadly sculpture in Emily's grasp, Kira couldn't even safely comfort the girl. Finally, a wavering smile flickered on Emily's face.

Either way, Kira had lost.

Chapter Twenty

S ULKINESS INVADED KIRA'S MOOD AS ZAC TOOK ENTIRELY TOO
much pleasure in dissecting the pros and cons of each of
the secondary bedrooms with Emily. She decided on a
bright terracotta and turquoise room with a horse theme, the walls
decorated with a lasso and horseshoes. A long dresser proved the
perfect spot for her to set up the dragon, and she fiddled with the
monstrosity, spinning it this way and that until satisfied. Then she
plopped onto the bed, making herself at home, and checked the
mountain view out the large window.

"I've never had such a nice room before."

Gee, kid, thanks for twisting that dagger.

Honey, the old yellow Labrador, jumped onto the mattress and
snuggled beside Emily.

Zac fingered the bed's comforter. "We can repaint and get different bedding if you want. Pink, purple, plaid, you name it."

Kira crossed her arms. "You have time to think about it, Emily.
You won't be living here for several months yet."

Zac eyed her. Oh, had she sounded bitter there? Too bad.

"Well..." He rubbed his palms together. "If we're going to head
out this evening, we should eat an early dinner before we go.
What's everyone in the mood for?"

She delayed following him and Emily out to the hallway long
enough to strip her glove. Despite the marks on her skin nearing

their complete circuit, only a weak flame formed in her palm.

Darn. Tossing the iron dragon into a huge bonfire would have to wait.

Honey cocked her head at Kira, and she replaced her glove. "I wouldn't have really destroyed it. Even if I could."

Probably.

After an early meal, Zac saddled the horses while she called Moose and let him know she wouldn't be back in time for the evening crowd at the bar. This supervised-visit gig was eating into her income stream, but what choice did she have? If she interfered with Zac and Emily's relationship, she'd face Zac's negative emotions *and* risk losing guardianship of Emily.

She called Emily over to reorganize their supplies into a saddle-bag. "Can you grab the water bottles from the freezer?" Emily complied, and Kira passed the girl her hat. "You ready for this?"

"I think so. Candy seems nice."

"She does. She'll take good care of you."

"You promise?"

"I do. And she promises too."

Out by the barn, Emily's first few minutes in the saddle were iffy, the ground suddenly much further away. After making sure the girl was okay, Kira mounted the horse Zac had picked out for her, a younger mare named Daisy, and Zac mounted Bullet, his stallion.

He showed Emily how to use the reins and stirrups and led her around the corral for a few circles. "We're all going to stick together, so you shouldn't have to do too much for turning her or changing her speed. Mostly, you just need to sit there."

Emily gave a nervous laugh. "I might be able to do that."

"You'll do great."

They headed toward Cave Creek Regional Park at the edge of Zac's property. Unlike city parks, this was a natural desert park, wild and unimproved other than a few trails and picnic areas.

No grassy fields or play structures awaited those who went off the trail. The saguaro cacti the Arizona desert was known for sprung up every hundred feet, their arms reaching toward the deep blue sky. Along with the saguaros, puffy-looking cholla cacti and low scrub covered the landscape, threatening to scratch and poke clothing and skin alike.

Kira settled into a rhythm with Daisy, and she took the rear position where she could keep an eye on Emily in the middle of their pack. The air was warm after being baked all day, but the rays of the dipping sun weren't too brutal.

Once they made it to the main trail Zac wanted to loop around, Kira called for a halt, ambled next to Emily, and handed the girl her water. "Are you up for this?"

Zac took a swig from his drink and gave Emily a solemn nod. "It'll take a bit less than an hour from here. You can do anything for an hour, right?"

A brave smile curved across Emily's face. "I think so."

Kira put their waters away and returned to her position at the back. As the sun fell in the sky, the lengthening shadows made the various outcroppings stand out against the hillside.

She had to admit this had been a good idea of Zac's. She so rarely got to connect with nature—a travesty for a faerie.

Deserts, even one as filled with growing things as Arizona's Sonoran Desert, didn't cut it for most faeries and their affinity for greenery and forests. That's exactly why she'd chosen this location as a child, the better to escape Lirdeag's notice. She'd gotten used to the emptiness and lack of lush growth long ago.

Now her senses reached out, relishing the contact with the life around them. A hawk swooped along the air currents, and a rock squirrel kept lookout on top of a boulder, where it chattered greetings to her as they passed. In her presence, the plants grew healthier, and a handful of prickly pear cacti nearby opened their blossoms in her honor.

Beyond what she could see, her senses also picked out a pair of mule deer foraging in the shade of a boulder pile. A coyote pack was shadowing Kira's group, eager for an audience with her. The horses weren't happy about the latter, but contained their skittishness.

So far, so good. They finished the loop faster than she expected, her thoughts distracted by their surroundings, and they headed back down the trail that would take them to the park's boundary behind Zac's house.

He pointed out the slope beside them. "A few weeks ago, this hillside was covered with wildflowers. Yellow and orange every—"

A squeal snapped Kira's attention to Candy. The horse stomped and half-reared, and Emily's scream ripped through the thick, hot air. Before Kira could prevent it, Emily fell out of the saddle and landed with a thump on the edge of the rocky trail.

Blinding fire burned down Kira's arms and stole her energy.

Death stalked nearby. Eager. Impatient.

Chapter Twenty-One

*S*HIT! KIRA IGNORED HER WEAKNESS. THE BROKEN PROMISE that crippled Emily's trust in her would only get worse if she didn't fix this.

What should have been a single, fluid motion was instead an uneven slide off Daisy and a stagger to Emily's side on the ground. "Are you okay?"

Emily's tears started before she got a word out. Kira knelt back on her heels, relieving her wobbly legs, and scooped Emily into her lap.

Several joints of a cholla cactus had attached their spines to Emily's back and arms. Chollas had earned the name "jumping cactus" because they snagged anything in the vicinity. Kira picked up two nearby sticks and slid them between the cactus pads and Emily's skin. Using the sticks as levers, she pried off the cactus pieces and tossed them aside. Emily screamed with each one.

"I'm sorry. I'm sorry. I'm almost done."

Each long spine bent at the tip like a fishhook, causing more pain. If not for her gloves, she didn't know how she'd pluck out the remaining spines without puncturing herself too.

Zac rushed back and grabbed the reins of the horses. "What happened?"

She finished with Emily and looked up, his confusion echoing her own. Impressions of pain bore down on her from nearby—not just from Emily—and she searched for the other source. Candy shifted a few inches on the path, favoring one of her legs.

Kira tuned out Emily's sobs and Zac's questions. Something rustled a few gravely pebbles off the trail, and she sent out her senses like radar. The something *rattled.*

"Candy's been bitten by a rattlesnake. That's why she freaked out." She groaned at their bad luck. Admittedly though, Emily could have been hurt much worse. "I saw a coyote pack nearby, and Candy was probably paying attention to them rather than looking out for snakes."

Hell, that's what she'd been doing. Non-mammals like rattlesnakes didn't trip her senses as much as other animals, so she hadn't noticed the reptile either.

Zac checked Candy's leg. "I don't see signs of swelling at the puncture site yet, but it's early. We can hope it was a dry bite without venom." He stood and caught Kira's eye. "No matter what, she's too lame to carry a rider. Even one as light as Emily. She's going to have to ride with one of us."

Emily squealed and thrashed in Kira's arms. "No! You promised. You promised. You promised."

Kira fell back on her ass, her limbs hot and heavy. Emily's panic seared through her, stealing her hold on life. She gasped and fought the urge to peel off her skin.

Damn it. She couldn't afford crap like this. She didn't have any energy to lose, and her magical marks were already too close to their destination, her body dangerously near to forcing her to return to her homeland for a recharge.

The cacophony of emotions from the animals wasn't helping either. The coyotes and the horses all expressed their guilt and apologies. The snake sneered that it couldn't care less about stupid faeries.

"Shut up." She meant for all to hear her directive. She needed a moment to recover.

Zac alone protested. "Don't—"

She glared at him. "You. Shut it." She ignored his reaction and squeezed Emily, careful of her injured back. "Shh. I'm not going to make you do anything you don't want to do."

Thoroughly wiped out, Kira sucked in desperate breaths and

concentrated on consolidating the energy she had left. Okay, options. What were her options?

Yips drew her attention to a low wash off the trail. The coyotes had circled the rattlesnake and killed it. She didn't have anything against snakes, despite their refusal to form a treaty with the fae, and normally wouldn't condone the death of an animal under any circumstances, but she was too tired to do anything but nod a thanks to the coyote pack.

After a minute, she finally had the air to speak in sentences again. "Fairy, Candy's very sorry that she wasn't watching the trail as well as she should have been. A rattlesnake bit her on the leg, and the pain made her jump. I know that doesn't fix things, but she didn't mean to break her promise." She tilted her head toward the wash. "The snake's gone now. The coyotes killed it to try to make things better."

"It doesn't." Emily's words were muffled against Kira's shoulder.

Red welts had risen on Emily's arms where the spines had punctured her. When they got home, Kira would have to double-check the area, or any remaining microscopic spines could cause infection. Her heart ached for the girl.

"I know. But we still have to get back to the house." Her slide off Daisy had dumped their half-frozen water bottles from the saddlebag. She lightly pressed a chilled bottle against Emily's welts and tried eliciting a smile. "I don't know about you, but I'm not planning on spending the night out here."

"I'm not doing it." Emily shook her head, still sobbing. "I'm not getting up there again."

"Not even if you're riding with me?"

"No." Emily looked up, and her eyes blazed, fierce and dark. "You promised it would be okay, and it wasn't. It wasn't." Tears trickled down her stiff jaw. "Why would I trust you this time?"

"I understand." What else could she say? Arguing with the girl would only cause additional negative emotions to burst across their connection. "So how do you want to get back?"

Emily's gaze turned weak and pleading. "Can't you carry me?"

Kira's eyes closed. Of course that was what Emily wanted. Normally, the request wouldn't be an issue, Kira's strength more than enough to carry Emily's weight, but she was running on energy reserves—reserves she didn't have.

She didn't have a choice though. Disappointing the girl even more would drain her completely.

"Is that the only way you'll be comfortable?"

Dark pigtails bounced with Emily's nod.

Then lugging the girl the half-mile to the house was what she had to do. "Okay. I'll carry you."

Her agreement rebuilt enough of Emily's faith in her that she somehow managed to get her feet under her. The world tilted, dizziness nearly sending them crashing to the ground again. She focused on deep, steadying breaths and waited for the swaying to stop.

Zac filled her vision. "What are you doing?"

"What does it look like I'm doing? I'm carrying Emily back to the house."

Proving to herself that she could do it, she took one step, and then another, and another. Through sheer force of will, she kept her legs solid under her.

After gathering the fallen water bottles, Zac paced her, still holding the reins of all the horses. "You look like you're about to pass out."

"Then maybe you should stop distracting me."

He muttered under his breath, low enough that Emily might not have heard it over her sobbing. "Just carry her on the damn horse."

"I *won't* make her do something she doesn't want to do."

"This isn't like forcing her to do something that's going to hurt her. She'll get over it."

He was quite likely right that Emily would "get over it." Eventually. But her loss of trust would destroy Kira in the process. She didn't have the luxury of taking the long view.

"I won't do it."

He held his arms out and whispered, "Then let me do it. Let her blame me."

Her connection to Emily didn't work that way. Being a co-conspirator would trigger Emily's feelings of betrayal all the same.

"No."

He grasped her bicep, forcing her to face him. She and Emily almost crashed to the ground at the disruption of her carefully balanced steps. He pushed and tugged on her arm, steadying her.

"Look at you. You really *are* about to pass out." His hand tightened. "I'm not giving you a choice. Give her to me."

The horses retreated, smarter than this human who dared manhandle her and give her orders.

"You're *touching* me."

"I'm trying to help."

"Get. Your. Hand. Off. Me."

"I will if you agree to give her to me."

"*Now.*" Her glare could have ignited a forest fire. "Or I *will* hurt you when this is over."

"I won't let you kill yourself for this. Give her to me."

He had it all backwards. The only thing keeping her going was Emily's trust that Kira wouldn't back down. If she gave up, she'd lose even that.

He was only making things worse, and that didn't help her mood.

"After you've gotten your way and kicked me out of the picture, you can decide when to ignore your daughter's wishes, but until then, get the hell out of my way."

He snatched his hand back like he could suddenly feel the heat that had burned under her skin a few moments before. She didn't wait for his response, instead resuming her slow steps back to the house.

By the end of this torturous hike, she might wish she *had* died.

Chapter Twenty-Two

EMILY'S TEARS KEPT UP A STEADY STREAM AND DAMPENED Kira's shirt as they returned to Zac's house. Zac somehow managed to get Emily to drink from her water bottle without disturbing Kira's steps.

Good thing. The girl surely needed the water. He offered to do the same for Kira, and she shook her head. No doubt she should stop and drink too, but her arms were full, and she didn't want to risk halting again. At least she didn't sweat and lose moisture that way.

By the time they crossed the park boundary and entered Zac's property, Emily's sobs had quieted, and if possible, she grew even heavier in Kira's arms. Every limb burned with pain, and her jaw ached at how hard she was gritting her teeth. Almost there.

Alongside the barn, Kira peered through the twilight at Emily. "We're back. Let's walk the rest of the way together."

The girl's eyes remained closed, and she didn't stir.

Lovely. Kira's gaze landed on her bike at the front of the barn. She couldn't get Emily home on the Harley with her asleep.

She twisted toward Zac. Maybe she could ask for a ride.

He spoke before she got a chance. "She sleeping?"

"Yeah. It's been a long day for her. Could you—?"

"I need to check Candy for signs of venom and give the vet a call before I do anything else."

Oh, right. She was so tired she wasn't thinking straight. Her focus had narrowed so much during her trudge that she'd forgotten the cause of her hike.

He nodded to the house. "Why don't you lay her down inside while I'm dealing with this?"

He walked the horses into the barn before she could answer. Uh-huh. Another couple hundred steps. Just what she needed.

Once inside, she headed for Emily's soon-to-be room. That bed made as much sense as any other.

She laid the girl down on her side and checked the cholla injuries. The welts weren't quite as big and swollen as before, but they were still an angry red shade.

Kira's legs wanted nothing more than to buckle under her. She forced them to carry her to the kitchen, where she dampened several paper towels and stuck them in the freezer while she gulped water.

If she had her full powers, she'd be able to heal the girl, but she wasn't about to wish for the magical pathway under her skin to complete its circuit. Even if she could survive the maturation process without returning to her homeland, the benefit of tapping into the power of her clan was outweighed by Lirdeag's ability to trace the energy flow.

Instead, healing would have to happen the old-fashioned way. Back in the bedroom, she checked for any missed cactus spines and lightly pressed the chilled paper towels to Emily's puncture wounds.

What a disaster of a day. As if the fall from the horse—Emily's fear du jour—wasn't bad enough, she'd had to endure a close encounter with a jumping cholla cactus. Kira didn't blame the girl one bit for losing faith out there. Not one bit.

Kira's legs finally gave out, and she lay on the floor beside the bed. Honey settled beside her and gave a sympathetic lick to her chin. Despite everything, Kira resisted falling asleep. If she didn't get energy soon, she might not wake up. At least not on the Earthen plane.

What was she supposed to do now? She had to find an emergency energy source while stranded on the edge of civilization. No problem. No problem at all.

A couple of hours later, she sensed someone watching her and rolled over. Zac stood in the doorway, his eyes boring holes into her. Was he upset to find her here? What had he expected?

Kira stroked Honey's fur and whispered in the dog's ear, "Let me know if Emily wakes up."

Then she pushed herself to her feet—not without difficulty—and staggered toward Zac. He tilted his head, inviting her into the hallway where they wouldn't disturb Emily.

She followed him around the corner of the doorframe and took control of the conversation first. "How's Candy? Did the vet see her?"

"She'll be fine. There's no swelling, so it looks to be a dry bite. The vet gave her antibiotics and a tetanus shot for the puncture wounds and will check on her tomorrow."

"I'm glad it wasn't worse."

"Me too." His hair glistened in the low light, still damp from a shower. Thank goodness she repelled dirt and didn't sweat, or she'd feel gross in comparison. He leaned back and glanced through the doorway. "How's she doing?"

"She's out. Probably for the night."

His expression became even more unreadable, sending tingles down her spine. He focused on her, his eyes locked in place. The intensity of his gaze crackled across their connection, igniting flutters in her heart. She didn't want to think about what either of those reactions signified.

"And how are *you* doing?"

The innocent question caught her by surprise, and she stepped back, deeper into the hallway. "I—I survived. But we could use a ride home since I can't take her on my bike like this."

Emotions rolled off him like a tidal wave, and he paced her retreat. "That was bloody stupid of you."

That was the attack she'd expected. Screw him. She didn't need that. She only needed energy. Desperately.

"I didn't ask for your approval." She straightened, a sudden wave of surprising strength renewing her determination. "Until you kick me out of her life, what I say still goes."

His expression darkened, and the hair at the back of her neck stood up in response. He took another step, entering her space.

"Kicking you out of her life *isn't* my goal."

"Goal or not, that's going to be the result, isn't it?" She didn't let him answer. "Can we get a ride home now, or do I need to call a cab?"

He moved even closer, crowding her between him and the wall. His scent, still primal despite his fresh shower, invaded her senses, and she found herself breathing deep, savoring his smell and the emotions it carried.

He planted a palm on the wall above her shoulder and caught her eye. "I want you to stay."

I want you to stay. His words crashed into her, shoving her back, amplified by the force of his emotions.

His desire.

Holy hell. She'd been strong enough to spar with him these past couple of minutes because she'd already started sucking that passionate energy from their connection, even without touching him or being aware of his mood.

And now the ultimate energy source stood inches from her. Daring her. Taunting her with its nearness. Its convenience. Its a-quick-touch-couldn't-mess-things-up-too-much temptation.

She didn't have a choice, right? She'd just whip off her glove and press her fingertips to his temple for five seconds. Ten seconds tops.

He wouldn't remember such a quick contact. She wouldn't lose control in that short a time. She'd get an emergency burst to carry her through the night.

And she'd make sure this *never* happened again.

During her internal debate, her fingers had already started inching off her glove. Her hand ached to touch him, yearning for what he could give her. Before she lost her concentration, she ripped the material off the rest of the way and touched his temple.

Energy slammed into her, and she slumped against the wall, her head tilting back. The taste of his desire was exquisite. Delicious. Better than she could have imagined.

A deep voice broke her concentration. "Does this mean I can touch *you*?"

Her head snapped up. Zac met her gaze with clear thoughts.

No glazing over. No trance. No memory modifications.

Her arm dropped from his face, and her jaw fell open. Gravity shifted, dragging her thoughts into the bottom of her stomach where they landed heavily and churned her insides. Her heartbeat fluttered like some of her faerie flies had taken up residence in her chest.

She was screwed.

At her non-answer, he licked his lips, and his eyes searched hers. "Let me touch you."

She was tempted. Oh so tempted.

Even without her hand on him, she sensed his desire build, pressing against her like a physical force. The need for contact seduced her, coaxing her to say yes.

It would be bad to give in though, right? Something told her that, but she couldn't remember why.

He moved closer, his breath heating her face, his desire enveloping them. "Come on, Kira, tell me I can touch you."

She gasped, and her body responded, almost before she understood why. He'd used her name.

Her true name.

He knew. He remembered. He controlled her.

If she wasn't so close to agreeing anyway, she might have been able to ignore his use of her name. After all, he knew only the first part, and she could overcome that amount of control if it was a matter of life and death. But as it was, she couldn't muster the willpower to deny what they both wanted.

Unable to resist, she swallowed and answered him. "Yes."

So for the first time, a human caressed her face.

And she liked it. Craved it.

Would even degrade herself to *beg* for it.

Chapter Twenty-Three

ZAC REACHED OUT WITH JUST ONE HAND, THE BETTER TO pretend he could control himself. The truth lurked in the corner of his brain, where ignorance was bliss. Even if he could stop himself this instant, this single touch to Kira's cheek was the dumbest thing he'd ever done.

He was supposed to be proving himself a good father for Emily, not getting hot and heavy for her foster mom. When whatever this was between them went south—and it would—his relationship with his daughter would be in danger.

Yet on its own, his other hand caught Kira's face as well, cradling her head, tilting her mouth up. Wide violet eyes met his. Her expression matched his churning thoughts. Apprehension. Anticipation. And most temptingly, desire.

Heat spread from his chest to his limbs, and every nerve ending overwhelmed him with exclamations of her nearness, her smell, her body warmth. She was off-the-charts amazing, her inner strength matched only by her capacity for giving. When she'd refused his help and insulted his intentions, his emotions had battled between fury, worry, and hurt before settling on admiration—and something else he couldn't identify, but it made him want to get closer to her.

How could this woman be such a stubborn hard-ass and yet be so soft and seductive? How could this woman—who was definitely not his type, with her wild hair and motorcycle lifestyle—manage to hit all his buttons like no one he'd ever known?

If only he had a rewind for life. Or they could take an unbreakable vow of no consequences. He'd screw her brains out to get this fascination with her out of his system.

She panted, her mouth parting slightly. His thumb stroked her lush, dark lips with each idea provided by his imagination. If only...

If the circumstances were different, he'd take her, right here against the wall. He'd strip those concealing clothes off her and suck and lick every inch of skin covered by her tattoos. He'd make her beg for more and bury himself in her until neither of them could see straight. If only...

A quiet moan vibrated her lips, and she shuddered. Her gaze seized his.

"Is that a threat or a promise?" Her tongue peeked out and ran along the length of her mouth, brushing the pad of his thumb. "Or maybe it's both."

Were his thoughts that obvious? He swallowed, whether from embarrassment or desire, he wasn't sure. Then again, she hadn't shied from him—or what she could guess of his thoughts.

He moved close enough that friction formed between their clothes. "Are you daring me?"

"I think you're daring *me*. What if I agree?" Her lashes lowered, and she looked up at him, a mixture of innocence and vixen. "No consequences."

Bloody hell. His body didn't give him time to answer, or even wonder how they'd become so attuned that she knew the exact *wrong* thing to say.

Without thought, his lips sought hers, and he thrust his way into her mouth. Delicious spiciness surrounded his tongue. She met him eagerly, her kiss warm and welcoming. Oh God, he could get used to this.

He didn't think. He didn't question. He just *felt*. Control slipped away from him.

He pressed his body against hers, her breasts giving softly at his chest. She slipped her hands up to his head. Tingles spread from his ear, where her fingertip brushed his skin.

The sensation snapped him out of his surrender to emotions.

He *needed* to keep control, needed to restrain his feelings, needed to protect himself from disappointment.

He interrupted their kiss and *tsked*, a grin breaking across his face. "No you don't, Kira." He pinned her wrists to the wall. "This is my chance to pay you back for all the times I wasn't allowed to touch you."

"Please." She stretched forward, as though to resume their kiss. "I *need* to touch you. Skin to skin."

Since when did she crave touch? The "let's play Opposite Day" comment made him want to thwart her wishes, and the desperation in her voice urged him to tease her even more.

When it came to his daughter, he had to follow Kira's rules, but here, with her promise of no consequences, he intended to run the show. This was his one chance to get the upper hand with her, and he wasn't going to let it slip away.

Especially as controlling the situation was his best chance for keeping *himself* in control.

"All in good time, sweetheart." He inched his grasp down her shirt cuffs from her wrists so no part of his fingers connected with her bare hands. "All in good time."

Now... What else could he do in this position that *wouldn't* give her what she wanted? Sweet torture sounded good for their first course.

Her breasts heaved against his chest, giving him an idea. He kept her wrists pinned and stepped back enough to bend down, and then he circled his nose around the tip of her breast. The fabric of her shirt slid along her skin, creating sensations without direct touch. Her head fell back to the wall, her protests silenced.

He opened his mouth over her breast and sucked on the material until thoroughly damp. The fabric stuck to her skin and the skimpy bra he felt underneath. He grasped both layers in his teeth and slid her bra down below her nipple. Now only her shirt lay between his mouth and her breast. He dragged the cloth in a circle with his teeth. Wet friction roughened the movement of the cotton over her skin.

She whimpered and slid an inch down the wall.

"You like?" He lightly bit her nipple.

Her gasp ended on a moan. "It's not supposed to..." She panted through another of his nibbles. "Feel like this."

Most of his attention focused on her breast, and he barely held her wrists. Despite that, she didn't fight his grip. He'd won.

He caught her nipple between his teeth and worked his tongue over the tip.

She sucked in another breath. "I'm not supposed to *feel*."

He almost laughed at her nonsensical statement. "Then you've been doing it wrong." He blew on the damp fabric, and her already-erect nipple hardened even more. "I'm going to fix that."

"Please."

He covered her breast with his mouth again, waiting for her to elaborate, but no words followed. "Please what?"

She didn't answer, and he drew back, looking in her eyes. Conflict played over her expression, like she couldn't find the right words to voice her thoughts.

"Tell me, Kira. Tell me what you want."

Even in the dim light of the hallway, the rainbow sparkles in her eyes seemed to flash. She pinched her eyelids closed for a second and then met his gaze.

"You. I want you." Her fingers clenched, and she grimaced, but she still didn't struggle against his grasp. "I want you to take me. I beg you. Take me and make me feel."

Her breathless, honest declaration sent shivers down to his cock. Her raw desire ignited every urge he had. No one had ever expressed such vulnerable, desperate *need* for him before.

He pulled her arms to his neck and dove into a kiss. She moaned into his mouth, threaded her fingers into his hair, and pressed her body against his. He grabbed her ass and lifted her hips to his waist. Her legs wrapped around him, erasing all distance between them.

Yeah, time to ditch the clothes. Still buried in their kiss, he carried her down the hall to his bedroom. They'd be way too noisy for the hallway outside Emily's room.

He kicked his door closed behind them, elbowed the switch for the mood lighting, and laid her out on his mattress. It was time to break in this sex-on-a-stage bed.

Her eyes popped open and widened, like she hadn't realized he'd been moving her elsewhere. Her gaze took in the massive bed, with its tree-trunk-sized carved posts at the corners, leather head-board, and ironwork above. She recoiled, staring at the star-shaped iron design connecting the tops of the posts.

"What? You're afraid I'm going to tie you up to that?" He chuckled at the speed her rounded eyes landed on him.

BDSM stuff was not his kink, but her reaction gave him ideas. Ideas that would have made him blush under other circumstances.

She licked her lips. "Please. I'll do anything you want, just promise you won't ever let any of your metalwork touch me."

Anything? Something flickered along the edge of his mind at the odd request, but her vow to do anything he wanted over-whelmed the thought. The game perfectly fit his current mood. The opportunity to expand this one area where he had power over her was too tempting to miss.

"I'll make that promise if the offer is good for multiple uses."

He could think of a few ways to take advantage of that situa-tion. His imagination served up several visuals to sweeten the deal. A small voice at the back of his mind reminded him that this was supposed to be a one-time thing to get her out of his system.

Well, it was good to have a backup plan in case it would take more than once. And he strongly suspected it would. Maybe even hoped.

A sensuous smile drew her mouth into a curve. "Unlimited use. No expiration date. For anything you want here in the bedroom." Her hand slipped under his collar, and her thumb rested on the skin over his heart. "But you have to take the promise seriously."

Negotiations for kitchen counters, swimming pool, and the billiards table could happen another time. "I promise."

"Say the whole thing—promise you won't ever let your work touch me—and swear on..." Her brow furrowed. "Swear on your life. So I know you're serious."

So *that's* how she wanted to run this game. Fine. Her request was beyond odd, but it wasn't worth interrupting the mood to debate with her, and the hallway scene had proved he could play dirty too. After they finished these power negotiations, he'd show her just how much.

"I swear on my life, I promise I won't ever let my work touch you."

She looked up through her eyelashes again, temptation personified. "I accept. I'll do anything you want here in the bedroom."

Tingles radiated in his chest, her thumb injecting her submission straight into his heart. She couldn't have hit every button he possessed any harder. She hit buttons he didn't even know he had. Heat flowed through his body, his blood simmering at her words.

The connection between them lured him into a black hole of unrestrained craving. Flickers twinkled on the edges of his vision. His muscles tightened, wanting to take her this instant.

No, this game was supposed to be about her needing *him*, not about his need for *her*.

Or for anyone.

Fighting the tightness in his chest, he untangled her arms from his neck and stood from the bed. He gulped air, drowning in the needy sensation, and his hands balled into fists. The skin on his legs itched, like they longed to run away, and his throat burned with the urge to yell at her to leave—to prove that he didn't need her here.

Before he could decide what to do, she placed the bottom of her boot on his chest. "I think you were going to strip me next. Something about licking and sucking."

Her teasing calmed him enough to regain his distance from the situation. Sure, he wanted her, but need? No. He'd never need anything from someone else again. He forced in a deep breath to relax the heavy sensation behind his ribs.

This was a game to scratch an itch. Period.

"Strip you? Is that so?" He slid her black motorcycle boot off her leg. Her other foot stretched up, and he eased that boot off too. "That sounds about right."

His fingers made quick work of unfastening her black jeans. She lifted her hips, and he tugged the material over her generous curves and down her thighs. More of her intricate tattoos wove down the outside of her leg. Yes, *that's* why he'd placed stripping her naked high on the list. Did she have them everywhere?

He tossed her jeans aside. Swirls and curves that put his work to shame wound from her hips to her ankles, each leg's design perfectly symmetrical with the other. Spirals that almost looked alive decorated the wavy lines along their path. The tattoos covered her outer thighs and calves and then encircled her ankles.

They seemed so much like a living thing he was afraid to touch them. Yet even though tattoos had never appealed to him before, he ached to explore these. "They're beautiful."

She didn't answer.

He glanced up and caught her biting her lip. "They are." A thought occurred to him. "Have others disliked them?"

"You're the first human to ever see them."

Several things struck him as *off* about her statement, but the feel of her under his palms distracted him from focusing on what they were. Her skin was so soft it was nearly like velvet, stimulating his nerve endings far more than it should.

In fact, she had on entirely too many clothes. He slid her to the edge of the mattress and stood between her thighs. He tugged off her remaining glove.

Like her other hand, this one also had a tattoo on the palm. The design's flower-like circle of flames reminded him of a henna tattoo of a mandala circle.

Despite the urge to caress her all over—or maybe in defiance of that urge—the fun of her earlier torture was too good to resist continuing. She might want skin-to-skin contact, but this game was about control. He *would* stay in control of the situation, of her...

And of himself.

He unbuttoned her shirt without letting her experience his touch at all. She arched her back, encouraging the material to slide down her sides.

"No cheating." He grasped the plackets and pretended to pull them closed. Instead, he rubbed the fabric over her skin.

Her breaths quickened, and she half-grumbled. "You know exactly what you're doing to me, don't you?"

"Mmm, I like to think so. You *did* want me to make you feel, didn't you?" Without touching her skin, he stretched her bra below her other nipple and stroked the stiff hem of the shirt placket over the erect buds.

"I'm starting to think..." She gasped at his light pinch on the tips of her breasts.

"No thinking. You shouldn't be able to think while I'm doing this."

She finished her thought between pants anyway. "This much feeling without touch must break some laws."

"Oh, I've just started, sweetheart."

Proving his point, he sank to his knees onto the floor. Thank goodness he'd gone for carpeting rather than his original thought of hardwood flooring in this room.

In front of him, her silky black panties covered the apex between her thighs. Her delicious scent filled his senses. This would be a feast of torture.

He blew slow, hot air over her panties. As he expected, her legs wriggled under his arms. He pressed his triceps down, holding her thighs to the mattress, and he moved her hands out of the way before reclaiming his hold on her shirt.

"Here are the rules for my first use of the Anything Promise. You're not allowed to move—no thrusting, arching, or twisting. You're not allowed to speak first unless you're begging me. And most importantly, you're not allowed to come until I give you permission."

Those "rules" weren't harmful in any way, but would prove her willingness to play along.

Or not.

She rose up on her elbows and rolled her eyes. "Am I to call you Master Zachary too?"

Apparently her definition of doing anything he wanted didn't include holding off on the sarcasm. Just to teach her a lesson, he smiled, slow and wide.

"Excellent idea. When you speak, you are to call me Master Zachary." He licked her panties, stroking between the lips, and then met her shocked gaze. "You understand and will abide by all the rules, won't you, Kira?"

She shuddered and dropped her head onto the mattress. "Yes, Master Zachary."

God, he could get to love this.

A part of him was horrified at his treatment of her, but another part of him—the part he needed to remain strong and in control of his emotions—justified all the rules. He'd get what he needed, and she'd get more than she thought she wanted. Win-win.

His goal was to bring her to orgasm without direct touch, and he'd settle for nothing less. Within a few minutes, her panties were drenched, both from his efforts and her response. He thrust with his tongue, stimulated with teeth, teased with his lips, and sucked with his whole mouth.

At the same time, he continued giving attention to her shirt-covered luscious breasts. Soft and pliant, her magnificent curves were all her. He loved that she wasn't a thin little stick, loved the feeling of sinking his hands into her, kneading, pinching, and squeezing. And he couldn't wait to use those hips to grab onto and grind into her.

Her thighs quivered, and he reminded her, "Not yet, Kira."

So far, she'd followed his instructions perfectly. Better than he'd expected in fact. But he wanted this woman's stubbornness to submit, completely and unreservedly, to him. She'd never allow it to happen anywhere else, which would make his victory all the sweeter.

Her panting breaths quickened. "Please, Master Zachary."

"Please what?" He sucked and dragged the silk over her hardened bud.

She gasped and whimpered but didn't answer. The lips under her panties became swollen, and her whole body shivered.

"You know what I want to hear, Kira. Don't fight me." He rolled her nipples in his fingertips. Only her stubbornness stood in the way now. "Let me give this to you."

"*Please.*" A moan ripped from her, and her muscles tightened. "Please, Master Zachary, I beg you. *Please* let me come. My body is yours to do with as you wish. My body is yours to command. My body is yours to serve your desires."

Fuck. His cock hardened so fast he almost lost it. She couldn't have worded her submission better if he'd given her a script. She was perfect in every way.

One time definitely wouldn't be enough. Not even close.

Chapter Twenty-Four

K IRA'S MUSCLES TREMBLED, WAITING FOR ZAC'S PERMISSION. She was so close, but her body followed his rules without thought. All she could do was hang on for the ride.

Damn him.

"My sweet Kira..."

She stopped breathing, perched on the precipice.

"Come for me now."

She crashed through the crest, shattering into pieces. Her fingers fell upon a nearby pillow, and she grasped it and muffled the scream tearing from her throat. Every muscle spasmed, wringing ecstasy from every cell. No part of her body was under her command anymore. Shudders shook her from head to toe, each one bringing a wave of pleasure, of euphoria, like nothing she'd ever known.

Sometime later—she had no idea how long—her consciousness settled back into her jelly-limbed body. Happy hormones kept her compliant for even longer. Gradually, those faded too, leaving her with nothing to do but face the truth.

Holy hell.

Which was worse? That Zac knew her name and kept using it to control her? Or that her traitorous body didn't mind?

She'd escaped the Mythos plane to get away from Lirdeag and the threat of living under his control. Now she faced the same problem here.

Granted, Zac hadn't used her name to hurt her yet, but that was just a matter of time. As soon as he realized the extent of his power, he'd abuse it.

Only the pretense of the Anything Promise had kept the secret so far. Playing along with his rules had made her submission seem like part of the game, but how long could she maintain that façade?

The only good thing about the circumstances was that she'd manipulated him into a faerie oath guaranteeing her safety from his iron.

Her traitorous body reminded her that she'd also gotten an exquisite orgasm out of the deal. With his expertise of both force and finesse, the man was a master in every sense of the word.

Shut up! That *wasn't* the point. The point was that Zac had control over her, something she couldn't allow.

Her stomach tightened, the facts of her predicament churning her insides. For reasons she couldn't fathom, he responded differently to her magic than any other human. He'd seen her faerie flies, and he was immune to her short-term trance and memory modification abilities. So she couldn't make him forget her name, she couldn't flee and leave Emily here, and she couldn't avoid ever seeing him again.

The puffy coverlet on the bed crumpled in her fist. Nothing helped her make sense of the chaos her life had become.

And worse, she hadn't even gathered much energy from his efforts.

Yet her body thrummed in anticipation for the potential of what was still to come, and its reasons weren't about the energy she'd gain. Traitor.

Between the reality-shattering orgasm and her internal argument, a moment or two passed before her breathing returned to a normal level. Once her gasps settled, he released her shirt and stood, a cocky smile curving his mouth. He leaned over her, his palms beside her shoulders on the mattress.

"And here you thought you needed skin-to-skin contact." He *tsked.* "Do you now trust that I know best how to give you pleasure?"

Trust. There was that word that nearly gave her hives. Circumstances had forced her into trusting him too much about too many things. Yet she couldn't deny that when it came to pleasures of the flesh, he knew what he was doing—and that her body wanted him to do more of it.

"Yes, Master Zachary."

He groaned and straightened. "Mmm, you are..." He pursed his lips and then broke into a smile again. "You're delectable."

His smile lifted into a shape suspiciously like the smirks she hated on the college tourists at Moose's bar. She couldn't begrudge his attitude though. He'd *earned* the right to be arrogant.

"Stand up." He motioned. "Let's get those clothes off you."

Finally. Nakedness had to result in skin-to-skin contact, right?

He directed her to a spot a few feet from the bed. But rather than helping her undress, he left her alone while he sat on the mattress.

"Strip for me. Slowly. Sensually."

Sensually? The building desire she sensed inside him proved an adequate barometer for meeting his demand. While he looked on approvingly, she removed her bra from under her shirt and tossed it to him. He twirled a strap around his finger and flipped her bra to the other side of the bed.

Next, she inched her soaked underwear down her legs and laid it at his feet. Finally, she let her open blouse slip off her shoulders and onto the floor.

She fought the urge to cover herself back up again. Exposing herself to a man who controlled her would make any woman feel vulnerable. It didn't help that no human had ever seen her like this.

She'd always worn long clothes for protection, never trusting another to keep her safe from iron. At least Zac's promise had changed everything in that regard. She didn't need to trust when she had the power of a faerie oath enforcing her safety.

Her body encouraged her to accept the situation. Energy, orgasms, and no risk of iron exposure? Hell to the yes-she'd-take-some-of-that-please.

Yeah, let's see if her body was so eager when he used his power over her name against her.

His gaze slid over her form, a hungry glint in his eye. "Spin around for me. Slowly."

After she completed her leisurely turn, he stood and circled her.

His hand was close enough to feel the heat on her skin, but he still didn't touch her. He had no idea how much of a tease he was being. How much his energy called to her. Seduced her.

Maybe taunting him would encourage contact. "Please, Master Zachary, I won't bite unless you want me to."

"Anticipation isn't something to rush, sweetheart." He stopped behind her and threaded his fingers into her blue locks. "Mmm, I'd have thought your hair would be dried out from all the coloring, but it's not."

The stroking of his fingers in her hair elicited a moan. *This* was sensual.

His hands froze mid-lift, and he parted the strands behind her ear. "Your tattoos go *under* your hair? Did you shave your head for those?"

Luckily, he didn't seem to expect an answer. Instead, his fingertips made contact with her skin, tracing the lines of her magic. Finally.

Energy soaked into her with each swirl and curve he followed. He started at her eyes and temples, slid through her hair to the sides of her neck, and out to her shoulders, where the lines split into a *Y*, one branch angling across her chest, one across her back, and the last stretching too close to completing the circuit of her magic with the power nexus on her palms.

Her heartbeat drummed loud in her ears, even this simple touch filling her with more energy than she could process. She gulped it in eagerly, hungrily.

He circled around her once more, and his fingers continued tracing, following the lines through the *X* across her chest and back, to where they joined at another *Y* at her hips. "These almost seem alive. As though they were vines unfurling across your body."

Her gaze shot to his face, and a serious expression met her eyes. An urge compelled her to answer truthfully, and she just barely managed to restrain herself from admitting even more. "Yes, that's a good way to describe them."

In fact, she'd thought of them in those exact terms many times.

"What do they mean?"

She spoke before he could add her name to the question and

force a straightforward answer. "What makes you think they mean anything?"

"You act as though you don't like them, and yet you have them." From behind her, he rubbed his lips on her neck. "You must have them for a reason."

He had her there. She swallowed and gave a vague response. "My heritage requires them."

His lips lifted from her skin, but he didn't pry further. Instead, he nibbled behind her ear, and she nearly swooned back into his arms. He caught her and drew her to his chest.

"So much for anticipation." His hands greedily branded her body as his possession, one squeezing her breast and the other slipping between her legs.

Her muscles quivered, unwilling to support her weight. She slumped against him, her body like putty in his hands.

He rumbled beside her ear. "That's right. Give yourself to me."

Between his control and her body's reaction, she didn't have a choice. She allowed him to lead her toward the bed.

The conflict of his internal debate crackled over their connection. Like her, his body and his mind wanted two different things. She wasn't sure of the details—something about sexual positions.

An image flashed in her mind, strong enough in his thoughts to fully form on her end as well. He imagined them face-to-face, slow, intimate, a loving gaze passing between them.

She almost recoiled from his touch. Intimacy was *not* something she'd signed up for. She'd already relinquished her clothes, and relinquishing what little remained of her sense of self wasn't in the plan. Heck, face-to-face wasn't even something she'd done before.

When she'd bothered with anything other than a mental simulation, she'd been more of a "purr, stir, thank you, sir" kind of gal, a simple straddling of her bike for a quick poke from behind. No stripping—or intimacy—necessary.

Anger built in him, from what she could tell, anger at himself. Without warning, he shoved her forward, bending her over the mattress. "I'm going to take you. Use you. And you're going to like it."

"Yes, Master Zachary."

Thank goodness they weren't doing the face-to-face thing. Most women wouldn't be thankful for a guy with intimacy issues, but she wasn't most women.

No matter what her body thought, she was here for an energy boost. That's it. And with this much agitation inside him, his release would be sweet indeed.

"Spread your legs, and then don't move."

She obeyed and kept her arms on the bed. Clangs and thumps accompanied his clothes dropping to the floor, his belt buckle and boots impacting heavily. The scrape of a drawer and a crinkle of foil assured her that their game hadn't distracted him from remembering a condom. Good thing too, as she *had* forgotten. Heat prickled on the back of her legs, signaling his return.

His palms skated over her skin, his energy laced with a manic edge. "You've been driving me crazy all day, you know." His finger dipped between her legs. "I heard you this afternoon, with your little 'fuck me' whisper. Teasing time is over, you understand?"

"Yes, Master Zachary." She wasn't proud of the fact that her answer came out breathy and excited.

"This time, Kira, don't whisper." He rolled her sensitive bud between his fingertips, and her knees threatened to buckle. "You have to beg me."

Even her mind couldn't protest his treatment. The feelings that her body craved mixed with the irresistible energy of his desire-fueled self-torment. She moaned and licked her lips.

"Please, Master Zachary, fuck me."

"Again." He removed his hands and adjusted himself behind her, lining up his length at her folds. No part of his body touched her, but oh, was he close.

The anticipation nearly undid her remaining control. "I beg you, Master Zachary. Fuck me, fuck me, fuck me."

On her last plea, he plunged into her. She cried out at the burst of energy between them. This wasn't the healthy but overly sweet energy she'd survived on lately, and it wasn't the unhealthy junk-food energy she'd experienced with her other targets.

This was raw, primal, and limitless. Like sinking her teeth into a juicy steak.

So much for being a vegetarian.

Faeries usually replenished their strength with occasional trips to their clan's protected glen, each one the heart of an element's energy from Mythos itself. Avoiding Mythos because of Lirdeag had kept her from that source, but Zac's energy almost made her feel like she wasn't missing a thing.

"God." He stopped and gripped her hips. "You feel so good I could stay here forever."

She could have said the same thing. He filled her so completely nothing could feel better than this.

He pulled her against him, ensuring he was all the way in, and then started a slow, sensation-filled slide apart. When just his head remained inside, his fingertip teased her sensitive bud again. Shocks zinged down her limbs, and her inner muscles squeezed him, wanting more. She whimpered.

"Yes, my sweet Kira?" His other hand pinched her nipple, igniting a craving in her body.

"More please, Master Zachary." She couldn't help circling her hips and trying to press back against him.

"You need me?"

"Yes, Master Zachary, I need you. *Please.*"

The last of his restraint vanished, and he yanked her down on him. Over and over, he pounded into her. Colors danced in her vision, the influx of energy and sensation sending her right to the edge.

His fingers dug into her hips, as though trying to force them to become one. Her muscles grabbed onto him with each thrust. She was so close, and yet, unlike before, she didn't want this to end.

It wasn't just the energy. The feeling, the sensation, satisfied her like nothing she'd imagined.

Too soon for her new appreciation, he ordered, "Now, Kira, come for me."

A cry ripped from her, and she bit down on the comforter to smother the noise. Her muscles clenched in an orgasm that nearly turned her inside out. Every part of her body seemed to scream for joy.

He followed with a grunt and a squeeze of her hips that would leave bruises on a human. His shaft pulsed inside her with an explosion she could feel despite the condom separating them.

Energy burst across their connection, filling her beyond what her body could hold. Light flashed before her eyes, and her skin tingled all over. Hell, her nerves, her muscles, and her brain tingled all over, the excess energy exciting every cell.

Between the sensations and the energy shooting through her body, her orgasm echoed again and again. Aftershocks sent spasms of pleasure that continued long after he'd finished. Her descent back into her consciousness took a leisurely drifting path, like a still-burning cinder floating to the ground.

Her thoughts and ability to think straight felt even less substantial than that cinder. She wasn't sure she could remember her name anymore.

A giggle threatened to break the mood. Maybe it was a good thing he knew her name. After all, he'd known her name for days and never used it against her. If this was all he did with his control over her, how much should she mind? Because that...

That was indescribable.

Domination and submission weren't her thing—and she could tell from his emotions that it wasn't usually his either—but for tonight, the game fit their needs perfectly. It was a win for both of them, and as far as she was concerned, she'd hit the jackpot.

Her knees gave out, and if it weren't for his grasp on her hips, she'd have slipped to the floor.

"Easy." He hauled her onto the bed alongside him and tucked her into a spooning position in front of him. "I take it that was good for you?"

After a minute, she got her breathing to a normal-enough level that she could speak. "Thank you, Master Zachary."

No use of her real name compelled her to say that. Only her honest gratitude for the experience.

And with that truth haunting her, she slipped into a long-overdue sleep.

Chapter Twenty-Five

THE ROAR OF AN ENGINE GUNNED THROUGH ZAC'S SLEEP, AND he sat up in bed. Shit. Kira's motorcycle.

He sprinted from the room and skidded down the hall. The closer he got to the front of the house, the quieter the engine throbbed. Maybe he should have worried about running into Emily in his still-naked-from-last-night state, but no one met him on his path. He plucked a cowboy hat off the hook at the entrance, covered his privates, and yanked open the front door.

He was too late. Morning sun illuminated only gravel on his driveway. Empty, except for a set of quail parents escorting their brood across the dirt.

Bloody hell. He slammed the door closed and tossed his hat back onto its hook. So much for no consequences.

Not that he could blame her.

He'd treated the foster mother of his child like a goddamn fuck buddy. No, worse.

What the hell had gotten into him last night? Sure, the "no strings" attitude had been his normal philosophy ever since Crissy had proved commitment was a waste of time, but he'd never pulled that ordering-around crap on anyone before. So why the *hell* had he gone that route with Kira, of all people?

He trudged back to his room, surveying the scene of the crime. No evidence remained of the evening, not even the used condom he'd tossed aside. He was tempted to pretend the whole thing had been a dream. A good dream or a bad one, he couldn't decide.

None of her clothes remained behind, so she'd apparently found all the pieces. Too bad. And other than a bit of rumpling, the bed didn't even look slept in, as they'd fallen asleep on top of the coverlet, right where they'd collapsed post most-incredible-*and-most-fucked-up* sex of his life.

Rather than scratching an itch and getting her out of his system, his attraction to her coiled deeper into his being, with an even more desperate urgency than last night. Something about her, something beyond just looks, made her more knock-out gorgeous to him than the groupies that used to star in his teenage fantasies of living the rodeo cowboy life. She knew just how to hit his buttons, including several he hadn't known existed until she'd triggered them in electrifying fashion.

And now...

Now he'd done God-only-knew-what damage to the situation.

Would she still take his calls? Would she let him near Emily again? Would she report to Renee Cushman that he was an aggressive asshole, unsuitable for fatherhood?

His stomach dropped into a churning abyss. He tugged at his hair and growled loud enough to elicit a whimper from Honey, who sat in the doorway of the room, her head cocked.

"Yeah, I know. I screwed up, and I have to fix this. Somehow."

If he remembered correctly, Emily had several therapy appointments today, which meant he had a whole day to kill before he could try to talk to Kira. Maybe that meant it was the perfect time to throw himself into his work.

Several hours and several hundred swings later, he'd hammered out his frustrations, even shunning the power hammer that auto-mated the process on simple pieces. Most blacksmiths couldn't work while frustrated, as their work required precision. However, precision came naturally to him, so the addition of his emotions— which were more out of control than ever—added artistry and drama beyond what he'd thought himself capable of designing.

For the first time since learning about Emily, he was ahead of schedule on commissioned projects. A quick shower to wash away the day's sweat, and he was as ready as he'd ever be to go to

Moose's bar and face Kira.

The parking lot was already full of motorcycles parked willy-nilly, forcing him to park his truck down the road. Neither Kira nor Moose were around inside, and he slipped onto a bar stool against the wall.

Moose emerged from the back a minute later and spotted Zac, his eyes widening. "Didn't expect to see you. Fairy's not here."

"Actually, I'm here to talk to Prin."

"They should be back soon. Don't you have her cell?"

"This is an in-person kind of talk."

"Don't tell me, you need to dig yourself out of a hole." Whatever expression Moose saw on Zac's face answered his curiosity, and he shrugged. "It happens. Took longer than I expected, to be honest."

The back door scraped open, and the pair entered. His daughter's foster mom was more stunning than ever. Almost otherworldly. In the dim light of the bar, she nearly glowed, as though she was her own light source, glittering and translucent.

Today, even though he couldn't imagine when she'd had time to dye it, her hair was a deep, solid black, darker than Emily's. The color framed her face perfectly, yet a broad grin directed at nothing in particular lit up her expression, ruining the goth look.

At the draft beer dispenser, Moose plunked down a glass he'd only half filled. "I'll be damned." His gaze cut to Zac. "You wouldn't happen to know what put that smile on her face, would you?"

Zac's mouth opened and closed several times. He didn't know what to think.

Moose called out to them. "How are my girls today?"

Emily slid from Kira's arms and skipped toward Moose. "The therapist gave me a sticker. Wanna see?"

Moose *oohed* and *aahed* over the image of something Zac couldn't make out from his corner stool at the other end of the bar. "Someone must have been good today." Moose looked up at Kira. "And what's cranked your happy juice?"

"I had a good night's sleep." Kira's chin dipped. "That's all."

Emily bounced. "I got the sticker because I didn't freak out about staying at Daddy's last night."

Moose's brows shot up, and he stared at Kira. "You stayed at..."

Before Zac could make himself disappear into the wood paneling, Moose's gaze snapped to Zac's corner of the bar. Kira followed Moose's line of sight and noticed Zac for the first time. Her lips parted, and she stepped back.

Zac gave a feeble wave. "Hi, Prin. Hi, Emily."

Before he could say anything else, Emily skipped over and stuck out her arm. "Hi, Daddy! See my sticker?" Apparently, he managed to give the right reaction to the cartoon character he didn't recognize, as she changed the subject. "Is Candy doing okay?"

"She'll be fine. The vet checked on her today and said she'll be back to normal in a couple of days. I'm glad you're okay too."

Kira approached, her face tight, all trace of her smile gone. "This is a surprise. I didn't see your truck."

From his spot by the wall, he spied customers throughout the bar sneaking glances their way. Maybe they were waiting for the famous Prin fireworks. For that matter, so was he.

She gave a side-eye look to Moose and tilted her head. He led Emily to the other end of the bar, leaving them in relative privacy.

Kira beat him to getting in the first word. "Thank you."

Her flat-toned statement caught him off-balance. Was she being sarcastic?

"For calling me Prin," she offered as way of explanation.

That's what was at the forefront of her mind? "Of course."

Last night with just the two of them had been a special situation, and he had no intention of outing the truth to others. Betrayal wasn't his style.

He leaned forward, ignoring his body's excitement at having her near again, and kept his voice low. "I'm sure you have your reasons for secrecy."

"I do. Reasons more important than you can imagine."

"Then I'll keep the secret. Trust me."

"I seem to need to trust you about quite a bit."

"I don't break promises. I've been on the wrong end of broken ones too many times."

Her eyes scrunched, like she was deep in thought, and then she breathed deep. "Care to make an oath with that promise?"

"Sure. I—"

"No, I have to offer something in return. That's how it works." Her lips thinned. "What do you want me to promise?"

Several thoughts streaked naked through his mind, mostly variations on how he could share a bed with her again and still maintain his "no strings" rule. But listening to ideas from that part of his body was what had gotten him into this mess, forcing him to face the possibility that she might not let him near Emily anymore. Besides, he didn't trust himself to keep his emotional distance if he allowed a repeat of last night to occur, and distance was something he required.

"Promise you won't keep Emily from me because of something between us."

She peered over her shoulder, but no one was close enough to hear their conversation. "You mean not keeping her from you as punishment for something you do or say to me?"

"Exactly."

She angled her body toward the wall, hiding her movements from everyone else. One of her gloves landed on the bar's top. "One hand on your heart."

He suppressed a chuckle at how seriously she took her promises—even more seriously than he did. Her acquiescence to all of his demands last night had already proven she'd keep her word, no matter what. He placed his palm on his chest.

"Under your shirt." After he followed her instructions, sliding his hand between his shirt and the skin over his heart, she grasped his other hand with her now-bare fingers. "Okay, say it."

"I swear on my life, I won't reveal your real—"

"True. True name. Start over."

His brow popped high at her nitpicky-ness. Whatever would make her happy, he guessed. He wanted this promise just as much as she did. If not more.

"I swear on my life, I won't reveal your true name to anyone, ever."

"I accept. I won't keep Emily from you or use her to punish you because of something between us."

The skin over his heart heated. What the—? He jerked his hand away, but warmth continued to flow from his heart to his limbs.

Before he could ask Kira if she felt the same thing, she removed her hand from his and slipped on her glove. The warmth faded.

Weird. One more thing to add to the Kira *X Files*. Had he imagined it or not?

Even though his logic wanted answers, his instincts told him to accept her as she was. Besides, what clarification could he ask for without looking like a crazy person?

Kira lifted her chin. "We good now?"

Wait... "You're not mad about last night?"

"What's there to be mad about?" She sucked in a breath, and an amused expression grew on her face. "You thought I left angry." She crossed her arms on top of the bar and leaned closer, her proximity sending tingles over his skin. "Emily had an early appointment this morning, and I didn't want to disturb you. Last night was exactly what I wanted—needed—and if I need it again, I'll let you know."

His shoulders dropped. That sounded like a *don't call me, I'll call you* dismissal.

He could live with that. "Okay."

She didn't owe him anything, and her brush off was better than the angry alternative. More to the point, with how much she tempted him, it was safer to leave her in charge of potential future rendezvous. He barely resisted telling her that he'd take her call anytime, day or night.

She stepped back and stacked dirty dishes in a plastic tub. "No offense, but I need to get back to work. I have Emily in more therapy sessions than the state's foster system covers, and with all of the supervised-visit activities, I've missed out on too many hours lately."

"Right."

Kira probably didn't hear his acknowledgment though, her stride already carrying her halfway to the door to the back, the tub in her hands. He was standing to leave when the big picture struck him upside the head. He was an idiot.

Kira returned from the back, and he hustled toward her. "Hey, one more question."

She didn't lift her gaze from her work. "Shoot."

"Would it help if I paid for all of Emily's therapy?"

She stopped and met his eyes. "You'd do that?"

"Sure. Official custody or not, I *should* be financially responsible for my daughter, or else I'm no better than a deadbeat dad." He hooked a thumb toward the table closest to the open end of the bar, where Moose had set up Emily with coloring pages. "And I'll leave you in charge of telling me when you can get away from work for activities. Otherwise, I'll come here in the evening and help you watch her. If I sit at that table with her, that's supervised enough, right?"

Kira's fingers rose to her mouth, and she didn't say anything.

"Uh, is that a problem, or would that be okay?"

She dropped her hand. "Yeah." Her blinks quickened. "Yeah, that would work great."

A smile spread her lips wide, and he'd swear she glowed from within. He retreated to Emily's table before he could say anything to mess up the situation.

Maybe it was wishful thinking, but she seemed happy with him. Damned happy. And that was a heck of a lot better than the fight he'd thought was waiting for him this evening.

Chapter Twenty-Six

Zac pulled into his usual spot in the back, between Kira's trailer and Moose's bar. The scent of rain-soaked creosote bushes saturated the air, and monsoon clouds piled thick and dark, threatening to bring the rain closer any minute. He glanced at the spotless finish of his new truck and sighed. It had to be broken in sometime. Hopefully he could drag Kira and Emily out to see his surprise before the storm hit.

Winds kicked up dust, and he crossed the parking lot with his eyes half closed. Inside, Kira and Emily hadn't arrived from the day's therapy appointment yet, but Moose waved a friendly greeting to him. In the couple of months since Zac's agreement with Kira, he'd become a regular in the place.

The arrangement had worked out better than he'd hoped. The frequent time with Emily at their corner table had accelerated their bonding. They split time between completing the educational workbooks Kira had picked up for Emily and playing every kind of game either of them could think of, from Candy Land to poker. As a bonus, he was around to help Kira tuck Emily into bed each night, and his daughter had graced him with a couple of hugs and goodnight kisses.

At first, Kira had seemed torn about his presence, but her mood gradually improved, probably as the strain of being a single parent dissipated. If only she called him for regular rendezvous, life would be perfect.

Zac shook his head and headed for his and Emily's table. No, he shouldn't wish for that. The intervening months hadn't dampened his interest in Kira. If anything, he was even less likely to keep his emotional distance during another bedroom encounter.

The last time he'd let himself seriously think about the possibility—over a month ago—the sum of his history had shouted warnings about getting too close to her as it was, about how it was only a matter of time until she betrayed him, just like everyone else he'd ever known. That voice from last month had convinced him it was better to stay where he was. No strings, no hurt.

The next burst of wind pelted the window with water drops, and rain drummed the roof above. As Emily would say, the storm had unleashed "full-grown cats and dogs" and not just "puppies and kittens."

Zac dialed Kira's cell, but the call went to voicemail. "Hey, it's raining pretty bad here. Give me buzz if you want me to pick you up."

While he grabbed a glass of water from behind the bar, his phone vibrated on the table, and a rock version of "The Good, the Bad and the Ugly" echoed off the back wall. He lunged and answered the call after just a few notes, but the distinctive *wah-wah-wah* had already turned heads, as though inflicting the cowboy song on the bar's crowd was a major crime. Like an idiot, he kept forgetting to give Kira a custom ringtone.

"Sorry," he announced to no one in particular and adjusted the phone at his ear. "Hey, need me to pick you up?"

"Is this Zachary Chase, son of Sandra Benally, *Tódích'íi'nii*, born for *Kinyaa'áanii*?"

"Uh..." Between the fact that the caller *wasn't* Kira and that he was throwing around Navajo clan terminology Zac hadn't heard in years, it took him a minute to answer. "Yes, this is Zachary Chase."

"My name is Sani Benally. I am *Kinyaa'áanii*, born for *Honágháahnii*. I am your *shicheii*—your grandfather."

"Oh, uh, hi." His gut tightened, a sudden burst of questions gnawing holes in his stomach.

"We received word that you have a daughter. Your grandmother and I want to meet her."

Zac pulled the phone back and stared at the screen. That was it? No, hi, how are you? No, how have you been doing? Just... *We want.*

He lifted the phone again. "It's not that simple."

"We have collected the paperwork to enroll her as a Diné tribe member, and we need you to bring her birth certificate."

And *this* was why his father had issues dealing with his mother's side of the family. Family loyalty and respect he could understand—hypothetically at least. But whether they meant for it to happen or not, his grandparents' single-minded focus on Navajo matters ended up feeling disrespectful to others. Then again, he had his own major problems with his father, so most likely, neither side was blameless for the bad history.

Was what they were asking for really so bad? After all, he didn't have a problem with Emily enrolling in the tribe. If nothing else, the official designation might help with scholarships down the line. And it's not as if he was likely to initiate the process on his own.

He sighed. Maybe he just needed to help them figure out the social niceties expected by those off the reservation.

"Okay, we'll make plans to come up. I'll let you know when we'll be there."

"That is acceptable."

Before Zac could answer, the back door opened to admit a drenched Kira and Emily. By the time he returned his attention to the phone, his grandfather had hung up.

Zac put his phone away and kept his gaze firmly away from Kira's curves revealed by the clinging, wet material. For a distraction, he grabbed a towel and draped it around his daughter's quivering shoulders. While he wiped Emily's face and brushed down her clothes, being careful not to crowd her and trigger fears, Kira grabbed another towel from the back and dried off her leathers but didn't bother squeezing out her hair.

Today, shades of blue, from blue-green to Caribbean blue, streaked through Kira's locks. If it weren't for all of the black below her neck, the wet strands would look like they belonged on a mermaid. Somehow, she managed to complete her task without getting a single smudge of the temporary hair dye on the terrycloth.

He finished with Emily and dumped both towels in the back.

Just as he returned to the table, Kira hung up her phone. "Looks like you reached my voicemail right as we were coming in, so we almost beat the storm." She gave Emily a smile. "You feeling better? You're not going to melt, are you?"

Emily giggled and shook her head. A call from Moose about missing his daily hug sent her running toward the bar.

Zac laid his phone on the tabletop and tapped the screen. "Actually, I'd called a few minutes before that. You'll never guess who I was talking to when you arrived."

Kira's expression darkened. "Renee Cushman?"

"No, but we should be hearing from her soon." He picked up his cell and swiped through the screens. Advice for the perfect way to bring up the subject didn't magically appear. "My mother's father. Up on the reservation."

She slid into the booth across from him. "I thought you weren't in contact with your grandparents."

"I wasn't. Renee's digging to track me down probably notified the tribe about Emily, and they passed along the information." He braced himself for the protest. "My grandparents want to meet Emily and complete the paperwork for her tribe enrollment."

"Have you set up the visit yet?"

"No, uh, I wasn't even convinced I should take her."

"There's no reason not to enroll her."

"I know." His explanation died in the silence.

"You're not sure how much you want to see *them*." Her guess sounded more like a statement.

"It'll take several hours to drive there, their house makes your trailer look luxurious, and although I have fond memories of my grandmother, my grandfather always treated me like the half-breed I am. Is it any wonder that I'm not sure I want Emily exposed to the potential of even worse behavior?"

"We should go this week."

"What?" He thumped the table. "Were you even listening to me?"

"Of course I was listening. That's why I made my suggestion." Her hair, already appearing smooth and dry, slid behind her shoulder. "The time to do this is while I'm still in the picture. I can make sure Emily's okay during the visit, and if necessary, I can run interference between your grandfather and either of you."

He didn't answer. None of her reasons explained why they had to decide this very minute. Especially as she still had the mistaken impression that he'd ever kick her out of the picture.

She gestured to Emily at the bar with Moose. "Besides, she starts school next week, and then it will be harder to get away for a couple of days."

Damn, *now* she had a point. The Navajo offices would be closed on weekends, and schools around Phoenix started in early August to allow for longer breaks during the cooler months. And between the start of school and Emily doing so well lately, they'd scaled back her therapy schedule, so he couldn't use that as an excuse either.

"All right. If we drive up tomorrow, I could hit the Vital Records office Wednesday, and then we'd have a day to drive back before her Friday therapy session. I'd need you to bring her birth certificate. I don't have a copy yet." He scanned the calendar app on his phone and made sure he wasn't forgetting any client meetings. The last of his excuses evaporated on the empty screen. "Are you sure you want to do this?"

"Only slightly more than you do apparently, but this is the best time to go. I'd rather go now than for this to happen later and me not be there for her." Kira's voice deadened on the end of the sentence.

"There's no 'not going to be there for her.' Emily and I aren't going anywhere." He tried to elicit a grin from her. "You probably didn't notice because of the rain, but I just got a new truck—an extended cab. Would I buy that if I was planning on kicking you out of the picture?"

She didn't crack a smile. No matter how many times he reassured her that he wouldn't prevent her from seeing Emily after the custody transfer, Kira still acted like he was taking his daughter to the other side of the globe and wouldn't be able to visit. Hell, she had to recognize how much easier it was with his help these past few months, so her assumption that he wouldn't welcome her help in return didn't make any sense.

Emily slid into the booth, and Kira filled her in on the plan. He stared, amazed, during Kira's explanation. Not only did Emily *not* freak out, but Kira also managed to make the trip sound like so much of an adventure even *he* almost felt a thrill of excitement.

How did she do that? He'd paid attention to her techniques for months, attempting to pick up parenting insights, yet compared to her, he was still a bumbling novice.

Rather than the passing of time leading to him needing Kira less, he was needing her more. And needing her in more ways than one.

He waited for panic to set in at that realization, waited for the voice of his history to start the klaxons again. *Needing* someone—especially to that level—went against everything he'd promised himself years ago. *Trusting* someone had seemed even more impossible until she'd proven him wrong. But the panic didn't come, and the klaxons didn't sound.

His heartbeat stuttered a bit, but didn't accelerate. His breathing remained normal other than a slight hitch. The only change was the sensation of his throat growing so thick breathing required concentration.

Was that a new sign of panic? Or of something else?

Chapter Twenty-Seven

EVEN THOUGH SHE'D PEEKED JUST A MINUTE BEFORE, KIRA checked again on Emily in the back seat of Zac's no-longer-shiny truck. Still sound asleep in her new booster chair. How that child managed to snooze through the bumps and waves of this dirt road, Kira couldn't understand.

"Sorry your new truck is getting broken in a bit too well."

"Yeah, I'd forgotten about this part of life on the reservation. Probably because I wasn't driving yet the last time I was up here."

Zac had fretted during the drive, warning her about everything from his grandparents' beliefs in the old ways—right down to having a dirt floor in their one-room hogan—to his guess of how his grandfather would treat her, the outsider. If not for the inconvenience, Zac would have arranged for them to stay in a hotel in Flagstaff, a few hours back.

He threw his scrawled-out directions across the bench seat. "If we're not lost, it'll be a miracle."

She almost gave in to the urge to reach over and comfort him. Damn. For months, she'd kept her distance, refusing to act on her impulses, using Emily as a crutch to keep her hands off Zac. This trip, with hours' worth of close quarters—especially when Emily snoozed through much of it and Kira couldn't use her to *create* that distance—was causing havoc on her resistance.

Caring and gentle, sexy and dominant, loyal and honest, the

facets of his personality appealed to her in every way possible. Her hand clenched, and she looked down at her glove, as though she could see the magical lines slowly but surely drawing ever closer to their destination through the leather. The reminder that she had no future was never far away.

She dragged her gaze away from his profile. Outside, clouds gathered into towering cotton balls in the distance, and flat, high scrub desert with occasional rock outcroppings surrounded them. Dirt roads crisscrossed at random angles every half-mile or so, most of them seemingly leading nowhere.

Going by what she'd seen so far, their hometown of Cave Creek—at a whole five thousand people—was as big as any town in the Navajo Nation, and Navajos didn't have a major metropolitan area like Phoenix for a next-door neighbor. Instead, most seemed to live out here in the nothingness, scattered across the land, grazing sheep or surviving through other rural activities. She would have asked Zac about the specifics, but her last question about the houses they'd passed had led to a twenty-minute rant about poverty on the reservation, with many of the houses lacking a kitchen or indoor plumbing.

"I don't even know if they're aware we're coming." He shut off his cell phone, and she followed suit. Neither of them had any coverage, and there was no use draining their batteries when they didn't know what the electricity situation would be. "My grandfather used a neighbor's phone to call yesterday. The neighbor gave me directions and said he'd pass on the message, but..." Zac's voice trailed into the darkness of his mood.

Without warning, the dirt road dead-ended at a homestead that had blended into the landscape. The main house looked like a six-sided log cabin, its low-sloping roof rising to a stovepipe at the center. Many of the other hogans they'd passed hadn't looked lived in, lacking a real door or windows, but this one wasn't for ceremonies. Other hogans made of packed dirt, probably the ceremonial ones, sat along the edge of the cleared yard.

"Did we find it? Is this their place?"

Before he could answer, an elderly woman in a long skirt with a scarf tied around her hair emerged from the home and smiled. Zac waved in return. Apparently they hadn't gotten lost after all.

Kira twisted toward the back. "Wake up, Fairy. We're here."

She scooped a groggy Emily into her arms, and Zac grabbed their bags. The next few minutes passed in a flurry of words she couldn't follow at all. An older man with a black cowboy hat, turquoise-accented bolo tie, and a proud face joined them, adding to the language chaos. They were obviously being warmly welcomed, but she couldn't make out specifics.

Finally Zac held up his hands. "I didn't understand most of what you just said. I think I remember a grand total of five Navajo words. Prin and Emily don't know any." He lowered his hands. "Please, can we stick to English?"

The man nodded to Kira. "She wears our sacred colors. I thought she was educated. Not that our beliefs were being appropriated for fashion."

Zac stared at her hair as though he hadn't noticed—quite a change from how he used to react to her colors. Today she'd gone with black except for the tips, which were a mix of turquoise, yellow, and white.

"She wears different colors every day. She means to honor you."

Kira crossed her arms over her heart the best she could with Emily on her hip and bowed. "I can change the colors if they offend."

The man's eyes narrowed. "How do you identify yourself if you have no clan?"

Maybe she understood the Navajo culture better than Zac expected. Clans, she could relate to just fine.

"Among my ancestors, I'd be known as a member of a clan called Flarea, the fire clan." True enough, except for the implication that her clan no longer existed.

"Fire clan. A member of the people of the light. I am honored."

"It is I who am honored."

And with that, Zac's grandparents welcomed her as the foster mother of their great-granddaughter. Zac shook his head, a grin curving his mouth.

The inside of their hogan was plain, she'd guess to keep the inhabitants in contact with nature. A wood stove sat in the middle of the room, a few rolled mats leaned against the wooden walls, a cabinet stood in one corner, and an in-process weaving spread inside an upright loom propped on the dirt floor. While preparing dinner, Zac's grandmother, Doli, explained that her husband, Sani, was the local medicine man, and they lived without electricity or other modern conveniences to keep his connection to the spirits pure.

As Kira had suspected, Zac's grandparents weren't just backward relics. They had a reason for their simple lifestyle.

Zac didn't seem ready to give up his childhood attitude, his mood barely an improvement over surly. In his defense, his grandparents interrogated him throughout dinner about his history and the story of Emily's birth to a woman who wasn't his wife.

Despite her intention to run interference, Kira didn't come to his aid. What could she say? State how he was a wonderful man and they should be proud to have him as a grandson? Anything she said would reveal her growing vulnerability to him. Not a good idea.

When the topic veered into sensitive issues, Kira took Emily outside. The lack of electricity at the homestead and the fact that the nearest neighbors were far in the distance meant the darkening sky held more stars than she'd seen in the middle of the night near Phoenix. They lay down in the back of Zac's truck to take in the sight.

The broad, open plain held nothing but silent stars. Unlike on Mythos, these stars didn't dance or sing.

After several minutes, Emily interrupted the unimaginable silence of the evening. "I don't think Daddy likes them very much."

Kira chuckled. "You noticed, huh? What do you think of them?"

"They seem okay to me so far."

"They might be okay, or they might not be, but I think your daddy is upset by their choices about how they live and how they treat others."

"I'll keep an eye open for that." Emily's voice sounded so matter-of-fact and grown-up that Kira had to swallow a chuckle. "Should we see if Daddy needs saving?"

"Good idea."

The best, in fact. If she rose to his defense at Emily's urging, her own emotions on the matter could remain hidden.

Chapter Twenty-Eight

BACK INSIDE THE HOGAN, KIRA CUT OFF HER PLANNED DEFENSE of Zac, as sleeping mats were now laid out on the dirt. Apparently, they'd agreed to disagree, and a single-room home with no electricity didn't allow for variety in sleeping schedules.

Zac and his grandfather's mats were on the south end of the room, and the rest were on the north end. Emily received a warm *goodnight* from her great-grandparents, and everyone claimed their mat.

However, between the sleeping accommodations and her long nap, Emily didn't want to settle. She thrashed around, rolling off the sleeping mat and into the cupboard, the loom, the wall—everything.

Finally Kira dragged her close and whispered, "Want me to tell you a bedtime story?"

With all of Emily's rustling about, Kira suspected the others were awake too, but no one shushed them or said a word. Now, what story to tell?

Her mind naturally went to the stories of her kind. Especially as the fae world didn't feel as distant as it had before.

Even with the energy she'd gotten from Zac months ago, her magic's connection to the faerie homeland had continued to grow, calling like a siren's song. Her daily boosts from Emily's pure emotions were only slowing down the spread of mystical circuitry under her skin, not stopping it completely. And the deadline of losing Emily in the courts loomed closer every day. Her time on the Earthen plane was running out.

Before, she'd fought to hold off the growth of her lines for her own sake and the sake of her people. Now she accepted the inevitable and simply hoped to remain here long enough to see Emily safe. The horrors she'd have to face after she was forced to return to Mythos were best left unconsidered.

Would she be able to fight Lirdeag and his control of her name? Would she be able to keep her people safe and free despite his power over her ruling magic? She shoved away the questions.

Instead, for her sanity, it was better to think just about her Earthen plane hopes and dreams. And with Zac in Emily's life, Kira almost felt at peace about meeting her fate. If only a bit of herself could live on in Emily, she might be able to accept losing her life here.

Warmth spread from her chest. *That* was the story to tell. Her story.

Maybe hearing a literal faerie tale would help Emily hold on to her sense of the good and the magic in the world. If Kira could give the girl strength to deal with the future, that gift of herself could survive.

She stroked Emily's hair and took a deep breath. This would take a while.

She kept her voice low, her story meant for Emily alone. "Once upon a time, a princess was born to the faeries. Faeries don't have many children, especially not in the royal family, so she was cherished—and a little bit spoiled.

"Her parents, the king and queen, ruled well, and they were loved among the faeries. The princess's clan had ruled since time began, and only the royal family knew all the magic to keep the faeries safe. Then rumors spread among the fae that someone was trying to steal the kingdom."

Emily tensed at her side. "Uh-oh."

Kira kept her tone level, the storytelling device giving her distance from the emotions she'd lived through. "The king wasn't worried. His guards, the Red Wing, were loyal and true, and they would protect the royal family. He didn't know that Lirdeag, the head of the Red Wing and his most trusted guard, was the faerie who wanted the kingdom for himself.

"Lirdeag had others pretend to try to hurt the royal family, and then he rushed in to save them. The king was so grateful he granted Lirdeag one wish. Lirdeag wished for the princess's hand in marriage, and the king had no choice but to agree."

"The poor princess."

"Well, the princess was only five years old and didn't plan on marrying anytime soon."

"Ew."

"Exactly. Worse, no one knew that Lirdeag didn't want to wait. He wanted the kingdom *now*. That meant he would have to kill the king and queen and convince the young princess to marry him. He came up with a horrible plan."

Wrapped up in the story, Emily gasped but didn't say anything.

"The princess had always loved Lirdeag like a favorite uncle, best friend, and protector all in one, so she figured she'd like the idea of marrying him—once she was a grownup.

"Her trust in him made it easy for Lirdeag and his invincible gargoyle army to capture the king and queen. Then he forced the princess to watch while he hurt her parents. She was shocked. How could one of her favorite faeries in the world do this to her? But she never figured out why.

"He planned to keep hurting her parents until they gave him what he wanted, the princess's true name. You see, faeries keep their true name a secret from all others. Anyone who knows their true name can control them, force them to do things they don't want to do."

"Like marry the bad guy."

Kira smiled in the darkness. "You're so smart. Yes, if Lirdeag found out the princess's true name, he could make her marry him, and he wouldn't have to wait."

"Couldn't they use his name against him?"

"If Lirdeag was his true name, yes, they could. But Lirdeag was his title for being head of the Red Wing, not his true name."

"Oh." Emily's response sounded like a pout.

The girl's reaction helped Kira continue treating the story like a fairy tale, and not the story of her life. This part of the tale would have reduced her to tears otherwise.

Even so, she swallowed hard to keep her voice level. Memories of her parents' last hours flashed before her eyes. She shoved the visions away, but not before images of their faces twisted in pain, their limbs crushed in the gargoyles' unbreakable—and unburnable—clawed grips, invaded her thoughts. That wasn't how she wanted to remember them.

"Anyway..." She cleared her throat and pushed herself to continue the story. "After all of Lirdeag's torture, the king and queen were near death. The princess cried and cried at how much her parents were hurting. Magic from the clans' spirits prevents faerie children from revealing their true name until they're old enough to understand the danger, so only her parents could give Lirdeag what he wanted. She begged them to tell Lirdeag so he wouldn't hurt them anymore.

"Finally, her mother couldn't take the pain. She told Lirdeag the princess's first name. Faeries have very long names, so knowledge of only one of those names wouldn't give him complete control, but it still made him very dangerous to the princess.

"The king didn't want Lirdeag to learn any more of the princess's name, so he used his magic to remove his and the queen's tongues before they could say anything else. Lirdeag was so furious he killed them both, right in front of the princess."

Emily shuddered. "That's horrible."

Maybe this wasn't an appropriate story for bedtime after all. Too late now. Besides, human fairy tales were filled with gruesome elements too.

At least she hadn't gone into the details of how her father had removed their tongues. That *was* horrifying.

"The princess knew she didn't have time to cry. The fae's only chance to escape Lirdeag's rule was to make sure he couldn't marry her. If they married, he'd become king and gain access to the ruling magic. She decided to use trickery, like he had.

"When Lirdeag used her first name, she didn't try to resist. He fell for her trick and thought he had complete control over her—after all, she was only five years old. Certain she couldn't outsmart him, he released her from her restraints.

"But the princess was willful and stubborn and had been waiting for the opportunity to fight his orders. She used her magic to leave the faerie homeland, going to the last place Lirdeag would look, a land nothing like her home.

"He wasn't going let her go that easily. He was powerful enough to track her use of that magic, and he almost caught her right away. Luckily, a stranger in the new land heard her cries, and he banished Lirdeag back to the faerie homeland. By the time Lirdeag recovered, the trail left by her magic was gone. She'd escaped."

"Yay!" Emily's reaction was a bit too loud, and Kira tucked her closer, muffling the sound. The girl returned to her whisper. "What happened to all the faeries she left behind?"

"For many years, the princess lived in peace and made friends in the new land. She worried about the fae back home, but she knew staying away was the best thing she could do for them. The new land didn't have a king and queen, and the people there found other ways to survive. She hoped the fae were doing the same in the absence of a ruler in their homeland."

"Then what happened?"

Kira swallowed, but her throat tightened anyway. Going into these details wasn't good for a happy ending, but maybe she wanted some part of Emily to understand why she'd have to leave her.

"As she got older, the pull of her homeland's magic got stronger. When the magic completely wove itself through her body, she had to leave behind her friends, all those she'd met and cared about in the new land, and she was very, very sad. The magic forced her to return to the faerie homeland and face Lirdeag."

Kira paused. This part of the tale still felt all too real. An ache in her chest grew tight at the thought of leaving Moose and Emily—and Zac.

She pushed the thought away. This was just a story. A true story. But just a story. Yet how could she end the tale when it didn't yet have an ending?

Emily prompted, "She was stronger then, right? Strong enough to beat the bad guy?"

The girl's eternal optimism, even in the face of everything she'd endured, plucked at the ripples of worry Kira tried to ignore. Emily showed bravery and embraced life despite her fears. Her progress over the last couple of months proved just how far she'd come.

More importantly, she was right. Every fairy tale deserved a happy ending, even if Kira didn't believe in it for herself.

"That's right. She was stronger, and she learned her magic was strong enough to defeat him." Kira grimaced at the lame ending. "And the faeries lived happily ever after."

Emily snuggled against her. "That was a good story. I hope the princess got to visit her friends again after everything was over."

Kira kissed Emily's temple. "I hope so too."

If only it would be that easy.

Chapter Twenty-Nine

THE NEXT MORNING, KIRA WOKE TO DAWN LIGHT SPILLING through the open, east-facing door of the hogan. Ugh. More early risers.

Zac packed their stuff in preparation for the hours-long drive to Window Rock, location of the Navajo Nation's government offices. He didn't seem to be listening to the pleas of his grandparents, who begged him to let Emily stay behind for the day so they could visit with their great-granddaughter.

Kira sensed another argument and stepped between them. "I'll stay here with her."

Zac tilted his head away from the truck, indicating she should follow. Once across the yard, he whirled on her. "Are you crazy? You want me to leave you and Emily here *alone* with them? All day?"

"It'll be fine." Her reassurance didn't convince him, so she changed strategies. No matter what he thought, spending another day beside him in the truck felt like the bigger risk. "Think of it this way, you're not likely to come up here for another visit, so this might be their one chance to get to know her. Put yourself in their shoes for a minute. Wouldn't you want to spend time with her?"

He removed his hat and swept his hand through his hair. "I hate when you're logical."

"No, you hate it when I'm right." She couldn't keep the smile off her face. "Which is all the time, so it's no wonder that you're always grumpy."

A laugh burst from him, loud enough to draw the attention of his grandparents beside the hogan. "I don't know what I'd do without you." He sighed and replaced his hat. "All right, if you think it'll be okay. You're the one who knows how to work magic with Emily anyway." His dimple appeared. "Until your bedtime story for her last night, I didn't think it would be possible to get her to sleep in a strange place with no bed."

Her grin faltered. He'd heard her whispers?

Hopefully, he'd just heard enough murmurings to know she'd been talking. She didn't want to think about Zac overhearing the private story of her life. Somehow it felt more intimate than sharing it with Emily.

She rearranged her expression into one of confidence. "Go. Turn in that paperwork. We'll be fine here."

A few minutes later, Zac left them alone, a cloud of dust following his truck. His grandmother, Doli, wasted no time inviting Emily to join her in morning chores. His grandfather, Sani, approached, his gaze taking measure of Kira.

"I need your help."

His abruptness didn't bother her. "With what?"

"Emily has seen too much badness in her young life. We Diné believe that we must walk in harmony with all around us. I would like to perform a healing prayer for her. We must restore healthy balance to her life."

"And you want my permission to do this with her today, while Zac's gone." She didn't need to ask, as his emotions shone as clear as the early morning light around them. Almost as clear as her perception of Zac's thoughts. "What would be involved?"

"The full ceremony would last for days." He held up a hand. "I know we don't have that much time. Instead, I ask only for a couple of hours for prayers."

"I must be present at all times."

"That..." He dropped his head with a shake. "That is not possible. I do not permit outsiders."

"I respect your beliefs far more than you assume, but if I can't be there—no deal."

Just like her technique with the college boys at Moose's bar, after dropping that bomb of a statement, she walked away. She strode toward Emily and Doli at the sheep pen. The sheep looked up from the food Emily and Doli presented and rushed to greet Kira at the far end.

The old woman knocked on the feed bucket. "Where are you going? Your food is over here."

Emily giggled. "Animals always do that around Prin. She talks to them."

Despite the wide eyes of Zac's grandmother, Kira couldn't ignore the animals' welcome. Yeah, the woman would think she was weird. What else was new? Her tattoo-like lines made that the default. Just as she embraced her ability to change hair colors, she wasn't going to hide this aspect of herself either. Especially not with humans she'd never see again.

Kira bowed to the sheep. "I am honored to meet you too. I'll be here all day. You should get your food."

A little one stuck his head through the fence, eager for her attention. She stroked his ears, about to repeat her teasing. Instead, his wild thoughts came through at the contact. *Seer.*

She sucked in a breath, inhaling her planned words. Seer. That's what the lion had warned her about too.

She bent down to the lamb's level and whispered, "What's a seer?"

The animal broke eye contact and bleated, scampering away. That was new.

And weird.

Sani appeared beside her at the fence. His lips pressed into a thin line, and his arms crossed over his chest. She knew what he was going to say before he said it and cut off his argument.

"No, I won't consider changing my mind. And don't think you might have a better chance with your grandson after all. I have full custody of Emily. What I say goes."

Even if Zac were here and agreed to the prayers, she'd still insist on being present.

"I see." His tone was sharp enough to inflict damage on anyone else. Good thing she wasn't anyone else.

She again walked away from him. The sheep followed her along the fence, still ignoring their food. Doli had resorted to speaking to the sheep in the Navajo language, but they stayed at Kira's side, joining the lamb in their warnings. Their worry was suffocating—especially because none of them could express their thoughts with enough detail to do any good.

Finally she leaned over the fence. "Thank you all for the information. I'll be fine. You should get your food now."

After they repeated their warning one last time, they returned to Doli and Emily at the food bucket. She felt Sani's gaze and met his eyes. Instead of the confrontation she expected to see in his face, an incredulous stare dominated his expression.

Uh-oh. As she'd often thought with Zac, he seemed to see—and understand—too much.

He erupted in a stream of Navajo words, speaking to his wife. She replied in Navajo as well. Kira couldn't understand a thing they said, but she sensed from Sani's emotions that they were talking about her.

She narrowed her focus to Sani. She didn't want to touch him, but maybe if she concentrated all her attention on him, she could get the gist of their conversation.

He gestured toward her body, a flash of black from his thoughts. Her black clothes? Then he pointed to her hair, which was red with yellow streaks today. An image of flames. A thought of something Zac had said to her before he left.

The sheep had again interrupted their eating and were bleating at her. Not a good sign.

Should she grab Emily and run? To where?

The torrent of words ended, and Sani gave her a nod.

"I would be honored for you to attend my singing." He ended the sentence with a word in Navajo that sounded like a title of some kind.

Lovely. She'd gotten what she'd asked for, so she couldn't very well say *no* now. Besides, she was stuck here for the day and had no way to get a hold of Zac. With no cell signal, she'd even left her phone powered off in the truck.

"Emily has to agree as well. I don't force her to do things that make her uncomfortable."

"The explanation is part of the prayer. She will understand then."

Ugh. Stubborn man. "Fairy?" She waited for the girl to look up from the sheep. "Your great-grandfather would like to say some Navajo prayers for you. Do you want to go along with it and see what he has in mind or say 'no thanks'?"

Emily's nose wrinkled. "Prayers? I guess."

"Good." Sani met Kira's gaze, challenging her to dispute the plan. "We will start after lunch."

"I look forward to it." That was the truth, even though apprehension—rather than eagerness—dominated her thoughts.

Sani excused himself to make preparations. Doli returned her attention to Emily. "Before the prayers, let me teach you how to weave."

The remainder of the morning passed without incident, and Kira had to admit that Doli was a doting great-grandmother. Emily was having a ball learning to weave a Navajo rug and cook traditional dishes.

After lunch, Sani called Kira and Emily to one of the ceremonial hogans, shaped similarly to an igloo made of packed dirt. He now wore traditional clothes—leggings and a colorful woven poncho-like wrapping draped over his simple top. Turquoise stones decorated accents around his neck, wrists, fingers, and waist.

He beckoned them to sit across from him, on the other side of a pile of sticks in the middle of the hogan. In a singsong tone, he began his explanation of how bad things happen to those who do not walk in beauty, those whose lives are not in balance. His prayers would call the Holy Ones to heal Emily and protect her from evil.

"The Holy Ones are not gods like what the white man believes, but powerful spirits who are always around us. Long ago, the leader of the Holy Ones gave us the sacred words and songs that call them to do as we ask. Do you want their help?"

Emily shrugged. "Okay."

Sani gave Kira a few sticks and a stone. "As the one presenting Emily for healing, it is your responsibility to start the fire."

What? She stared at the tools in her grasp. Earlier he didn't even want her here, and now she was being given a job with no direction? She—more than anyone—wouldn't know how to start a fire with these crude implements.

"Um, how?"

He mimed rubbing them together. His emotions clearly gave away that this was a test of some sort.

Uh-huh. Forget that.

She half-heartedly rubbed the tools as he directed over the starter pile of twigs and tilted her palm down. Magic gathered in her hand. Her fire magic wasn't yet powerful, but it would be enough.

Tingles prickled her palm. A spark leaped to the twig pile, licking the wood with flames. Hopefully her hand had blocked the humans' view of the magical flash.

Sani nestled the baby flames into the larger woodpile, his eyes glinting in the low light. "I knew you would be able to start the fire."

"Thank goodness for beginner's luck." She scooted back a couple of feet, but slightly ahead of Emily so she could still head off any issues.

The beat of a drum started at Sani's hands, and he sang along with the *thrum thrum thrum thrum*. The Navajo words to the chanted prayer wove a rhythm in the small hogan. The air grew thick and warm, the fire adding to the heat of midday. Each pound on the drum vibrated every molecule in the room.

Beside Kira, Emily stared into the fire, entranced. Understandable. Most fires were rather hypnotic.

Kira couldn't help a smile. Of course, their hypnotic qualities increased when a faerie of the fire clan was nearby. Unable to resist, she let her magic weave its spell over the fire. The flames danced—literally.

Under her control, the blaze pulsed in time with the drum and moved along with her imagination. The flames paired off, one twining around another and then unwinding, only to switch partners for the next verse of the song, like an elemental square dance.

Sometime later—Kira had no idea how long—Sani threw herbs onto the fire. Sweet smoke drifted through the hogan.

Between the mesmerizing flames and the smoke, her consciousness didn't feel attached to her body anymore. Instead, her head seemed to float several feet above the dirt floor, swaying from side to side. Her thoughts spun along with the curls of smoke.

"Holy One, I have called. Do you answer?"

The sudden burst of English words in Sani's song brought up her gaze. He was staring at her.

"Do you answer?" he repeated, each word emphasized on a drum beat.

Was he talking to her? Was she supposed to interrupt his song with an answer? What kind of answer did he expect?

Maybe a whisper, just in case she misunderstood. "I don't know the question."

"She-who-is-one-with-Black-Body, do you promise to watch over Emily?"

She had a native name now? She didn't know whether that was cool or ominous, and she certainly didn't want to agree to a promise she didn't understand. Promises had power.

"I've watched over Emily for months, but I can't promise I'll always be around."

Emily jerked, her eyes snapping to focus on Kira.

"I won't live forever, Fairy, and we don't know what will happen with your daddy. But you know I'll be there for you as long as I can." Sometimes telling the truth sucked.

Sani resumed his singing in Navajo and threw more herbs onto the fire. The air—and her thoughts—became even more clouded. Several more verses resonated through the hogan.

"Holy One, I call you to watch over Emily for as long as she walks in beauty. Do you answer?"

Holy One? But Sani once again stared at her, prompting for an answer.

"I can't promise that."

"I've used the sacred words. You must answer."

"I *am* answering. I can't promise I'll always be here for her, no matter how much I wish I could."

"Why not?"

Maybe it was the heat in the hogan, maybe it was her aggravation with Sani's expectations, or maybe it was the smoke making her thoughts woozy, but something loosened her tongue enough to give him a sense of the truth.

"A force more powerful than I can resist is calling me to be elsewhere."

A scowl gathered on his face. As if any of it was her choice.

"I see."

Like earlier that morning, his tone was sharp enough to leave scars. This experience was quickly crossing from "sure, I'll go along with that" to "how can we escape?" But he didn't say anything else, and the smoke lulled her into relaxation again.

The *thrum thrum thrum thrum* of his drum continued. A few minutes later, a headache started building inside her skull in time with the beat.

Sani groped into a dark corner with his other hand and dragged forward a leather bag. From within its depths, he withdrew a handful of leaves. He chanted several more verses in Navajo and threw the new herbs onto the fire.

Smoke mushroomed from the flames, filling the hogan. The pain in her head stabbed both temples, and nausea crept up her throat.

What—

The smoke seemed to thicken, the hogan's interior growing darker.

—the—

Her head swam, unable to tell up from down.

—hell?

She lost control of her limbs and collapsed. The dirt floor clouded up, her impact disturbing the packed soil.

Darkness embraced her. Darkness tricked her. Darkness betrayed her.

Chapter Thirty

ZAC DROVE UP TO HIS GRANDPARENTS' PLACE AND GROANED. Another night on a dirt floor was the last thing he wanted. The day had already been long, what with hours and hours of driving for ten minutes worth of filing paperwork. He climbed out of his truck and prepared for another evening of dealing with his grandparents.

Emily tore across the yard toward him, arms flailing. "Daddy, Daddy! Prin. I think she's *dead*!"

His chest cinched so tight his legs stiffened under him. *No...*

No, she was exaggerating. Had to be. He gathered his balance, preventing a stumble, but before he strode more than two steps toward his daughter, she dug her fingers into his arm and towed him forward.

"Hurry!" Her urgency clenched his chest tighter.

"Wha—?" He gasped, replenishing the breath that had abandoned his lungs. "What are you talking about? What happened? Where is she?"

"She's in there with Grandpa Sani." Emily gestured to the dirt hogan past the house, her destination for the attempt to drag him with her. "She was sitting next to me, arguing with him, and then her eyes got all weird, and she fell over."

What was Kira doing in the ceremonial hogan? Chills swept over him, even though the sun hadn't yet set. Fears and *what ifs* tangled around his legs like sludge. He forced his feet to propel him forward and left Emily behind.

He yelled back to her. "Go wait in the truck, and stay there until one of us gets you."

A sickly sweet smoke met him at the doorway of the hogan and stung his eyes. He blinked and dove into the darkness.

The dim light inside strained his vision, and he willed himself to see. Something. Anything.

A low fire in the center of the hogan produced more smoke than flames. Kira lay crumpled on her side, her eyes open but unseeing. Only a slight rise and fall of her chest gave away that she *wasn't* dead.

She *wasn't* dead.

Thank God. His chest expanded, able to take a full breath again. Zac rushed toward her side.

"Do not touch her." The sharp instruction from his grandfather cut through the dim, smoky interior, but didn't interrupt the drumbeat he sounded at his spot across from her.

Zac hesitated. Did his grandfather know of her aversion to being touched? Was that what they'd been arguing about?

He spun toward his grandfather. "What did you do to her?"

"She is unharmed. I am attempting to help her. She said she is being forced to leave Emily—this is the work of a *chindi,* an evil spirit."

Zac didn't know whether to laugh or shake the nonsense out of his grandfather. "There's no evil spirit. She's just worried about the custody case. For no reason, I might add." He glanced at her unmoving form. "So I ask again, what the hell did you do to her?"

"She is not what she seems, as you should well know from seeing her true self. Have you not noticed how the world comes alive around her? How the animals listen to her? Are you not my grandson who can *see* the work of spirits around us? You yourself said this morning that she knows the secrets of the spirits, what white men call magic."

What? He'd said no such thing. He replayed the morning's conversation, trying to make sense of his grandfather's words. Uh, he'd said Kira could work magic with Emily, but that couldn't be what his grandfather meant, could it? That was nothing.

Less than nothing.

Weight gathered in his stomach, swarming. Of course that wasn't how his grandfather would interpret it. The weight lashed out, churning his insides. This was his fault. He was the one who'd painted a target on Kira for his grandfather to see.

Zac paced, torn between wanting to strangle the man and wanting to help Kira—if only he knew how. "That was a figure of speech."

"I *saw* her work the medicine of the spirits." His grandfather's tone implied that was all the proof necessary. "You would see it too if you opened your eyes to the truth. We are seers—you and I. We see what others cannot."

"I am *nothing* like you."

"You saw the spirits when you were little. That's the true reason your father kept you away from me. His own son terrified him."

The accusation punched Zac in the gut, and he stepped back. His throat clenched so tight he couldn't speak the words to disagree. To defend himself. To rationalize his father's attitude.

He didn't want to believe his grandfather could be right about anything—especially not right now. Kira had her quirks, but he didn't need to fall back on spiritual mumbo-jumbo to explain why.

Whatever expression his grandfather saw on Zac's face prodded the old man to his feet, the drum forgotten on the dirt. "She-who-is-one-with-Black-Body admitted that she is of a clan of light, of fire. She started this fire by working with the spirits."

"She-who-is—what? What spirits are you talking about?"

"Her hair is as red as flames, like Black Body, our god of fire. She wears all black on her body, like Black Body. She has connections to the spirits and is powerful. Do you not recognize how dangerous this moment could be if I don't finish the prayers? Can you not see that she is a Holy One sent by Black Body? She has the power to destroy us all or the power to protect Emily." He stood over the fire and opened his palms. "Her spiritual medicine can burn away the badness in Emily's life, and it's my job to call her to do so."

His grandfather's gesture to the fire revealed the weapon he'd used on Kira. Zac scanned the amount of smoke in the hogan, less now than it had been a few minutes before. Less than what she'd been exposed to. Less than what had filled her lungs with God-only-knew-what toxins and chemicals.

He'd—? He'd *drugged* her?

His stomach heaved in protest at the idea. Kira, innocent Kira, had been forced into a nightmare.

"You did your *job* by drugging her? How could you *do* that?"

Of all the crazy-ass stuff his grandfather had done, this was the worst. All for even crazier beliefs. Thinking Kira a supernatural being with magical abilities? Only knowing his grandfather thought this would help Emily kept Zac from hurting the man.

His grandfather ignored the question, instead focusing on Kira and beating on his drum again. "Why would you leave Emily?"

Kira moaned, her face tightening into a grimace. "Magic pulls me away."

"See? Either she's admitted she's connected to evil witchcraft, or she's using white man's language, and *magic* refers to the spirits. Admit I am right." His grandfather didn't wait for Zac's answer. He sat and pounded out the rhythm for his chant. "What is stronger than this *magic?*"

"Nothing." Kira's voice sounded strained.

Zac circled the fire and reached out to snatch that damned drum.

His grandfather dodged the attempt. "Something *must* be stronger. Talking God gave us the words to the songs and ceremonies. What are the strongest words you know?"

A whimper drifted from her lips. "My true name."

Zac's gaze snapped to Kira, and he sucked in a breath, his promise to never reveal her *true* name pounding in his ears. A fist tightened around his heart, threatening to halt its movement.

He lunged to her side. If his grandfather asked the question Zac suspected was imminent, he had to protect her. He owed her that. At least that. He'd gotten her into this ridiculous situation.

The drumbeats continued, proving his grandfather wasn't done with his interrogation. "What is your true name?"

Zac slapped his hand over her mouth and drew her against him. He had to get her out of here.

"What are you doing? You cannot interrupt the prayer. You

would put Emily into danger."

Zac rose to his feet, and a growl burst through his clenched teeth. "*You're* the only danger here."

Ignoring his grandfather's repeated threats, Zac carried Kira into the fresh air. He still didn't know what his grandfather had done to her, but hopefully it would wear off on its own.

His grandmother emerged from the main hogan. "You're back." Then she noted his direction, straight to his truck. "Why are you leaving?"

"Ask your husband why he drugged a guest." His tone was accusing, and he didn't care. He was beyond done with both of them. Leaving Kira and Emily alone with them had been a colossally bad idea.

Thankfully, Emily was inside the truck, just as he'd instructed. And since he'd packed up their stuff this morning, when he'd figured they'd make the drive to Window Rock together, nothing stopped him from leaving this minute. He laid Kira on the front bench seat and sprinted around to the driver's side.

The setting sun silhouetted his grandfather against the flat landscape. He folded his arms and lifted his chin, his body language screaming defiance. "You have put Emily into danger. She will remain in danger until She-who-is-one-with-Black-Body promises to stay and protect her. If you open your eyes, you will see that is the truth."

A sudden cool breeze raised the hairs on Zac's arm. Could his grandfather be right?

He shook his head and got into his truck. No potential future college scholarship would make what had happened here worth it.

This whole trip had been a mistake. So much for Kira always being right.

He couldn't help saying the one thing he knew would hurt his grandfather. "Now I know why my mother did drugs. Did you drug her against her will too, until she got addicted?"

His grandfather's arms fell to his sides, and his face opened, his mouth slack. "We do not speak of the dead."

"Yeah, a convenient way to forget past mistakes." He slammed his door and looked back at Emily, whose wide eyes exposed the depths of her fear. "Prin's alive. Get into your booster seat, and buckle your seatbelt. We're leaving."

His tires threw up dirt and rock in his hurry to get away from the man who thought it acceptable to drug a near-stranger for his beliefs. Heat pulsed through his body, his muscles quivering with barely constrained urges to rip the life out of someone.

Fifteen minutes later, they were onto a paved road, and he felt like he could breathe again. He checked on Emily. "You okay, Fairy? I'm sorry about all that."

"Is Prin going to be okay?"

"She's alive, she's breathing, and she even said a few words. I think she's just really sick from all the smoke, so I hope she'll be okay."

"What happened?"

Damn. How to explain that craziness? "My grandfather decided it would be okay to drug Prin to make her do what he wanted. But just as Prin and I have told you that you have the right to say what happens to *your* body, the same goes for everyone else. But he didn't care. He hurt Prin's body, and he hurt her."

A horrifying thought brought his head around, and he eyed Emily in the back seat.

"How are you feeling? Did the smoke bother you?"

"I feel okay. Prin was sitting between me and the fire."

Of course she was. Kira's thoughts were always about what would be best for Emily. And look where that got her. The woman was a damn saint. If only he'd been there. He'd never have allowed this to happen.

He punched the dashboard. A squeak from Emily echoed the *thwack.*

Damn it. He took a deep, calming breath. He had to hold it together for Emily's sake.

"Sorry. It'll be okay. Flagstaff is a few hours away. We'll get a hotel room there for the night." He glanced down at Kira, who was still lying, glassy-eyed, on the seat next to him. Stabbing pain nearly broke his chest in two. He had to fix this. "Can you dig through the bag back there and find Prin's water?"

They were in the middle of nowhere, and he didn't have a clue how to deal with her drug exposure. But getting fluids into someone out in the desert was a no-brainer.

Emily passed Kira's water to him. Now, how to get it into her without stopping the car?

He slid Kira closer, lifting her head onto his lap. She didn't react to his touch. The proof that she was completely out of it weighed down his shoulders.

A few locks of her hair trailed over her face, and he swept them out of the way. He kept half an eye on the straight, empty road and gave her the rest of his attention. Between the bumpy tar patches on the asphalt, he tipped the bottle toward her mouth. Dribbles slipped between her lips, and she coughed.

Quieter than Emily could hear, he whispered a desperate wish. "Come on, Kira, talk to me."

She coughed again and moaned. "My true name is Kiratania Serafiskra Zarylina Lidashka Maksyna."

Tingles swept through Zac's limbs. The back of his neck burned as if a scorpion stung him. Instinctively, he rubbed at the spot and felt nothing.

At the same time, a million thoughts collided in his head and jumbled together. Kiratania was the most beautiful name he'd ever heard. What the hell kind of name was the rest of that? Thank God he'd gotten Kira out of there before she'd said all that in front of his grandfather—no doubt he would have taken it as yet more proof of his crazy ideas. Luckily, Emily had been digging through the bag for her own water and hadn't heard a syllable.

And most importantly, he prayed Kira wouldn't remember any of this. She'd kill him if she knew she'd revealed that much to him.

"Shh." He stroked her face and placed a finger over her lips. "Fight these drugs, Kira. You're stronger than they are. You're going to be okay." His chest tightened, and he clenched his jaw. "You have to be okay."

He couldn't lose her. Not now. Not ever.

Chapter Thirty-One

ZAC TUCKED THE COVERS AROUND EMILY, KEEPING THE SCRATCHY hotel bedspread away from her face. "I'm going be right on the other side of that door, okay?"

"You're going to make Prin all better?"

He hesitated, questioning his decision to skip the emergency room for the hundredth time. Only the knowledge that *she* wouldn't want to go there—where dozens of strangers would touch her, poking and prodding—kept him from packing them all up into the truck again. That, and the fact that after he'd shushed her, she'd settled into sleep for the rest of the drive.

"I'm hoping she'll feel better when she wakes up, and I'm going to stay with her all night in case she needs anything."

Emily wrapped her arms around him and pulled him close for a kiss on the cheek. "Thank you, Daddy."

His heart melted, and he returned her hug and kiss. Despite everything, they were making a life together. "I want her better just as much as you do."

Possibly even more.

He switched off Emily's light and tiptoed into the connecting hotel room, shutting the door between their rooms behind him. A crash from the bathroom brought up his gaze from the doorknob. Kira wasn't on the bed where he'd left her.

"Prin?" He stepped into the dark bathroom and tripped over a lump.

The impact elicited a moan from the lump, and he flipped on the light. Kira sprawled across the floor, the shower curtain half-yanked onto her.

He didn't know whether to be alarmed, relieved, or amused. "Good lord, woman. I leave you alone for five minutes, and look at the trouble you get yourself into."

"Cold." Kira shivered, emphasizing her statement. "Dirty. Hate dirty."

True enough. One side of her face was covered with sand, probably from the floor of the hogan when she'd passed out. Most importantly, she was speaking about normal things again.

A shaky sigh bubbled up his throat, sounding almost like a laugh. "So even though you're half-unconscious, you thought you'd take a shower? Can't it wait until morning when you have the energy to stand?"

"Cold. Hot shower. Get clean. Logical."

Now a laugh did escape him, his chuckles resonating in the small tiled room. Even in this state, she was arguing with him.

"I can't believe I underestimated your stubbornness." He fixed the shower curtain. "All right, I'll get the water going for you."

After the water was nice and warm, he stepped back. "There you go. Try not to drown."

She caught his leg and tugged. "Help."

He froze. Help? As in, help her take a shower? At the thought, his cock rose to attention, happy to volunteer.

No, he must have misunderstood. Kira never asked for help. He wouldn't have thought it possible.

He swallowed, as though he could push his blood flow away from the body part determined to distract him. "Help?"

"Help me. Shower. Not drown."

Bloody hell, he *hadn't* misunderstood. She wanted to kill him.

He wasn't usually one for swearing, but given the situation, he couldn't help muttering, "Fuck."

"Not yet. Clean first."

His gaze snapped to hers. Was she delirious?

Even though her head was angled to the side, a grin broke across her face, and her eyes danced with mischievousness. The expression didn't help him decide whether she was still under the influence of whatever drug exposure she'd had, was messing with him because she could, or was serious.

He closed his eyes and braced himself against the wall. Messing with him. That was the safest choice to believe. And if that failed, definitely under the influence.

That sealed it. There could be nothing physical with someone incapable of making a clear-headed decision. He opened his eyes, his focus landing on the top of his jeans. *You hear that? Nothing is going to happen tonight. Nothing.*

He unbuttoned his shirt. "Okay, Miss Trying-to-Kill-Me, do you need your hair washed too?"

"Everything." She nibbled on her lip and giggled. "Everywhere."

Yep, no question. Still drugged out. He adjusted his attitude, ditching any annoyance or frustration. This wasn't her fault—or her choice.

After he'd removed everything but his underwear, he turned his attention to her. "I'm going to undress you now unless you tell me not to."

As though inviting him, she flung her arms wide and smacked her knuckles on the wall. "Ow."

"Just..." He sighed and bent down at her feet. "Just let me do it."

"Yes, Master Zachary."

Bloody fucking hell. He kept his gaze on her boots, focusing on his task of removing her clothes, and forced his expression into a chastising scowl. "That's not helping."

"Oh, unhappy. Want him happy. Want his dimple. Love his dimple."

Her confession tugged his mouth into a curve. He wouldn't take physical advantage of her, but he didn't have the willpower to resist using the opportunity to explore her thoughts.

"You do, do you?"

"Yep, yep. See dimple. Good goal."

As he'd suspected, she purposely teased him to make him laugh. He fought the impulse now and stopped his hands halfway through undoing her shirt buttons. "If you're a good girl and don't make this harder for me, I'll show you my dimple after we're done. Deal?"

"Deal."

He slipped off her shirt. "Anything else you love about me?"

Bad idea. He ground his jaw, ready to kick himself for asking such a question. A voice in the back of his mind tried to rationalize that he just wanted to know what else he could use to rein her in tonight, but that was a lie.

She didn't say anything, and he met her eyes, expecting a snarky retort. Instead, her expression was serious. Intense. Her palm, freshly bare from her glove, rested on his cheek.

"Everything."

Emotions surged through him, foreign and yet familiar. The ache of longing. The crush of denial. The grip of fear. He sucked in a breath and strove to rise above the wave overwhelming his thoughts.

Her arm fell back to the tile, and his mind calmed enough to remind him that she was under the influence. She didn't mean anything she said. Especially not anything she said in seriousness.

A shudder from her body brought his attention back to the task. "You're freezing."

He rushed through getting her pants off and barely acknowledged what he was doing. Now that she was down to just her bra and panties, he carried her into the shower.

"No. No clothes. Dirty."

He set her on the floor of the tub and adjusted the spray. Then he grabbed shower supplies and a washcloth from a shelf by the sink. "You'll get clean enough with your underwear on."

"No. Lirdeag earth clan. Hate him. Hate dirt." The foreign word rang a bell, but he couldn't place it.

Clonk. She'd bent forward, trying to take off her bra, and banged her head on the side of the tub.

"Usually repel dirt. I'm broken. Ow."

He sat down behind her. She was broken all right.

"Listen, I'll make you another deal. Let's get you warm and your hair washed first, and then we'll talk about washing the rest of you."

"Hate being dirty. Hate being broken."

"I know." His chest burned, the wish sharp in his heart that he could have prevented this from happening.

He squeezed shampoo into his palm and worked the liquid into lather in her hair. She moaned and swayed in his hands. He tried to block out the sound. By the time he'd rinsed the shampoo and was working on the conditioner, his cock ached.

"Feels so good. Never washed before."

"You mean no one's ever washed your hair for you before? Not even your mother?" His knuckles stroked her back with each finger-comb of her hair.

"Nope. Didn't need to. We should again. You and I. Even if not broken."

"Yes." His voice came out thicker and rougher than he expected. "We should do this again when you're not broken." He closed his eyes and breathed deep, letting his hands rest on her back while his imagination ran with the idea. His throat thickened even more. "I'd like that."

She moaned louder and fell back against his shoulder. "Yes, that's what I needed—raw passion."

That was the longest and most complete sentence she'd said yet. Maybe being under the spray was clearing her mind. His cock twitched in hopefulness.

Settle down. One sentence doesn't prove anything.

She sat up and twisted to him. "Can you help me stand so I can rinse it well?"

Okay, two sentences.

"Uh, sure."

She was still asking for help and still encouraging him to touch her. Whatever that meant.

He stood and helped her to her feet. Her legs wobbled, and she held onto him for support. Their wet, slick bodies pressed against each other.

Standing together was worse. Much worse.

She tilted her head back, looking up at him. Just when he thought she was expecting a kiss, she arched her back and ducked under the spray.

God, she was unbelievably gorgeous. And she was here, in his arms. And he couldn't do a damn thing with any part of her body. This was a heavenly sort of hellacious torture.

Her brow lifted, and she locked onto his eyes. "Hold me. I'm going to let go."

She swept the fall of water through her hair, rinsing the last of the conditioner. The flame-red color and yellow streaks of her hair remained as bright as ever, none of the dye going down the drain.

He still hadn't figured out how she managed the trick with the temporary colors she must use every day, but that oddity was just a footnote in the list of things that made her an intriguing mystery. No matter how strange the quirk, she somehow made the weird seem natural—at least natural enough that he accepted her as she was.

She straightened and locked her arms around his neck. "It's time to wash the rest of me. Are you going to remove the rest of my clothes like I asked? Or do I have to risk life and limb to do it myself?"

"It's that important to you?"

"Yes." She didn't offer an explanation.

Maybe he should have argued with her more, but the return of her speech abilities probably meant that she was only going to be more stubborn than before, not less. He unhooked her bra, and she released one arm at a time from his neck, allowing him to remove the soaked material. One less barrier between them.

She met his gaze and nodded. The underwear had to go too.

He crouched down, and she braced herself on his shoulders. The damp fabric didn't want to slide down, and she shimmied her hips to help. The movement released the material, but it didn't help him. Thoughts crowded his mind about this being his personal strip show, and he shoved them away.

She lifted one foot and then the other. The last of her clothes.

He closed his eyes. He didn't want to face her naked.

He didn't want to know that he couldn't have her.

And keep her.

Chapter Thirty-Two

THE SPRAY OF THE SHOWER SPECKLED ACROSS ZAC'S SKIN, BUT he kept his eyes closed and tried not to feel anything.

Kira's fingers slid into his hair. "Are you okay?"

Her voice, gentle and caring, surprised him enough that he looked up. A vision of perfection awaited him. He loved everything about her. He could worship her.

Her thumb rubbed his lips, and he shook his head. He couldn't do this. If anything, his feelings for her provided even more incentive to do the right thing and not take advantage of her.

He picked up the bottle of body wash and the washcloth from the edge and stood. She plucked the washcloth from his grasp and tossed it over the shower curtain.

"What—?"

"That cloth looked too rough. You can use your hands." She blinked slowly, water drops falling from her lashes in a picture of innocence.

He groaned. "You know, if I die, I can't keep you from falling."

She gathered her hair in front of her shoulder and locked her arms around his neck again. Her breasts pressed against his chest, and she smiled. "Then don't die."

"Easy for you to say."

He aimed the water away from them and filled his palms with the liquid soap. He spread the body wash over her back, stopping above the curves of her ass.

She breathed against his neck. "I need to be clean everywhere, remember?"

He ignored her for now and dipped to one knee to get both sides of her legs. Her inner thighs were a no-go zone as well. In his head, he quantified a series of mathematical angles for how to reproduce the curves of her tattoos in his ironwork, doing everything he could to *not* think about the feel of her body under his hands.

After he finished washing her feet, he couldn't ignore the rest of her body anymore. He rose and exhaled a loud sigh. "Everywhere, huh?"

"I can't have a grain of dirt on me."

This time, he analyzed the pattern of logarithmic spirals along her tattoo lines. It wasn't enough. The soft curves of her ass still tempted him to spread his fingers, feel more of her.

At least she was silent, not teasing or goading. He could pretend that this chest-to-chest position wasn't as intimate as it was. He could pretend that he didn't want more.

She lifted her face, and to his surprise, her expression was one of simple gratitude. "Thank you." Her head dipped, and he thought he caught a ghost of a smile. "Now for the front."

She twisted in his arms, spreading the slippery soap over his chest as well. His hands froze on her hips. She bent over, her ass pressing against his cock, hard and throbbing in his underwear, and then she straightened, the bottle of body wash in her grasp.

"Open your hands."

He squeezed her between his forearms to keep her steady and lifted his palms. She drizzled more body wash into his hands and then dropped the bottle unceremoniously over the edge of the tub.

"I didn't want to bend down again," she explained, acting the innocent.

Uh-huh. Either she knew exactly what she was doing to him, which might mean she was mentally recovered, or she was still so out of it she didn't realize the consequences of the game she was playing. He couldn't take that chance.

She held on to one of his arms and extended the other for him to wash. He kept his thoughts of what he was doing under a tight rein again.

She couldn't possibly know that he wanted their next encounter to be more. That he didn't care about her submission. That he wanted more than just her body. That he also wanted her mind, her heart, and her love.

That he wanted her. All of her.

Maybe on a different night he could tamp down those expectations and be satisfied with just the physical. But not tonight. Not with his emotions so raw after the close call with her life.

Tonight, he was vulnerable.

He finished with her other arm and rubbed her belly, delaying the inevitable need to wash the rest of her body. Her hands slid down from their grip of his forearms and intertwined with his fingers.

"We'll do it together," she whispered with no trace of teasing or guile.

She moved their hands together, her palms on the back of his hands, to her breasts. They rubbed in circles, her tight nipple catching on the edges of their fingers every rotation. She moaned, and her head fell back to his shoulder.

"I'm sorry. I can't help it. It just feels so good."

She squirmed, her body slipping across his chest. He started mentally walking through the steps for hand forging a scroll. *Hammer the rod tip to a taper.* He pictured every strike, every adjustment, every angle—anything to prevent him from thinking about the reality in his grasp.

She moved one of his hands down, working his palm on the inner thighs he'd skipped before. *Form a straight edge at the tip.*

She directed his hand to the tops of her thighs. *Take in the sides of the taper.* She pressed his fingers between her folds. *Lengthen the taper.* She slid his fingers in and out and shuddered in his arms, her moan vibrating against his cock. *Bend the tip with gentle brushing strokes.* She squeezed his other hand, forcing him to pinch her nipple. *Hammer and roll to tighten the spiral.*

He should stop this. He should stop her. But damn, there was no part of this he was directing, so he certainly wasn't taking *advantage* of her.

Besides, just because he refused to take her under these

circumstances, when he wanted more than she would—or could—give, didn't mean he needed to prevent her from enjoying herself.

She increased the speed of his fingers in her, her breaths coming in short gasps. *Brush and roll the iron to extend the scroll.* She writhed against him, like sex itself in his arms. *Adjust and keep scroll central.* She arched back, and her lips parted, a cock-hardening moan on her breath.

Clean up the piece. No, wait. *Blend into the straight edge first.*

Nibbles caressed the underside of his jaw, startling him. "You're holding yourself back. That's not fair."

His voice came out a growl. "You're in no position to talk about *fair.*"

"I need to feel your passion."

"And I need..." He closed his mouth and drew away from her.

She crumpled without his support, her knees buckling.

Damn it. He caught her just in time, his lunge shoving them under the water spray. The soap rinsed from their bodies, and she spun to face him.

"I'm vulnerable tonight too." She stroked his jaw. "Tonight I can give you what you want. Let me give it to you."

A sense of gentle tenderness bloomed where she touched him. The feeling spread through his body, promising him tonight. Promising him his secret wish and deepest desire. At least for one night.

Unbidden, his hand imitated the caressing gesture on her cheek. He couldn't resist her offer. Her insight into his mood proved she was mentally all there, and her confession stroked his need for more.

How did she always know what to say that would break through his defenses?

"I want you. All of you. No holding back."

"Ditto, ditto, and ditto."

Her agreement burst through the last wall of resistance, and he let his gaze sweep over her for real this time. His cock rose in victory.

"All clean and rinsed off?"

At her confirmation, he shut off the water, snagged a towel, and carried her out to the bed, leaving drips in their wake. He went to offer her the towel first, but she already looked dry, even her hair.

His hands made quick work of removing his wet underwear and drying off, and he crawled into bed beside her. She snuggled up to him before he could even indicate that's what he wanted. Her behavior wasn't normal, and maybe he should be concerned about that. Or maybe they were both just feeling vulnerable and open to each other for the first time.

He stroked her lips with his thumb. "This isn't going to be like last time. You understand that, right?"

She met his gaze, honesty apparent in her open expression. "Tonight I need you. I need a connection. I need to feel that I'm not alone."

Her words weren't quite a match to his commitment, but he'd take what he could get. "You're not alone. You never have to be alone again."

Tonight he was going to make love to her.

Tonight he was going to love her.

And hopefully, she'd let him continue in the morning.

Chapter Thirty-Three

WHATEVER ZAC'S GRANDFATHER HAD DONE TO HER HAD taken its toll. Kira felt drained. Empty. Vulnerable.

The specifics of what had happened up until the infusion from Zac's passion in the shower were vague and dreamlike. A suspicion lurked in the back of her mind that Sani's methods in the hogan were meant to strip her mental defenses bare, but for what purpose, she didn't know. She probably didn't *want* to know.

Another suspicion strutted around openly: Whatever he'd done was still having an effect. Words kept spilling from her mouth without thought.

Did she mind? She inhaled the scents and emotions surrounding her from Zac's body holding her tight. His passion tingled her senses, his animalistic aroma edged past the sharp smell of body soap, and his own vulnerability called out to hers, enticing and alluring.

No, even though it was definitely a bad idea to encourage him like this, she didn't mind. Not as long as she was getting what she wanted, an energy infusion and an understanding of her current needs.

A tiny voice whispered from the fringes of her thoughts. *That's not all you want.*

She snuggled closer, pushing the idea away. She couldn't afford to think like that—not when the end was so close.

Although... Maybe that issue was exactly why she should embrace this situation. She was likely to die at Lirdeag's hands soon after the Mythos plane yanked her back, so why not enjoy this opportunity? Maybe this strange, dream-like state was just what she needed to fully appreciate the experience without fear.

No fear of her vulnerability. No fear of the future. No fear of intimacy.

The hard planes of Zac's muscles rippled under her palms, and she stroked his back, her fingers stretching and exploring. His rough hands caressed her in return, surprising gentleness in his touch. Her body thrilled, like prickles of electricity, everywhere he laid claim.

The sensation wasn't unpleasant by any stretch of the imagination. Why not give herself over to the feeling?

She nibbled the underside of his jaw. He angled his head and met her lips. The soft skin of his mouth pressed on hers. His tongue brushed her lips and then dipped inside, sweeping and possessing.

At the same time, his hands skimmed her back and drew her closer. Their skin touched from head to toe—literally—and every cell in contact with his savored the sensation. Yes, she didn't mind this kind of closeness at all.

She teased back with her tongue, flicking the tip along his mouth. Her fingers dove into his hair, and she moaned, nestling her hand in his smooth, damp waves. Ideas filled her head for all the ways she could remain burrowed in his long locks while enjoying the upcoming activities—a far cry from her usual desire to keep her distance and turn her back to a partner. But this was no ordinary night.

He broke off their kiss and looked into her eyes. The bathroom light provided enough illumination that she could search his expression. His gaze was wide and unblinking.

"You feel it too, don't you?" His voice was low and soft. "A connection so strong it's like magic."

Her chest tightened. Had he been feeling her emotions just as she felt his? Just how mentally bare was she?

"Shh." He stroked her face. "Don't pull back. I'll keep you safe. I promise."

A rush of his determination swept over her, encasing her in his emotional bubble. His strength drove away her momentary urge to flee. She settled against him and sank back into her *no fear* attitude.

Consequences could wait.

She traced the angles of his jaw and the cut of his muscles. Her palms thrilled at the smooth planes of his body, a sculpture of the ideal man. Powerful legs, even more powerful arms, and a chiseled chest connected all those limbs to a strikingly handsome face—not even counting his adorable dimple.

She memorized it all. And he understood every intention, every wish, every desire.

Their bodies moved in perfect rhythm to each other, synchronized to their shared emotions. No awkward nose bumps or fumbling hands interrupted the flow. Every brush of his lips and every squeeze of his hands elicited maximum pleasure. The constant energy outpouring from him was just a bonus.

Soon, a condom that she'd once again forgotten to insist on covered his length, and he was propped over her on the mattress. His intense gaze caged her just as effectively as his arms and weight. Rather than feeling trapped, she felt safe. Protected. Cherished.

Time seemed to stop, frozen in this moment, until the differences between this time and last time took on a life of their own. The situation gathered meaning, growing heavier, pressing him down onto her in slow motion.

She held her breath, waiting for when he'd finally enter her and make them one. The idea that she'd want this face-to-face would have been preposterous just twenty-four hours ago. But right now, she couldn't imagine any other way.

Slowly, deliciously, his length slid into her, filling the emptiness—literally and figuratively. The unhurried motion added even more significance to the act, highlighting how it wasn't about the physical but about the two of them together, sharing.

When he was all the way in, he paused again, and she drank in the enjoyment of the sensation. In a strange way she couldn't explain, this felt like home. Like despite the fact that this wasn't even her world, *this* was where she belonged.

Her throat grew thick and dry, and at the same time, moisture stung her eyes. How could such a simple thing feel overwhelming?

He dropped down to his elbows and stroked her temple. His eyes glistened in the low light.

"Thank you." He pulled himself partway out, just as leisurely, sending tingles down every limb. "Thank you for letting me love you, Kira."

His first use of her true name in months zinged straight to her heart, and she couldn't help her jaw going slack. Especially because he hadn't used it to control her or hurt her, but to thank her.

If possible, the connection between them wound even tighter. A drop of liquid trickled from the corner of her eye, as if squeezed out by the bond tying them together.

His thumb at her temple caught her tear. "It's okay. We're going to fall together."

Energy built in the blooming anticipation. She wasn't afraid. Not right now.

He kept his gaze on her, steady and stabilizing, and drove himself deep once more. Slowly at first, and then faster. Gentle at first, and then harder.

Over and over, he plunged into her. She gasped, the sensations bursting through the center of her being. This was no superficial pleasure, but an electric power that gave birth to her soul. Deep, primal, elemental.

She gripped him hard and focused on his face, solid above her, desperate for something to keep her from shattering into so many pieces she'd never find them all. Tension shook her muscles, the strain of trying not to fly apart taking its toll.

He lifted himself higher, sinking even deeper into her. A whimper escaped her with the perfection. He echoed a grunt, and if possible, his eyes darkened even more.

"You're safe. I promise I'll catch you." His dimple dented his cheek, erasing the last of her control.

Her muscles gave up and shuddered their release. An explosion rocked through her, and she nearly screamed at the powerful force. He groaned and drilled deep into her one last time. Her walls squeezed around his surge.

Ironclad Devotion

Energy blasted into every cell, rumbling along with their shared moan. They clutched each other, falling together, and rocked with the waves of heavenly sensations.

She wasn't sure she'd ever be able to let go. Maybe being in his arms was the only thing keeping her from burning up in a puff of smoke.

The energy burst rewrote her essence from the inside out, shedding light on the truth. It was only now, when faced with the real possibility that this was her last time to experience sex at all, that she understood the meaning behind the act. That she recognized the potential for truly "making love." That she realized the beauty in one bared soul bonding to another.

And only Zac could have made it possible. She would be forever grateful, but no amount of gratitude would be enough for what he'd shared with her.

Eventually, their trembles settled, and he collapsed and kissed every inch of her face. "Oh God, Kira, thank you." He drew back and rose on his elbows. "I lo—" His eyes focused on her, and his brows pulled down. "Do you know you're glowing?"

Uh... Her mind was still floating somewhere near the ceiling, and she was in no shape to form words.

Luckily, he shook his head and snuggled back down with her. "Don't mind me. I think you made me delirious." He tucked her against him. "Deliriously happy."

Energy continued to flow through their connection, and she soaked in every drop, like a greedy addict. This source—his emotions—was as complete as an all-you-can-eat buffet, and she was going to gorge and enjoy. She never wanted to let him go, and she never wanted this to end.

She'd always thought the post-face-to-face time would be awkward and self-conscious. But all she felt at this moment was fulfillment. If only it could stay like this forever.

If only...

Chapter Thirty-Four

K IRA BLINKED, SLOWLY RISING TO WAKEFULNESS. EARLY MORNING
light leaked under the thick hotel curtain and illuminated
the fact that she held Zac's hand at her breast. A smile
crept over her face. Who'd have thought she'd be okay with letting
herself be vulnerable?

Last night had been the perfect way to experience true happiness at least once before she met her fate at the hands of Lirdeag.
Could she extend this vulnerability party just a little bit longer? Or
would that ruin the memory?

Zac lay face down beside her, his features soft in his sleep,
reminding her of the unguarded moments they'd shared. She lifted
herself a few inches, propping her cheek in her palm. Unable to
resist, she slid her fingers into the curls at the back of his neck.
Her fingertips twirled, allowing the locks to wrap around in gentle
circles.

A dark spot on his skin caught her gaze. She elbowed herself up
to a sitting position for a better look and swept the hair at the back
of his neck out of the way.

She sucked in a breath so fast she almost choked. *Effing A.* She
was dead meat.

There, on the back of his neck, a tattoo-like mark had burned
beneath his skin. A mark that matched the unique design on her
palm. A mark that could indicate only one thing: He had power

over her.

No, no, no. She withdrew her hand and slid from the bed before her trembles could wake him. This couldn't be happening. How— or why—was that mark even there? Was it because she'd let her guard down last night?

Please not that. She bit her lip and paced across the hotel room floor.

No, from everything she remembered, the only thing that could give someone enough power over her to create that mark was if they knew her full true name. She stopped mid-stride. Her full true name.

A hazy memory of Sani asking for her true name floated into her mind. Did she answer him? Did he know it too? Damn her for trusting him to have only Emily's best interests at heart.

She pressed her fingers to her temples. Okay, what did she remember about full true names? Her fingertips dug harder against her skull, as though she could rip the childhood knowledge from her brain. *Think.*

Something about how only one being could have full control over a faerie. After all, being a slave to two masters would cause problems if they gave conflicting instructions.

Right. So just the first person to learn the full true name would gain that total and complete power.

Her gaze landed on the tousle-haired hunk indenting the pillows. Zac.

Zac had the mark, so he had the power and control. He—for all intents and purposes—owned her.

What the hell was she going to do? What *could* she do?

It had been hard enough to trust that he'd never use her name against her when he knew one-tenth of it. Now he knew the whole thing.

There was trust—which wasn't one of her strengths anyway— and then there was *trust.* No one could be trusted with that much power.

She couldn't even guess how he'd react. Had a human ever known a faerie's full true name before? And Zac was unique. He always seemed to know too much as it was.

No... He always seemed to *see* too much.

Zac—and likely Sani—were the *seers* the animals had tried to warn her about over the last couple of months. *Warn* her. Like they were a threat. And now one of those seers held her life in the palms of his calloused hands.

What powers did a seer have? She rewound the past few months in her mind.

The obvious abilities—seeing her magic, immunity to her magical manipulations, and a stronger emotional connection— were potent, no doubt. But what if there was more?

Her limbs shook as the truth vibrated in her ribcage. Everything she'd run away to avoid on the Mythos plane had instead come true here.

The air conditioning unit under the window clicked on, humming in the silent room, and her bare skin pebbled in the cool breeze. The sense of exposure didn't help her mood. She dug through the bag at the foot of the bed and yanked out every piece of clean clothes she had.

No more naked time. No more vulnerability. No more trusting.

Chapter Thirty-Five

A SHIVER WOKE ZAC, AND HE REACHED FOR KIRA TO SNUGGLE closer. Only an empty mattress met his hand. His eyes popped open, and a sense of dread seeped through him. Something was wrong.

His heart rate accelerated, memories of their last "morning after" flashing through his mind. He lunged to the door to the connecting room, about to rip it open, and then stopped. No, Kira hadn't been mad last time, and things were going to be okay this time too.

He took a deep breath and forced his heartbeat to settle. The pounding in his ears quieted enough that he could make out voices beyond the door.

See? She hadn't left.

So why did the sense of dread remain?

He took his time getting dressed, running through various scenarios in his mind. But he couldn't prepare for the situation when he didn't have a clue what awaited him in the other room. Only one way to find out. He held his breath and opened the door.

Kira and Emily were sprawled across the bed, nibbling at a tray of food. Emily glanced up first.

"Good morning, Daddy!" She bounded out of bed, nearly toppling the glasses of juice, and wrapped her arms around him as far as she could reach. "Look, Prin's all better. You fixed her."

He squeezed her and scanned for Kira's reaction. She hadn't moved off the bed to greet him, and her tight smile was more of a grimace.

That was what he'd been dreading. A wall crashed over his heart, half smashing it and half protecting it. His throat tightened so hard a sour taste rose in his mouth.

He focused on Emily and stroked her hair, already gathered into the pigtails he could never get even. What had he expected? That last night had been so good he'd win Kira over permanently?

He pinched his eyes closed. Yes, that's exactly what he'd hoped for. It wasn't Kira's fault that she didn't live up to his expectations. Or more accurately, that she exceeded his expectations in every way but returning his feelings for her. Logic was all well and good—of course her purpose in life wasn't to fulfill his desires—but it still hurt like hell.

But that was his problem. Not hers.

He forced a smile to his face and met Kira's gaze. "How are you feeling this morning?"

"Much better. Thanks." She motioned to the tray of food. "I ordered room service and charged it to the room. I hope you don't mind."

"Good thinking."

He sat beside her and selected a breakfast burrito. She stood from the bed and moved away.

Damn, it was going to be a long drive home.

They hit the road half an hour later. Silence descended in the truck cab, especially as Emily attempted to read a kids book about Navajo life his grandmother had slipped to her sometime during the disastrous visit. Finally, he couldn't stand it any longer.

He kept his voice low, just loud enough to reach Kira's ears over the engine and freeway noise. "Did I do something wrong?"

She twitched but didn't turn away from the passenger window. He was about to repeat his question when she gave a loud sigh.

"No." She rubbed at her palm through her glove. "Not on purpose anyway."

Not on purpose? That wasn't comforting. "What can I do to fix things?"

She clenched both hands, the gloves' fabric bunching in her

fists. After a moment, her shoulders hunched, and then she crossed her arms.

"How about we talk about what all happened while I was out of it?"

Uh... His stomach sank. How much time did that cover? Not last night. *Please* not last night.

He'd swear up and down that she hadn't been "out of it" then. He wouldn't have touched her otherwise.

"You mean from the time I arrived at my grandparents until...?"

"Until I woke up in the shower."

He slowly released his breath. Not last night.

"I think I made it back to their hogan shortly after you passed out. Or whatever that was. You were still talking, and your eyes were open, but you were definitely out of it."

In the rearview mirror, he checked that Emily was still absorbed in her book.

"Emily grabbed me as soon as I arrived. I went into the hogan and saw you. I don't know what my grandfather did exactly. I think he burned something to drug you with the smoke." The steering wheel squeaked under his clenched fingers. "I was ready to kill him—I might even mean that literally—but decided it was more important to get you out of there."

She narrowed her gaze. "You're skipping over things. What did he say? What did he ask?"

Prickles rose up his arms, and a bad feeling unfurled in his gut.

"Uh, he thought you could protect Emily and that he could force you to do so."

"How did he plan to force me?"

His stomach dropped, leaving only emptiness behind. She knew.

"He asked for your true name."

Silence.

"I didn't let you answer. I covered your mouth and carried you out. We didn't even say goodbye to my grandmother. We just left." His jaw hardened. "I'll never forgive him for what he did to you."

She'd twisted toward the side window, and her shoulders had risen even more.

Her voice was a whisper. "Then what happened?"

His limbs went numb. Only one thing had happened between then and the shower that would upset her. Only one thing that he'd hoped she wouldn't remember. But on some level, she did. She knew everything.

"I didn't know what to do for you, especially out in the middle of nowhere. Other than your eyes being open, it was like you were unconscious."

"And then?"

"I tried to get you to drink some water and to talk to me—let me know you were okay."

She spun toward him, her eyes as hard as amethyst.

"I'm sorry. I didn't mean to. I swear I never asked you the question. But when I begged you to talk to me, you told me your name. Like since I hadn't let you answer before, those words were still on the tip of your tongue." He took his eyes off the road long enough to meet her gaze. "If it makes you feel any better, it sounded like a big mishmash of syllables, and I doubt I could remember any of it."

Her face pinched into an expression of sadness. A wave of bleak despair washed the color from the world and pressed down on his heart. It still didn't make any sense why the issue would be so important to her, but somehow, he felt her pain tangibly enough to grasp. She considered it a life-and-death situation, and he had to respect that.

"Hey, hey." He reached across the truck cab but stopped short of touching her. "I promised not to tell anyone your true name. That goes for your *whole* name. If you want, I'll even make the promise again."

She pulled up her legs and curled into as tight a ball as she could, given the constraint of the seatbelt. She shook her head, today's colors of black with green tips brushing the headrest.

"A new promise wouldn't do any good. I have nothing left of myself to give you in return. You already own everything I have, everything I am."

An odd sensation filled his chest, as though either his heart or his stomach had flipped over—maybe both. Dizzy, he focused on the road.

What had she meant by that? Was that a convoluted way of saying that she'd already given him her heart? That she *loved* him?

But if that was the case, why was she upset?

A quiet voice in the back of his mind answered: Just because she loved him didn't mean she trusted him not to break her heart.

Hell, if he let himself listen to the worries, he'd be cautious too. But Kira's attitude—the fatalism toward her situation with Emily post-court-case—had driven him to focus on her fears instead of his. Maybe she worried enough for the both of them.

He waited until they were safely past a semi-truck to lean toward her. "I want you to listen to me."

She unburied her face from her knees and looked at him, her gaze raw.

"I know—believe me, I know—how hard it is to trust someone. But I *promise* I will never hurt you with this information."

Her eyes closed, and this time her face wasn't contorted by pain. Finally, she opened her eyes and nodded.

Her voice was flat, grim. "Thank you for trying." She released her legs. "I don't blame you for knowing. You didn't ask to be in this position. Honestly, I don't even blame your grandfather. His heart was in the right place." A weak smile curved her lips. "But more than you can possibly imagine, I hope you're able to keep that vow."

She extended her hand to his. A few rock-opera-ish notes played from her phone and interrupted her movement.

She cleared her throat and took the call. "Hey, Moose."

Moose's voice boomed through the cab from the speaker of Kira's phone. "There you are! Renee and I have been trying to get a hold of you since yesterday. Why haven't you been answering your phone?"

"Uh..." She adjusted the phone on her ear. "Remember, I told you we were going to the Navajo Nation. No cell service up there. I just turned my phone on forty-five minutes ago."

Zac picked up his phone and held the power button, switching on his as well. Had Renee been trying to reach him too? He couldn't make out Moose's words anymore. Kira must have lowered the volume to save her hearing.

"Yeah, we're driving down from Flagstaff now." She paused and then screeched, "*Today?*"

The squeal even pulled Emily from her book, and she leaned

forward, curiosity on her face.

Kira's head fell back to the seat, her eyes open and unseeing. The sight too closely recalled her sickness, and he paid about as much attention to her as to the mostly empty road. But then she mumbled, "Yes, I understand," and flicked off the phone.

"What's up?"

She dipped her head, and her hair fell, covering her face. Her hands lay unmoving on her lap. Regardless, tension crashed into him from her.

He gave her a minute while negotiating the curves coming down Mogollon Rim. But even after the freeway straightened, she'd still not moved or spoken. His phone picked up a signal and blinked with messages. He ignored it to focus on Kira.

"Okay, talk to me. What's wrong?"

She twisted in her seat and caught Emily's eye too. Her expression was tight and determined. "We have to drive straight to the Superior Court. The custody hearing is today."

His muscles relaxed, and he shoved away the weight on his chest. Damn it, this was *good* news. Why did she have to act like this was the end of the world?

Emily slowly sat back. "What does that mean?"

He jumped in before Kira could ruin the moment. "It means a judge will decide if you should live with me." He stared at Kira through the rest of the explanation, even though she'd twisted away again. "This isn't the end of anything, though. This is just the beginning. Other than you sleeping at my house at night, nothing else has to change. We can still all be together."

"You mean Prin will still be my mommy, and you'll really be my daddy?"

He met Emily's gaze in the rearview mirror. "Yes, I'll officially be your daddy. But it's seemed like that for a while already, hasn't it? That's what I mean about how nothing will really change."

"And Prin?"

He raised his voice. Maybe he could knock through whatever wall of negativity Kira had erected in her corner of the truck cab. "*Nothing* will change with Prin either."

No reaction.

How could he get through to her? How could he make her see

that he had less than *zero* desire to kick her out of the picture? In fact, he wanted her there just as much as he wanted Emily. And not just as a visitor, but as a partner. A friend. A lover.

A... Something more.

He risked her wrath and stroked her hair back from her face to catch her profile.

"I want her to stay with us forever."

She didn't say a word, but a tear rolled down her cheek.

Chapter Thirty-Six

K IRA BLINDLY FOLLOWED ZAC AND EMILY TO THE COURTROOM. From her brain to her toes, numbness had taken hold. Walking down the halls of justice felt appropriate. Just the thing for someone being sentenced to death.

No, that wasn't accurate. How close she was to Emily didn't matter anymore, so she should be happy to witness the girl safely placed with her father before magic stole everything she valued.

And she was. Mostly.

A part of her wanted to trust Zac. Another part of her hated that she *had* to trust him.

Yet he'd dealt with her honestly, and that meant she had to be honest with herself too. Whether or not Zac kept his word wouldn't change anything. She was dead either way. Lirdeag would stop at nothing to control her people, and her existence was an inconvenience to his plans.

The drama with Zac's grandfather—and Emily's worry over whatever she'd witnessed happen to Kira—had pushed her power lines to their limit, millimeters away from their destination. Her palms itched with the imminent connection between the circuitry of her magic and their power center. If Emily hadn't bonded with Zac over the past couple of months, the news of the custody hearing in the truck might have been Kira's last words. The next crisis would be the end of her.

Renee and Moose were waiting for them in the hallway outside the assigned courtroom, and Renee pressed her hand to her heart. "Thank goodness you made it."

Moose gave Kira a bittersweet smile and opened his arms. "Can I get a hug from my girls today?"

After Emily moved forward, Kira let him engulf her too. Twitches, from his rapid blinks to his bouncing feet, made it seem like he needed a hug far more than she ever would.

He released her quickly, not pushing his luck, but his beefy fingers lingered, squeezing her shoulder. "Big day today, huh?"

"I'm happy for them." True enough. And that answered his real question anyway.

He pressed his lips together and nodded. "I'm proud of you, Princess."

A sudden thought flashed in her mind. Would this be the last time she saw Moose? Her eyes stung, and her mouth scrunched like she'd eaten a lemon.

Unable to stop herself, she hugged him again. "Thank you," she whispered. "Thank you for everything."

The words were inadequate to cover everything he'd done for her. How he'd kept her safe, didn't ask questions—and most of all, how he'd given a helpless orphan a loving home.

Before tears rolled down her cheeks, she stepped away. She didn't—wouldn't—look up to catch his reaction.

A whispered curse from Zac grabbed her attention, the distraction a welcome one. He strode down the hallway toward a professionally dressed older man who looked familiar. She didn't need to see Zac's face to know he wasn't happy about something. Even beyond his stiff posture, tension jumped over their connection, nearly strangling her.

This wasn't a good surprise, and she couldn't take any bad ones.

She tossed a warning to Moose. "Trouble. Keep Emily away."

She caught up to Zac in time to overhear his growled question to the man in the suit. "What the hell are you doing here?"

The older man gave Zac a smile she knew well. In fact, it was Zac's smile. On this man, it didn't look nearly as charming.

"I'm petitioning the court for grandparent visitation rights."

Her stomach clenched harder than a rock. Before she disappeared, she at least wanted to know Emily would be safe. The last thing the girl needed was a stranger—male, no less—forcing himself into her life. This *wasn't* part of the plan.

Seething anger spilled over her bond from Zac. "You bastard. Leave. While you still can. I'll never let you near my daughter."

The man *tsked*. "That's no way to address your father. Besides, it's up to the judge, not you. My very pricey lawyer will be here any minute, and she's assured me that I'm well within my rights."

"Like you've ever cared about the law."

The man ignored Zac's comment and focused on her. "You must be Zachary's new girlfriend." He cut a sideways glance to Zac. "Not raising your standards, I see."

She pasted a carnivorous grin on her face. "Actually, I'm Emily's foster mother. And if you want the judge to care about your little petition, you'd need my recommendation because she's in protective custody."

That probably wasn't how the hearing would proceed at all, but he might not know that.

His eyes widened, and he straightened. "Ah, my mistake. So sorry." He cleared his throat. "Well, you should know that I'm a respected member of the business community. I've owned several financial investment firms for over thirty years."

Zac crossed his arms. "Ask him how many he ran while staying within the law."

"I've never been on the wrong side of the law."

"Only because they didn't have enough evidence to prosecute you."

"I wasn't going to bring it up, but since you opened the subject..." His father scratched his cheek and focused on her. "Are you aware that Zachary's been convicted of criminal fraud? He's the one you should be worried about, not me."

Wouldn't something like that come up in his background check? "No, I hadn't heard that."

Zac rubbed his face with both hands and then looked up toward the ceiling. "No one would have heard about it because those records were sealed."

Her gaze shot to him, and her hair stood up on the back of her neck. What did that mean? He was a convicted *felon*?

Granted, she knew plenty of convicted felons within the biker community. It just wasn't something she'd expected from *him*. Regardless, for Emily's sake—and her sanity, needing to trust that the girl would be safe—she wanted to know the truth.

She took off her glove and pretended as though she was seizing his hand out of anger. "You want me to trust you? Explain."

Images poured through the strengthened connection of their physical contact while he sifted through memories, debating where to start the explanation. His father, red-faced, insisting that Zac give up his artistic dreams and do something solid with his life. His father, sneering, comparing his art to that spiritual crap his loser of a maternal grandfather did. His father, haughty, manipulating him into going to college for investment banking.

She started to pull away, having seen enough, but Zac held her tight. "My father pressured me to go to college and join his company. After I asked about some accounting irregularities I discovered, the records were changed—"

"Allegedly." His father lifted a finger in protest.

"—to implicate me. After I was arrested, the Feds offered me a plea deal and sealed records if I turned state's evidence. I *had* to plead guilty."

Zac dipped his head. Only sincerity and shame crossed the connection between their clasped hands.

"The evidence of fraud was clear, but there wasn't enough proof of tampering to prosecute, so my father wasn't convicted of anything. Even though he was the only one with deep enough access to the books to make the changes."

"That's because there *was* no tampering." Zac's father examined his fingernails. "I'd hoped you would have matured enough to take responsibility for your mistakes. Apparently not. Perhaps the court would be interested in my testimony on your suitability for custody of a child at all."

Her vision narrowed, her pulse pounding at the edges. No wonder Zac had trust issues. Set up by his father to take the fall for his criminal fraud? What kind of father would even let his son be *arrested*—much less convicted—for the parent's crimes? And judging by the smirk on the older man's face, he suffered no guilt from his actions.

Her skin tightened, his slimy presence crawling over her like ooze. Compared to her own father's bravery, Moose's compassion, and Zac's devotion, this man didn't deserve the title of father. Or grandfather. Even Zac's grandfather, with his drugging manipulations, had at least *thought* he was doing the right thing for his family.

Worse was what this man's attitude meant for Emily. No white-collar crime was ever "victim-less," especially not in a case like this. Zac was a victim of more-powerful criminals just as much as Emily was.

There was no way in hell she'd let this man near a helpless little girl. And she didn't have the time to make sure things played out properly in court.

She tugged her hand from Zac's grasp and pressed her fingertips to his father's temple. A week ago, she wouldn't have the power to do this, but her strengthening magical circuitry was a double-edged sword—all the risks of being forced to face Lirdeag and a bonus of stronger magic. She just hoped to every Mythos and Earthen god that this would work better on him than it did on Zac.

"You're going to forget this petition. You're never going to contact Zac or Emily. If you have any thoughts at all about either of them, you will feel violently ill from your sense of guilt for what you did to Zac. But you will know that you don't deserve to be part of their life. And you will stay far, *far* away."

His glazed-over eyes reassured her that she'd succeeded, and she shoved him, stumbling, toward the exit. She replaced her glove and wiped her palms together. There. One crisis averted.

Zac stared at her. Yeah, way to reveal her abilities in front of the one man who already knew *way* too much. But the stakes were too high to stand by and do nothing, and her impending death fueled a sense of now-or-never recklessness.

His mouth had completely dropped open. "What the hell did you just do?"

"Just because you don't find me intimidating doesn't mean others don't." She forced a casual shrug. "When a scary-looking tattooed chick tells you to do something, you do it."

His eyes scrunched. "I've never known him to be intimidated before."

"He hadn't met *me* before." She winked and gave him a smile, sticking to her no-big-deal claim.

Zac's lips quivered into a shy curve, and he caressed her cheek. Beyond his confusion, thoughts of worship and adoration drifted from his gentle touch.

The flutters of faerie flies rippled up from her stomach to her limbs, and her knees nearly buckled. Not what she'd expected—or prepared for. She ignored her hammering pulse and arched her brow, the most she could manage for feigning annoyance at his presumption.

His cheeks flushed, and he released her. "Sorry. I mean... Thank you, I just—I've never been able to deal with him. We're so different that I've never known where to start to get him to listen to me."

"Do something for me." She waited until he met her gaze. "Pay me back by always being different from him. Be the type of father to Emily that he wasn't to you."

He crossed his heart. "I promise."

He held her attention captive, his focus so sharp she felt it like a caress. Tingles excited her skin at the thought, and she almost wished he'd shove her up against the wall and kiss her senseless. Right here, right now.

His eyes darkened, and he stepped closer. "And I want you beside me to ensure I keep that promise."

Yes. The answer sat on the tip of her tongue. But she couldn't make that promise. She couldn't even promise one more night.

A sheen of moisture unfocused her vision, and she couldn't help placing her gloved hand on his chest. "I'd like that."

That was the truth. And that was her wish.

But that was never going to happen.

Chapter Thirty-Seven

K IRA BASKED IN THE HAPPINESS FLOWING FROM ZAC AND EMILY, while the simple task of everyone pitching in to unload the truck turned into family time. The custody hearing had concluded without a hitch, and Emily hadn't experienced a single twinge of panic. Not even when they'd swung by the trailer to pick up her things to move to Zac's house.

Zac and Emily's smiles and laughter buoyed Kira's thoughts. If this kept up, maybe her magic circuitry wouldn't complete for another week—or a month. She might get to see Emily off to her first day of school, and more time with Zac would be the good kind of dangerous. Hope was always a risky emotion, but being a part of this family was enough to make her believe.

They piled the plastic bags filled with Emily's clothes, books, and toys at the front gate of the house. Emily grabbed her stuffed animal and backpack, and Kira picked up the canvas bag from their trip north. Zac groaned, breaking the good mood.

Kira froze. "What's wrong?"

"While we were out, we should have stopped at the grocery store to pick up food for a celebratory dinner."

A shaky laugh escaped her throat. No crisis. "I think we'll live."

"Nope, I insist we celebrate tonight." He raised his voice to Emily, who was halfway across the courtyard. "What do you want for a big dinner?"

She cocked her head. "Navajo tacos?" She continued up the walk before Zac could stop her.

He looked at Kira and arched his brows. "Navajo tacos are her idea of a big dinner?"

"She's a kid." She shrugged. "Besides, that was our first meal with you, so in a way, it's fitting."

"Navajo tacos, it is. I'll have to pick up the lettuce and tomatoes."

"If you want to run out for the food, Emily and I can handle taking all these inside."

"You sure?"

"The kid doesn't have much, I'm afraid. We can handle it." She wanted some alone time with Emily to check how the girl was doing anyway.

"All right. On my way back, I'll see if the neighbors are home yet for me to pick up Honey."

"We'll be here."

She shouldered the bag, started up the front walk, and gave his departing truck a wave. She probably should have closed the gate to keep the javelinas out of the courtyard plants, but no way was she going to touch that iron handle.

Luckily, Emily had left the front door wide open. Bad for air conditioning, good for avoiding contact with the wrought iron accents. She nudged the door halfway closed with the sole of her boot for a happy medium.

With her making herself at home while Emily moved in and Zac ran to the grocery store, the scene felt damned domestic. A nice, comfortable feeling for a change.

She dropped off their trip bag at the laundry room and decided to start the washer. The image of hers and Zac's clothes tumbling together prompted a chuckle. She caught up with Emily in the hallway.

"How's my Fairy doing?"

"Good. I'm glad everything is 'ficial." The girl's bright smile settled any remaining worries, and they headed toward the front door for another load. Then Emily's brows drew together. "What bedroom will you be sleeping in?"

"Uh..." Kira's stride faltered, and she propelled herself forward, covering her surprise. "We haven't figured that out yet."

Apparently Emily had made a lot of assumptions. Not unexpected, to be honest. Kira had been rather vague about her plans. *She* didn't know what was going to happen.

She stopped in the foyer and rubbed her forehead. "Listen, Fairy. You want me here, your daddy wants me here, and *I* want to be here. So I'll be here for as long as I can. But at some point, I'm going to have to leave."

"Why?"

That was the million-dollar question. How could she explain it in a way that wouldn't cause a panic attack right now? She'd love nothing more than to put this discussion off, but she wanted to make sure that when the time came, Emily wouldn't blame herself or Zac, and she didn't know how many more one-on-one opportunities she'd get for this conversation.

"Not because of anything you, your daddy, or I do. It won't be anyone's fault. Believe me, if I could prevent it, I would. I don't *want* to leave, but there are things I can't control."

Emily frowned and looked serious. "Would it help if I made you promise to stay?"

"I won't lie to you, Fairy. That's not a promise I could keep."

She shifted her weight, her legs restless. A need itched at her to say more, to say something she'd felt for a while but hadn't shared. She needed to come clean with her emotions—at least with Emily.

She bit her lip and crossed her arms. "I'm telling you this because it's important for you to know..." She swallowed. "To know that I will always love you. No matter what happens."

Dizziness swirled her head. More damn vulnerability.

She forced her arms open for a hug. "But I don't want to be sad or thinking about that day yet, so let's hold on to our good mood, okay?"

Emily stepped into Kira's embrace. "I don't want you to have to leave."

Kira squeezed her tight and kissed the top of her head. Her throat thickened, and her words nearly came out like a croak. "Neither do I, Fairy. Neither do I."

She breathed deep, savoring the trust in Emily's grasp. Back when she'd first picked up the girl from the Department of Child

Safety, she'd thought the arrangement was mostly one of convenience. Love wasn't part of the plan. Yet she wouldn't have it any other way.

After a moment, Emily fidgeted, and Kira had to release her. She took a deep breath and gathered what remained of her strength. That was enough baring of her soul for one day.

"Okay, let's get the rest of your stuff in here."

They walked outside and squinted against the bright sunlight. Emily took off running. "Race you to the gate!"

Kira laughed and half-heartedly jogged, letting the cheater get a head start. The girl needed a good run after being cooped up in cars and courtrooms all day.

A flash of movement beyond the courtyard wall caught Kira's attention, but disappeared before she could identify the animal. Hopefully it wasn't the javelinas already trying to sneak into the courtyard after they'd left the gate open. She'd never hear the end of it if they munched Zac's landscaping to the ground.

Emily rushed through the gate and raised her fists. "I win!"

Arms emerged from behind the wall and seized Emily. Her shriek split the air.

Kira's world broke.

Heat seared her palms, and only her momentum carried her through the gate, her stagger nothing more coordinated than falling to her knees. She collapsed, face-first, onto a plastic bag of Emily's clothes.

No!

But there was no denying the signs.

Not now.

But her body knew better than she did that her time had run out.

Not yet.

She still had too much to do, to say, to share. She'd never told Zac that she forgave him. That if anyone had to know her true name, she was glad it was him. That he'd taught her how to love just as much as Emily had.

But she'd never get the chance. It was too late. It was too late for anything.

Fire blazed through her veins, her connection to the Flarea

clan's magic complete. The pull of her homeland crushed her chest. She resisted, even though the battle ripped her body in two. *Emily...*

She managed to roll over and sought out Emily. The need to protect the girl fought with the demands of her magic. Leaving wasn't an option. Not yet.

The murderer of Emily's mother stood off to the side of the gate and held a struggling Emily in his arms. Tito sneered down at Kira, looking more menacing than when she'd last seen him. A shaved head and a new gang tattoo on his cheekbone now set off his thick eyebrows.

Emily alternated between a scream and a sob. "No, no, no..."

Kira gasped for breath. "Tito, let her go. She can't help you."

"Who says she can?" He stroked Emily's cheek. "Maybe I just want my baby doll back."

Nausea pressed on Kira's throat, burning just as effectively as her blood. Her pulse raced, her blood's flames licking every cell, calling her home to seal the connection to her clan's energy. Not yet. Please not yet.

"Prin!" Emily reached for her, arms flailing. "Help!"

Kira braced herself, directing every ounce of concentration toward standing to confront Tito. Her joints and muscles wobbled and gave way under her. She sank back into the pile of bags.

Damn it, no! She was powerless to stand, much less fight Tito.

At the edges of her blackening vision, dark shapes closed in, vastly outnumbering her. Tito hadn't come alone.

Her heart pressed more heavily in her chest. How could she defeat them all? And how long could she resist her homeland? Seconds? Minutes? Would Lirdeag or someone from Mythos come for her before then?

No time. She had to do *something* now.

She ripped off her glove. Her palm glowed with the full power of her magic. She lifted her hand and ignored the pain burning her from the inside out.

The initial energy burst powering up her magic might be enough. It *had* to be enough.

The years of drawn-out pain would be worth it if her magic could be good for something. She blinked, forcing her focus to cooperate, and concentrated on the other gang members.

A fire bolt shot from her palm and forked into the chests of each approaching thug. Flames enveloped them from head to toe. Wind roared by her ears and whipped her hair, the nearby air sucked into the unnatural bonfires, fueling them like a mini-sun. The blaze consumed their bodies instantly and then disappeared. None of them even had the chance to scream. Ash trickled to the dirt driveway and drifted on the wind.

She couldn't muster guilt for killing gang members who would kidnap a little girl for their own sexual pleasure. Killing them quickly was more mercy than they deserved.

Her skull thudded onto a bag of books, her body nearly fainting from the energy expenditure. Darkness pressed on her head, and her homeland's draw weighed down her body. She couldn't move against the burden.

Hang on a little bit longer. Just a bit longer.

Zac...

Tito dropped Emily, his jaw hanging open, and his gaze darting around the now-empty front yard. Emily, smart girl that she was, ran for the house.

Kira called after her. "Lock the door, and call 911." But her voice didn't carry very far.

Tito lunged at Kira and held a knife at her throat. "What did you do? What happened to them?"

She coughed, the blade's steel singeing her skin. "Hell was impatient and took them early."

"You bitch!" Tito hauled his arm back for the final blow.

She pushed what little remained of her energy into her bared palm and shoved it against his face. *For Emily.*

He screamed, his skin burning to the bone under her hand. But it wasn't enough to stop his thrust with the knife.

Steel pierced her skin and ripped her body from the Earthen plane.

The world disappeared and went dark.

Zac...

Chapter Thirty-Eight

DREAD DARKER THAN ZAC HAD EVER IMAGINED BEFORE clouded his vision. He froze mid-swipe of his credit card at the grocery store and glanced up, expecting the lights to flicker with a brownout from the high electricity demands of the hot afternoon.

The lights above were fine, but the world around him looked dimmer for a second. If he was one to believe in premonitions, he'd think something horrible had just happened.

"Sir?" The cashier eyed him. "Did you change your mind? Did you need me to grab ice or stamps for you?"

He shook his head, both answering the young woman and banishing the worries to the corners of his mind, and then he finished swiping his card. Apparently, visiting his grandfather wasn't dangerous just for Kira. The man's talk of spirits had been a bad influence on his mental health too.

Even so, he rushed home more than usual, squeaking through the left-turn light just before it switched to red. He also punted on picking up Honey from the neighbors right away.

That was logical though, right? The milk and juice he'd purchased along with the veggies shouldn't sit in the car too long, and his neighbors would want to hear all his news about Emily.

A few driveways before his own, he had to swerve around a man stumbling across the road. The guy didn't look familiar, but his hoodie was pulled up, even in this hot weather. Any other time, Zac would have stopped to see if the man needed help, but he needed to assuage his fears first. Prove to himself that these worries were crazy.

He should be happy. Kira had finally relented. He shoved away the dark thoughts with plans for how to take the next step with her.

Could he propose to her right away? Or should he wait a while, give her time to adjust?

He didn't doubt that marriage was the next step. It was rather perfect, in fact. Emily would have a loving mom and dad for real, and he'd get a woman he knew beyond a doubt would always impress him with her goodness. The last remaining question was the timing.

Maybe he'd give her a day or two, until this weekend. That would give him enough time to plan a proposal too.

He wiped his hands on his jeans and grinned. That plan assumed he could keep the secret for two whole days. His truck bounced up his driveway, and he stopped at the open gate.

Emily's pile of bags was still there.

His heartbeat turned sluggish, and chills zinged over his body despite the heat. No, that didn't mean anything. Any number of innocuous reasons could explain why they hadn't finished moving in Emily's stuff yet. He rolled his shoulders back and forced slow movements.

Switch off the engine. Take the key. Grab the groceries. Slide out of the truck. Elbow the door closed.

All nice and slow. Controlled. Calm.

An odd scent met his nose. No, not an odd scent. Singed hair—he'd smelled it plenty of times during his blacksmithing apprenticeship. Just an odd scent for out here, away from his workshop.

He walked around the pile of bags. The scent sharpened and changed. Copper and burnt pork and charcoal aromas lingered around the gate.

Despite his determination to keep his worries under control, his stride quickened up the front walk. "Emily? Prin?"

He thumbed the front door handle. It didn't open.

"Prin? Did you lock the door?"

No thinking. Mustn't think.

He juggled the grocery bags and maneuvered the key into the lock. No one met him inside.

They had to be here though, right? Someone had to have locked the door. This *wasn't* a rerun of Crissy's disappearance.

He forced steady steps to the kitchen and put the groceries away. Only after he was done did he call again.

"Prin? Emily?"

He climbed the stairs to Emily's room. Maybe she was having a delayed panic attack and that's why they hadn't brought in the rest of her stuff yet. That would be logical. Normal. Nothing to get too worried about.

"Fairy? You okay?" No answer reached him in the hallway, and he rounded the corner into her room.

They weren't huddled on the bed.

Dizziness pressed on his skull, and the back of his throat ached, acid jumping to fill the space. He tried to swallow the sour taste down, but those muscles refused to work. Then the rest of his muscles joined the strike, trembling and out of control, and he grasped the doorframe for support.

He opened his mouth to call them again, but no sound escaped. Like a nightmare where he couldn't yell, his voice had gone silent. If he never called for them again, he'd never have to face the cold lump in his heart. Never have to face that they weren't here.

No thinking. No feeling. No pain.

He stumbled to the bed. The mattress squeaked under him.

An echoing squeak sounded from the closet door.

He whipped his head toward the noise and bounded to the closet. He yanked the door open, and Emily screamed. Her expression eased from terror to relief, and she dropped a phone from her ear.

"Daddy!" She leaped from the closet floor and threw herself at him.

His strength broke, and he crumpled to his knees. "Emily. Thank God you're okay." He squeezed her tight and rocked her against his chest. "You're okay. You're okay. You're okay."

Tension drained from his gut, and he closed his eyes. Thank God.

But she didn't recover. In fact, her breathing turned into

hyperventilating.

He stroked her hair back. "Easy." He gripped her shoulders and met her eyes. "I'm here. I need you to breathe slowly, okay?"

He demonstrated with a calm inhale and exhale. Her breathing didn't change. Where was Kira? She was so much better at this.

A tinny voice sounded from the floor. "Mr. Chase?"

"Keep breathing nice and slow, Fairy." He picked up the phone from where Emily had dropped it on the carpet. He needed to figure out what the hell he'd missed, and Emily wasn't going to be able to tell him anytime soon. "Who is this?"

"This is the emergency 911 operator. The police are on their way."

911? Police? His stomach tightened harder than ever.

"What happened? What's going on?"

"Sir, I have to warn you that the intruder might still be around. Please find a safe place until the police arrive."

Intruder? Even though he hadn't seen anything, he didn't argue with the woman.

He picked up Emily and strode to his bedroom, checking around corners as he went. The gun safe in his closet offered plenty of options for dealing with anyone trying to harm his daughter. His decision to turn state's evidence had made him paranoid his father might take revenge. Paranoid enough that he'd fought to retain his civil rights as part of his plea deal so he could stock up on training and protection.

"It's okay, Fairy. I won't let anyone hurt you." He tucked the phone under his ear and selected a Glock 17, something he could easily handle with one hand while still holding Emily. He tilted his chin to speak into the phone. "Okay, we're safe. Now tell me what's going on."

"Emily's your daughter?"

"Yes, she's six."

"She called 911 about ten minutes ago, saying that someone named Tito was at the house, trying to kidnap her. Does that mean anything to you?"

"Yes, Tito..." He glanced down at Emily and wasn't sure she'd even hear his words over her sobbing. "Tito's a suspect in the murder of her mother."

Why the hell the man was still walking free was a question he'd have for the police.

His stomach clenched even more. Was that where Kira was? Attempting to chase him away? The new worry etched itself into his muscles.

"Emily said he showed up with about eight others and grabbed her outside."

Eight others? And Kira was facing *all* of them?

His instincts tore him in two—protect Emily or help Kira? He forced himself to stay put. Kira would kill him if he left Emily unprotected.

The emergency operator continued, "And then, to be honest, I'm not sure where the truth ends and the fairy tales of a very scared little girl begin."

"What do you mean? What did she say?"

The woman cleared her throat. "She said a fairy princess with glowing hands threw fireballs at all the other men, and they burned up. And then the princess burned Tito, and he ran away."

The only part of those sentences that made sense was "princess." A small voice in the back of his mind noted that he *had* smelled burning outside, but he shoved the nonsensical detail away. He needed facts.

"Did she say where Prin—Princess—is?"

"She said Tito stabbed the princess, and she disappeared."

His heart stopped, and he sucked in a breath. "Stabbed? Is she okay?"

"I'm sorry, sir. I'm just telling you what she said."

Emily burst out with a stream of words between sobs. "She killed the other bad men, and Tito dropped me. I hid in the courtyard. She tried burning him too, but there wasn't any flames. It just took away his face. Then he stabbed her. And she disappeared."

Zac closed his eyes and spoke slowly, enunciating each word. "What do you mean, disappeared? Like she limped off somewhere? Or she chased after Tito?"

Emily collapsed against his shoulder, and fresh tears streamed down her face. "She told me something was going to happen. Why did she have to leave?"

His eyes popped open, and his chest cinched hard enough to prevent speech. She'd left?

He forced a steady breath into his lungs. "Fairy, I need you to explain. Prin could be in trouble or hurt. Which direction did she go? Toward the mountains, my workshop, the road, or the barn?"

"None." She started bawling harder, cutting off any chance for clarification.

What the hell did that mean? Possibilities scrolled through his mind.

Kira had been seriously ill just a day ago. She might be delusional again. Or she might have wandered off to seek help. Or she might even be unconscious in the desert somewhere.

Lies. A tremor from his fears invaded his thoughts. *Emily's the delusional one.*

No, he didn't want to believe that. But what was he to make of her claim about glowing hands and fireballs?

Emily's in denial. She's making up stories to hide from the truth. Kira ran off just like Crissy and left you. Left Emily.

But there had to be an explanation for what Emily saw. He *had* smelled burning.

What...like your grandfather's spiritual bullshit was right?

His muscles tensed so hard his very soul felt raw and exposed. The straightforward explanation offered by his fears overwhelmed every other thought. Unless he accepted his grandfather's idea that Kira was a "magical holy spirit" or whatever, the doubts clawing out of his ribcage argued that Emily was lying—potentially about everything. But that would mean...

Face it—Kira left you.

His chest exploded with pain worse than being kicked by a horse, and his breath abandoned his lungs. He doubled over, and the phone slipped from his shoulder.

Heat swept through his body, hardening the strength of his fears, and he ground his teeth. He'd fallen for it again.

He'd believed she was different. Better. Believed she was someone he could trust.

Lies.

For months, the woman had hinted that she wasn't going to be around after he gained custody. Yet he'd stupidly believed she was different from Crissy. Different from his mother. Different from his father. Different from his grandfather.

He'd believed she was the exception to the rule. He'd believed she was good. Unlike anyone else. He'd been wrong.

Everyone was the same. Liars. Cheaters. And worse.

Everyone.

Life had seen fit to hurt him over and over—the pain stronger and deeper each time—trying to teach him that lesson. And like an idiot, he'd refused to listen. Refused to learn.

And now he'd let himself be hurt again.

Only this time the pain was worse. Much worse.

Chapter Thirty-Nine

IRENS WAILED OUTSIDE. ZAC TUCKED THE GLOCK INTO HIS
waistband after checking the safety and picked up the
phone from the floor, where the 911 operator had been
calling for him. "The police have arrived." His voice was a flat
monotone. "I'm going to hang up now."

He clicked off the phone and headed downstairs. Half his focus
still watched for an intruder, but at this point, he didn't know how
much of Emily's story was true. Maybe she'd made the whole
thing up to explain to her six-year-old brain why her foster mother
would have abandoned her.

A tiny voice interrupted the black hole of his thoughts and
fears. *Or maybe you should give them both the benefit of the doubt.
Kira might be injured and need help.*

Maybe...

With a supreme effort that felt like he was attempting to control a stampede, he yanked his bitterness back into looking only at
the here and now. The woman he'd been ready to propose to just a
half hour before deserved more than giving in to his fears at the
first suspicion of betrayal. For all he knew, Emily might have seen
something too odd to explain. He'd never known her to lie before,
so maybe she was just very—*very*—confused.

He shifted his daughter to his hip and opened the front door.
Two police officers stood there, about to knock.

"Are you the homeowner?"

"Yes, sir. Zachary Chase." He indicated Emily at his waist. "This is my daughter, Emily. She was here with Prin while I was at the grocery store. I was still at the store when Emily called 911, so I don't know what's going on." He swallowed. "I don't know if Prin is injured somewhere or..." He cut off the rest of the thought before his fears took hold again.

"We'll do a full search of the area. Mind if we take a look around inside, make sure the intruder isn't here?"

Zac stepped aside and let the cops on the front walk enter. Another pair was circling outside with dogs.

He kept his mind blank—the better to keep his worries under control. Time passed without meaning.

Emily's tears quieted, probably more from exhaustion than anything else. He carried her into the kitchen and fetched her a water bottle, which she gulped down until she choked. They sat at the kitchen table in silence, hunched over the tabletop.

Sometime later, the two police officers who had been searching the house entered the room. "Mr. Chase?" The female officer waited for Zac to glance up. "I need to ask your daughter some questions. Is that all right?"

Zac eyed Emily. She'd stopped sobbing and fallen into a near-catatonic stupor. Rather like him. "You can try."

The woman sat across from him. "Hi, Emily. We found something burned beside the bag of clothes in the courtyard. Can you tell us how it got there?"

Emily didn't pick up her head from the tabletop, but she rolled her neck and looked at the cop. "That's Tito's face. Prin burned it off when they were fighting."

"Prin—Moose's daughter, right? And she's your foster mother?"

That was life in a small town. All the local police were likely familiar with the motorcycle hangout, but Zac wanted the record straight for the police report.

"Actually, I was awarded custody of Emily a few hours ago. I'm her biological father."

The officer barely acknowledged him, continuing to meet Emily's eyes. "Can you tell us how Prin burned Tito?"

Emily stared at her palm and spread her fingers. "Her hand was glowing. She touched him, and he screamed."

Zac rubbed his temples, but Emily's story refused to settle into any kind of sense. Kira always wore gloves. Emily couldn't have seen Kira's hand, glowing or not.

The cop didn't dispute the nonsensical statement. "Is that the same thing that happened with the men he'd brought with him?"

"No, she didn't touch them. She just threw fire at them until there was nothing left."

"Do you know where Prin is now? We'd like to talk to her if we could."

Fear that she'd really left and worry that she might be in trouble battled in Zac's chest, and his breathing became shallow. "Have you checked with Moose?"

The officer focused on him. "My partner already called him. Moose hasn't seen her."

"What about searching the area?"

"The dogs couldn't find her scent beyond the courtyard. She didn't walk away."

Zac sat back, his stomach sinking to his toes. "The local hospitals?"

"We checked. They don't have anyone close to her description."

His throat tightened against the nausea roiling in his chest. What had happened to Kira?

Emily took a shaky breath. "She saved me. Then Tito stabbed her, and she disappeared. Like a magic trick."

His head jerked toward Emily. Like a magic trick?

Memories of the faerie fly apparitions Kira had made filled his mind. She hadn't done anything else like that in the time since, and he'd forgotten about that talent. Was this another time he should just accept that not-normal things happened around her?

His fears spoke up again. *Now you're sounding like your grandfather. So what if she used a magic trick to disappear in a puff of smoke. That doesn't change the fact that she left you. On purpose.*

He shuddered, recoiling from the idea of being like his grandfather in any way. But why would she go through the trouble of faking a reason for her disappearance?

Moose burst through the kitchen doorway. "I came as soon as I heard, Fairy."

Emily's face twisted into a pained grimace, and she stumbled to him. Before Zac could say anything to either of them, the police officers stepped toward the hallway. "Can we speak with you a minute, Mr. Chase?"

Moose seemed to have things under control with Emily, so Zac followed them out of the kitchen. The cop crossed her arms. "Whether or not her answers make any sense, your daughter has the facts right."

"What did you find?"

"Tito *was* here. When we came in, we found a man unconscious just down the road and called it in to our reserve unit. A few minutes ago, they radioed that Moose"—she tilted her head toward the kitchen—"positively identified the body."

"The body?"

"He died. Severe third degree burns to his face, right down to the bone. I'll give you one guess what the burn pattern resembles."

He wrung his fingers through his hair, but nothing could yank sense into the situation. "A hand?"

"The K9 unit also found a woman's leather glove and a chunk of charred flesh out by the driveway. If there's any DNA left, we can run a test to be sure, but I'll bet those results will place him here, at your house."

His arms dropped to his sides. He'd only been gone a few minutes. How the hell had the world turned upside down so quickly?

"During the K9 unit's sweep of the area, they also found three vehicles parked just past your property. All belong to gang members known to be affiliated with Tito and wanted for armed robberies and murders. But there's no sign of the vehicles' owners or passengers." Her lips thinned, and she shrugged. "In short, Mr. Chase, your daughter's eyewitness account is right on too many levels to ignore."

She gave him a card and indicated the kitchen. "Listen to whatever Emily says about this, and let me know. No matter how out there her comments seem to be."

He nodded, and then a wild thought took hold in his head. Say Kira really had killed all those men somehow, would she have faked her disappearance because she feared prosecution for the murders?

"What would happen to Prin if you find her?"

"We have no bodies as evidence except Tito, and only ten minutes before you returned to allow for the supposed disposal of several bodies. We have no weapon or even a guess of a weapon to look for one. And no eyewitness except a six year old whose testimony would be thrown out of court for being unreliable." She tossed up her hands. "I never know what the prosecutor will or won't decide to take to court, but if you ask me, unless new evidence shows up, there's nothing usable to pursue a case."

Zac swallowed and stroked his knuckles against his chest. His bitter doubts grumbled, but he decided the answer was good news. He thanked the officer and returned to the kitchen.

Moose held Emily's hands and sat knee to knee with her beside the table. "And when she disappeared, did you see anything else? A flash of light?"

Emily straightened. "Yeah, it was all around her."

"Almost like the light sucked her inside?"

"Yeah, it did."

Zac circled his fingers on his temples, where a killer headache was waiting to strike. "Why are you encouraging all this glowing hand, fireball stuff?"

Moose startled and then lifted a brow. "I'm *listening* to her. And if you have any desire to figure this out, you should listen—and believe her—too."

Zac's mouth opened. Moose actually *believed* all that wacky stuff? He'd never have guessed Moose had so much in common with his too-out-there-for-words grandfather.

The big man leaned back and crossed his arms. "Okay, College Boy. What do *you* think happened?"

His fears took hold of his mouth. "I think Prin was upset about losing custody and used the attack as a cover for running away."

He pinched his lips closed. This was not a conversation to have in front of Emily, especially when he wasn't sure what he *really* believed.

Before he could take back his words, Moose pounded the table and stood. "You think Prin would have abandoned Emily after everything she's done for this little girl?" He growled and bent down to Emily. "I can't stick around and listen to this crap, but I'll always listen to *you*, Fairy, and I'm only a phone call away." He barreled around the table and knocked into Zac's shoulder on the way out. "If that's what you think of Prin, you never deserved her anyway."

Zac sank into a chair, his knees weak. The battle in his chest continued, one part of him agreeing with Moose and the other part bitter with the echoing betrayals of his history. He wanted to give Kira the benefit of the doubt—especially if she was in trouble and needed help—but he was frozen, unable to take the leap of faith that could lead to pain and anguish.

Emily sat across from him, a frown of disappointment on her face. He couldn't blame her. Dealing with Kira's disappearance, Emily's panic attack, the police investigation, Tito's attack, and now Moose's accusations—it had been the worst possible first day of custody.

A lump that he couldn't swallow away blocked his throat, and he grimaced. The situation had to improve, right?

He couldn't imagine how things could get worse.

Chapter Forty

K IRA WOKE ON A SOFT LAWN, THE MOONLIGHT OF MYTHOS
gentle on her face. Her fingers stretched and dug into the
grass, drawing strength from its life force. She wasn't dead.

Her lips parted at the realization, sucking in a breath that felt
like the first one in a while. She'd thought for sure that knife
would be the end of her.

Her hand went to her stomach, and she explored the gash in
her shirt. The skin was tender but partially healed underneath, like
a several-days-old scab. How? Would she be able to return to
Emily and Zac on the Earthen plane if she finished healing?

She tasted the magic surrounding her, filling her. Flarea clan.

The maturation process with her power lines had pulled her
straight into the protected glen of her clan, the heart of all her
magic. Only such a place could have started the healing process
from an invasion of metal. Like a doting mother, the glen took care
of all faeries of the Flarea clan whenever possible.

If she had to be stabbed, apparently getting stabbed right as
magic took control of her body was good timing. Go, magic.

She lifted her hand, the one without the glove, and stared at her
palm. Her circuitry completed, a thread of gold flowed through the
black lines like blood within veins. She was now powerful, as her
magic against Tito's gang had proven. With her royal lineage, she
was among the most powerful fae alive.

At least, she would be when she'd finished recovering.

Her whole body protested at her attempt to sit up. She grimly chuckled under her breath. *Just wait 'til I stand up.* Then her body wouldn't think sitting to be such a big deal.

The glen, like Mythos in general, didn't seem to change with the passage of time. It appeared the same as it had during every visit her family had made for the spring equinox celebration, as her parents and the rest of her clan replenished their energy for the upcoming year.

A circle of stately trees kept watch over the protected magic source, the hamadryads embodying them waving their branches in welcome. A pedestal at the center of the glen elevated the giant ruby connecting the Flarea clan's magic to all of Mythos.

At least the ruby *should* have been there. Instead, the pedestal was empty.

She painfully scrambled to her feet and looked around, as though the gemstone could have rolled off the altar on its own. But the ruby wasn't going to be nearby. It had been taken.

Only those of the Flarea clan could enter the grove. Had a traitor stolen it? Why would anyone doom their own kind?

As the ruling clan of the fae homeland, if Flarea fell, the land would fail. The spirits inhabiting plants, animals, and the land itself would weaken. Without the gemstone in place to connect the land to the source magic of Mythos, only the protected glen of each clan would escape the decay. Everything outside the glens would die.

Everything would die.

Her heartbeat heavy, she raced past the ring of trees and into the forest enclosing the glen. Her abdomen ached at the exertion, threatening to reopen the wound. But she had to see. Had to know.

Beyond the forest, giant stone columns encircled the entire grove and marked the edge of the Flarea clan's protection. The soft grasses and glittering flowers ended at the stone markers enclosing the circle of the glen.

The land on the other side was barren and gray. Dried plants coated the ground like straw, boulders slept as lifeless rocks, and leafless trees stretched their spindly branches into the hazy sky. Hill after desolate hill rose into the distance, sharing the same fate.

She sank to her knees, and her stomach roiled, mixing denial and terror into a noxious stew. Her nails cut into her palms, and her arms curled over her chest. She squeezed her eyes shut, but she couldn't make the truth disappear.

She'd done this.

In her attempt to protect her people, she'd doomed them. Maybe Lirdeag wouldn't have been able to track her magic if she limited her Mythos visits to only the Flarea glen. She should have at least tried.

If she'd checked on a regular basis, she would have been able to find and reclaim the gemstone almost immediately. But she hadn't been here to prevent it, to stop it, to fix it. And so she'd hurt the spirits and all of the fae—and who knew how long this intolerable situation had been going on.

How was her neglect any better than Crissy's? Her hands clenched into tighter fists. It wasn't. She'd told Emily to not live in fear, to be strong, and all that time, she'd been too afraid to take even the smallest risk.

Her fears—no matter how well founded they were—had still condemned her kind to a land that stank of death and decay. Being the last ruler meant she was the only one with the power—the magic—to prevent this. To fix this.

She pressed her palm to the bare dirt beyond the stone enclosure. Green spread from her touch like wildfire. Grasses grew strong and healthy, the hamadryads in the nearby trees woke, and the haze cleared to reveal the moonlit night.

She lifted her hand, and the color faded from the land again, just as she'd expected. She *could* fix this, but only if the ruby was returned to make the magic permanent.

Her wound throbbed in time with her accelerating pulse, and she wrapped her arms around her stomach. Lirdeag had probably collected partial true names of others in the Flarea clan to create a loyal army to do his bidding, such as stealing the gemstone. Maybe he had enough power over her to do the same.

But she had to reclaim what the land needed. And that meant she had to face Lirdeag, her intended, the holder of her true first name, and the murderer of her parents. For the fae.

She stood, squared her shoulders, and brushed the dirt off her palm. If he had other Flarea under his control, it was only a matter of time until they discovered her here in the glen anyway. Better to take the fight to him before he expected her move.

She concentrated on finding the signature of the ruby's energy before her muscles could start shaking from what she was about to do. No matter what Lirdeag had done with it, the talisman of her clan couldn't hide. A vibration in the Mythos magic pinpointed the gemstone.

It was now or never.

She called on her magic and transported beside the ruby. At her command, a wall of flames materialized and encircled her and the gemstone. A few screams sounded from those who had been close enough to burn. Too bad. She wasn't going to stand there unprotected while trying to figure out her next step.

Only now that she was safe did she take the time to look around. Shadows of her surroundings were visible through the flames. Behind her, two thrones overlooked the great hall of her family's palace. Interesting choice, though not unexpected.

Lirdeag had wanted to seem as legitimate a ruler as possible, despite his lack of ruling magic. So he'd set up shop in the palace used by faerie rulers for countless centuries.

Shouts echoed off the marble walls and columns of the hall, and she pivoted back to the gemstone. As she'd expected, Lirdeag hadn't left the ruby unprotected. What she hadn't expected were the iron chains.

Iron? In Mythos? In the fae homeland, no less? Was Lirdeag *trying* to kill them all?

Iron didn't naturally occur anywhere in Mythos, so someone must be importing it from the Earthen plane. Someone powerful enough to exchange material between planes. Someone able to touch iron without consequence. Someone not fae.

Spears tipped with steel emerged through the wall of flames, swinging to and fro, providing answers sooner than she wanted.

Unicorns. Iron and steel didn't bother the shapeshifters, and they knew the techniques for working with metal.

Her stomach sank hard enough that her wall of fire thinned for a second. Unicorns weren't quite the mortal enemies to faeries that dragons were, but millennia ago, it had been close. And apparently,

Lirdeag was working with them. She was screwed.

She strengthened the flames protecting her and hoped it would be enough. The sharp steel tips swung toward her rather than sweeping aimlessly. *Effing A.* The weakening of the fire wall for a second had allowed them to pinpoint her location.

She ducked and moved to the other side of the ruby. She couldn't afford to be stabbed again. Next time, her magic wouldn't automatically carry her to Flarea's glen.

How could she get the gemstone out of here? She carefully poked a bare finger through the chains and tried to transport back to the protected glade.

She released a sigh that ended on a groan. No dice. She didn't transport and neither did the ruby. Not surprisingly, the iron interfered with her magic.

Fire magic was easy for her. Transporting took a bit more effort. And this stress wasn't helping her wound.

Maybe if she got rid of the column below the gemstone, it would leave a big enough opening in the chains. She placed her hand on the marble column.

A spear point lodged behind her ear. She froze.

The touch of steel to her scalp drained the magic needed to maintain the fire wall, and the flames vanished. A collection of fae and unicorn warriors—the latter in their shapeshifted humanoid form—surrounded her.

Why would he use unicorns for his army instead of gargoyles? In fact, no gargoyles stood as sentries in the hall. Had something happened to all of the gargoyles protecting their homeland?

The group parted and allowed a large male faerie through.

Lirdeag.

Her throat thickened so much that gravity seemingly dragged it into her stomach. She was one step away from hyperventilating, and the look on his face accelerated her breaths.

Long, straight black hair framed his icy blue eyes, where one dark brow cocked high. "What a pleasant surprise, Princess." He motioned to the ruby. "I must admit that when I first took this, I'd thought to lure you out of hiding, but you were more stubborn than I'd imagined. I'd grown satisfied with my limited power. However, now that you're here..."

He moved to the second throne and stroked the gold-covered frame. Nausea burbled at his implied familiarity. The invitation was clear. He still intended to be the king to her queen.

The steel at her ear burned her hair with a stench that would live in her nostrils for days. Worse, the metal prevented her from transporting away. She was stuck.

Lirdeag had captured her.

Her jaw ached, the clenched muscles protesting. Anything to prevent showing her terror.

He stepped close and whispered in her other ear. "I'm very pleased you came back to me, Kiratania."

She recoiled and nearly gouged her skin on the spear at her opposite side. "I didn't come back here for *you*." She rocked her mouth into a sarcastic smirk. "Unless you're referring to my plan to kill you."

"We'll see how you feel about things after a month in the dungeon." He stroked her cheek. "Locked in iron manacles."

She sucked in a breath, and her legs weakened. Her whole chest—from her heart to her wound—throbbed in time with her racing pulse. He'd updated his torture methods with new weapons. She was going to die here.

Lirdeag's cruel cackle followed her down the stairs as the unicorns led her by a phalanx of spear points into the bowels of the palace. His laugh still echoed in her ears as the faerie soldiers tugged back her sleeves and jeans and the unicorns locked her neck, wrists, and ankles against a stone wall, half-circles of iron preventing her from moving so much as an inch. After the guards left her alone in the stone cell, the echo rolled on in her thoughts, taunting her with what could have been. What she'd lost.

She didn't even know if Emily had escaped Tito. And Zac—what would he think of her disappearance? Would he think she'd rejected him? Poor Moose would be devastated.

Tears blurred her vision. She'd never see any of them again.

If she moved or slumped, the iron rings—just barely larger than her limbs—would burn her skin, weakening her more. A month of not being able to move? And what about sleep? She would die here, and she was tempted to speed up the process.

A part of her wanted to hope. Hope that her captors would

screw up, that escape would be possible, that she would survive this. That part of her told her she had to keep herself as strong as possible to take advantage of any opportunity.

But a bigger part of her admitted defeat. Admitted that the happily-ever-after ending she'd told Emily two nights ago was impossible.

In truth, hope would just prolong her torture. Hope was a lie.

Which would she embrace? The lie? Or her death?

Chapter Forty-One

NINE A.M., AND ZAC WAS ALREADY AT HIS WIT'S END. "EMILY, you *have* to get dressed. Your therapy appointment is in half an hour. We need to leave *now*."

Emily sat on her bed, petting Honey, and completely ignored him. The dog was one-hundred-percent devoted to the girl. Good for helping her settle in. Not good when being a distraction.

He clapped, getting the half-deaf Lab's attention, and pointed to the door. "Out."

Honey gave a *humph* and a final lick to Emily's chin and then slunk to the door. Emily crossed her arms. Her pout was deep enough to look like an upside-down smile.

"You take away everything I care about." She smacked the bed, one step away from a temper tantrum. "It's only a stupid appointment, and we should be looking for Prin. What if she needs our help?"

He jerked back and swallowed a curse. This *really* wasn't helping his mood. He'd spent half last night calling hospitals and blindly wandering the desert nearby, hoping against hope that he'd somehow find Kira. The other half of the night, he'd slept like crap—dreaming that he'd die if he fell asleep. So his temper was as short as his sleep.

"There's nothing we can do. Now get dressed."

Emily stood and opened her closet door, but instead of picking out clothes, she glared at him. "I *hate* you."

Then she slammed the door, shutting herself in the closet.

He pressed his knuckles against his forehead. Bloody perfect. He stood outside the closet door and thumped his skull on the wall. Now what?

His inability to find Kira last night had strengthened the ache in his chest and burrowed deep into his fears. How could someone disappear so completely unless they didn't want to be found? Giving her the benefit of the doubt wasn't an option when maintaining *hope* hurt too much. Now he was just angry—at her, himself, and the whole damn world.

He'd never planned on doing this alone. Hell, he was man enough to admit he wasn't cut out to do it alone.

He needed Kira, and *damn it*, she wasn't here. Honestly, he felt like throwing a temper tantrum himself. In fact, he would if he thought it would help.

A bitter laugh threatened to burst from his chest. Maybe he and his daughter were more alike than he thought. If so, the argument was unwinnable.

"Okay, Fairy, I'll call and cancel this morning's appointment."

Her voice was tiny and muffled. "You'll look for her?"

He rested his temple on the doorframe. Encouraging hope was a dangerous game, but he didn't know what choice he had. "If you can figure out where we could look."

The door cracked open. "You promise?"

Giving a promise to Emily was just as serious as promising Kira, but no alternative had popped into his head in the last minute. "I promise."

The door opened the rest of the way, and Emily emerged and gave him a hug. "Thank you, Daddy."

An hour later, they were huddled around a table at Moose's bar, the big man himself taking up the whole bench on one side. The bar wasn't open yet, but pans clanged in the back, where the kitchen staff readied for the lunch crowd.

Moose crossed his arms over his chest, and he jerked his chin, releasing his long beard from under his forearms. His expression couldn't be more skeptical, his anger from yesterday still on display.

"Let me get this straight. You're here—not because you think Prin might not have left voluntarily—but because you made a promise to Fairy."

Zac opened his palms. "Honestly, I don't know what to think. But whether she left of her own free will or not, I spent hours last night searching for her without finding the slightest clue, so I'm hoping you can help me."

"And what are you going to do if you find her? Treat her like the family member she is? Or make her feel like a criminal?"

Zac flinched, the question swirling around him like the mini-tornado of a dust devil knocking him off his feet. His answer depended entirely on the circumstances. If her disappearance *was* a betrayal, that wasn't going to be forgotten in a chorus of "Kumbaya" around a campfire.

"I'd listen to her. Just as I'm listening to Emily and you right now." He'd listen long enough to determine which of his instincts were correct—that she'd abandoned them all or that leaving hadn't been her choice.

"That's a start." Moose dropped his arms. "Second, you need to stop thinking that everything is about you. She didn't leave as *payback* for losing custody. I can guarantee that."

Zac swallowed and scratched his neck. With Kira just being the latest in a long line of people to betray him, his heart sure hurt like it was all about him. But she'd never tried to interfere with his relationship with Emily, so his blurted accusation yesterday was way off base. This *wasn't* about her trying to get revenge after losing custody.

"You're right. I let my fears run away with my mouth yesterday, and I was wrong, and I'm a jerk. But how does that help? If I'm going to listen to her, I first need to find her. Where should I search?"

"That's the problem." Moose slid his focus to Emily at Zac's elbow. "Fairy, I think you're right that she's in trouble, but I don't know how to get to her. I wish I did."

The man's voice dipped so low on that note Zac almost felt it resonate in his ribcage. "What do you mean, you don't know how to get to her? Is she out of the country already or something?"

Moose played with a gold coin in his fingers. "Fairy? What do you think?"

"I think..." She sat on her hands and mashed her lips tight.

"It's okay." Zac held out his hand in case she wanted to hold something. "I'm listening, remember?"

She met Moose's eyes. "I think she's not *here* anymore."

Moose nodded, slow and deliberate.

Zac turned from one to the other. "What do you mean, not *here*? Yeah, she's not in this bar, but she has to be somewhere." He pulled back his arm, and a cold shock shot up his spine. "You're not saying she's dead, are you?"

"No, not dead." Moose continued flipping the yellow coin between his fingertips. "But not *here*."

Zac gestured, pushing away his frustration, and grunted. "I'm trying to be patient. I'm trying to listen. But neither one of you is making any sense."

Moose slid the coin across the table to him. "Take a look at that."

He picked up the coin, its weight unexpectedly heavy. It was *real* gold? He didn't work with gold very often in his shop, but this matched his memory of the density.

Up close, it didn't look like a coin at all. A circle of interlocking loops created a golden flower with petals. The craftsmanship was astounding.

"What am I supposed to see?"

"That's a solid—and I do mean solid, *zero* impurities—gold decoration. I had it appraised once. The guy said he couldn't put a price on it. Thousands of dollars maybe."

Moose held out his hand, and Zac returned the piece. Even beyond how this conversation didn't seem to have anything to do with topic at hand, Zac couldn't help scanning Moose's bar. Was the big guy one of those "millionaire next door" types who didn't flaunt his money?

Moose rubbed his thumb over the golden surface. "Prin gave it to me the night we met."

Zac's attention jerked back to Moose. "What was she doing with something like that?"

"That's the thing with Prin." Moose gave him a tight smile. "Sometimes it's better to observe than to ask questions."

He fell silent after that, as though making a point. Kira didn't like answering questions, so a person was more likely to learn if they paid attention and didn't jump to conclusions.

In other words, if they listened to their instincts. The same instincts that had improved Zac's artistry. The same instincts that he'd rejected as being too close to his grandfather's way of life. The same instincts that told him to trust in Kira.

The walls crumbled from the fortress of his bitter fears and distrust. "Okay, I get it. But *talk* to me so I *can* listen and learn."

"You sure you're ready to hear what I have to say? 'Cuz I've never told anyone this story. Not even Roxi knew all of it." He set the golden disc on the table. "But I think it's time."

Chapter Forty-Two

ACOLD SHIVER AND A HOT FLASH SWEPT OVER ZAC'S BODY IN rapid succession. *This* was the lie he'd suspected from Moose from the very first time they'd met. The information he held back from everyone, including Kira.

Zac met Moose's gaze across the table. "I'm ready."

"I'm going to trust you on that, son."

The anger seemed to have dissipated from Moose's attitude, and Zac gave him a nod, acknowledging the difference. Moose stroked his beard and took a deep breath.

"About twenty years ago, I was closing up late one night when light flashed in the front lot." He tilted his head to the windows. "A bright light, like lightning, right by my bike. I didn't know what it was, but no one's allowed to mess with my bike, so I grabbed a metal bar a salesman had left as a sample—you know, trying to convince me to buy those wrought iron window security bars. Anyway, it was on that window sill, and then I ran outside."

His finger traced a loop on the gold circle.

"I was ready to beat the shi—" He glanced at Emily. "Crap out of someone, but instead a little girl was crouching beside my bike. No one else was around, so it was odd enough that she'd be out all by herself, but her appearance was even odder. She was wearing what I assumed to be a fancy nightgown, and her hair..."

He looked away, as though embarrassed to tell the story.

"Her hair was like dancing rainbows, multiple colors that didn't stay still."

Zac's mouth opened, more out of surprise than with a desire to comment. What the hell *could* he say to that? Moose eyed him, as though daring him to say something. Zac closed his mouth and pressed his lips together.

How many times had he seen Kira's quirks and accepted them as natural for her? He needed to do the same for this story.

Moose shrugged. "So I bent down, said hi, and asked her what she was doing all by herself in the middle of the night. She told me she was escaping the guy who'd killed her parents. I looked around to see who was after her. Nothing. So I asked where she'd come from, and she just said, 'far away.'"

He tapped the table with his fingertip. "I believed her, especially the *far away* part. Her accent was like nothing I'd heard before. Foreign..." He scratched his cheek. "In my head, I always described it as *regal*, almost musical."

Emily leaned forward. "Like when she talks to animals."

"Yeah, Fairy. Just like that."

Tingles started at Zac's fingers and toes. He knew exactly what Moose described. He and Emily had heard it plenty at the zoo, and come to think of it, when she was serious too—like with her promises.

Moose opened his palm. "Anyway, believe it or not, none of that is the weird part. But that's all I ever told Roxi. She was back in the trailer with two of our foster kids and never saw any of this." He gave his beard a couple of strokes. "So right then, in the middle of this conversation, I heard a sizzle over in that end of the parking lot"—he waved to the left—"and another bright light flashed. This time, I smelled it too. Smelled like a metallic chlorine scent, like ozone."

Emily frowned. "Chlo—what's that smell like?"

"Kind of like the printer in Miss Renee's office."

"Oh yeah." Emily straightened, obviously pleased at not being left out of this conversation. "I smelled that after Prin disappeared."

Moose nodded, unsurprised. "When the light faded, a man—a man who wasn't there before—stood right where the light had been. He was a big guy—tall, built even more than you. His clothes were all black leather and like something out of that Renaissance

Festival down Highway 60, a warrior type. Something about him struck me as intimidating as hell, even to a guy like me."

Moose's lips twitched. Most likely, he knew damn well he was usually the one intimidating others.

"Then the little girl cowered behind my bike, and I knew this was the guy she'd tried escaping. And if *I* was intimidated, I could only imagine how she felt. So I called out, 'You're on my property. State your business or leave.'"

Moose's mustache stuck out, his pursed lips setting the hairs at odd angles. "He didn't take that real well. He said, and I quote, 'This is none of your concern, *human*. Deliver the princess, and I might not kill you.'"

Human? Princess? The tingles spread up Zac's arms and legs.

Moose chuckled and spread his arms over the top of the seat bench. "Likewise, I didn't take to that threat real well either. But right about then, I was wishing I had my shotgun and not just that metal bar. My mouth wasn't in on that problem though, and I think I said something dumb like 'over my dead body' or 'come and get her' or something lame like that. Not my finest hour, I know. In my defense, it's not often I'm intimidated."

He sat forward and curved his hand, palm down, on the tabletop in front of him. "Then the guy closed in, but not by walking. More like he was surfing on a wave, except with the ground." Moose demonstrated by sliding his cupped hand across the wood. "I started losing my you-know-what at that point, and so did the girl. She hid behind me, clinging to my jeans like I was her last hope in the universe."

Emily inched closer, and Zac wrapped his arm around her shoulders.

Moose lifted his arm. "I held up the iron bar. It had one of those thin edges for attaching to a building, but that's nothing like a sharp knife. I thought I was done for." Moose swung his arm. "When the guy got close enough, I took a crack at him. He grabbed the bar before it hit him, but then he screamed and collapsed to the parking lot."

Moose opened his palms, as though apologizing for not having a better fight story. "I didn't know if he was faking it or not, so I just stood there for a minute, kind of in shock. The girl peeked around my leg, like she couldn't believe it either. He saw her and rolled, reaching out for her. At the same time, he said, and again, I quote, 'You *will* marry me, Princess.'"

Zac froze. The tingles now rose to his neck, where his hairs stood on end. Something about this story felt familiar, but that was impossible, right?

Moose spread his hands, implying a large circle. "Then the ground shifted under me, like quicksand. The girl screamed and tried to run away, but the dirt swallowed her legs. I didn't know what the hell was going on, and quite frankly, I didn't care. This guy was obviously bad news. Talking of marriage with a little girl was creepy enough, much less all the other crap. I bashed him with the bar, over and over—I couldn't tell you how many times. I was a bit out of my mind by that point, to be honest, up to my knees in gravel."

Emily shivered beside Zac, and he squeezed her close. This story was bound to give her nightmares, but it was too late to stop.

"Then, all of a sudden, light surrounded him, and he disappeared like he was sucked into the flash. He vanished, right in front of my eyes, with only that singed ozone smell left behind." Moose tilted his head. "I climbed out of the hole, which became solid under me as soon as I was out, and helped the girl too. I wasn't sure if I was going to call the police or the funny farm at that point, so I started a conversation with her just to calm myself down."

He sat back and smiled. "She said the craziest thing when I asked what her name was. She said, in that odd accent of hers, 'What a rude question. You don't ask someone their *name.*' As though after everything she'd witnessed, *this* was the final straw." He chuckled. "Then I asked what I should call her if I couldn't ask who she was, and she said, 'I am the faerie princess, of course. You may call me Princess.' Then she gave me this piece of gold"—he waved to the decoration on the table—"and asked me to promise that if that guy came back, I'd make him go away again. I agreed and then took her to meet Roxi."

He placed his palms on the table, announcing the end of the story. "And that's how Prin came to us. We were already approved for fostering, so the state let us keep her while they figured out what to do with her. They never figured out anything, so she stayed. She learned quickly and was a good kid. By the next morning, she'd stopped her hair color from rippling, picked up our accent, and started wearing long clothes and some gloves from a Halloween costume she found in a closet. Not even Roxi ever suspected the truth."

Moose didn't state what the truth was. He didn't need to.

Too many things fit, from her changing hair color that never ran when wet to the promises she'd elicited from him—keeping his metalwork away from her and protecting the secret of her name. She *was* a faerie princess.

Emily curled up next to him and whispered, "She told me. She told me, and I didn't listen."

"What do you mean, she told you?" But even as he asked the question, he suspected he knew the answer. That there was a reason all this felt so familiar.

"When we were at Grandma Doli's, Prin told me a bedtime story about a faerie princess who had to leave home after a bad guy killed her parents. She said the princess's magic was forcing her back home and that she'd have to fight the bad guy, Lir— something or other."

Now even the hair on the top of his head stood at attention. "Lirdeag."

All the pieces fell into place, including her drugged-out answers to his grandfather and her insistence for the shower because she hated being dirty, hated Lirdeag of the earth clan, the faerie who could control the ground, the faerie who'd killed her parents.

He'd seen it *all*—including her magic with the faerie flies—and he knew her truth because his grandfather was right about one thing. He *was* a seer. He'd always seen her for what she was but dismissed it because he didn't want to believe in things the world couldn't explain. He didn't want to believe in *her.*

His chest tightened, and his facial muscles twisted into a grimace. He'd been wrong. Horribly, horribly wrong.

He'd allowed his disrespect for his grandfather to blind him to the signs. He'd allowed his fears to lie to him and rationalize away the truth. He'd allowed his history to make him doubt her—think the worst of her, think she'd abandoned him and Emily, think she was as bad as Crissy. Instead, she'd shamed him with her goodness again.

She *knew* the situation with Tito would be dangerous for her, but she'd worried only about Emily. She'd saved his daughter and paid for it by being stabbed—metal *in* her body. What had that done to her? She'd done all that even though she knew what was waiting for her on the other side.

Moisture gathered in his eyes, burning, and his lips wavered and thinned. She was so much better than he'd ever given her credit for, than he'd ever imagined. She was the woman he admired most in the world, the woman who exceeded his expectations, and the woman he loved.

Moose leaned forward. "So you believe me?" His tone was worried and hopeful at the same time.

Zac breathed deep. "Every word."

God help him, but he'd fallen in love with a faerie princess who now needed rescuing. He rubbed his anxiety into his jeans at his thighs. Fairy tales usually had happy endings, right?

"How do we help her?"

Moose sat back, and his mustache curved with a frown. His hands curled, and he tapped his fists on the table. "I wish I knew, son. I wish I knew."

Despite the impossible situation, he wouldn't abandon her to the torture and forced marriage waiting in her homeland. If he gave up now, after learning all this, he'd be worse than everything he'd assumed of her. He'd be worse than anyone he knew. He didn't want to be that person.

Before, he'd wanted to do the right thing because he didn't want to be like his parents or his grandfather—simply proving what he wasn't. That was before Kira inspired him, taught him about selfless love. Now he wanted to do the right thing because *that* was the kind of person he wanted to be.

For Emily. For Kira. For himself.

He *would* figure out how to create a happy ending for her. Somehow.

Chapter Forty-Three

ZAC HAD SPENT THE REMAINDER OF THE DAY RESEARCHING everything he could find on faeries. Ninety-nine percent of the information out there was utter hogwash about tiny pixie creatures with wings.

The only aspects that seemed to have any basis in fact—although the whole idea that *any* part of faeries could be factual still struck his logical side as beyond crazy—was their vulnerability to iron or iron mixtures and the importance of their true name, like with the story of Rumpelstiltskin.

That last thought was still on his mind as he lay in bed that night. Nothing he'd learned had brought him closer to finding her, and he tried not to think of what torture she might be enduring.

"Help me, Kira. Help me know how to help you."

Exhaustion finally overcame his worry and frustration, and he drifted into oblivion.

Images came to him in dreams. Images and thoughts and emotions and sensations that didn't belong to him.

A large stone room, like something out of a medieval dungeon, surrounded him. A low fire burned in a pit on the other side of the room, sending flickering shadows over the rough walls.

His stomach hurt like it was on fire, and his whole body ached, longing to move, but if he shifted an inch, he knew the iron manacles at his limbs and neck would burn him. Again. Eventually, he'd stop healing and die. He was too damn close already. Only sheer stubbornness had kept him from giving up already.

A door opened, and a warrior-built man clad in black leather stepped into the room. His glacier-blue eyes shone bright against his skin, which was the rich color of dirt. Nausea rose at the sight of him, filling not-Zac's mouth with excess saliva. He approached and stroked not-Zac's cheek.

"Ready to submit to me, Princess?"

The body that wasn't Zac's spit in the man's face, a good use for the extra stuff. Then Kira's voice sounded, weak but obstinate. "You wish, Lirdeag. Never going to happen."

Lirdeag wiped away the spittle, and his eyes glittered. "We'll see."

The stone behind Kira swelled, pressing her limbs deeper into the iron manacles' curves, closer to the deadly metal. Sharp, hot pain shot from the side of her neck, and she straightened her head. Her muscles protested at the movement.

The vision before Zac in the dream wavered, tears springing to Kira's eyes. And yet, she thought nothing about giving in to Lirdeag. The only temptation before her was giving up, letting death take her.

Please don't. Give me time. Let me figure out how to help you.

Warmth swept through Kira's body. He didn't know whether she'd heard him or understood, but her resolve strengthened.

Lirdeag glared. "Submit and marry me, Kiratania. Before you die for no reason."

Her heartbeat seemed to stop for a second, and then resumed with greater strength. Her stomach fluttered and lightened. She laughed, not sarcastic or bitter, but with joy and happiness.

"Oh, this is *perfect.*" Her cheeks stiffened as she fought a smile. "No."

He frowned, his brows drawing low. "Have you gone mad? I ordered you to submit to me, Kiratania. That's nothing to laugh about."

She giggled. "Yes, it is."

"I see. You've become stronger, so your first name is no longer enough." His gaze scanned her face. "No matter. I'll just find someone else you care about—on the Earthen plane if I have to—and torture them until you give me more of your name."

Pressure squeezed her ribs for a second, and then she shook her head. "I could tell you my full true name, and you still couldn't make me do anything." Another giggle escaped her. "Don't you see? You don't own any part of me anymore. Someone else beat you to it. When he learned my full true name, any magical control you had over me broke. He's the only one with power over me now." A sly mood curved her mouth. "Face it, Lirdeag. You. Lost."

"I don't believe you." He pressed his lips into a thin line. "But even if you are telling the truth, your choice doesn't change. Marry me and give me the ruling magic, or stay here until you die."

"Oh, it must be so frustrating." Mock sympathy flavored her voice. "To have this grand plan thwarted by a *child*. And then she comes back, and you think everything is in your grasp once more, only to have her thwart you again." She clicked her tongue. "Such a sad failure for an evil genius. They never win, you know."

His hand shot out and slapped her hard enough that her other cheek hit the stone behind her. The iron at her neck burned her far more than his palm. Regardless, the taunt was worth the pain.

Zac's consciousness coexisted in her body, simultaneously fascinated and horrified by her attitude. He *knew* just how much the iron had hurt her, and yet he couldn't help admiring her strength. If only the risk weren't death, he'd be cheering.

"Temper, temper." She *tsked*, inviting Lirdeag's wrath again. "I must have cut close to the truth."

He clenched his fingers into her cheeks and forced her neck into the iron. Burning agony sliced across her throat. Energy drained from her as he continued the torture, second after excruciating second. Nausea rose in her throat, searing her from the inside and adding to the pain.

"No." He released her. "That's what you want, isn't it? To escape this torture. It drove your parents mad, and you don't want that to happen to you."

His gaze swept over her from head to toe. An expression halfway between a leer and a sneer shadowed his face.

"Forget marriage. You're not good enough for that anyway. I'll just force you to carry my child and have *it* give me the magic."

Zac's hatred ran cold. Even Kira's façade faltered, her heart sluggishly beating through the nightmarish scenarios playing in her mind.

She hid her fear from Lirdeag. Maybe his temper and her logic would trick him into doing something stupid. Stupid for him.

"Too bad this iron would get in the way of you raping me."

"Don't worry, Kiratania." He squeezed her breast hard enough to bruise, driving more bile up her throat. "I'll figure out how to get what I want by tomorrow."

At that threat, he stormed out of the stone cell, and the door clanged behind him.

Her dread escaped on a shaky laugh. "Well, most of that was fun. At least I know he can't use my name against me anymore." Warmth filled her chest, and she murmured into the emptiness. "For that alone, Zac, I think I love you."

He melted, his conscious spreading into every limb in a bizarre out-of-body, metaphysical embrace. *And I* know *I love you.*

He gasped and sat up in bed, awakened from the dream.

Or not a dream.

He pushed away thoughts of Lirdeag's threat and focused on everything he'd learned. He had power over her? A vague memory rose to the surface, and he rubbed the back of his neck. After Kira had told him her full name, a sharp sting had numbed his neck, like from a scorpion. But the pain had faded so quickly, he'd forgotten about it.

Were they somehow connected? Was that how he'd sensed that she'd left?

On a hunch, he grabbed his phone and started the camera app. A part of him hoped to see a mark, proof that the dream was real. That she was alive. That he might be able to help.

He lifted his hair off his neck and took a picture. There, on his cell phone's screen, was proof enough to convince anyone. A tattoo-like mark about an inch-and-a-half in diameter covered the back of his neck. He zoomed in on the design, and his breathing hitched.

It was *her* mark. The one on her palms. The same palms Emily had seen glowing.

He straightened and took a deep breath. Now what? How should he use this information?

If he called her here, would that literally *pull* her through the iron manacles? Or would the iron interfere? Maybe it would be safer to see if he could use her name to go to her.

Okay, time to plan.

Twenty minutes later, he'd dressed, selected two lighter Glocks for his shoulder holster, and filled extra magazines for his belt pouch. If faeries couldn't take iron-mixed metal inside them, the steel-jacketed, hollow-point bullets he'd gotten on discount might be the best weapons imaginable.

He checked the clock, almost three a.m. That couldn't be helped—he refused to wait hours for others to waken naturally, all while Kira struggled to live. He called the number Moose had given to Emily.

"'Lo?" A shuffling noise came through the speaker. "Fairy? What's wrong?"

"This is Zac. I think I figured out how to find Prin. I need..."

The truth was that he was heading into an unknown environment as an outsider. He had no idea if he'd make it there, much less back. By going, was he choosing Kira over Emily?

That wasn't a choice he could make. That wasn't a choice *anyone* could make. All he knew was that if he didn't try, he *was* condemning Kira, and that *really* wasn't a choice he could make. Besides, he needed to show his daughter that he'd do anything—anything—to protect those he loved.

"I need you here with Emily."

"I'll be there in a couple of minutes."

True to his word, Moose arrived a few minutes later. Zac gave him a signed if-anything-should-happen-to-him document. Moose read it and paused at the sentence about him taking custody of Emily, his face grim.

"I haven't taken on a kid since Roxi died. You'd better be packing. I want you coming home in one piece."

"I am, including a backup gun and extra ammo."

"Good. What's your plan?"

"I spent the day trying to remember everything she'd said, in case she'd left clues in innocent comments." True. "As I was falling asleep, I remembered words she'd told me that I think have magical power." Mostly true. "I'm going to use them to follow her to wherever she is and help her escape." All true.

No one else needed to know the details of her full true name. She might think she was safe from anyone else learning her name, now that he possessed it, but he wasn't in a rush to test that theory.

"You're going to tell Emily first, right? She deserves to know."

Zac peered up the stairs. Yes, Emily deserved to know. He trudged up to her room and woke her with a gentle shake to her shoulders.

She rolled over and rubbed her eyes. "Daddy? What's wrong?"

"Nothing's wrong, Fairy. I think I figured out how to find Prin, and I'm going to try to get her now. Moose is here with you, okay?" His voice sounded robotic, unconvincing.

Her gaze skated over him, her brows tight. "It's going to be dangerous, isn't it?"

"It might. But I'll be careful." He swallowed, dreading the decision he felt obligated to place before her. "I think it's important to try to help Prin, to protect those we love, even though it will be dangerous. But if you don't want me to take that risk—"

"Prin saved me, and you need to save her, Daddy." Her lips scrunched tight. "How can I help?"

"Grow up to be just as brave as you are right now, Fairy." He hugged her close and placed a kiss on the top of her head. "My brave, brave girl."

Moose dragged over an armchair. "I'll stay right here the whole time, Fairy." Before he sat down, he held out a hand for Zac. "Bring our girl home, son."

"I will, sir."

And with that, Zac seated his cowboy hat on his head, left his cell phone on Emily's dresser, and stepped into the hallway. Wherever he was going, he doubted they'd have cell service.

He drew one of the Glocks in preparation for whatever he'd find at his destination. The hallway's privacy allowed him to recite Kira's full name without worries of eavesdropping.

"Take me to Kiratania Serafiskra Zarylina Lidashka Maksyna."

The fact he remembered that mouthful was additional proof of the connection between them. His memory alone certainly wasn't responsible.

Tingles swept over his skin. Magic *was* real.

Chapter Forty-Four

AGIC WHIRLED AROUND ZAC AND SUCKED HIM INTO A vortex. His gut and the air in his lungs remained somewhere back in the hallway, and rather than being ready to surprise an attacker, he arrived—wherever—gasping and choking, loudly.

After he coughed and swallowed his stomach back to where it belonged, he finally took in his surroundings. A low fire smoldered in the corner of a dim stone cell, empty except for Kira, who was held immobile by iron half-circles securing her against the wall.

"Prin..." She looked beaten, even more out of it than after the fiasco with his grandfather. Her hair hung listlessly, only a pale non-color shading her locks, and her skin had an unhealthy tinge. She didn't look up at his call.

No, no, no... His stomach roiled again, and chills burned through his body.

He couldn't be too late. Lirdeag's torture couldn't have killed her. The magic had brought him here, right? Had using that magic drained her? Would it have worked if she was—?

He cut off the thought, holstered his gun, and ripped his sleeves down his arms. Step one: Protect her from further damage from the iron while he figured out the next steps. He stuffed fabric wads between her skin and the cuffs at her limbs.

She didn't stir until he got to her neck. That cuff was so tight he had to press on her skin to get even the thinnest strip wedged inside. If proximity alone was enough to damage her, the iron had been draining her energy since the dream, and that didn't count whatever healing she'd had to do after Lirdeag's torture.

She opened her eyes and struggled to focus. Instead of the happy expression he'd been hoping for, she groaned. "No. Can't fall asleep. Must wake up."

Once he had her neck protected, he held her face in his hands. "You're not sleeping. I'm here. I'm going to get you out of this."

"Can't be here. Dreaming. Must wake up."

He stood close enough that she'd feel his heat. "I'm here. I'm real. I used your name to bring myself here."

She searched his eyes, hope warring in her depths. "Kiss me."

He didn't need to be told twice. He slid his lips over hers, caressing, licking, meshing. The past two days worth of emotions—the drama, tension, anger, hurt, and above all, desire to have her with him forever—burst through their connection. In spite of fighting his instincts too long, he'd found her, and he wasn't going to let her go again.

She moaned. "You *are* here." Her moan turned into a groan against his lips. "You shouldn't be here. It's not safe for you."

Her color looked a bit better already, her cheeks flushed. He gave her another kiss and then pulled away. "I'm not leaving. But I need to figure out how to get you out of this."

He searched the cell for what he could use. Iron bars caged in the fire pit, probably to limit the magic of a faerie of the fire clan, like Kira. The frame wasn't attached to the dirt floor, so he tipped the cage off the fire.

A few of the iron bars had weak joints, and he spun the contraption so one of those bars was horizontal above the ground. He stomped on the middle of the rod. After two attempts, the bar's welds gave, and iron rod broke free. The metal clattered against the bottom side of the cage, and he glanced toward the door. He fingered the grip of his gun in case guards were outside.

A moment passed without visitors, so he picked up the freed iron rod. Perfect. The bar already had a thin end from where the inept smith had tried the joining.

He returned to Kira, and a quiver fluttered in his stomach.

Taking a bar of iron closer to a faerie didn't seem like a good idea, but he didn't have a choice. The least he could do was protect her though. He unrolled the ends of her sleeves and jeans up to the edge of the iron cuffs.

"I'm going to test how well these manacles are attached to the wall. It can be difficult to maintain friction in stone."

"Not for Lirdeag."

He ignored her pessimism and shoved the bar under the flange of the metal cuff at her right ankle. The uneven rock wall curved inward enough to get the tip of the bar between the iron and the stone face.

"Or the metal might be brittle if they didn't use the right mixture or temperature for forming these pieces."

If the holes for the bolts were larger than necessary, the bolts might simply slide out. That was also the safest area to attack, away from her skin.

He rocked the iron bar behind the flange, wedging it deeper against the stone. The cuff moved a couple of millimeters and then stopped. He switched to the flange on the other side. This one slid out with a few double-handed yanks on the bar. The hinge on the other side swung the whole cuff out of the way.

"See?" He glanced up, but her eyes had closed. "We'll get you out of here, I promise."

He went to work on the rest of the cuffs. Her other ankle was soon free, but the bolts on the other cuffs were too solid. Lirdeag had probably strengthened that area when he'd expanded the stone in the dream.

The next weak point to attack was the chained loop threaded through the locking holes at the middle of each cuff. His stomach tightened more at the risk to her. He needed to cover up her hands, so she at least wouldn't have any exposed skin. He scanned the cell again.

Her guards had removed her boots and socks to lock the ankle cuffs around bare skin. He slipped the socks over her hands. That should help a bit.

The chain loop securing the cuff at her right wrist already separated between the ends, so he slipped the iron rod in the link and levered the bar against the stone with sharp tugs. He'd give anything for a gripping tool right now. His yanking bent both the rod and the C-link. Almost. He pulled once more and landed on his ass, the rod slipping through the separation between the ends. Finally.

He rotated the loop until the opening faced the cuff's locking holes. The iron link slid off the cuff, and he freed her hand.

Her muscles fought his grip. He gently stroked her wrist, where the skin was raw and red. "It's okay to move this arm now. Feel my fingers on your wrist? This cuff is off."

He massaged the rest of her arm, stimulating her blood circulation. She'd slipped back into a half-conscious state. Damn it. He needed her help for the next part.

The other two locking chain links were tighter, so only the tip of the iron rod would fit into the loop. That wouldn't create enough leverage to pry the ends apart. He needed a brighter light to search for anything else he could use, or at the very least, so he could better see what he was doing, and there wasn't a stack of fuel for the fire in the room.

He stroked her face. "Prin, I need your help. Wake up."

She stirred and smiled, her happiness washing over him like a warm hug. "You're still here."

"Of course I'm still here. I'm not leaving without you. I have three of the cuffs off, but I need your help for the last two."

"How?"

"See that fire over there? I removed the iron from around it. You belong to the fire clan, right? Does that mean you can make that fire brighter?"

"Tired. Too tired."

"I know you're tired, but if you can do this, I'll have you out of here in just a minute."

Her eyes closed again.

On a hunch, he kissed her until she responded, and then he drew back. "Please try, Prin. I don't want to have to use your name, but I will if I think it would help you."

"I'm going to need a lot more kissing."

He chuckled and rubbed his thumb over her mouth. "That's the Prin I know."

He braced her still-secured neck and left wrist with his hands. If she hurt herself during the kiss, that would be a real mood-killer.

"I don't know if I've told you this…" He kissed her eyelids. "But I love you." He covered her forehead with kisses. "I mean *really* love you." He next got her nose and chin. "Like, an I-would-do-anything-for-you type of love." Then her cheeks. "Like, an I-worship-you type of love."

He finally landed on her lips, and she met him eagerly. Her moans vibrated through him, and despite their precarious situation, he couldn't help his arousal.

His tongue swept into her mouth, stroking, sucking, licking. Her free hand gripped him hard and pulled his body closer. He didn't resist. Her breasts pressed against his chest, and his erection found a soft curve on her belly.

Then something in her mood shifted, became serious. She pushed him away a fraction. "Is Emily okay?"

"Yes, she's fine. Moose is with her right now."

Air burst from her lungs on a shaky exhale. "I'm–I'm glad. Honestly, if it weren't for you and Emily, I'd have killed myself here." She met his eyes. "But I wanted to survive and return to you. I want to be part of your family—you and Emily."

A wave rippled through his chest, like the rest of his organs made room for his expanding heart. His knees weakened, and he leaned more heavily into her for balance, knocking his hat off-kilter. Warmth filled him, and he wanted nothing more than to release her from the cuffs so he could hold her in his arms.

Their kisses deepened, more tender and yet more passionate. He loved every aspect of this woman.

She released him and grinned. "Yep, *that's* what I needed."

She gave him one last kiss and then lifted her free hand, flinging the sock off her fingers. The dim light made it hard to be sure, but her tattoos seemed to glitter like golden threads. Brightness gathered in her palm, glowing with a golden light, and the flames in the fire pit became taller.

"You don't need hotter, right? Just brighter?"

"Right." He straightened his hat. "I want to search for something I can use to pry the ends of these last two links apart."

"Okay, done."

He scoured the stone cell for anything he could use to help bend the metal but came up empty. Not even a spare nail or bolt.

Damn.

This was wasting time too. A guard could check on her at any minute.

He'd just have to use the same bar and be extra careful about not letting the metal slip with the iffy leverage and touch her skin. He brought the rod over to the chain link on her wrist's cuff, once again ignoring the apprehension in his gut, and wedged the tip into the loop.

A slow rocking motion worked the rod deeper into the C-link. After a minute, brute force opened the loop, and he slid the chain link around and freed her left wrist, massaging the muscles as before.

"Almost, Prin. One more just like that."

He turned to the remaining cuff at her neck. His stomach protested again, and this time, his heart clenched, skipping a beat.

At the other cuffs, her arms and legs hadn't stuck out into the area where he was working. Here, he couldn't yank or rock the rod from side-to-side without risking a touch to her neck or chin, and there was no way to protect her exposed skin like he'd done with the socks on her hands.

He'd just have to be really, *really* careful. Despite the boycott setting up shop in his chest, he forced himself to slip the tip of the other bar into the center of the link. He worked gently, slowly, with controlled movements. No brute force for this one.

She closed her eyes. "You know if you scratch me with the iron, I'll probably die, right?"

His mouth went dry, and he froze.

"No pressure though."

A deadly chill threatened to make him shiver and move the iron. "Right. No pressure."

Her lips twitched. "I guess this means I trust you."

"Don't remind me."

He wasn't sure anyone deserved that much trust.

Chapter Forty-Five

THE MORE ZAC TRIED NOT TO THINK ABOUT THE DANGER TO Kira if he messed up, the more that's all he could think of. His heart beat so loudly in his ears he swore he could hear each valve opening and closing. Each time the rod slipped a millimeter, he cursed himself. He held his breath for so long his lungs ached and dizziness crept into the edges of his vision.

"Damn it." He stepped back before his frustration caused a careless mistake.

A growl worked its way up his throat. This wasn't going to work if he couldn't get a grip on himself.

Her voice sounded, low and concerned. "Are you okay?"

"No, I'm *not* okay." He wrenched his hands through his hair, cursing himself again for raising his voice. "I feel like I'm going to have a heart attack, I'm so worked up about this."

She gasped and slapped her palm against the stone wall. "The promise."

"What promise?"

"Remember when you promised you'd never let your work touch me? You swore on your life."

His brows slammed together. "That was *literal*?"

Her lips pressed tight, an apologetic frown answering his question. "A promise to a faerie is very powerful." She slid her hand into his shirt. "I'll release you from that promise."

"Wait." He grasped her forearm. "Can you release me for five minutes and not permanently? I just need to *not* have a heart attack long enough to use this iron to free you."

Her mouth opened and closed without words for a moment. "You'd *do* that? You'd keep the promise even though you know the cost of failure is death?"

His gaze caressed her face. "I want to keep you safe. As long as the promise doesn't kill me right away, this freak out can be like an early warning system to help me protect you from metal." A thousand horrible scenarios stampeded through his brain of all the ways he could unintentionally hurt her. "This promise is the best way to prevent accidents. I'd never forgive myself if I damaged you."

"You're..." She gave him a smile brighter than the fire at his back. "You're amazing." She added a wink. "I'll give you *ten* minutes."

He chuckled. "Such a generous jailer you are."

Her palm rested over his heart and heated. "For the next ten minutes, I release you to bring your metalwork near me."

His heartbeat stabilized, and his stomach eased its grip on his chest. Concern still wove through his thoughts, but at a normal level for the situation. He was trained. He was patient. He could do this.

The loop on her neck cuff required steady, gentle pressure to separate the ends of the link. He set aside the iron bar, slid the loop around, and opened the manacle at her neck.

She wavered a second and then fell into his arms. He held her close. "Easy. I've got you."

He carried her to the far corner alongside the wall with the door. If any guards came to check on her, he'd get in a couple of free shots while they searched for her. He set her down and massaged her leg and shoulder muscles. They trembled under his touch.

She curled into a ball and held her hands to her stomach. "Note to self—don't get strung up after being stabbed."

Damn. He'd forgotten about that injury. "Here, let me see."

She opened her arms, and he tugged up the hem of her shirt. A red and swollen scab lined her right abdomen. The skin and muscles there had healed better than a human would with no medical attention, but being immobile in a strained position for a day and a half had damaged their progress.

"What can I do to help?" He gently tucked her shirt down. "Can we leave here now? Get you back home where you can heal in peace?"

"I'm not strong enough to transport us anywhere right now. That magic doesn't come as naturally to me as fire magic." She indicated the door. "We're going to have to break out of here first."

"Okay." He helped her into her socks and boots. "Any ideas for how to get out of here?"

She shook her head. "Out there, we're likely to find other faeries Lirdeag has control over—"

He patted the guns at his sides. "These are steel-jacketed bullets."

"Glad you're on my team." She shuddered. "And we'll also probably run into unicorns."

"*Unicorns?*" Were all myths true in this crazy place? "They're fighters? Why would they be on Lirdeag's team?"

"Oh please." She rolled her eyes and grimaced. "Don't tell me you fell for their innocent and pure crap? I don't have a clue why they'd work for faeries though. Usually, we don't get along very well." Her hand waved away the idea. "Anyway, they look human unless they shapeshift. Hope they don't. They're much bigger than horses. Either way, steel bullets won't stop them. Although one straight to their heart might slow them down."

His brain struggled to keep up with her new honesty and explanations for this bizarre world. Shapeshifting, potentially dangerous unicorns—what was the world of fairy tales coming to?

Scraping drew his attention to the door. *Damn.*

The door opened, and a man entered, his focus on a cup in his hands. He seemed to be alone.

"Princess, time for your..." He looked up at the empty wall. The cup tumbled out of his hands, scattering liquid on its descent, and thumped to the dirt floor.

In the time it took for the man's shoulders to slump and process that she wasn't there, Zac had slinked toward the fire. The man's gaze would reach him before completing the circuit to Kira in the far corner, and from this location, Zac could watch the door too.

He took aim but didn't fire. On top of the fact that a shot would echo down the hallway through the partially cracked door, killing wasn't on his list of preferred things to do. Just because he'd trained to shoot didn't mean he was eager to.

As expected, the man's head swiveled, searching the cell. Zac took charge of the moment before his imminent discovery.

"Don't move."

Despite the instruction, the man startled, and his pale blue eyes locked on Zac, widening even further. His gaze stopped on Zac's cowboy hat, and his brows scrunched together. At the movement, something on his cheek glistened in the low light. He didn't even look toward the gun, as though he didn't recognize what one was.

Zac glanced at the Glock for a fraction of a second. "This is a weapon that will shoot a mixture of iron into your heart. You move, you die. Understood?"

"You are a…" The man hesitated over the word. "Human?"

"A human with a deadly weapon." Zac indicated the door. "How many others are in the hallway?"

"I am alone."

Right.

"It is early morning." The man must have interpreted his skeptical expression. "The others are still sleeping."

Maybe that was a believable explanation. "You're going to sit and face that wall and answer some questions. If you try anything, I'll either shoot you or lock you in those irons. Understand?"

The man answered by following Zac's instructions and aiming his body toward Kira's empty cuffs. Zac sidestepped across the cell and closed the door so they'd get warning of any other visitors. Kira had slumped against the wall, eyes closed again. Maybe faeries weren't morning people in general. If the others were asleep now, this guy might be their chance.

He sidled back to his place where he could watch the man and the door. "Why are you working for Lirdeag?"

"I don't. I work in the prisons. Lirdeag just happens to use them."

Good answer. "I need to get the princess out of here. Will you help?"

The guard gasped, and his head twitched, as though he wanted to spin around but stopped himself. "The princess? She is alive?" He wiped his cheek. "You didn't kill her with your weapon?"

His voice sounded downright hopeful. Zac lowered his gun a fraction.

"I'm the one who set her free, and now we need to escape. Will you help?"

"Yes. On one condition."

Zac groaned. Faeries and their tit-for-tat promises. "What condition?"

The guard turned and met his gaze. "Free my wife, and take us with you."

Zac's arm drooped. "Your wife is imprisoned here too?"

"That's why I work here. So I could still see her." His lips pressed into a thin line. "I'd hoped to discover a way to free her, but I'm powerless against her shackle, and the unicorns have their own agenda." His eyes flicked to the open cuffs on the wall. "You, however, are a man of iron, yes?"

"Yes." Zac weighed his options. Delay longer and risk detection while freeing this man's wife, or be on their own for finding a way out? "You're certain you can get us out of here?"

"Positive. I've had every aspect of our escape planned except for the iron."

The man sounded sincere, and they wouldn't get a better opportunity. Zac holstered his gun.

"Deal." He risked turning his back to the man by going to Kira in the corner. He crouched down and gently lifted her head. "Prin? It's time to go. This man's going to help us escape."

She stirred, opening her eyes enough to scan the cell. She gasped and backed further against the wall. "He's earth clan, like Lirdeag."

Zac peered at the guard, who had the same blue eyes and dirt-colored skin as Lirdeag, disputing the all-white parade of faerie depictions by human artists.

The man's chin dropped to his chest. "I ask you not to judge us all by the actions of one, Princess. For millennia, we have been loyal and honorable in our service to the royal family. Some have followed Lirdeag, but many of us consider him an outcast."

She gave a small nod, her expression tight. Zac helped her to her feet, and she stumbled on weak legs. All right. Not up for walking.

After a minute of negotiating, he got her to ride piggyback style. That way he could carry the iron rod he might need for freeing the guard's wife and still have access to his gun without endangering Kira.

The man led them down the hall. Torches lit the dark stone pathway. A few hallways down, the guard opened another cell and stepped inside.

This was a smaller cell, about the size of a bathroom, and a woman was sleeping on the stone floor. An iron cuff circled a wooden collar, and a chain connected the locking loop on the cuff to another loop in the wall.

The man bent down to the woman and cradled her head. "Beloved, I have found a human to free you."

Her eyes, light blue like her husband's, opened and then scrunched at the scene, where Kira was attached to Zac's back. "He's captured the princess? And yet you trust him?"

Zac set Kira down in the most protected corner like before. "I'm rescuing the princess from Lirdeag." Trying to anyway. "Let's get you out of this so I can succeed."

He knelt at her side, waved her husband down to her other side, and angled the rod through the center of the partially open top chain link. The man caused the dirt at Zac's knees to harden, bracing one end of the bar.

This magic stuff wasn't going to seem normal anytime soon. Although, maybe from their perspective, his ability to touch iron was near-magical too.

A quick minute later, Zac opened the loop and snapped off the wooden under-collar that had protected her from direct contact with the dangerous metal. This woman was just being held, not tortured like Kira.

Sounds reverberated from the hall. All eyes except Kira's looked toward the door. *Bloody hell.*

The guard helped his wife to her feet. "Come. Others are waking. We must leave now."

Zac nudged Kira awake again. "Time to go, Prin. Up on my

back."

Situated once more, Zac carried Kira and followed the guard and his wife. The man led them on a zigzagging path of torch-lit stone hallways and then ducked into an alcove with a two-foot-wide, stone-rimmed well. "Quickly. Jump in. The water at the bottom is an underground stream that runs along a cave."

His wife hoisted her legs over the edge of the well and slid down, proving she believed her husband's claims. A quiet *sploosh* sounded when she hit the water.

A shout echoing from several halls back announced their escape. Footsteps pounded on stone in every direction.

The guard grasped Zac's arm. "I'd hoped to go with you, but it's too late for that. I'll mislead them instead. Tell my wife I'll see her where we first met, an hour after sunrise tomorrow." He gestured to Kira. "I won't ask for a promise from the one who is helping the princess, but will you watch over my wife for me, *please*?"

Zac met his eye. "I'll do everything I can."

"Give the princess time to drift away from the bottom before following her. Float with the river to a sinkhole where you can climb up. Then look for the cave marked with a rock cairn. I stocked it with supplies. Thank you, human."

The guard took off before Zac could thank him in return. He hesitated for only a second and then set Kira on the stone edge. "Your turn."

Kira grabbed the back of his neck and kissed him. Hard. "Be safe and come back to me. I *want* to be owned by you."

Before her words sunk in, she slipped down the well. Her splash covered up his grunted "Huh?"

Owned? Was that really what him knowing her full name amounted to? What did that mean for *them*?

Stomps brought up his head. A man with wild-streaked hair rounded a corner at an intersection thirty feet away, his gaze locking on Zac.

The guard shouted over his shoulder. "They're—"

He never finished his sentence. He never would.

A thunderclap filled the stone hall, reverberating through the narrow passages. A projectile struck the guard and knocked him backward. The hollow-point bullet expanded as designed, lodging itself in the man's body. The force, the damage, and the steel all combined to kill him before he hit the ground. His body dissolved, sparkling like glitter, and nothing remained to land on the stone.

A metal grip quivered in Zac's hand. Was he responsible? Had he killed?

More shouts and running steps sounded from down the hallway. He slid over the edge of the well, lifted his arms so his shoulders fit, and allowed himself to fall.

Water swallowed him whole.

Chapter Forty-Six

ARMS HAULED ZAC ABOVE THE SURFACE OF THE WATER. A soft glow shone from Kira's palm.

The guard's wife dragged him closer as they floated with the cave river's flow. "Where is my husband? Is he behind you?"

"The other guards were closing in. He was going to mislead them and catch up with you an hour after sunrise tomorrow where you first met."

The woman swallowed. "Did anyone witness the escape route?"

Zac lifted the gun above the water and let the barrel drain. Kira's gaze followed the movement and stopped at his expression. He could only shake his head.

The witness hadn't survived. Even if the others found a glittery residue or the bullet, he'd died in an intersection of hallways. Others wouldn't know where the attack had come from unless they found the bullet's brass cartridge by the well and understood its significance. Otherwise, the other guards would know only that they'd escaped. And were dangerous.

He'd done what needed to be done. He hadn't had a choice. He knew that. But...

Trembles started deep in his chest and flooded his body. He spun away, pretending to scan their surroundings in the water-filled cave. In reality, he saw nothing.

Kira slipped her arm around him and placed his soaked—but rescued—hat on his head. He ducked his chin. Drips *plinked* onto the water's surface from the brim. Like life in general, ripples swept out, spreading the impact to other areas.

He'd killed. And he'd never be the same.

Soft fingers slid along his jaw. Warmth, acceptance, and appreciation flowed from Kira's touch. She didn't judge him. She felt only gratitude tinged with an edge of guilt.

How did he know her emotions? Now that he thought about it, he'd sensed her feelings before now too. His brain wasn't in any shape to figure it out for certain, but he'd guess that ability came with his knowledge of her name.

She gave him an understanding smile. "Thank you." Her lips twisted into an apology. "You didn't know you were going to be stepping into the middle of a war, did you?"

He opened his mouth—to say what, he didn't know. Yeah, he'd had a vague idea that Lirdeag was bad news, but that wasn't quite the same as knowing the depth of his takeover.

He cleared his throat. "No. But I'd still have come for you, even if I knew."

"I know you would." She kissed him long enough to send heat through his body.

Reluctantly, he pulled back. "We should lie on our backs to float faster. He said we'll be able to get out at a sinkhole downstream."

Soon, the flow of the underground stream carried them away from the prison. He held his hat on his stomach—Glocks nestled inside—with one hand and kept a grip on Kira floating beside him with his other hand. She created a glow in her palm to allow enough light to see the ceiling above the river's surface. His body had adjusted to the chilled water, and now only a near-silent journey accompanied his thoughts.

He shoved away the memory of the shooting. Of the man's body disappearing into nothingness.

Instead, he distracted himself by analyzing their surroundings. Sometimes the ceiling came perilously close to the water surface, but it never closed off completely. If they were on Earth, he'd describe the river's path as an old lava tube, solidified and now flowing with water. They weren't on Earth though—at least, he didn't think so—and he had no idea if volcanoes even existed here.

After floating for so long that he'd started shivering again, light finally shone from up ahead. The river's flow jumbled, and the tube widened at the bottom of a sinkhole. He led them to the side, and a pale yellow sky appeared above them, where the ground had collapsed alongside the river's path. Crude steps marked the side of the sinkhole.

"Everybody up. I think we're almost to a place where we can rest." He hoped anyway.

Kira eyed the stairs warily.

He squeezed her hand. "I can carry you again if you want."

"No offense, but I'll take my exhausted balance over your normal balance any day."

It wasn't worth an argument. "I'll still go behind you in case you slip."

Kira climbed onto the first step, behind the guard's wife. "You just want to stare at my ass."

His gaze shot up to hers, skimming said curvy ass on the way. Her grin gave him hope that she'd eventually recover from her torture.

He shrugged, surrendering. "Well, now that you mention it..."

At the top of the sinkhole, he stood on firm ground and got his first look at Kira's world.

Damn. He gave a low, sad whistle.

A barren landscape of stunted, dead trees and blowing sand lay before them. It appeared like the special effects he'd expect from a post-apocalyptic, nuclear winter sci-fi movie. Weren't faeries supposed to live in green, enchanted forests?

Kira sighed heavily beside him, and her jaw worked its way back and forth. Even though he wasn't touching her, he sensed shame-filled anger rolling off her.

"You like what Lirdeag has done to the place?"

Right. This wasn't how things were supposed to be here. This *was* post-apocalyptic. This *was* war.

The wind gusted, creating odd sounds behind them, and he turned. They stood at the foot of a cliff riddled with openings of every size. Some niches were no more than a dent in the rock big enough for a person, and some looked like entrances to larger caves.

Kira faced the wind and closed her eyes. Moans and *whooshing* sounds, like from conch shells, resonated from the air blowing along the cliff's openings. She tilted her head, as though hearing music from the vibrations.

The breeze brought the stench of decay and the grittiness of airborne dirt. The dry air evaporated the water off their skin and, together with the eerie sounds, raised goosebumps on his arms. They needed to find cover.

Zac scanned the cliff face, searching the cave openings. Somewhere along here was one marked with a cairn, but which one? There were hundreds as far as he could see in both directions.

He circled the sinkhole, stepping back from the rock wall and broadening his field of view. The cliff waved, bowing in and out, rather than running in a straight line. If he were setting up a base in a hidden yet easily reachable cave, which one would he choose?

One possibility a few hundred feet away and partway up the wall caught his eye. At first glance, it appeared like one of the shallower openings, just a few feet deep, but odd shadows on the back of the niche didn't match, like one side of the back wall was deeper than the other. A passageway could be hidden perpendicular between them, similar to the snail-style shower entrance in his master bathroom.

"Stay here. We need to find a cave with a rock cairn, and I'm going as far as that tree trunk to take a closer look at one. Let me know if you see any openings with a stack of rocks."

Kira didn't acknowledge him, still listening to the wind, and the guard's wife sat down in a heap. They all needed rest. The women had been imprisoned, and he'd slept only one or two hours last night before waking from the dream and hadn't done much better the night before.

During the walk, he shook out the remaining water from his Glocks. Good thing water didn't hurt them.

By the time he'd traveled halfway to his destination, he thought he could make out a stacked pile of rocks at the edge of that opening. The next question was how they'd climb up. Nothing revealed itself until he reached the foot of the cliff below the cave. Only then could he see shallow hand and foot holds zigzagging up the rock face. Perfect. Hopefully the women would be able to make the climb.

He returned to Kira and the guard's wife. He needed a better name for the woman, but how did a society that kept names secret handle identification? Asking her name would be rude.

"All right, I found the cave with supplies. It's about thirty feet up the cliff near that tree trunk. So there's the walk and then the climb. What are each of you up for?"

The guard's wife refused all offers of assistance and stumbled her way across the landscape. He insisted on carrying Kira so she'd have energy for the climb. The going was slow, especially because Kira climbed with her sleeves pulled over her hands, as though she didn't want to touch the rock face, but they eventually all made it up to the cave opening.

As he'd guessed, the back wall overlapped and hid a passage to a rear cavern. A stack of supplies sat in a far corner. He sorted through the pile—firewood, simple fabric clothes, water canteens, fur-lined sleeping mats, and woven bags of dried fruit, hard cheeses, and crackers. The supplies were obviously meant for two people and not three, but would suffice for a day while they recovered.

The guard's wife spread the two sleeping mats on either side of where Kira started a fire. Luckily, the honeycomb structure of the cliff sucked the smoke deeper into the rocks and wouldn't fill the cavern or give away their location.

His stomach rumbled at the smell of the food. He delivered a canteen and an assortment of food to the guard's wife, who had already laid claim to one of the sleeping mats. Kira scooted to the end of the other mat, making room for him, and he brought over two more canteens and food piles.

He nibbled on some of the hard cheese and eyed the guard's wife. "If we don't see your husband again, please thank him for sharing his supplies with us."

The woman burst into tears. *Oh hell.* His chest sank. He was in no state to comfort her. He didn't even know her name, for crying out loud.

Kira set down her food and sat beside the woman. "Arda, your husband is safe."

Arda? The woman's designation or title maybe.

Arda sucked in a shuddering breath. "You know this for certain, my princess?"

"The river told me that no one suspects him because of the iron, and the wind told me that they're so concerned about my escape that no one is paying attention to yours. You'd been imprisoned for so long no one even remembers who was in your cell. Dut is completely safe."

Arda crossed her arms over her chest, Egyptian mummy style, and bowed. A memory flickered at the back of his mind. Kira had bowed like that to the animals at the zoo.

"Your word is better than a promise, my princess."

Kira bowed in return. "You honor me with your loyalty."

"Thank you for not judging us all based on Lirdeag's crimes."

"The Flikea clan has always been loyal to my family—I don't know why he's different. If he was always a traitor who just pretended to be my friend, or if he changed for some reason."

Arda set down her cracker. "You don't know?"

"How could I? I left when I was five."

Arda's face tightened, and her chin dipped. "He blames your family for the death of his love and his daughter."

Zac swallowed his cheese before choking on that tidbit. Somehow, the fact that Lirdeag's actions were personal—and not just those of a generic power-hungry bad guy—made him more threatening. If anything, the truth explained his treatment of the land: Destroy everything valued by his enemy just as the things he'd cared about had been destroyed.

Even in the warm firelight, Kira looked paler than usual, and she rubbed her chest. "*Were* my parents to blame?"

He had to give her credit for not being defensive about the possibility.

"That"—Arda sighed—"is up for debate. Might they have done more to protect our land from the Lamians? Perhaps. Although rumor has it the Lamians had help from the gargoyles. Regardless, it didn't come out until after their deaths that he'd even *had* a lover or a daughter."

How many enemies were around this place? While Kira nibbled on her lip, he interrupted. "Who are the Lamians?"

Arda glanced at Kira and then answered when it didn't seem like she'd heard. "The Lamians are serpent people."

"We've never been able to establish a treaty with them." Kira winced and rubbed the back of her neck. "Remember the snake that bit Candy? They don't like faeries and cause trouble for no reason."

Zac did a double take. Candy had been bitten because of a feud *here*?

Kira's shoulders hunched. "I wonder if an apology would help. Whether my parents should be held responsible or not, I still regret that anyone suffered."

"No." Arda shifted, angling away from Kira. Her voice was low, barely carrying across the cave. "We do not like to speak of it, but we Flikea are vicious when our trust is broken. That's *why* we're loyal and honorable to others—the cost of failure is a bloody nightmare. I don't think you could change his mind."

On that depressing note, they all forced down the now-even-more-tasteless food. After the snack, Arda looked up shyly. "Forgive me for asking, my princess, but what will you do now? I worry Lirdeag is searching for you."

"Yes, and he's strong enough to track my magic, no matter where I hide. Once I rest, I'll leave you, so as not to draw him here." She glanced at Zac. "I have a plan."

He rubbed his temples. He knew that look. That was the and-I-need-your-help look.

"Something tells me we won't be going home right away, will we?"

Her lips pressed into an apologetic line. "I need to fix things here first."

His head drooped, his entire body held down by an invisible weight. Exhaustion drained the protests from his throat.

He had a daughter to get home to, and Moose would be worried by now, which meant Emily would be panicky. This war wasn't his concern.

And yet...

And yet on top of having no way besides Kira to get home, he wanted to help her too. Abandoning Kira to her fate here would be just as bad as what his mother had done. That would be like stating he didn't want a future with Kira, and he wasn't prepared to do that. Even thinking the word *abandon* twisted his stomach.

He'd come with the intention to help her, and yes, he'd rescued her from the prison, but until Lirdeag was taken care of, the threat still existed. The only real way to make her safe was to get rid of the threat. And that meant this war *was* his concern.

He stroked her hair, which was starting to regain pale colors, and sighed. "Consider me drafted to your cause."

She held his palm to her cheek. Gratitude beyond words flowed through their connection, erasing all tension in his muscles. Gratitude and something more.

Something that quickened his heartbeat until his pulse thumped in his throat. Something that sent tingles to his nerve endings and made the hair stand up on his arms despite the warm fire.

Something that strengthened his hope for their future.

Chapter Forty-Seven

KIRA WOKE, WARM AND SAFE IN ZAC'S ARMS. HOW HAD IT come to this?

There was no longer any question that she loved this man. He'd literally come to her rescue, risking everything for her. At every turn, he'd exceeded her expectations. Refusing to be released from her promise. Putting her needs first. Becoming a killer to keep her safe. Yes, there was no question.

She loved the one person in all the world with the power to utterly destroy her.

And as a seer, that threatening power came easily to him. Far more easily than it would for most humans.

A couple of mornings ago, she'd freaked out over him knowing her name, but at least then he didn't *know* he knew it. And he certainly didn't know what it meant. Now he did. Now he knew the power he held over her. Now the risk was sharper, deeper, more dangerous.

Her body stiffened, and she clenched the fur mat in her fist. Ugh. She *hated* this.

She loved him but hated what this situation meant for her. Would she now be more concerned with pleasing him than with what she wanted? That shouldn't even be a question. How could she be sure she even *did* love him when his control meant she could deny him nothing he wanted from her?

Zac stirred at her back and stroked her hair. "How are you feeling?"

"Better."

In fact, she was probably strong enough to transport. She lay quietly, trying to figure out the best way to approach Zac with her alternate proposal. That alone chafed her sense of independence. She was an act-first-ask-forgiveness-*never* kind of person, not a planning-how-to-get-*permission* kind of person.

Twilight reflected around the narrow path to the cave opening, and the fire had burned low while she slept. Now was the time to leave before she needed to use magic here. That was the least she could do to keep Arda safe.

She'd carefully kept her body on the sleeping mat, no stray fingertips touching the cave floor to give away her location. The ruling magic within her meant that in addition to being able to speak to all the *spirits* of the faerie homeland, she could also speak to all the *elements* of the faerie homeland.

Others—including Lirdeag—assumed the ruling magic gave her control over everything. That was far from the case. The deeper elemental magic of their homeland wasn't something to control, but something to use in forming alliances with the local elements.

Unfortunately, the stone in the prison had sided with Lirdeag, so she'd been unable to speak with the rock wall holding her restraints. Given his power, he might be allied with all the earth of her homeland—the element of his clan. If so, whether she used her magic or not, he could determine her location if she touched any dirt, stone, or rock with her bare skin.

Arda emerged from a deeper alcove, wearing fresh clothes, and bowed upon seeing Kira awake. "I hope I did not disturb you, my princess. I wanted to start my journey as soon as dusk fell." Her gaze dropped to the floor. "How much food should I leave for you and the human?"

Kira sat up, folding her limbs on the sleeping mat. The woman was thin from her years-long imprisonment, but Kira suspected those outside the prison didn't fare much better under Lirdeag's control.

"Take as much as you wish. Once we leave, I'll be able to acquire more." If nothing else, a quick supply trip to the Earthen plane might be possible.

Arda's eyes lit up. "Thank you, my princess. That is most generous."

Kira bowed. "It is your husband who was generous to share with us. His kindness will not be forgotten."

This couple proved that the war wasn't clan against clan, but good against evil. And just as evil appeared in many faces, so did goodness.

Zac helped Arda pack up the remaining food and water by wrapping them in the other set of clothes. After the woman left to journey to the meeting place for her husband, Zac stood over Kira, where she hadn't moved from the sleeping mat.

"All right, what's our plan?"

"Drag over the other mat. We can talk about that while we give her time to get away from here."

Zac slid the other animal skin to lay side-by-side with hers. He sat and looked expectantly at her.

Damn. Now what?

"Tell me what happened after I was stabbed. Emily's truly safe?" Yeah, it was a delaying tactic from the issue, but she really wanted to know too.

"I got home shortly after that." His brows scrunched together. "I *felt* when you weren't there anymore. Like darkness clenched my heart."

She gripped the fur under her hands. He could sense *her* emotions now, even when they weren't together, just as she'd been able to do with him. That wasn't something she'd anticipated from their connection.

"Emily had locked herself in her closet and called 911. The cops came and found a chunk of burned skin by the gate. Tito died out on the road around that same time."

The memory of his cruel expression when he'd stabbed her flashed in her mind, and her stomach hardened. "I won't say I'm sorry."

He gave her a grim smile. "I wouldn't expect you to be."

He cleared his throat and looked down. "I need to confess something." His finger twirled in a circle around the fur's hairs. "When I came home and you were gone..." He swallowed. "I thought the worst of you. I didn't want to give you the benefit of the doubt. I'm sorry."

Surprise caught the air in her throat, and she choked. *That's* what he thought he needed to "confess"?

She waved to their surroundings. "Believing in any of this would be far beyond 'the benefit of the doubt.' I can't say I'm surprised."

He breathed deep and looked off to the recesses of the darkening cavern. "It wasn't just about you. You know enough about my history—Crissy, my father, my grandfather—to guess I don't take betrayal well. You can add my mother to that list. She abandoned my dad and me when I was eight to go live in her drug fantasy world. By the time the cops came to report her death a couple of years later, I couldn't even make myself care." He shrugged. "I don't have a lot of patience with people who create their own problems."

"And that's what me disappearing looked like." She didn't voice it as a question. "Betrayal, abandonment, and self-destructiveness all rolled into one."

"I wouldn't blame you if you hated me for thinking that about you."

"Are you kidding me?" She held his hand. Maybe his ability to sense her emotions could be helpful after all. "Hello? You're talking to Miss Doesn't-Trust-Anyone here, and yet I trust you with... Well, *everything.* I don't blame you at all for your reaction. I probably would have felt the same in your place." She swung her arm, exasperation turning the movement into a wild gesture. "You're here *now.* And that's what matters. So what? You're a trust-but-verify kind of guy. I *respect* that."

One corner of his mouth quirked up. "As soon as Moose told me about the night you showed up, I stopped denying the truth."

"So he *does* remember." She sat back. "He was so good about keeping quiet I wasn't sure."

"Did you think he'd forget about the time a guy materialized in front of him and turned his parking lot into quicksand?"

"No, I guess not." She chuckled. "He might even remember better than I do."

He clasped her hands. "I won't doubt you again."

She was sure he meant the sentiment to be romantic, but her sensitivity to anything even sounding like a promise forced her to see past the heartfelt words.

"Yes, you will. But next time, you'll be able to ask me about it, and I'll explain right away. So it will be a small doubt followed quickly by facts." She gave him a wink. "I can live with that."

"Yeah, getting an explanation out of you? This is a new experience for me."

She couldn't help her smile. He knew how to make a girl feel like she still had some power in the relationship. At the thought, her smile drooped.

"What?" He scooted closer. "Did I say something wrong?"

"No. It's not you."

She pressed her lips together. How could she explain the problem?

"Ever have your heart and your head arguing about how you should feel or think?"

"I think everyone has."

"Well, imagine that times a hundred." She circled her hand around her head. "You can't see it, but there's an epic war going on in here right now."

"What are the two sides saying?"

"My heart..." She shrugged. "My heart wants to trust you and love you."

"And your head?" Tension jumped between them, and his expression tightened.

"My head reminds me that you already own me and that the last thing I should do is give you my heart too." She tucked her chin. "It worries that it's only a matter of time before I do something to piss you off, and then you'll use my name to control me. That whole 'absolute power corrupts absolutely' thing."

He rubbed the back of his neck. "I'll be honest—I don't understand this *owning* thing. What does that even mean?"

"You have complete control over me. And don't get me wrong— I'm glad you have this power and not Lirdeag. If I have to be owned by someone, you're my top choice. But it still sucks."

She plucked at the fur on the mat. The only way to explain why this bothered her so much was to be completely honest, even though it made her more vulnerable.

"Even if you don't use my name, the connection between us makes me inclined to do what you want. If you *do* use my name, I don't have a choice." She met his gaze. "You could order me to kill myself, and I would."

His mouth hung slack, and he blinked slowly. "That..." He jumped up and paced in a circle at the edge of the sleeping mat. Pebbles crunched under his agitated stride. "That's horrible. If I were you, I'd *hate* me for having that much power." He stopped and frowned at her. "No one should live under someone else's whims like that."

She gestured to her head. "Yeah, as I said, epic battle."

He sat across from her again. "There *has* to be a way to release you from this."

"Short of death? No."

His face fell. Through their connection, she sensed his grasp of how messed up this made things between them. How she'd feel compelled to change herself to meet his unspoken desires, even if he never used her name. How she'd eventually lose everything that made her who she was inside.

"You'll never be able to love me, will you? Not for real. Not untainted by this."

He didn't want an answer. She gave him one anyway. "Not long term. And *that* pisses me off. I can't have what I want because all this other crap is in the way."

"But..." He looked away and ground his jaw. Despite the low flames, firelight glinted in his eyes. He focused on her, energy pouring out of him. "I love you *because* of your strength and your opinions and your independence. I don't want to be the cause of destroying that in you."

Tears stung her eyes, and she swallowed, her chest suddenly too small for her heart. *This* was why she loved him. No matter what her stupid head thought. These feelings weren't about any power or control he had over her, but about the power and control he wanted to *give* to her.

He bounced closer, the energy between them now crackling. "That's it."

Her heart rate elevated from his excitement, even though she didn't know what he meant. "What's it?"

"On the drive down from Flagstaff, you said we couldn't do another promise for your full name because you had nothing left to give. But you do, don't you see? You can give me the real you, untainted by this *slavery.*" He spit out the word. "So you promise to give me the real you—all your opinions and sarcasm and strength—and I'll promise never to use your name."

Dizziness swirled in her mind with the speed of her thoughts. Could that work? *Would* it work? He would *do* that?

As that last thought crossed her mind, she growled at herself. Of course he would give up control over her. Her head might fear what the power would do to him eventually, but he was still the man she loved today. And the man she loved was exactly who he claimed, one who didn't want to destroy who she was.

She gave him a big grin, eagerness to put the issue behind them spilling out of her. "As soon as we're safe, we'll give it a try." His mouth opened, and she held up a finger. "But I just need you to promise that you'll never use my name *against* me. After all, it was only because you *were* able to use my name that I was able to escape the prison."

"Got it." He joined her grin. "But I don't want to wait. I want you free now. I insist."

Gratitude clogged her throat, and she could only nod.

"Hand on heart and touching you, right?" He held out his left hand and slipped his right hand into his shirt.

She impulsively kissed his knuckles. *Please let this work.*

His thumb stroked her fingers. "I swear on my life, I promise I'll never use your true name against you."

"I accept. I won't let your knowledge of my true name change who I am, not my thoughts, emotions, actions, or behaviors."

Magic flowed through them, joining them, winding their promise into reality. She breathed deep, her shoulders straightening, strengthened against the vulnerability of her name. The warm flow filled her heart and spread through her limbs.

Zac's eyes closed, and his hand pressed against his chest. He felt the magic too.

Effing A. Magic.

She jumped to her feet and towed him up alongside her. "We

have to go. Now. I forgot. Lirdeag will be able to trace the magic I used for that promise."

"Okay." He pivoted toward the cave entrance. "Let's go to wherever you can finish healing."

She tugged him back and embraced him. "Thank you. I *do* love you."

To hell with her head's worries. She stretched and sank her lips against his. He tightened his hold on her, pressing their bodies together. His tongue stroked her mouth, demanding entrance, and she was all too happy to oblige.

Passion raged through their connection, and she didn't want to interrupt their make-out session to transport them. Her magic whirled around them, holding them in its grip, and she focused on Zac's workshop on the Earthen plane. The iron there might hide her energy signature.

Nearly all her energy drained at the exertion. Just when she wasn't sure she'd make it, a wave of fresh energy embraced her, and the ground solidified under her feet.

The pressure of Zac's body disappeared. She opened her eyes, looking for the source of the mysterious energy that had rescued her.

Instead of Zac's shop, she was in Flarea's protected glen, and he wasn't with her. He wasn't anywhere.

An invisible band constricted her chest, holding in the scream clawing its way up her throat. Her clan's magic—apparently eager to help her finish healing—had brought her to the safest location, but that meant she'd left him behind.

With Lirdeag.

Chapter Forty-Eight

Z AC OPENED HIS EYES, ARMS STILL CURVED TO HOLD KIRA. A Kira who was no longer there.

He spun around and groaned at the sight of the empty cave. What had this crazy world done now?

Magic was to blame, no doubt. Electric energy had sparked through his body, and then an odd sensation of vertigo had swirled his head a second before an invisible force had shoved against him.

The question was, had it been Kira's magic? Or Lirdeag's?

He counted the seconds. If it had been Kira's magic, he needed to stay here so she could find him again. If it had been Lirdeag's magic... He didn't want to think about that, especially as a dark feeling grew deep inside him like an oozing mass.

Heaviness pressed on his heart as time passed, and he took slow, deliberate breaths. The situation required calm. As the number of seconds rose, familiar doubts knotted his stomach. He ignored them and added the last of the firewood to the coals. But the brighter flames didn't chase away the inky blackness in the cave, much less the sense of foreboding.

His fears taunted him once more. *She left you—just like all the others.*

He set his jaw and pushed the voice of his history away. He trusted her, and he *would* trust her.

He didn't deserve her if he couldn't believe in her. And he

believed in her more than anything else—in either world.

His worries were only about the growing sense of failure spreading from deep inside. Had Lirdeag recaptured her? His muscles hardened at the thought. He'd waited long enough.

Even though he didn't want to use her name again, something was definitely wrong. "Take me to Kiratania Serafiskra Zarylina Lidashka Maksyna."

Magic gathered around him and sucked him inside. A second later, the vortex spit him back out in the cave with a hard shove, and he swung his arms for balance.

Chills crept up his spine, freezing him solid. Wherever she was, he couldn't get to her.

Crackles sizzled from the opposite side of the fire. Bright light blinded him. Tension left his muscles in a rush, and he staggered forward. *Kira.*

A figure materialized in the blackness, taller than Kira. Bulkier than himself. He couldn't discern any details beyond that due to the aftereffects of the blinding flash.

"Where is the princess?"

He stopped mid-stride, and his stomach sank under the splash-down of an iceberg. "She's not here."

"You are the human who freed her. You must be the one with power over her name."

Before Zac could figure out whether that fact made him a target, a low murmur crept across the blackness. Buzzing snaps filled the cave, and Zac shielded his eyes just in time to avoid fresh blinding from the lightning-like flashes.

Shit! Lirdeag was calling others to his side.

"Capture the human. Preferably alive. I want the princess's name from him before he dies."

Ice sliced through his veins. Lirdeag would torture him just like her parents to try to gain control of her name.

Zac drew one of the Glocks and shot anything that moved closer. But as fast as they disappeared in a glittering cloud, new light bursts signaled more taking their place. Lirdeag was calling their names, forcing them to do his dirty work and die in his place. Torture and death for both him and Kira stood twenty-five feet in front of Zac, leaving no time to consider the devastating effects of his actions.

The first Glock's magazine emptied, and he tugged out his backup gun. The constant flashes of arriving faeries thoroughly blinded him, and the gunshots reverberating in the small cave deafened him.

He pulled the trigger again, and the slide jumped back, unable to chamber the next round. Empty.

One hand dumped the magazine from the Glock, and the other grabbed the next off his belt. He lined up the magazine by touch, unable to see in front of him.

Vague shadows closed in from the sides, and he backed toward the rear wall to buy time to finish the reload. His legs struggled in the quicksand-like dirt he'd sunk in up to his ankles without noticing. He felt more than heard the click of the magazine snapping into place and flicked the slide to load the first cartridge.

Recoil up his arm rewarded his effort. He pulled the trigger again, and another moving figure disintegrated. Shot after shot and magazine after magazine met the same fate. His hands fumbled only when he reached for the second to last magazine. This standoff couldn't last forever.

The light bursts hadn't let up the whole time—meaning none of the bullets had reached Lirdeag. Zac took out the closest figures and then risked allowing the faerie wave to move closer, instead aiming in the direction he'd last seen Lirdeag. With only one magazine remaining after this one, his only chance was to stop the flow of additional faeries.

Besides, these name-slaves weren't the enemy. Only Lirdeag.

Muffled thunderclaps punctuated the ringing in his ears with each shot. The front edge of the wave swept closer. One more second. Muzzle fire lit up the cave like a strobe light, illuminating the faces brighter than the red splotches in his eyes for a millisecond.

There. Zac found the face of the man he'd seen in his dream.

Had the slide opened for the next magazine yet? He hadn't been paying attention to his shots, only the target. He put his finger on the trigger.

Nothing.

Empty.

Shadows reached his flanks. Hands seized his arms and slammed them against the cave's back wall. Pain shot down his limbs, and the impact knocked the Glock from his grasp.

Warbles like underwater sounds vibrated his eardrum, but he couldn't make out the words. He struggled against those holding him, bending and putting his weight into the fight. They wouldn't take him. He wouldn't let them.

He had to get free. He had to save Kira. He had to get home to Emily.

His upper-body strength overpowered his captors, and he broke free of his attackers on his right side. Almost.

Red-hot agony stabbed his shoulder, and his right arm stopped working. His back arched, and he sucked in desperate breaths. New spots, spots caused by pain rather than searing light, blotted his sight. The overwhelming messages from his nerves were more than he thought possible.

He looked down, using the less-blinded edges of his vision. A wooden spear drove through his shoulder and into the rock wall behind him.

His arm... The arm he used for his job, for holding his daughter, for making love to Kira. His arm was dead.

His heart sunk into the acids churning his stomach. Numbness crawled through his body, blessedly diluting the pain. A scream tore from him, and his other arm swung to connect with one of them. Any of them.

A matching blow ripped through his left shoulder, pinning him in place. His knees weakened at the additional agony. This was it. He was helpless. Dead.

Two more strikes pierced his hips for good measure. Between the quicksand and his shattered hips, his weight slumped, shredding his muscles on the spears.

His body trembled uncontrollably, and he tipped his head back, needing more air. Although for what, he didn't know. Death would be a welcome relief compared to this.

A large shadowy figure stood before him, Lirdeag no doubt, and warbled more incomprehensible sounds—probably demanding Kira's name. Zac took a deep breath and used the last weapon he had—his tongue.

"Unlike some losers, the princess doesn't have to enslave people to gain loyalty." At least, that's what he thought he said. He couldn't hear himself well either.

Slashes cut his face, neck, and body from unseen weapons. Too many to count. Too many to feel. Too many to acknowledge the pain. He was nothing more than a numb hunk of meat, suspended and draining blood.

Apparently he'd pronounced the words close enough to succeed with the insult. He'd call that a victory. The only victory possible now.

Warm liquid poured over his left eye, more dripped off his chin, and still more slid down his neck. The tangy taste of copper filled his mouth. His throbbing pulse leaked out of dozens of lacerations.

The hot flash of adrenaline faded in a dying gasp. Cold swept over him like a wave of frost crystals covering a window.

Cold. So cold.

I'm sorry, Kira. I tried. Tell Emily I'm sorry. I'm sorry I couldn't be there for her.

So tired.

I never lost faith this time. I'll always love you.

Dark.

Chapter Forty-Nine

KIRA ATTEMPTED TO TRANSPORT BACK TO ZAC FOR THE TENTH time in the minute since she'd been torn from him. Her effort resulted only in the tenth failure. Dryness stung her throat with her wheezing breath, evidence of her determination, but it wasn't enough.

Her heart thudded dully, pressing sourness up her chest. She was too damn weak, and he would pay the price.

She was an idiot of epic proportions. Trying to transport into the heart of iron in his workshop had taken *way* too much energy. Her remaining strength was barely enough to keep standing, much less transport back to Zac.

This was her fault. She'd misjudged. Badly. And now she'd condemned him.

After she'd stupidly painted a target on Zac by boasting of how someone else knew her name, Lirdeag would torture him, and most likely kill him, long before the glen restored her ability to transport back to him. And Zac—who wasn't even a faerie, much less a member of the Flarea clan—couldn't enter the protected glen, even if he used her name.

She should have taken him straight to his house, where he could live out the rest of his life without having to deal with these risks. He'd never asked to be in this war, and he was too good of a person, who loved her too much, to deny her request for help.

She'd thought she'd loved him before, but in truth, she'd been selfish. Real love wouldn't have thought only about how she could best make her proposal to get what she wanted—with no consideration about what would be best for him. She was no better than Lirdeag. And now her selfishness had sentenced him to death.

Nausea turned her stomach, and she wished for the impossible. The ability to undo her mistakes. A miracle to save his life. Emptiness overtook her soul, devoid of everything but hopelessness and futility.

She shook her head, banishing the thoughts. Just like she'd taught Emily about how to be brave and believe in magic, there had to be a way.

She stumbled past the center ring of trees. If she left the glen, maybe he'd use her name to find her again. This wasn't the end.

He'd have a future. She had to believe. Had to hope.

Her vision wavered behind a sheen of moisture, and instinct led her over the flower-strewn grass. The glen was a circle—any direction would take her to the edge.

Her lungs burned at each staggered step, her inhalations sharp and labored. Her legs threatened to give out any second. She didn't have the energy for this journey, but she couldn't let him die.

She had to hope he'd use her name once she made it outside the circle of protection. He would. He was smart.

He'd be okay. He'd be okay.

A tidal wave of clammy adrenaline flooded her, Zac's emotions still connected to her through their bond. She lurched off-balance and reached out for a tree trunk that wasn't there. Dark news poured into her awareness.

Lirdeag had found Zac. And he'd brought his army.

It was too late.

No... She crumpled to her knees.

She couldn't lose him. Not now. Not like this.

She'd abandoned him, betrayed him, and his troubles were all her doing. Just as he'd feared.

Her stomach caved, the truth gutting her in half, and she doubled over. Tears dripped from her cheeks, laying a path of blame. She dug her fingers into the ground, and tremors wracked her body. She'd done this.

Please no... There had to be a way to fix this. To save him. But nothing came to mind.

Salty tears drowned the sleeping flowers at her knees. Sobs choked her throat, and her chest shrunk too tight to breath. She'd failed in every way possible.

What good was it to be alive if she couldn't save the man she loved? Her fingers clawed deeper into the dirt, but were powerless to affect members of the earthen clan. Faerie magic had limits, and she'd found them.

Tingles lifted the hair on her scalp. That was it.

Faerie magic couldn't help her, but maybe other magic could. There were other sources of mystery in the world, like the *medicine* of Zac's grandfather, and here on Mythos, the deeper magic of the *elements* might have the power to help her.

She pushed away the knowledge that the elements of her homeland had no reason to come to her aid. They'd formed no alliances. She had to try. For Zac.

She rose to her feet, stretched her arms to the sky, and invoked the ruling magic of her family. "I, Kiratania Serafiskra Zarylina Lidashka Maksyna, call upon the elements. Hear my cry and attend me."

A tempest of wind and sand and rain and fire twisted around her, swirling her hair and clothes. A voice that was not a voice—sounds of whooshes and rumbles and waves and roars—reached her ears. "Why have you awoken us?"

Uh-oh. She swallowed her surprise. These weren't just the elements of the faerie homeland. These were the elements of Mythos itself. In her desperation, her ruling magic had reached a bit too deep. Oops. Too late now.

"I ask for your assistance."

"The fleeting lives of those who spread across our realm are of no concern to us."

Of course not. The elements were more immortal than immortals. What *would* they care about?

"This land is dying. The spirits of the wind and the earth and the water and the fire are weakening. Sleeping."

"All will be well in the end."

Oh sure, a million years from now.

Then again, maybe she could make that immense perspective

work for her. "What I ask for is less than a blink to you." She added under her breath. "A teeny-tiny, easy-to-grant favor should be no problem, right?"

The voice didn't answer her, but the whirlwind didn't disappear either. Patient. Eternal.

Did the elements ever get bored with their existence? Maybe the magic of a promise would intrigue them enough to grant her request out of sheer curiosity. If she couldn't keep the promise, that meant she was dead anyway.

She lifted her chin and gazed into the encircling maelstrom. "Restore my power, and I promise to restore this land."

"We also want something else." The swirling chaos coalesced into a horizontal cyclone aimed at her heart, ready to inject her with power if she accepted.

She didn't know what their counteroffer was—something they couldn't put into words apparently—but it didn't matter. Whatever the terms were, the situation was do or die.

For Zac. She closed her eyes and spread her arms. "I accept."

The power of the elements penetrated her chest. Electric shocks zinged through her body, her muscles seizing and spasming. The sensation overwhelmed any thought of pain or hot or cold.

She was not her body. She was spirit. She was essence.

The impact lifted her off the ground and flung her limbs outward. She hung, suspended, in the column of elemental energy. And she knew what the price of this promise would be.

Someday, she'd owe them a favor in return. A favor for something beyond even their power.

Someday. Not today.

She relaxed into the hurricane within her and around her. She could live with that promise. The cost was worth it if she could save Zac.

At her acknowledgment of the bargain, the tempest streamed out of her and continued up to meet the heavens. The stars silently witnessed the agreement and then resumed their nightly dance in the sky. The elements left her alone to fulfill the first part of her vow.

She landed gently on the ground, a puff of air easing her fall. Her limbs felt unfamiliar and yet part of her at the same time. She didn't have time to analyze what the elements had done to her.

Before she could plan how to defeat Lirdeag and restore Flarea's gemstone to the glen, she had to save Zac's life, no matter what threats surrounded him. Zac needed her.

She didn't have a plan for that either. She'd just be real quick-like.

She reached into her power to transport, and the magic tasted different, like the air of the tempest that had possessed her.

A vortex of whirling energy—unlike normal faerie transportation magic—spun her to his side. She didn't analyze the situation in the flickering darkness. The smell of sulfur, copper, and ozone told her enough. She enveloped her arms around him and whisked them away before the unseen others could react. Two seconds, in and out. *Thank you, elements.*

Her transporting spiral released them beyond the iron gate outside Zac's house on the Earthen plane. She needed time to heal Zac, but Lirdeag would no doubt follow her. And as she'd learned too well, her magic couldn't breach an area surrounded by iron, so the safest place for a time-out was inside an iron fortress.

Of course, she had to get in herself first.

"Moose! Emily!"

The liquid coating her arms told her not to look at Zac. Not to see what Lirdeag had done to him. Not to let herself lose hope.

The seconds of waiting for help dragged by like hours. She didn't even have gloves on to risk a quick touch. Honey answered her call first, the dog running from behind the house.

"The gate. Open the handle."

The yellow Lab stretched up and nudged her muzzle on the iron latch and handle. As soon as the latch moved, Kira kicked her boot's sole on the gate. She lifted Zac into her arms and carried him into the courtyard.

"Close it, Honey."

The gate clanged behind her at the same time that Moose yanked the front door open, his eyes latching onto her hair. "Prin, thank God! We've—" His gaze finally left her hair and landed on the burden in her arms. "What—?"

"No time. Close the door behind me and bring loose iron—decorations, chairs, whatever—into the living room. Check that the back gate is closed and keep Emily up in her room for now."

She entered the living room and laid Zac on the rug. Now she had to look. Had to see.

Nausea rose in her throat, and she closed her mouth to keep from hyperventilating. Her pulse beat as fast as a hummingbird's wings, and dizziness pressed on her head.

If she didn't know—couldn't *feel*—that this was Zac, she'd never recognize him. Blood from hundreds of slashes covered him from head to toe, disfiguring his face, his clothes, his body. Portions of wooden spears stuck through his shoulders and hips, their jagged ends ripped from the rest of the stake when she'd taken him with her.

Even her parents hadn't been tortured this bad. Tears burned her eyes, and she wiped them away.

A whisper fell from her lips. "I'm so sorry, Zac."

Behind her, a growled curse reminded her of the continuing threat. She twisted toward Moose, who stood, shell-shocked, with a wrought-iron chair in his hands.

"Pile the iron in a circle around me. I need time to heal him before the others arrive."

She left off the words *try to*. Failure to heal him wasn't an option, but the iron so close might weaken her magic. Yet she needed to hide the energy signature of her efforts as much as possible to give them more time.

She faced Zac again, leaving Moose to the preparations. A *clunk* sounded from the chair he set down, and then screeching signaled the glass-topped iron coffee table being dragged into place.

She placed her palm on Zac's shoulder. "Zac, I don't know if you can hear me, but hang on. Give me time to fix this, and I'll heal you. Stay with me. *Please.*"

The top priority had to be preventing further blood loss. She burned away the wooden spear in his shoulder and cauterized the wound. The other three puncture wounds received the same treatment. She passed her hand over him, sealing the cuts and gashes one at a time.

Logically, cauterizing damaged even more tissue, but she'd rather stop the blood flow and have more to heal than to lose him entirely. That would be...

She shoved the thought away and concentrated on the task. His heartbeat was weak yet stabilizing, but his clothes hung in the way of seeing all the injuries. She ripped through the fabric, stripping him the best she could. The holster, magazine belt, and his jeans all remained, captive to steel buckles.

Another chair *thunked* beside her from Moose's grasp, the circle of iron now complete. She caught his gaze. "Help me out with the rest of his clothes. I can't touch the metal parts."

Moose's brow jumped up his forehead, but he did as she asked. Then he eyed Zac's underwear. "Unless you tell me the world's going to end if I don't, I am *not* touching those."

"Don't worry, I'm not asking you to." She waved to the iron circle. "Now that it's complete, see if you can find more of the steel-jacketed bullets he has somewhere."

"Yeah, I know where to look. He was in such a rush to get to you that he left his gun safe open in his room. Discovered that while I was bored silly waiting for you two earlier today." His tone was more teasing, covering his relief, than a complaint.

She matched his attitude. "So sorry to keep you waiting." She glanced up to the ceiling. "Hey, while you're up there, grab new clothes for him too."

He groaned. "Underoos too?"

She couldn't help a smile at his reference to the cartoon-themed underwear for young boys. "Yeah, a superhero pair would be perfect."

He snorted and resumed his mission. Once he left the room, she removed Zac's punctured and slashed undershorts and cauterized the wounds around his hips. Then, for Moose's sake, she covered Zac's privates with a throw blanket and sealed the rest of the lacerations on his body. A few gentle rolls ensured she hadn't missed any on his back. Now for the healing phase.

Cauterizing was easy, just a technique using her natural fire magic. Healing was another matter. She'd always felt the ability to heal others within her, but until her magic lines had connected with the nexus at her palm, she'd never had the power to do so. Theoretically, touching her skin to his would allow the transfer of energy into his body, where she could direct its healing efforts.

Theoretically.

Lightning-bright light flashed through the front window. More followed. Lirdeag and his army had arrived outside the courtyard.

The time for theory was over.

Chapter Fifty

NUMBNESS SETTLED OVER KIRA'S BODY AT THE INEVITABILITY. They'd gotten more time than she'd expected, to be honest. Maybe whatever the elements had done to her had changed her magic's signature, making her harder to track.

She swallowed the guilt clogging her throat. Now she'd not only dragged Zac into the faerie war, but she'd forced Moose and Emily into the middle of it too. Emily. In a war zone. She'd brought Zac here to heal him, and she hadn't even managed that yet.

Screw it. She didn't have time to heal Zac's injuries one by one. Moose wasn't around, probably upstairs gathering weapons. She stripped naked and lay on top of Zac, covering both of them with the blanket. A shiver overcame her at the touch of his cold body. She didn't want to think about what that meant.

The body-length, skin-to-skin contact would make him heal faster. She hoped.

She lined up her limbs with his and then closed her eyes and concentrated on his injuries. Her energy sank into him, joining their bodies, their minds, their souls. His cells danced to her choreography and played the song she conducted for them. Heal.

Under her direction, skin, muscle, bone, nerve, and blood cells all grew healthy and strong. They split and multiplied, spreading their number, filling the wounds. Yet his mind didn't stir.

Rumbles grew outside the courtyard. They were running out of time.

Her awareness went in search of his. Could she reach him if he lay in a coma? Nothing she did would matter if he never woke.

Zac, please talk to me.

Nothing.

Please, Zac, I love you. Don't leave me. Don't leave Emily.

His mind woke, but not to consciousness. Instead, his mind created a mental construct, like in a dream, of a white room. He appeared before her—he in all black and she, for some bizarre reason, appeared in a white goddess-style gown.

He stepped closer and stroked her cheek. "My beautiful Kira. I'm so sorry I failed."

She pressed her finger against his lips. "You didn't fail. I failed *you.*"

"No, you're here with me. And that means I failed to keep you safe."

His statements fell into a twisted kind of sense, and she gripped his arms. "I'm not dead. This is all just your coma-induced dream. I'm not dead, and you're not dead. I'm trying to heal you." She indicated the angelic dress that she'd never be caught wearing in real life. "Seriously? You think I'd wear this?"

His brows scrunched. "Now that you mention it, that dress doesn't seem like your style."

"Exactly. So wake the hell up. Lirdeag is outside your house right now. And Moose and Emily need you." She squeezed him. "*I* need you."

"If I'm not dead, how come I'm not awake?"

Ugh. She didn't have time for existential questions. "I'm lying naked on top of you right now. If that's not enough of an incentive for you, I give up. Figure. It. Out."

She pulled her consciousness away from him, hoping he would follow, and completed one last check of his physical state. Oh hello. *That* part of him was waking up.

She pushed up on the living room rug to remove her weight from him. Strong arms locked around her.

His eyes danced. "One kiss for the dead man. Prove to me I'm still alive."

She kissed him with a promise she hoped to live long enough to deliver and pressed against his length. Then she sat up and pointed to the pile Moose had left sometime during the healing process. "Clothes."

Blood coated both of them, and her own clothes were still gritty from when she'd been too weak to repel dirt. A shower celebration would be in order if they survived.

She got dressed in record time and stretched her bare hands. Gloves had been part of her life every day for two decades, but she couldn't use her magic with them on, and she had a job to do.

Zac stared at his clenched fists, as though trying to believe he stood whole again, and then peered out the front window. Flashes continued to gather near the gate. "Didn't I just leave these guys?"

"I know. I'm sorry for leading him here, but the iron around the yard made this the safest place for me to heal you. Their magic can't pass the courtyard wall."

"What's our plan?"

"How many more of those steel-jacketed bullets do you have?"

"If you'd asked me before today, I'd have said 'enough.' Now I'm not so sure. This guy acts like he has an unending source of name-slaves."

She'd never heard anyone refer to faeries with compromised names as name-slaves before, but the description fit. For a guy who didn't believe in faeries two days ago, he was damn insightful.

Ringing pealed from a phone that had been dumped on the floor during Moose's redecorating project. Zac gave her a look. "I should probably get that." He leaped over the iron circle and picked up the handset. "Hello?"

Good to know the healing had worked. He seemed none the worse for wear. Physically at least.

He wiped his hand over his mouth. "Yeah, sorry about all the bright flashes. I'm having a problem with a..." He lifted his hands in the universal gesture for not having a clue. "A pack of wild dogs. They're attacking my horses, and I was trying to scare them away." He rubbed his temple and paced to the other end of the room. "No, no. I don't need any help. In fact, can you call the other neighbors? I think I'm going to have to fire off some blanks, and I don't want anyone coming by and getting hurt." He nodded. "Right, or calling the cops. Thanks, Bobby."

The handset clicked off, and he gave her a grim smile. "You know, in movies, they never mention the worry of getting hit with misdemeanors for discharging firearms within town limits."

"Sorry." The apology sounded hollower every time she said it.

He offered her a shrug, like it was no big deal.

She yelled out, "Moose? You around?"

A moment later, Moose shuffled into the room, keeping his eyes downcast, but perked up when he noticed Zac standing near-by. "Glad to see you, Dead Man Walking."

"Yeah, I owe Prin my life."

She shook her head. "We'll have time to point out all the ways you're wrong later. Right now, we have to plan. Moose, you gathered all the steel-jacketed stuff?"

"There wasn't much left. I collected everything I could, and all the appropriate weapons."

"Good. I want you both staying inside the courtyard walls. I'm going to move Emily into this iron circle for extra protection while you're distributing the firepower." She pointed out the front window. "Zac, I want you to take out as many of them as you can. Keep Lirdeag busy. They won't be able to touch you as long as you stay inside the walls. Moose, I need you at the back gate with me. I'm guessing there'll be fewer of them there, and I want you to clear a path for me to get out."

Zac gaped at her. "Why the bloody hell would you go out there?"

"Because just as much as their magic can't touch you, I can't touch them from inside here."

"So what? That means they'd be able to get to you too."

"Yeah, but the only way to stop this without having to kill hundreds of innocent faeries is to stop Lirdeag."

His face fell. Over their connection, she sensed he knew exactly what she referred to and couldn't disagree. His jaw worked back and forth.

"Why can't I just target him? Keep you out of it."

"Have you looked out there?" She hitched her thumb toward the window, where the faeries' movement kept triggering the motion sensor floodlights on his barn. "See that big clump of them next to the wall? How much you want to bet he's hiding in the center?" Her lips pressed together with knowledge of her torturer. "As soon as he sees your strategy, that clump will only increase, not decrease."

Moose frowned. "I don't get it. What's this guy waiting for?"

Zac rubbed his shoulder, fresh with memories of Lirdeag's tactics. "He might be waiting for something, but I also think he's going for brute force at this point. I wouldn't put it past him to sacrifice several dozen on an attempt to shove through the gate."

"He's had at least twenty years to build up an army of slaves. Even at one a week, that's a thousand faeries under his control. The faster we can end this, the more of them we'll save."

Moose straightened and crossed his arms. "All right then. Let's go."

The men started for the door.

"Uh, guys? Can someone help me *out* of this iron prison first?"

Zac lifted her over the circle of wrought iron furniture, and then she ran upstairs. Emily peeped around her doorway. "Prin!"

Kira scooped the girl into her arms and squeezed. She'd been so wrong to lead Lirdeag here. The safest situation for Zac had created the least safe situation for Emily. Her throat grew thick with apologies.

"Fairy, I'm so sorry about all this."

Emily drew back. "That's Lirdeag outside, right?" At Kira's nod, the girl gave her a firm stare. "When I was in trouble, even my own mom wouldn't help me. But you and Moose showed me how people are supposed to help each other. It's your turn now, and you have help. So you'll be able to beat him."

Kira couldn't help chuckling at Emily's attempt at a pep talk. "You promise?"

Emily burst into a grin. "I do."

"Okay, let's get you somewhere safe." Kira led her to the stairs. "The courtyard walls should keep everyone safe because of the iron, but just in case they get through that, Moose built an iron fortress for you."

Downstairs, Emily crawled between chair legs and sat in the middle of the circle. She'd grabbed a wrought iron candle pillar stand for an emergency weapon.

Kira hated the thought of leaving her alone, but they didn't have a choice. This was the safest place for her in the middle of a fae war zone.

"Fairy, I need you to stay inside here." Even though the girl didn't need any more bogeymen in her nightmares, Kira added the line she knew would make Emily obey. "These faeries are even stronger than Tito. If you're outside this circle, you won't be able to fight them. If any try to get inside here, you'll be able to beat the crap out of them. So stay inside. Is that clear?"

Emily nodded, serious and mature. "I promise."

Kira walked backward out of the living room, keeping her eye on the girl for as long as possible. She'd done everything she could. She hoped.

Zac and Moose were in the kitchen, loading cartridges into magazines as fast as they could.

She hung back from the table. "How are things in here?"

"Not good." Zac's chin dipped to his chest. "When I stored all this stuff years ago, I mixed the steel and copper bullets in boxes together to save space. Most of the boxes *labeled* steel-jacketed are actually filled with a bunch of regular copper. I don't suppose copper hurts faeries the way steel does?"

"No, it's non-ferrous. No iron. The bullet itself might hurt them, but it won't be instant death."

"Yeah, I didn't think so. We don't have time to sort them, so we're just loading everything."

Kira's skin crawled. What *was* Lirdeag waiting for? She appreciated the time to prepare, but his delay wasn't for her benefit, she was sure.

She gave Zac a smile she hoped was more confident than she felt. "As long as the bullets slow them down, that will be helpful. Honestly, I'd rather not kill any of the others. They're most likely innocent."

"Agreed. At least we'll be able to pick you out of the crowd easily to make sure you're not hit."

Her brows tightened, and she looked down. How gross were these clothes?

He waved to her head. "Your hair?"

She pulled a lock forward. Each strand was gold—not just goldish-yellow, but bright, shimmering, metallic-looking gold. It felt like hair, but every other aspect appeared like spun threads of gold. That was possible?

Over the years, she'd made her hair into every color imaginable. This was something different. This gold wasn't a color but an essence, *and* she hadn't caused the shade to appear. Magic was at work, magic of the elements.

Okay, note to self—keep head out of view when trying to hide.

He motioned toward the living room. "Emily secure?" After she confirmed, he stood. "All right, let's go. Any time we spend loading more weaponry just gives him more time to build his army."

The way he took control—pulled the trigger, figuratively speaking—released the band around her lungs a notch. She really *wasn't* alone.

She snagged his collar and planted a kiss on his lips, memorizing the feel of his body against hers. The muscles of his arms held her tight, promising to do whatever he could to keep her safe. His well-built chest supported her like the strong foundation of home.

Her emotions burbled out of her and out of control. She threaded her fingers through his hair, tugging him closer, staking her claim. *This* was the man she wanted for her happy ending. *This* was her future.

But first, she had to escape Lirdeag for good. She reluctantly pulled away. "Soon."

He touched his forehead to hers. "Soon."

She gave Moose a hug. "Thank you for always standing by me."

His eyes glistened, and his mustache stuck out from his pursed lips. "I'm proud of you, Princess."

More went unsaid, but his quick glance at Zac told her Moose's every unspoken word, especially through her un-gloved touch. After everything he'd done for her, he'd do even more to help her reach her potential future.

A moment later, the mood turned grim, as Kira and Moose headed to the back door, and Zac started for the front, stopping by the living room for his moment with Emily. While waiting for Zac to take his position, Kira peeked out the window.

Faeries spread every few feet along the courtyard wall. She couldn't make a move without Lirdeag's awareness. He had a strategy—they just didn't know what it was.

At Zac's signal, Kira crept out to the backyard and kept below the level of the bushes. The back gate lay out of sight around the corner, and she made her way to the edge of the house. The sentinel faeries were clustered slightly thicker beyond the gate, but nothing that Moose couldn't handle. Their plan should work.

She caught Moose's eye through the back door's window and signaled. He disappeared for a second and then returned. A moment later, a commotion drew the attention of the faeries, all peering toward the front. Zac had received her message.

With Lirdeag occupied up front, he wouldn't send more faeries back here. She signaled again to Moose, and he stormed out, beard flowing, and howled like a wild troll. The faeries at the gate all stepped back, mouths agape, even before he brandished his pistol.

Something struck her as odd about their behavior, but quite likely, they'd never seen anyone like him and wondered what type of unpredictable creature he was. She took advantage of their distraction and darted to the courtyard wall closest to her position at the corner. Bent over, she crept to where Moose now stood before the gate. The wall's stucco base hid her approach, and she reached her destination undetected. She held up her fingers for a silent countdown.

Three. Two. One.

Moose got ready to open the handle with one hand and shot his first faerie with the other. Luck was with them, and the first bullet was steel-jacketed. The faerie disintegrated.

Even though she knew it was coming, the sight still took her breath. For all their magic and power, they could be so easily wiped out. Erased from existence with nothing to show for their life.

The other faeries around the gate reacted similarly, and they all retreated a few more feet. Moose belly-laughed for show. "That's right, you damn faeries. You're in my world now."

He popped off a quick succession of five more shots into the group. Chaos erupted, and he opened the gate. She slipped out while the sentinels were still figuring out whether or not they'd survived, and she skirted past the group.

Two were down and in pain. Good to know. The normal bullets *would* take them out of commission long enough for them to heal.

Ironclad Devotion

She stopped running at the edge of the driveway and crouched next to an overgrown sage bush, its branches casting a shadow from the floodlights. Moose had closed the gate again and gave her the thumbs up sign.

An argument broke out among the faeries, and she strained to hear their words. "Lirdeag" featured heavily and maybe "lose," but she couldn't pick out more than a debate of some kind.

Wait...

That's what was so unusual about their behavior. These faeries had free will. They weren't name-slaves. They were traitors.

Although... Their heated discussion suggested they might not be as tight with Lirdeag as their presence here would indicate. Maybe they were followers in general and not particularly loyal to him. In which case, they might turn.

How many more of the faeries here *weren't* name slaves? Could she convince a chunk of his supporters to abandon him?

The elements had done more than just restore her energy. Her golden hair and the speed and method of the transport she'd done with Zac proved that. Faeries transported in an electrical flash, not a whirlwind of power.

Maybe it was time to see what her new and improved magic could do.

Chapter Fifty-One

ZAC AIMED AT THE CLUSTER OF FAERIES TO THE LEFT OF THE gate, figuring Lirdeag hid in the center. Some faeries stoically remained standing after being hit, some doubled over, and only a few disappeared in an explosion of sparkles.

He tried to tell himself the lack of deaths was a good thing—after all, he'd reached the same conclusion as Kira long before she'd said anything—but his stomach still hardened a notch at each faerie he couldn't remove from Lirdeag's control.

Movement on a bougainvillea bush inside the courtyard caught his eye. The pink bracts along the branches wiggled, like an animal was crawling through the base. The heavy lump in his gut twisted a warning.

Before he could process what it meant, a blast of wind knocked him off his feet, and he landed hard on the landscape rocks around the courtyard plants. Sharp edges shredded his clothes and gouged his elbows. He shook his head and belatedly understood his gut's warning.

Lirdeag was earth clan—and he was powerful. He'd tunneled under the wrought-iron-topped courtyard wall, probably using brute force digging when his magic stopped working at the iron boundary of the fence. Kira's delay to heal him and save his life, together with their attempt to come up with an attack plan, had given Lirdeag time to breach their main defense.

Zac rolled to his stomach and blindly shot toward the bougain-villea. Even if his only target was the palm of that wind clan faerie sticking through a hole, he had to hold them back.

The bougainvillea wobbled and dropped out of sight, the tunnel's exit expanding. Iron. He needed iron.

He paused firing long enough to yell across the yard. "Moose! Have a minute?"

Had he heard Moose's blast of shots yet? Was Kira now out among the other faeries—mixed in where his bullets might fly? He kept an eye open for her golden hair.

A head popped out the hole, and Zac blasted through the skull and tried not to think about what he was doing. Another head followed and received the same treatment. His stomach churned at the visuals. He told himself to think of war or an especially violent version of the Whack-a-Mole game. Not the specifics.

A second bougainvillea bush slumped into the tunnel. What could he use to block the opening?

The hole was now wide enough to allow several heads to emerge at the same time. He held the group off, but this immediate threat interrupted his mission of focusing on Lirdeag himself.

"Moose!"

Another group popped through, and one faerie got as far as his biceps. That one found Zac's position on the ground and yelled to the others before he managed to take him out. On instinct, Zac scrambled over the rocks to the other side of a cluster of bushes.

A fireball streaked by, aiming for his previous location, and incinerated an oleander bush. He tugged his collar over his nose for protection from the plant's poisonous smoke. Ominously, the bush flamed violently enough to burn away before creating any smoke, demonstrating the power of Kira's clan.

Thank God for instinct. That could have been him.

"Christ!" Moose stepped back from where he'd careened around the corner of the house. "Zac?"

"Bring iron. The patio furniture."

The big guy lumbered off just before a fireball exploded a sage bush near where he'd been standing. Zac knocked out a few more shots. These guys were *really* starting to piss him off.

He kept one eye on the hole and another looking for an

opportunity with Lirdeag. Wherever the guy was. For all Zac knew, Lirdeag was down in the tunnel and unreachable.

Metal scraped against concrete, and he sneaked a glance at Moose, who dragged a full chaise lounge toward the front yard. Zac laid down cover fire, and Moose gave the bulky piece one more yank and then hoisted the chair in front of him like a shield.

"Try to get me now, you damn faeries."

Moose's temptation was too much for their attackers to resist. Several heads rose above the hole, and Zac shot them one after the other.

His path clear, Moose chucked the lounge chair into the tunnel opening. Screams proved he'd hit his mark.

Moose gave him a grin. "Nice shooting, cowboy."

Zac was about to joke in return when the biggest dust devil he'd ever seen whirled down the driveway. The brief smile of accomplishment dropped off his face. Bloody hell, now what?

Lightning shot from clear, star-strewn skies and gathered into fireballs stringing around the whirlwind like a Christmas tree. White pebbles landed and bounced, covering the area with popcorn-like weapons of ice. Some of the faeries cowered and howled in pain, the hail pelting them hard enough to leave bruises. Luckily, the courtyard wall kept the winds outside the gate.

The other faeries stared at the phenomenon too. Whatever this was, they were all equally clueless. Was there a faerie who could control *all* of the elements?

Golden hair coiled in the center of the dust devil. *Kira?* She floated above the ground, her arms outstretched. He shivered despite the adrenaline buzzing through his blood. Was she trapped?

A booming voice that was Kira's—and yet not Kira's—rumbled over the desert. "The elements have spoken. I am the rightful ruler of our homeland. I speak for all my clan when I say I'm sorry for Lirdeag's loss, and I regret that more was not done to prevent the Lamians' attacks, but his revenge against my family has destroyed *our* home. Now his time is over, and it is time for me to restore strength to the spirits."

Zac sucked in a breath, refilling his lungs after he'd apparently stopped breathing. Holy... That *was* Kira.

Despite her timely appearance, his scalp prickled in waves sent from a quiver in his stomach. He'd underestimated her yet again. She was powerful. She was amazing.

And she had *way* more important things to do than stay on Earth with him and Emily.

Several faeries rushed the whirlwind and were blown back before they got within ten feet of its base. A few lightning bolts shot out for good measure.

Zac tore his gaze away to check the tunnel exit, but her elemental-tinged voice drew his eye back. "We must move forward from this. Not as enemies, but as one. If you are not a name-slave to Lirdeag, leave now or be judged a traitor to the needs of our homeland. This is your only warning."

The fireballs unwound from the mini-twister and hovered above, making the intention to attack obvious to all. A suspended moment passed, and no one moved. Whether from fear, disbelief, or treason, he couldn't tell.

The lightning around Kira crackled louder and spread in an arc around the courtyard, a blanket of electric fingers thirty feet above the ground. The tip of each bolt zigzagged over a cringing faerie. Clear sky remained over other pockets of faeries who seemed unconcerned by the threat.

Of course. The name-slaves couldn't question their orders to be here, while those here as followers of Lirdeag would shrink from the danger. The specificity of her imminent attack also let them know that *she* knew who the traitors were.

A cluster of faeries huddled together, alternately flinching and puffing themselves with bravado. One of the fireballs over the dust devil shot out and engulfed the group.

Compared to the fireball that had nearly hit him, this one was more intense. Instantaneous. Consume and gone. Almost a dozen faeries erased in a blink.

A collective gasp swept over the yard at the demonstration. Suddenly, flashes dotted the area beyond the courtyard, handfuls of faeries fleeing the scene.

He rose to his feet and pumped his fist. "Yeah."

Finally, something that would save lives instead of take them.

Iron clanged from the tunnel exit, another chair tossed into the hole. Moose had sealed off the opening from magical attacks.

He gave Zac a grin. "That's my girl."

Zac returned the smile. He wished for the day when he could say the same.

Yet Kira's demonstration had made it abundantly clear that she was a faerie princess—soon to be a queen if he understood their society—who would have obligations and duties more important than ensuring he didn't feel abandoned, and he was...

He sighed, long and slow. He was a human. Living on Earth. And a blacksmith dealing in iron. Not the usual recipe for a happily ever after.

Flashes of departing faeries continued decorating the yard, punctuating her power. Another group of faeries sidled closer to Kira's cyclone and stopped at a point farther than the previous scouts had triggered her fiery attack. They clumped together, hiding something in the center.

"Prin, watch out!"

It was too late. The mob separated and threw something into the whirlwind. The barn's floodlights caught the object for a single horrifying second. The faeries had ripped a chunk of wood off his barn door—the chunk with the iron handle.

No! As if in slow motion, each twirl of the wooden plank hung suspended, dragging out the torture until it made impact. He stepped closer to the fence but had no way to prevent the inevitable.

The iron handle breached the edge of the dust devil, and Kira screamed. Whether from an iron injury or from the iron interrupting her magic, the winds dissipated instantly. She dropped from the sky and crashed onto the driveway with a sickening *thump*.

His heartbeat pounded double-time in his chest, and he lurched forward on weak legs. Before he knew what he was doing, he was at the gate and yanking it open.

"Zac, no!" Moose's just-out-of-reach grab from behind didn't break his stride.

His senses tingling, Zac ducked fireballs and jumped sudden icy patches. Near-superhuman awareness kept him safe from the faeries' magic. How, he didn't know.

Shots fired from behind him. Moose taking out the attackers, no doubt.

He reached Kira's side still in one piece—a medium-sized miracle. No time to worry about a neck injury. He scooped her into his arms and ran for the gate.

The mob along the driveway fell silent, and the attacks ceased. Lirdeag probably wanted the glory of defeating Kira for himself.

Even so, the gate grew tantalizingly close. Five steps. Four steps. Three steps. Moose gripped the handle.

The ground under Zac's feet buckled, like the flick of a whip. He landed on his back, bones crunching from the impact and Kira sprawled over his chest. The driveway sucked him down, the gravel suddenly like quicksand.

He rocked forward to sit up, but without anything to push against, his ass sank deeper, below ground level. Before he lifted his head more than a few inches off the gravel, a menacing chuckle sounded above his feet. "You cannot escape me, Princess."

Whatever sympathy Kira might feel for Lirdeag's losses didn't affect Zac. He wouldn't let her suffer for anyone's need for revenge. Unfortunately, between gravity, his attempts to get up, and Kira's weight, his legs and half his skull now lay below the gravel. Pebbles dribbled into his ears. Dying by drowning in dirt wasn't something he'd anticipated for his life.

When she didn't respond to Lirdeag's gloating—on account of being *unconscious*—he kicked, hitting both Zac and Kira, their limbs tangled together. "Wake up! You're not allowed to die until you give me a child."

He kicked again and again until she stirred and sucked in a breath, pain etched on her face.

The assault stopped for the moment. "Your apologies mean nothing. I want them back, and you can't me give that. But I'll take you and your womb as a poor substitute."

Zac's legs now sank completely under the ground. He struggled to keep his head above the dirt, but the best he could do was maintain his skull's half-buried state. Another thirty seconds and he'd be completely covered and unable to breathe.

"Moose! I need some help here, buddy."

A stream of swearing burst from beyond the gate. "I'm empty."

No more ammo. Their luck had run out.

Zac's arms were trapped between their chests from when Kira

had fallen on top of him. He pressed against her, trying to lift her above the liquefied ground. Just because he was going under didn't mean she had to die too.

Kira moved her head. No neck injury. She caught Zac's eye and whispered just above a breath. "Is that steel burning my chest, or are you really that hot for me?"

He froze. Everything had happened so quickly, he'd forgotten he still had the weapon in his hand when he'd run out and carried her. So much for helping.

Although... He distinctly remembered reloading after providing cover fire for Moose.

"Gun. Not empty." He matched her near-silent whisper.

She gave him a smile that lifted his heart. "I love you."

His muscles relaxed, warmth flowing from his chest. "I believe you."

And he did. This faerie princess wanted to be *with* him, so they'd find a way to make it work, no matter the obstacles.

She nodded a fraction of an inch and rolled to one side. In one smooth motion, he lifted his arm toward the silhouette at his feet and squeezed the trigger.

A thunderclap filled the driveway, and a smoky flare flashed from the muzzle. The bullet streaked through the now-clear shot, and Lirdeag's expression stretched into horror.

"No—" As the bullet hit him, a burst of light engulfed his body, and he disappeared, but the floodlight angled directly at Zac blinded the details.

Maybe luck had provided them with a steel-jacketed bullet right when they needed one. That kind of luck never seemed to happen in real life, but he'd take it.

Regardless, Lirdeag was gone, and the battle was won.

Wasn't it?

Chapter Fifty-Two

K IRA ALLOWED HERSELF A SMALL SMILE BEFORE COLLAPSING onto Zac's chest. Lirdeag might not be gone for good—the floodlight had blinded her from seeing any disintegration evidence, so maybe he'd just transported elsewhere—but they'd survived.

Gravel scraped around them, and she cracked her eyelids, seeking the source. Dozens of feet inched closer on the driveway.

Oh crap. The name-slaves. Maybe they weren't out of danger after all.

"Are you all right, my princess?"

She slumped, relief loosening her muscles. Whatever of the *D*s—damage or death—Zac had inflicted on Lirdeag had ended up freeing the name-slaves, at least of the *attack* command. That was the most important issue anyway, simply for being the hardest to overcome.

She met Zac's eyes, which were filled only with concern for her. He'd left the safety of the courtyard to save her, and she brushed her fingertips along his cheek, desperate for a touch. He was a hero in every sense of the word.

A smile grew on her face, matching his grin that stretched wider at every passing second that didn't end in their deaths. "I'm all right now."

She and Zac let the faeries help them to their feet. Every inch of her body ached, and she clutched Zac for support. He held her just as strongly. Maybe for the same reason.

They'd both need time to recover, physically and emotionally, from their respective tortures and injuries. With luck, they could recover together. But first, she had a job to finish.

She squared her shoulders and lifted her chin, and then purposely sought the pale blue eyes of an earthen clan member at her side. Her people's healing started with her refusal to succumb to prejudices.

"Spread the word that Lirdeag is gone, and I'll be returning tomorrow to set things to rights."

The faerie's mouth tightened. Before she could worry she'd misjudged, he offered, "There are unicorns, sent here by their previous ruler. We suspect they have been afraid to go home for fear of judgment."

The unicorns had a new ruler? She had so much she needed to catch up on before she'd be a good leader for her people. "Hopefully they'll leave on their own now that their ally here is gone too. If not..." She shrugged. "They will be dealt with."

He gave her a grateful smile. "It's good to have you back, my princess." He bowed. "We shall make ready for your joyous return."

At that, flashes dotted the yard following each faerie's bow of respect. She allowed Zac to lead them into the courtyard, where Moose enveloped them both in a bear hug. Honey's barks danced around them, and a moment later, little arms encircled the group.

"Emily..." Kira's throat burned, and she pulled away enough to lift the girl into the center of the gathering. "I'm so sorry I forced you into the middle of all that."

Dark eyes focused on her. "I'm not. You needed Daddy and Moose to win. I just wish I could have helped."

Kira squeezed her tight and closed her eyelids before the tears welling up could escape. "That's my brave Fairy. I'm so proud of you for everything."

They stepped into the warm glow of Zac's house, the light revealing tired faces around her. Despite their success, exhaustion muted their celebration. That, and dirt. She'd never felt so scuzzy in her life.

She leaned closer to Zac. "Think I could sneak in a shower?"

She wasn't sure if her delay in dealing with her homeland until tomorrow was more about sharing this win with those she cared about or avoiding public displays of filth. Either way, she wasn't going to take any chances.

"Let's put Emily to bed first." The twinkle in his eyes hinted that he'd join her.

A half hour later, Emily was out, despite her protests that she was too amped to sleep. Moose settled into the chair at her bedside in case nightmares struck her during the night. Grateful, Kira and Zac escaped to his room.

As soon as he closed his door, she violently stripped off her grimy clothes in the middle of the room. He arched a brow. "Well, *that's* no fun. No teasing this time?"

"I may have forgiven the earth clan, but I still hate dirt."

"Noted." He laughed and held out his hand. "Toss me your clothes, and I'll start a load so you'll have something clean to wear in the morning."

She cocked her head, surprised once more by how well he understood her. "You're amazing."

"I hardly think so, but if you insist." He grinned and left with her clothes.

On second thought, between the wrought iron door handle and her lack of clothes, she was trapped here. In his room. The horrors.

A giggle bubbled up her throat at the idea, and she checked out his master bathroom. Mini spotlights highlighted the dramatic space. Desert-colored travertine tile covered the floor and most of the walls, and the walk-in-closet-sized shower stood elevated in the center of the room like a glass-walled stage. Nice.

Even better, the moisture of the room meant the fixtures weren't wrought iron. She figured out the fancy faucet settings to start the water and followed the angled glass at the entrance to step inside. Arizona's summer temperatures already warmed up the stream.

She sensed Zac's return before spotting him in the doorway, transfixed. She acted like she hadn't seen him yet but exaggerated her sensual movements, letting her hand follow the trails of water down her belly and hip.

In a split second, he joined her under the water. "I hope you didn't start without me."

"Just rinsing off the worst of it. I saved the soapy stuff for you." His voice roughened. "My favorite."

His hands worshiped every inch of her, spreading body wash over her skin and diving into her hair with shampoo. She melted against him. She'd take showers every day—needed or not—just to experience this. Moans escaped her, unrestrained and unashamed.

The air in the shower hung heavy with steam and desire. Especially when she returned the favor and soaped down his body, giving extra attention to the member obviously happy to see her.

She hadn't the opportunity during their earlier encounters to appreciate his body nearly enough. All the other times they'd been together, her energy deficit had consumed too much of her thoughts. This time was simply for enjoyment. And enjoy it, she would. From his locks curling around her fingers to his sculpted body, she drank in the feel of him under her hands. Hard, muscular, and yet so caring and devoted.

Once only rinsing remained, he spun her toward the wall and pushed. She caught herself, pressing her palms against the tile, and awaited the feel of him behind her. This wasn't a replay of their first time together, when neither of them was ready for face-to-face vulnerability, but a replay of their previous time in the shower. And now, he'd do what she'd been too broken to attempt before. Now she knew the benefits of vulnerability—a connection with the man she loved.

The water spray drowned them both, but just a single finger traced the rivulets' paths. She fidgeted, impatient.

His hot breath caressed her ear, his chest close to her back. "You can't lie to me, right?"

Tingles shot through her at his deep, sexy voice, at his nearness, at the seductive danger inherent in the question. Hunger thrummed between them.

She angled her head and exposed her neck, encouraging his mood. "That's true, Master Zachary."

His chuckle warmed her skin. "You just answered the question of what you wanted before I asked it, didn't you?" He slipped his hand between her thighs and made her gasp and lean back toward him. "I'm allowed to use your name in this situation, aren't I? In fact, you *want* me to, don't you?"

"Yes, Master Zachary." She panted between the expert strokes of his fingers. "I want to continue the Anything Promise. I want you to take me and make me yours."

He added soapy nipple rolls and pinches to his sweet torture. "You want me to claim you?"

"Yes." Gasps made the word sound pleading.

"Own you?"

"Yes." Her muscles shook, waiting for him to release her. Even without him using her name, her body was his instrument to play.

"You're sure? Even though I'm a blacksmith and work with iron?"

"Yes, please yes, Master Zachary. I beg you. I trust you."

At her utter submission to vulnerability, he replaced his fingers with his length and thrust into her. She whimpered at the perfection of sensations inundating her. Yes, this was what she wanted. What she needed.

She needed him. She needed *them*. Together. As one.

After everything that had happened, she'd despaired of ever sharing this connection with him again. And now, she was getting more than she'd dreamed. No princess had ever been more spoiled.

Every thrust, he branded her. "My Kira. My Kira. My Kira."

Her chest expanded, unable to contain her emotions. She gave herself over to him. She trusted him with her body, her life, her heart.

He swirled his fingers in ways that made her nerves dance, and her body started shaking again. Just when she thought she couldn't stand another moment, he said the magic words.

"Come for me, my love."

Proving he didn't need to use her name to invoke his style of "magic," explosions burst inside her and carried her bliss to another level. Sensations flooded her limbs, overwhelming her ability to contain the ecstasy. Her emotions, her body, her very awareness broke into a million pieces. And yet, at her center, grounding her, strengthening her, he stood as her gravity. She would never falter again. Not with him at her side.

She loved him beyond words. Beyond explanation.

Her walls tightened, clutching him hard enough to stand in for her whole body. With each squeeze, she echoed, "My Zac. My Zac. My Zac."

His release came a second later, and he shoved into her with one last thrust. His emotions swept through her like fire, melting them into one. The energy between them redoubled and healed all their hurts and bruises. Together, they were magic indeed.

He pressed against her and held her tight. For many long moments, they stood at the edge of the shower's deluge and dragged in shaky breaths. Conveniently, the water's spray was curving away from them without her even consciously making the thought.

Finally, he straightened and slipped out of her. Already missing the feel of him, she spun toward him. "Thank you."

His eyes were still dark with desire. "Did you mean what you said? About making you mine?"

The meaning behind his question skittered just out of reach, but she'd stated the truth. "Yes. Absolutely."

"What about what you told your people? That you'd return tomorrow?"

Gravity tightened its grip on her limbs, and she sank into the soles of her feet. Manipulating him was out of the question, but also she didn't want him to give up on her—give up on them. He deserved to understand all aspects of the situation.

"Yes, I need to heal my world, and I need to..." Truthfully, she hadn't thought the next steps through herself yet. "I need to be the queen they deserve, but I have no interest in becoming a micro-managing sort of ruler. I want to find a happy medium where I can support their growth without needing to spend all my time handling every little detail."

She stroked his cheek and searched his eyes for a sign of comprehension. During her self-exile, she'd always hoped her people had found strength and independence without her presence. That was still the case, but now she'd not abandon them completely while they learned and transitioned.

"I intend to split time between the planes. This here—the Earthen plane—is my home too. I care about the work I do with B.A.C.A. and abused kids, I care about Moose, about Emily." She brushed her fingertip over his mouth. "I care about you. I love you."

His throat bobbed with a swallow. "So if I were to ask you to marry me, you'd say..."

He let the proposal hang in the air between them, still hot and vibrating from their passion.

She sucked in a breath, expecting to panic at the idea. A wife? Wasn't that what she'd run away from all those years ago?

But the air slipped from her lungs, refusing to stay locked tight. Was she scared of marrying in general? Or had she just been scared of Lirdeag and his threats?

The answer slid into her thoughts and then wouldn't let go. This was the man she would love for the rest of her life, and she never wanted to part from him again.

"Ask me for real and find out."

He bent down to one knee, his drenched hair curling in every direction, and gave a smile that spread into his dimple. "My dearest Kira, I want nothing more than to share the rest of my life with you, but I order you to answer from your heart and your head and not from my wishes. Will you marry me, a lowly human blacksmith, and become Emily's mother?"

"No." As fast as his smile dropped, she yanked him to his feet. "No *lowly* husband for me. I will, however, marry *you*, the heroic man I trust and love with both my heart and my head."

The dimpled grin returned to his face, and he stroked her cheek. "I adore you, my Kira."

His warm, wet lips found hers, and his tongue slipped into her mouth. The soft strokes promised years of bliss ahead of them. And if the fact that they both worked with fire was a sign, maybe they'd always share this abundance of fiery passion.

She wrapped her arms around him and let happiness carry her away. Despite their bodies pressed together, it wasn't close enough. She shivered at the tingles zinging through her limbs.

Even though she wasn't cold, he took the shudder as such. He shut off the water and led her to the bedroom.

He indicated the shower. "That was the appetizer. Now I'm going to make love to you."

She stepped into his arms, more eager for the face-to-face than she would have believed a scant few days ago. "I can't wait to discover what it will feel like to make love to my fiancé."

A rumble vibrated from his chest, and he scooped her into his arms. Blacksmith or not, he ensured she'd never felt safer, and as a bonus, his dimple was on full display.

Yes, she would like this marriage thing very much.

Chapter Fifty-Three

ZAC WOKE TO SOFT TOUCHES ALONG HIS TEMPLE, AND HE opened his eyes in surprise. Not only had Kira *not* abandoned him while he slept, but she also now lay facing him, stroking his hair. Early morning sunlight bathed her in a radiant glow, adding to the magic of the moment.

"Hi." His voice came out as a sleepy croak.

"I'm sorry. Did I wake you?" She nibbled her lip. "I couldn't resist playing with your hair."

Warmth flowed through him, filling him from head to toe. "I don't mind a bit."

The fact that she was still here—*that* more than anything—proved how much things had changed between them. But he could still tease her.

"Although my grandfather still has his hair, so I don't think there was any rush."

The black lines outlining her eyes crinkled with her smile, and a faint golden shimmer flowed along the pattern. Her skin was luminescent, even in the shadows of the sunlight.

He caressed the design at her temple. "You really do glow, you know."

"Only for you."

He gave her a wink. "I'm that good, eh?"

"No—well, yes, you *do* tend to give me an excess of energy."

She laughed. "But I mean, no one else can see it."

"Really? Is that because of our connection?"

"No." A *V* shape formed on her forehead. "You're special. You were able to see my faerie flies when you weren't supposed to, and that was right after we met. The lion at the zoo called you a seer."

His fingers stopped above her ear. "My grandfather used that word too. Said that, like him, I could see spirits when I was a child."

"I think he was right. About a lot of things." When his brow shot up, she gave a slight shake of her head. "I'm not saying what he did was right. Only that he understood more than we thought. He *was* right about my true name being the key to my rescue. In fact, if Tito hadn't stabbed me, I think you would have even been able to prevent the magic from calling me back when all these lines connected."

"I still want to strangle my grandfather for hurting you."

"No family reunions right away. Got it."

"Let me banish that image of you sick and unconscious from my memory first." A shiver of worry flowed from her over their connection. "There's something else, isn't there?"

Her lips twitched. "I was going to tell you when I figured it out myself." Her ribcage pressed against his with her deep inhalation. "I had to make a promise to save you from Lirdeag. A promise to the elements of Mythos. I don't know yet what it means, what they did to me, but you saw my hair and my magic over all the elements. And someday they're going to want me to do something for them in return."

"When that time comes, we'll deal with it together." He drew her close enough that he felt her worry dissipate, and they intertwined their limbs. "I don't want to talk about potential issues anymore. I want to talk about how much I love you." He caught the back of her head. "I didn't think I could ever love like this. That I would ever..."

No words seemed right.

She made an attempt. "Give up your heart to something you couldn't control?"

He chuckled. "Yeah, that."

"Oh, I don't know what that's like at *all*." Her eyes danced, imitating their banter. "It's terrifying and yet…"

As she struggled with finding the words, he jumped back in. "And yet you make me want to do it anyway."

A wide smile burst over her face. "Exactly."

They snuggled long enough for the sunlight to creep off the bed. She circled her fingers on his chest. "I suppose we should get going. I have to get to work on the next step."

"Ready to start planning the wedding already?" His voice rose in mock surprise.

She playfully pushed against him. "No, I mean, I have to go back today and fix that post-apocalyptic horror show of a landscape you saw."

"You can fix that?" At her nod, he marveled once again at this amazing woman. "Anything I can do to help?"

"I can't ask you to leave Emily again. Until I go back, I won't know if it's safe. If Lirdeag is really gone for good. If the unicorns left on their own. If the war is really over."

"All the more reason I should be there with you." When she opened her mouth to protest, he placed his finger over her lips. "This isn't about me choosing you over Emily or anything like that. I love you both—there is no choice. But she won't be in danger if I'm not with her. You *will*."

She didn't seem ready to give up her objection, her lips thinning.

"Listen." He stroked her hair behind her ear. "I couldn't live with myself if anything happened to you, and I wasn't there to help." He gave a wry smile. "And Emily would never forgive me either." He squeezed her closer. "So how can I help?"

"I love you." She tucked her head under his chin. "You might not be aware, but I have a history of manipulating people for entertainment."

He snorted.

"And I just wanted to make sure that I wasn't manipulating you." She caught his gaze. "You deserve better than that."

His chest expanded, allowing his heart to embrace her with their love. The man-chewing-up-and-spitting-out woman he'd first met was nowhere to be seen, replaced by honesty and concern for him. Just when he thought he couldn't respect her more.

Then her lips lifted into a sheepish curve. "But truthfully, your help would make the difference. I have to free the gemstone of my clan from iron chains so I can return it to the sacred grove. Once that's in place, I'll be able to heal the spirits of the land."

"Iron chains, huh? Sounds like a job for a blacksmith."

"Do you have someone in mind who could help with that part?"

"As a matter of fact, I do." He struck half a superhero pose, his free arm in a bicep curl.

She giggled and kissed his nose. "My hero."

He grabbed her and rolled them over the mattress until he came out on top, where he could demand a bigger payment. The gemstone could wait another half-hour. Maybe even an hour.

LATER THAT AFTERNOON, THEY STOOD ON THE BARE DIRT BEYOND THE Stonehenge-like columns ringing her clan's grove. He'd already rescued the gemstone from the iron chains in the palace, and they'd spent the better part of the day removing all iron and steel from faerie lands, including his abandoned Glocks in the cave. Revisiting the place of his torture hadn't been fun, but Kira had stayed close by his side every second.

Now Emily snuggled under his arm, and Moose stood next to them on the edge of the apocalyptic vision. Emily had begged to join them for this part, once they'd discovered the unicorns had left during the night and things seemed safe, and that meant Moose was there too, finally seeing the homeland of his foster daughter after imagining it for so long.

Kira had replaced the gemstone in the glen behind them, and all that remained was waking the spirits. She bent down and placed her palm on the ground.

Instantly, color washed over the world like a swipe of a giant paintbrush. Grasses grew green and healthy, leaves burst from the limbs of hundreds of bare trees, and sandy-grayness gave way to blue sky and fluffy white clouds. Even the boulders seemed brighter, and a brook nearby burbled louder.

Within a minute, color and life enveloped the world as far as he could see. His senses tingled, attuned to the faerie magic and able to *feel* the spirits inhabiting everything around him.

Emily and Moose echoed Zac's whisper of "Wow." Further words were beyond him.

But something was wrong. He sensed it from Kira at his side. Edges of the faerie lands had fallen into darkness over the years, and she was weakening.

He stepped around Emily and laid a hand on Kira's shoulder. According to the wind clan, his seer nature allowed him to see the truth of her world and exchange energy with her better than any other human.

In his mind—the mind of an artist, brimming with creativity— he imagined all those dark places being overtaken with such beauty that he'd want to make love to Kira in each spot. He pictured them running over sun-dappled hillsides and landing in a heap on soft grasses, her hair a multitude of colors spread over the ground. There, he would make her pant and squeal. Life itself would rejoice at their joining.

He shared his passion for the future with her over their connection. He'd learned enough about what would send energy her way, and this wasn't a job he minded at all.

Another wave of magic swept over the land, dialing up the brightness of the colors, and the air itself crackled with magic. Darkness was banished off the faerie shores. He felt that truth like a magical version of echolocation.

She'd won, and the faerie lands were whole once more.

Applause and cheers broke out from the gatherings of faeries spread over the hillsides. He recognized Kira's kindly prison guard and his wife in a clump several yards away, and he gave them a grateful nod.

The spirits of the land joined in the celebration. Trees waved their branches, water leaped above the brook, and flower petals swirled in happy breezes.

Kira rose, glowing from head to toe. "Now *this* is my homeland."

Between the brilliant colors, the gleaming palace on the horizon, and the knowledge that animals here *would* talk, the place was like a Disney movie come to life.

Moose took it all in and grinned. "Bringing a world back from the dead—that's pretty intense, Prin. What're you going to do for an encore?"

Emily squealed and yanked on Moose's hand. "Maybe we could go to Disney World."

Her parroting of a Disney commercial elicited a gruff laugh from Moose, which sounded out of place in the shining land. "Yeah, Prin could teach Tinker Bell a thing or two."

Kira grimaced, probably fighting a smirk.

Zac pulled her close, ignoring the disapproving looks from some of the faeries. The wind clan had declared he must have their blood in his ancestry to be a seer, but not all faeries were convinced any human should be bound to their queen. Good thing they weren't in charge.

He raised a brow at the wonder around them. "Nice work. I'm glad I could help."

She brushed her palms together and frowned at the ground at her feet. Then she leaned close.

"Uh-oh. I touched dirt again. You know what that means."

He barely held in a laugh. "Another shower?"

She met his gaze with a dead-serious expression. "Yep."

He lifted her up for a kiss. "Anytime, my love. Anytime."

The amazing woman in his arms was a faerie queen, and yet she loved him. The least he could do was show his devotion at every opportunity. In both his world and hers.

Be part of all
the love stories found in the...

Thank you for reading *Ironclad Devotion*! I hope you enjoyed meeting Kira and Zac. The next book in the Mythos Legacy series is also available. Read on to learn more!

~ Jami

- If you enjoyed being part of the Mythos world, sign up for Jami's email list at *jamigold.com/mail*. Learn when her new books become available and **take advantage of her pre-order-only sale prices**!
- At *jamigold.com*, find information for all of Jami's books, including extra content for this book, and connect with her on social media.
- Reviews help other readers discover new books! If you have a moment, please leave a review on Goodreads, Amazon, and/or your favorite online retailer.

Stone-Cold Heart, the fourth novel-length story in the Mythos Legacy series, features a **shapeshifting gargoyle hero** and a **recovering military vet heroine**. Go to *jamigold.com/sch* to learn more!